GENTLEMAN CAPTAIN

GENTLEMAN CAPTAIN

J. D. DAVIES

ISIS
LARGE PRINT
Oxford

First published in Great Britain 2009
by
Old Street Publishing Ltd.

Published in Large Print 2010 by ISIS Publishing Ltd.,
7 Centremead, Osney Mead, Oxford OX2 0ES
by arrangement with
Old Street Publishing Ltd.

British Library Cataloguing in Publication Data
Davies, J. D.
 Gentleman captain.
 1. Navies - - Great Britain - - Officers - - Fiction.
 2. Great Britain - - History - - Charles II,
 1660–1685 - - Fiction.
 3. Great Britain - - History, Naval - -
 17th century - - Fiction.
 4. Sea stories.
 5. Large type books.
 I. Title
 823.9'2–dc22

ISBN 978–0–7531–8620–6 (hb)
ISBN 978–0–7531–8621–3 (pb)

Printed and bound in Great Britain by
T. J. International Ltd., Padstow, Cornwall

To Wendy, with much love, and thanks for the
Theory of Everything

There were gentlemen and there were seamen in the navy of Charles the Second. But the seamen were not gentlemen; and the gentlemen were not seamen.

Lord Macaulay, *The History of England*

CHAPTER ONE

We would strike the rocks, the ship would break apart, and we would all drown. Of this, I was certain.

His Majesty's ship the *Happy Restoration* was beating up to Kinsale harbour, into the teeth of a hard northerly gale that had blown up with sudden, unforgiving fury. We had weathered the Old Head, somehow avoided smashing ourselves to pieces on Hake Head, and were now edging toward the chops of the harbour mouth itself. Vast seas drove the ship every way at once, the timbers screaming against the waters that sought to tear them apart.

On the quarterdeck, we three men tried desperately to keep our feet, clinging to whatever stood fast, fighting the bitter and freezing Irish rain that drove straight into our faces. There was the ship's master, John Aldred, splendidly confident in his ability to bring us safe to anchor, as drunk as Bacchus after a rough night in Southwark. There was the best of his master's mates, Kit Farrell, my own age, watching the shore and the sails and the rigging with a strange dread in his eyes. And there stood I, or tried to stand, clinging desperately to a part of the ship I could scarce, in my fright and inexperience, have named if called upon to do so. Matthew Quinton, aged twenty-one, captain of his Majesty's ship. Strange as it sounds, the prospect of my imminent demise was almost less dreadful to me than the prospect of surviving. Survival would mean having to report to my superiors that we had spectacularly missed our rendezvous with the Virginia and Barbados merchant fleets, which we were meant to escort to the Downs in that year of grace 1661. They were probably still out in the endless ocean, or sunk by the weather, or the French, or the Spanish, or the Dutch, or the corsairs, or the ghost of Barbarossa.

A torrent of spray ended my aimless reflections in time for me to hear Aldred's latest pronouncement. "Be not afraid, Captain! Plenty of sea room, if we tack but shortly. This breeze will die from the west as fast as it sprang up, as God is my judge."

Aldred's eyes were glazed, not from the salt spray that stung us mercilessly, but from too much victualler's ale and bad port wine. Kit Farrell moved behind him, braced himself against a huge wave, reached me and shouted above the roar of the sea, "Captain, he's mistaken — if we try to tack now, we'll strike on the rocks for certain — we shouldn't have had so much sail still aloft, not even in the wind as it was . . ."

But the tempest relented as he spoke, just a little, and a shout that Aldred would never have heard before now carried to his ears as clear as day. The old man turned and glowered at Farrell.

"Damn, Master Farrell, and what do you know of it?" he cried. "How many times have you brought ships

2

home into Kinsale haven, in far worse than this?" We would have the *Prince Royal* next, I feared. "Don't you know I first went to sea on the *Prince Royal*, back in the year Thirteen, taking the Princess Elizabeth over to Holland for her marriage? Near fifty years ago, Mister Farrell!" And next it would be Drake. "Don't you know I learned my trade under men who'd sailed with Drake? Drake himself!" And last would come the Armada: Aldred's drunken litany of self-regard was almost as predictable as dusk succeeding dawn. "Blood of Christ, I've messed with men who were in the Armada fight. So damn me, Master Farrell, I know my business! I know the pilotage of Kinsale better than most men alive, I know how to bring us through a mere lively breeze like this, and God strike me down if I don't!" And as an afterthought, as the wind and the spray rose once more, he leaned over to me, gave me a full measure of beer-vapour breath, and said, "Begging your pardon, Captain Quinton."

I was too fearful to give any sort of pardon, or to remind Aldred yet again that my grandfather had also fought the Armada, and sailed with Drake to boot. Drake was the most vain and obnoxious man he ever knew, my grandfather said. *After himself, that is,* my mother would always add.

The ever-strengthening wind struck us in full force once more, snatching a man off the cross-beam that those who knew of such things called the foretopsail yard. He flailed his arms against the mighty gale, and for the briefest of moments it looked as though he had fulfilled the dream of the ancients, and achieved flight.

Then the wind drove him into the next great wave bearing down on us, and he was gone. All the while, Farrell and Aldred traded insults about reefs and courses, irons and stays, all of it the language of the Moon to my ears.

Kit Farrell started to rage. "Damn yourself to hell, Aldred, you'll kill us all!" He turned to me. "Captain, for God's sake, order him to bear away! We've too little sea room, for all of Aldred's bluster. If we brade up close all our sails and lie at try with our main course, then we can run back into open sea, or make along the coast for the Cove of Cork or Milford. Easier harbours in a northerly, Captain!"

Uncertainty covered me like a shroud. "Our orders are for Kinsale —"

"Sir, not at the risk of endangering the ship!"

Still I hesitated. Aldred began to snap his orders through a speaking trumpet. After eight months at sea, four of them in command of this ship, I was now vaguely aware of the theory and practice of tacking. I remembered Aldred's tipsy and relatively patient explanation. *No ship can sail right into the wind, Captain, nor more than six points on either side of it. To go towards the wind, you must sail on diagonals. Like a comb, sir, like the teeth of a comb. Make your way up the teeth to the head of the comb.* I had seen it done often enough, but never in wind that came straight from the flatulence of hell's own bowels.

Kit Farrell watched the men on the masts and the yards as they battled equally with those few of our sails that were not yet reefed, as they said, and to preserve

4

themselves from the fate of their shipmate, our Icarus. Between the huge waves that struck me and pulled me and blinded me and knocked the breath out of me, I looked on helplessly at the activity about the ship. I could see only sodden men taking in and letting out sodden canvas in a random fashion. Farrell, bred at sea since he was nine, saw a different scene. "Too slow, Captain — the wind's come on too strong, and too fast — too many raw men, too much sail aloft even for a better crew to take in or reef in time — and the ship's too old, too crank —"

The spray and rain eased for a moment. I saw the black shore of County Cork, so much closer than it had been a minute before. Waves that were suddenly as high as our masts broke themselves on the rocks with a dreadful roaring. I ran my hand through my drenched and thinning hair, for both hat and periwig were long lost to the wind.

Aldred was slurring a mixture of oaths and orders, the former rapidly outweighing the latter. Farrell turned to me again, his face red from whip-lashes of rain. "Captain, we'll strike for sure — we can't make the tack, not now — order him to bear away, sir, in the name of dear heaven —"

I opened my mouth, and closed it. I was captain, and could overrule the master. But I knew next to nothing of the sea. The master controlled the movement of the ship and set its course. John Aldred was one of the most experienced masters in the navy. I knew nothing; I was a captain but four months. But John Aldred was a deluded drunk, lying unconscious in his cabin long

5

after this sudden storm blew up. I knew nothing, but I was a gentleman. John Aldred was old, with bad eyes even when sober. I knew nothing, but I was an earl's brother. I was born to command. I was the captain. Farrell's eyes were on me, begging, imploring. I knew nothing, but I was the captain of the *Happy Restoration*.

I opened my mouth again, ready to order Aldred to bear away as Kit had told me. "Mister Ald —" I began, but got no further.

A great wave more monstrous than all that had gone before smashed over the side. I shut my mouth a fraction too late, and what seemed a gallon or more of salt water coursed down my throat. My height told against me, for a shorter man would have been able to brace himself better. The ship rolled, I lost my footing and slid across the deck on my back. Farrell pulled me up, but my senses were gone for moments. I coughed up sea water, then vomited. I heard Farrell say, very quietly, "It's too late, Captain. We're dead men."

As I retched again, I opened my eyes. The men high on the yards were climbing down with all of God's speed — and falling, too, I saw with horror. The few sails we still had spread were loose, mere rags blowing free on strings. Aldred was clinging to the rail, staring at the shore. He was mouthing something, but I could hear barely anything above the roar of wind and the awful crashing of water on rock. Farrell took hold of me again, and as I lurched forward through the gale, I made out Aldred's words.

"Have mercy upon me, O Lord; for I am weak: O Lord, heal me; for my bones are vexed . . ." The sixth psalm of David. The old words were a comfort, now, at what I knew was the moment of my death, and I found myself mouthing them with Aldred, unheard above the thunder of the seas that gathered at last to crush us. *For in death there is no remembrance of thee: in the grave who shall give thee thanks? I am weary with my groaning; all the night make I my bed to swim; I water my couch with my tears. Mine eye is consumed because of grief . . .*

A vast wave struck our right broadside and turned the ship almost over, driving the hull across the water. We must have ridden up onto a great submerged rock, for our frames roared their agony, and I saw the deals of the deck begin to tear apart as our back broke. The foremast sprang with a loud crack. The force of the water and the impact of our grounding threw Aldred across into the nearest mast, the one that seamen call the mizzen, which folded him like paper around itself, crushing his innards and backbone as it did so. I saw one of his mates, Worsley, take the full weight of a cannon that had not been lashed secure, driving him off the deck and to his maker. I saw these things in what I knew to be my last moments, as my feet left the deck and I felt only water, and wind, and then water.

The old mariners on Blackwall shore will tell you that drowning men see their whole lives flash before them, and see the souls of all the drowned sailors of the earth coming up to meet them, no doubt as Drake's Drum beats out its phantom galliard to welcome them to the shore beyond. That day, as the *Happy Restoration* died, I learned more of drowning than most men. I heard no drum, saw no souls swimming to meet me, and the pathetic apology that was my twenty-one years of life did not flash before me. There was only the most unbearable noise, worse than the greatest broadside in the greatest battle, and the screaming of my chest as it fought for just one more breath. Then there was the face and horn of a unicorn, and I knew that I was dead.

"Take hold, Captain — God in heaven, sir, take hold!"

I opened my eyes again, and the unicorn bent upon me the unfaltering stare that only a creature of the dumbest wood can give. Kit Farrell was holding me fast, his other arm taut around the head of a wooden lion. Between us lay the harp of Ireland, the fleurs-de-lis of France, the lion rampant of Scotland and the lions passant of England. It was our sternpiece. Somehow, the proud wooden emblem of our country had broken free from the ship, and become our raft. Somehow — by a miracle of wind and tide or Farrell's kicks into the sea — we had come into a pool between two great rocks and wedged there, safe from the worst blasts of the storm.

I swallowed air as if it were ambrosia, and gripped my unicorn with all my strength. I looked at Farrell. He was looking beyond me, so I turned, and saw a sight that is with me to this day, as vivid as it was at that very moment.

My last sight of my first command was her bow. It reared into the air, and a great wave pushed it higher still, pushed it toward the heavens. Our new figurehead, the crown and oak laurels, was suddenly clear against the sun in the west, as the gale blew itself out and the sky began to brighten. Then the last great gusts blew the bow onto the western shore, where it shattered like so much kindling. A moment before, I saw dark shapes trying to crawl like ants up the deck, up towards our figurehead. The strike against the rock threw some into the sea, some against the teeth of the shore. The last of our men were gone. His Majesty's ship the *Happy Restoration*, formerly the *Lord Protector*, was gone.

I see that sight in my dreams, all these distant years later, as vivid now as it was that October day. I still see the sight, and I still reckon the cost. Upwards of one hundred souls, drowned or broken on the rocks. God knows how many widows made, and orphans cast onto the streets. All damned to oblivion by my ignorance, indecision, and pride.

Some hours afterwards, we were sitting on stools and swathed in blankets in front of a blazing fire. We were in a barracks room of the old James Fort, on the west side of Kinsale harbour. There were twenty-nine survivors from the wreck of the *Happy Restoration*. Kit Farrell and I were the only officers. The Governor of Kinsale had been attentive and sympathetic, sending over bowls of broth and jugs of a fiery Irish drink, both of which burned the throat in equally harsh measure. But the victuals served their purpose, and slowly, feeling returned to limbs, my cheeks began to flush, and I finally rediscovered my tongue.

I drew breath. "Mister Farrell," I said. "Thank you."

Perhaps I should have said more. This man my own age had saved my life, perhaps saved far more than he would ever know: the fate of an earldom, at the very least. But my throat and lungs were sore from the storm, the seawater, and the governor's largesse, and I had no breath for speeches. Nor in truth could I face unburdening myself to another at that moment, for God knows what depths of anguish and guilt might have spilled forth. Kit Farrell seemed to know this. He pulled himself a little higher on his stool. Struggling to speak, just as I had, he said, "It was the sternpiece, sir. It was carried away by the same wave that swept us from the deck." Then he smiled, the proof of a small private joke, and said, "Brazen incompetents, Captain. Corrupt as a Roman cardinal. Old treenails, probably, so they could take the new ones bought for the job down to Southwark market and sell them. Deptford shipwrights, sir. Villains to a man. Deptford yard refitted her when the king came back, and they took down Noll Cromwell's arms and put up the king's."

I took another measure of the increasingly attractive Irish drink. "So they cheated when they fastened the sternpiece?"

"And much else on that curse of a ship, for it to break apart as it did, but they saved our lives by doing so. God bless them, Captain Quinton."

"God bless you, Mister Farrell. But for you, I'd never have caught hold, and never seen this world again." I

10

thought of my wife and all that I had so nearly lost. I thought upon the scores of men who had perished. I felt an uncontrollable pain; not a wound, but something in my gut and throat that began to swell and tighten. I fought back my shame, forced myself to look my saviour in the eye. Then I raised my cup to him.

"My brother is an earl, and friend to the king," I said, awkwardly. This was entirely true. "We are a rich family, one of the richest in England." This was entirely untrue, though once, things had been different. "I owe you my life, Mister Farrell. We Quintons, we've always been men of honour. It's lifeblood to us. I am in your debt, and my honour demands that I repay you."

He was probably as embarrassed at having to listen to this appalling pomposity as I was in uttering it. A man of my own rank would have called me a fool, or boxed me about the head. But a man of Kit Farrell's rank would have known nothing of gentlemanly honour, although evidently he knew enough of sympathy and discretion. He sat silently for some minutes, gazing into the fire. Then he turned his head towards me and said, "One thing I would like, sir. One thing above all others."

"Name it, if it's in my power."

"Captain, I can't read or write. I see men like yourself taking pleasure from books, and I'd like to know that world. I see that writing makes men better themselves. Reading and writing, they're the key to all. I look around me, sir, and I see men must have them these days if they're to advance in life, be it in the king's navy or any other way of this world. Knowing words gives men power, so it seems to me. But I've never found anyone willing to teach me, sir."

I had a sudden memory of my old schoolmaster at Bedford — Mervyn, the meanest sort of little Welsh pedant — and wondered what he would have made of his worst pupil turning teacher. Then I thought of other men, of my father and grandfather, and in that moment I knew what they would have me say. "I'll teach you reading and writing, Mister Farrell. Gladly. It's the smallest of prices for my life, so I should not ask anything else from you in return." I retched up more Irish salt sea, and something grey and indescribable. I reached for the governor's fire-liquid and burned away the taste. "But there's something I'd have you teach me, too."

"Captain?"

"Teach me the sea, Mister Farrell. Tell me the names of the ropes, and the ways to steer a course. Teach me of the sun and the stars, and the currents, and the oceans. Teach me how to be a proper captain for a king's ship."

I held out my hand to Kit Farrell. After a moment, he took it, and we shook.

CHAPTER
TWO

"Like you, Matthias, I was captain of a ship at twenty-one," said my brother-in-law, "but unlike you, I did not lose her before I was twenty-two."

From most men, this would have been an intolerable goad and insult, worthy of a blade in the ribs at dawn. From Captain Cornelis van der Eide, it was a rare proof of the existence of his tortured sense of humour, generally thought to be as mythical as the gryphon.

"Cornelis!" His sister, my wife, admonished him, her eyes flashing like the broadside of a sixty-gunner. "You must not jest with Matthew over this. Many men died on his ship, and he feels their loss each day."

Although Cornelia was fully ten years her brother's junior, and as slight as he was bovine, she made him flush like a child caught stealing apples from an orchard. She could always bend him to her will in an instant, this proud, square-chested captain; a man who could stand up to the hardest burgomasters of Amsterdam and trade broadsides with the best.

Cornelis mouthed an apology and raised his glass to me in supplication. It was the first time that my brother-in-law and I had met since the loss of the *Happy Restoration*, six months before. Cornelis's ship was in Erith Reach, taking on supplies while her captain consulted with our Navy Board, for some reason unspecified. He was soon to sail for the Iceland fisheries, where he was to guard the boats that gleaned their rich harvest from that perilous sea. But for all his faults, Cornelis van der Eide took his family responsibilities seriously, and even the apparently pressing nature of his expedition could not prevent him paying his respects to his sister and his in-laws in our strange old house in the depths of rural Bedfordshire, fifty or more miles north of his berth.

In his ineffably dull way, Cornelis had been holding forth for much of the meal on the merits of training captains to the sea from the age of, say, nine, which was precisely how old he had been when he was first taken out beyond the Schooneveld shoals and into the North Sea by a *schipper* uncle. Then he had treated us to a profoundly tedious discourse on the sailing qualities of his new command, a strong forty-gun ship called the *Wapen van Veere*. He seemed particularly pleased with the sheer of the wales, and I wondered momentarily why he had such blubbery sea-leviathans fastened to the side of his ship. Cornelis went on to essay an opinion on the alleged superiority of the Dutch system of government, with its seven virtually independent provinces, five mutually suspicious admiralties, and countless squabbling factions.

I had heard Cornelis' opinions many times — most memorably at interminable length at my wedding feast — and merely nodded passively from time to time. My

14

eyes wandered instead to the decaying vaulting and beetle-eaten roof timbers of the cavernous hall in which we ate, and as I did at every meal, I contemplated the possibility of the entire structure crashing down to kill us all. My gaze moved down to Cornelia, to her clean and louse-free hair, her smooth, round face and delicate white bosom. She wore, in Cornelis's honour, a grand orange dress that I knew to be a political statement against her brother's dogged republicanism. She would have none of Cornelis's defence of their homeland. She had adopted the ways of her new country to a gratifying degree, and in any case was relishing the rare opportunity to resume her lifelong squabble with her sibling.

"Oh, come, brother!" she cried mockingly. "Surely even you can see that the present government of Nederland is a calamity? Holland against Zeeland, the other six provinces against Holland, Orangists versus Republicans, Amsterdam versus the world! And what of religion, Cornelis? A state that publicly preaches the dourest version of Calvinism imaginable, yet gladly tolerates Catholics, Jews, Devil-worshippers and God knows what as long as they make enough money to swell the coffers of that same state! If this is De Witt's 'True Freedom', brother, then God preserve us from it!"

Cornelis looked on her indulgently, as he always did, for in that, at least, we were agreed: we both loved this bright, impetuous, and forthright creature, and would defend her with every breath in our bodies.

Cornelis said, mildly, "Then what would you put in its place, sister?" Of course, he knew the answer perfectly well: the orange dress was eloquent enough.

"Why, monarchy, what else? Look at England, now happy again under her rightful sovereign after all those long, miserable years of emulating our foolish Dutch republic!" Knowing rather more than my wife of the discontents that swirled around the court, of the murmurings of the London mob and the emptiness of the royal exchequer, I raised an eyebrow. Cornelia continued, "The Prince of Orange should be made king, brother, and De Witt and all his acolytes in the States-General sent packing back to the Amsterdam brothels whence they sprang!"

Not even Cornelis could tolerate such a slander from his sister, who seemed thus to accuse Johan De Witt, Grand Pensionary of Holland and the man who held the entire shambolic Dutch state together, of being a whoremaster. Captain van der Eide drew himself up in his chair. "The prince is a lad of twelve, sister!" he said. "Make him king, and we will have a civil war to equal the one that tore England apart . . ."

Thus they continued, and I returned my gaze to the ceiling. As I did so, I contemplated the mystery of how this impenetrable pottage of rude, avaricious merchants, the United Provinces of the Netherlands, could dare to contend with England for dominion over the trade of the world. We had already fought one war, in the Commonwealth's time, and sometimes on the quarterdeck of the *Happy Restoration* I considered the likelihood of another, and the prospect of sailing into battle against my good-brother Cornelis. It was a thought that ever filled me with dread, for I knew full well that behind Cornelis's dull face and speech lay the heart and mind of a consummate seaman and ferocious warrior.

My mother, attired as always in black mourning weeds, stirred from her meditation of the fireplace. Perhaps she had experienced Cornelia's sharp mockery herself often enough to know that it was time to lead the warring van der Eide siblings onto safer ground. "Tell me, Cornelis. Your parents. They are well?"

Cornelia fixed her lively brown eyes on a particularly alarming piece of capon on her plate, then took up her knife and set about it mercilessly. Despite being, somehow, their child, my wife cared even less for Meinheer en Mevrouw van der Eide, of Veere in Zeeland, than did my mother. Cornelis van der Eide de Jonge contemplated the question as though it was a complex navigational problem. "*Ja*, my Lady Ravensden, they are well. Our father expects to become burgomaster of Veere this year, or the next. My mother is a little troubled by the rheum and the gout, but otherwise —"

"So are we all, Cornelis, at our age," said my mother with as much kindness as she could muster, cutting off any further discussion of Mevrouw van der Eide's symptoms. Mother had never been a patient woman, and the arthritic stoop and stiffened fingers of she who had once been the tallest and most striking of court beauties made her intolerant of the frailties of others. She looked at her son-in-law with her head cocked slightly to one side, an expression that she usually

17

reserved for the dullest of our tenants, or for Cornelia; it was a rare and welcome occasion, I thought drily, when the two of them could turn their fire onto a guest, rather than training their barbs against each other. My mother was silent for a moment, then glanced at her plate and evidently decided that the conversation had only one refuge left to it, if it was not to stray back to navies, politics or the van der Eide family.

"You found the capon to your liking, I trust?"

Naturally, she had not the slightest interest in her son-in-law's opinion of the capon. Although my mother never commented on the matter, I suspected that she had regretted almost from the first moment her agreement to marry her younger son into this tedious burgher stock. The marriage contract; born of Quinton desperation and penury in the bleakest days of exile, had given the van der Eides their connection to a bloodline of English aristocracy, allowing them to strut a little more proudly to the Grote Kerk in Veere each Sunday. To be fair, I had acquired a wife so pleasant, witty, musical, supportive, and utterly unlike her parents and brother, that I sometimes contemplated the impossible proposition that Mevrouw van der Eide had cuckolded her husband with some exotic foreign mercenary who chanced to ride through Veere in the autumn of 1638, on his way to the wars. For all my contentment with Cornelia in those days, though, the Quintons had never quite received the healthy dowry that was meant to accompany her, and which would have gone far towards retrieving our family's woeful financial state. For all his bourgeois stolidity, Cornelis van der Eide de Oude was surprisingly evasive on the matter. There was always some vague talk of problems on the Amsterdam insurance bourse, or of difficulties with cargoes from Smyrna. Or, on other days, Batavia.

Presumably ignorant of his hostess's doubts, Cornelis van der Eide contemplated his remaining piece of capon dubiously for a moment, then brightened as the correct answer presented itself to him. "Of course, my lady. As always, Ravensden Abbey provides a repast fit for a king."

Samuel Barcock, the ancient, lanky and puritanical steward of Ravensden, permitted himself a shadow of a smile from his position behind my mother's chair. The compliment from the brave and godly Captain van der Eide would get back within the hour to the abbey's cook and housekeeper, Goodwife Barcock, and within a day it would be all around the clucking gossips in their Bedford prayer meeting. I privately applauded my block-headed brother-in-law for learning enough of the etiquette of our home in his two previous visits to lie outrageously about the tough, cold, and over-cooked meat that invariably emerged from our kitchen.

Old Barcock cleared the plates as quickly as his ancient legs and uncertain grip would permit, shrugging off the feeble attempts at assistance offered by Elias, the imbecile that Cornelis perversely chose to employ as his servant. As Barcock tottered away towards the kitchens, Cornelis's minimal patience with the social pleasantries of an English table came to its inevitably early end; after all, he was but the son of an avaricious Dutch merchant.

"So, Matthias," he said, turning towards me. "You have no prospect of another command?"

Cornelia grimaced, but her brother did not see her expression. I said, as amiably as I could, "The commissions for this year's expeditions were issued long ago, Cornelis. Our ships are nearly all in the Mediterranean — Admiral Lawson's fleet against the corsairs, while my Lord Sandwich takes possession of Tangier and brings home our new queen. I cannot see how I would have had any prospect of a command this year, even if I had not lost my ship."

My beautiful, pert Cornelia defended me against myself, as she always did, and said quickly, "You forget, my brother, that Matthew may not need to seek further command in the navy. His heart is set on a commission in the Life Guards, which is what we all hoped for when the king was happily restored to his throne. Command at sea was the last thing Matthew desired, or sought."

This was true, though I could still hear the words in my head, still fresh in my memory: *Teach me the sea, Mister Farrell.*

"Now his brother, the earl, is using all his influence with his friend the king to secure a place for Matthew in the Guards, where he belongs," Cornelia continued. "It will be a fit position for a man of his breeding, away from all these rolling men with their strange talk of ropes, sails and bearings —"

My mother looked up from the last rigid remnants of her capon and said vaguely, "Of course, my dear Cornelis, your sister means no disrespect to your calling or your kind. In your country, the son of the next burgomaster of Veere can become a captain in a great navy that is the dread and envy of all the world. In our country, though, the navy is no place for a gentleman and a Cavalier. Commands here go to captains who served under Noll Cromwell, that incarnate Satan. If the king was to make the navy solely the preserve of our kind, as he has done with the army, I would be content for my son to serve in it. But at this moment — not."

Although they warred on almost every matter under the sun, Cornelia had learned rapidly to recognize my mother's absolutes, after which no further discussion was permissible and the subject of conversation had to be changed. Her brother, lacking both Cornelia's experience of the dowager countess and her unfailing good sense, blundered on regardless. "Then why, my lady, does your king appoint such Satanic captains, and put over them admirals like Sandwich and Lawson, who surely also served Cromwell and your Commonwealth? And have not men of breeding, as you call them, always commanded in your navy, during those times when you have had kings or queens? What of Matthias's grandfather, for instance?"

I braced myself for an imperious explosion from my mother, whose face was fast colouring to flame. Two subjects, and two only, infallibly drew such a reaction from her.

The first was the execution of King Charles the First of Blessed Memory, Saint and Martyr, in whose honour she lit an unconscionable number of candles on every anniversary of his birth, death, and certain other days of the year that she associated with his sacred memory. Towards those she held responsible for his death, she reserved depths of vitriol probably unique even for a Cavalier woman of her age and station.

The second was her father-in-law, my grandfather and namesake, Matthew Quinton, eighth Earl of Ravensden. He was there now, behind her. The vast portrait painted for the earl's eightieth birthday by Van Dyck himself was mounted on the east wall of the great hall, directly behind the countess's chair, so that she could eat without ever looking on the old man's face. There he was, arms akimbo and in a breastplate, attempting to look forty years younger and failing utterly, thanks to his own vanity in employing the greatest artist of the day, an artist who caught unerringly every line and wrinkle: this man who had sailed the seas with the likes of Drake, Hawkins and Raleigh, the darling of the London mob, who had won the heart of the great Queen Bess herself, and whose legend had been drummed in to me throughout my childhood years.

My mother, who had done none of the drumming, drew in her breath, and said, "Matthew's grandfather was a *mere pirate* — he nearly bankrupted and destroyed the House of Quinton with his lunatic schemes —"

Cornelia interrupted bravely. "My lady, Barcock is beckoning. The rhubarb fool, I think."

The dowager countess recollected herself. It did not do to tell tales to the servants of their social superiors, even a long-dead one whom Samuel Barcock had served for forty years, and whom he had heartily detested as a dissolute, godless rake. As the uncomfortably liquid rhubarb fool was served, I endeavoured to deflect Cornelis onto safer ground.

"The king seeks to put behind us all the quarrels of the late unhappy times, brother. Our past differences are forgotten, and not to be brought to mind. Reconciliation is our watchword, now — Cavaliers and Roundheads, all serving together, all loyal to king and England." My mother sniffed in disapproval, but, kings being infallible in her eyes, it was just possible that her displeasure was directed at the rhubarb fool, and not at Charles the Second. "Of course, some of those who served under Cromwell and the rest have been condemned —"

"The regicides, may they rot in hell for signing the death warrant of the blessed royal martyr," said my mother, straying dangerously close to bringing up her two greatest hates in the space of one dessert course.

"And justly executed, of course," I said smoothly, bowing to my mother. "But the king owes his throne to the likes of Montagu and General Monck, now the Duke of Albemarle. You remember how it was, brother."

Vivid in my mind was the garret room in the van der Eide house in Veere, on an April day almost exactly two years before. Cornelia lay asleep in bed alongside me, as naked as a Rubens model, her long brown hair spilling wantonly over the pillow. There was no rush to stir. There never was, for the penniless younger brother

of an exiled traitor. Then the deepest bell of the Grote
Kerk in Veere had begun to toll, slowly at first, then
steadily faster. Guns fired from some of the ships
further down the Veerse Meer, then from some of those
in the harbour. As the distant cheering started to draw
nearer, along the quay beneath our window, I got up
and pulled on my breeches. The crowd was running,
and shouting, and dancing, English, Scots, Irish and
Dutch all riotously happy together. Cornelia awoke,
pulled the sheets around herself and joined me at the
window. I recognized a few of our fellow exiles. There
was Sir Peter Harcourt, worth two thousand a year
before the wars, pouring small beer over his dirty face
and the rags of his last shirt. Old Stallard, who had
once been a cathedral dean and was brother to a
viscount, was pulling a protesting tavern wench into an
alley, lifting her skirts exultantly. I cried out for the
news, but no one could hear. The mob spilled past,
some towards the church, others towards the Campveer
Tower at the water's edge. Then I saw Cornelis. His
ship was at the quay, almost beneath our window, the
outermost of three van der Eide vessels readying
themselves for a voyage to the Levant. He was in the
bow, seemingly attending to a problem in the rigging.
He cupped his hands and called out to us.

"Your English Parliament has voted to recall your
king, Matthias. General Monck has won Cromwell's
old army over to it, and General Montagu brings his
navy to Scheveningen to take King Charles over. You
have a country and a home again, my brother." Thus
ended England's eleven-year interregnum, and we

24

exiles who had thronged every town of the Netherlands and Spanish Flanders could rejoice at our own, very personal, restorations.

Two years later, at table in Ravensden Abbey, the same Cornelis van der Eide nodded slowly. I continued, "Even if the king had enough Cavalier officers for all his ships, most of them would be men like me, young gentleman captains who barely know one end of a ship from the other. If he wants experience, he has to turn to Noll Cromwell's men, who are now Monck's and Montagu's. You know better than I how good some of them are, brother."

Cornelis nodded gravely, but said nothing. The first of the great wars between the Dutch and the English had begun ten years before, born of the perverse refusal of the Dutch to agree that English goods (plentiful) should be carried in English ships (few and expensive) rather than in Dutch hulls (many, and quite preposterously cheap). This war proved to be a very Armageddon on the North Sea, and after a few early Dutch successes, the Commonwealth's navy smashed their vaunted fleet almost into oblivion. Cornelis van der Eide had then been lieutenant on a forty-gun Zeeland ship, but in the middle of the ferocious Battle of the Gabbard Shoal, a cannon ball took off his captain's head and gave him instant and unexpected promotion. Although Cornelis had fought his ship out of danger with skill and courage, fifty of his men had died at the hands of a fleet under the same General Monck who now strutted the corridors of Whitehall as Duke of Albemarle: the man to whom the king owed his throne and who proclaimed loudly that he desired nothing more than a new war against the Dutch, thus finishing the job he had begun.

My good-brother and I were silent for a minute or more, perhaps both thinking of the men we had commanded who were now only memories, even for the fish who had consumed them. Then my mother turned back to us from a discussion with Barcock, coughed and clapped. "Now, Cornelis," she said, "what were you saying about your father becoming burgomaster?"

We were eating suspiciously green cheese, and Cornelis was once more regaling us with the town politics of Veere, when Barcock's daughter slipped into the hall and whispered something to her father. She was the youngest of the fourteen Barcock children, and with foreknowledge of her nature, her parents might have thought twice before naming her Chastity. She was about my age, and had been in love with me since we were infants. As she turned to leave she caught my eye, winked, and smiled wantonly. Her father, happily unaware of her ill-concealed lust, and of the fact that she was known to amuse herself with a steadily rising number of swarthy lads from the valley villages, patted her fondly on the head. Then he turned and began staggering slowly over to the table.

Reaching my mother's side, Barcock coughed loudly. "The man Phineas Musk is here, my lady. He has a message from the earl for Captain Quinton. I commanded him to remain in the antechamber, but he has made his way to the library." He gave another dry cough and muttered under his breath, "I anticipate there will be several books fewer after he leaves."

Barcock detested Musk, the steward of my brother's town house in London. Where Barcock was every inch the dour old Puritan, Musk was a crafty, carousing rogue with a suspiciously vague past. Cornelia was convinced he had once been a highwayman on the Canterbury road, albeit on no good evidence.

I made over-hasty apologies to my wife, my mother, and, with blessed relief, my brother-in-law, and almost sprang from my chair, such was my joy at this unexpected liberation. The library of Ravensden Abbey was a short walk away, down the corridor that had once been the east side of the cloister. The library itself had been the chapter house, just as the hall in which we dined was once the nave of the gloomy old abbey church, in which for centuries monks had prayed for the release of souls from a purgatory I imagined as only marginally less painful than a dinner with Captain Cornelis van der Eide and the Countess of Ravensden. My ancestor Harry Quinton, the fourth earl, had been granted the abbey lands and buildings by King Henry VIII when that sovereign brought down the monasteries, and how glad he had been to decamp here from the family's ruinous old castle across the valley. But we Quintons were multiply unfortunate with money, and never quite had the funds to replace the abbey with a great house after the latest fashion, or so the story ran. So the old church and its monastic offshoots survived, converted piecemeal over the years into a strange, rambling jumble of unsuitable rooms and corridors that ended inexplicably at poorly built brick walls. My mother, though, had a different theory to explain the oddity in which we lived. The Quintons had ample money, she said, before my grandfather lost it all. According to her, the house had stayed recognizably an abbey through the formidable will of Katherine, wife to the fourth earl and mother to the next three, who lived to be nearly ninety. She had been a nun early in life, and guilt at abandoning her vows for the bed of Harry Quinton made her determined to die in her very own, vast, private convent. Or so my mother said.

I found Phineas Musk in the library, studying my father's first folio of Shakespeare. He was a small, round man with a bald head, and a timeless, watchful face that might have borne any age between forty and sixty. As usual with Musk, there was no deference, only an uneasy sense that he was resuming a private conversation with himself. "Don't see the point in Shakespeare, myself. Went to see his *Hurricanoe* at the Cockpit just last week, attending on your brother. No, not *Hurricanoe* — some great wind or other. And that was all it was. Great wind. Couldn't follow it. Fell asleep. Give me John Fletcher any day. Plenty of bodies, plenty of blood. Now that's what I call theatre."

From the window, I could see the ruined choir of the old abbey church, where the grey stone table-tombs of the Quinton earls stood exposed to the weather. My grandfather was there, the old pirate, and I wondered yet again why his last act in life had been to hire this ignorant villain as the new steward for the London house. I said, "You've a message for me, from the earl, Musk?"

"Wants you to come to London."

"He could have written. Why send you?"

"Wants you to come to London straight away."

"Today? But it'll be night when we get there, man. We'll set off in the morning, early . . ."

Musk frowned. "I'd be for the morning, that I would. Ridden so hard to get here, I think my arse has turned to leather. But the earl wants me to turn right around and ride all the way back again, bringing you with me. Today, Captain Quinton."

"Why the hurry, man?" Even as I said the words, that oldest and darkest of thoughts came to me, striking like a shard of ice into my heart. "My brother — is he ill?"

Charles Quinton was not one to issue peremptory commands without need. My elder brother was a man who measured his words and his actions. He was, however, a man who for ten years had never been wholly well. Charles ill could so easily become Charles dying. And Charles dead would bring to me the nightmare of nightmares. I still remembered Uncle Tristram's words to me, a child of five, after we buried my father in the ruined choir of the abbey church. "Your brother Charles is the earl now, Mattie. The tenth Earl of Ravensden. You owe him all obedience and deference, under the king and God. But if, like your father, Charles falls in glory in this wicked war, then you will be earl. You are the heir to Ravensden now."

And the heir to Ravensden I remained. Heir to its debts, and its crumbling walls, and its querulous dowager. Heir to responsibilities that I never, ever wished to face.

Musk knew our family well — far too well — and read my face. "Your brother's well enough, Captain Quinton. As well as he ever is. You'll not be earl yet, not this little while."

My relief must have been transparent, but it was tinged with impatience. "Then what's so pressing that we have to leave for London now, man?"

Musk relished his moment. "The earl told me to tell you, sir. It is the king's especial and urgent command. You are to attend on His Majesty, in person, at the palace of Whitehall. Tonight, Captain Quinton."

CHAPTER
THREE

The apologies to my family were perfunctory, and the farewells took little longer. Cornelis shook my hand gruffly and bowed his head in the German fashion. My mother was inscrutable and sanguine, as always; she was well used to her menfolk riding off to their fates at a king's command, and she gave me but the merest peck of a kiss. Cornelia's tearful farewell embraced a mixture of pride in my summons from the king himself, and abundant apprehension at what that might portend. Dear, dear Cornelia, who in most things could ever mirror my own feelings exactly. *An immediate summons from the king?* Not even the attainment of my life's dream, a commission in the Guards, could warrant such urgency, I reflected, as I rode out through the gate of the stable yard and beyond the sight of those who worried for me.

Yet the paths of the Quintons and the Stuarts had often crossed, in ways that were by no means always clear to me, and it was hardly unusual for the one to call on the good offices of the other. My brother and the present king were the closest of friends, and Charles had often undertaken the most secret of tasks for his royal namesake, or so my mother claimed. My grandfather had been one of those most instrumental in bringing the king's grandfather, James of Scotland, to the English throne, or so my uncle Tristram proclaimed; and Tristram's own connections with the court ran deep, though somewhat opaque. Finally, of course, my father had made the ultimate blood sacrifice for the first King Charles, despite his original reluctance to fight for that or any other cause. After the unfortunate monarch himself, Earl James was the Royalist martyr par excellence, or so said Cavalier opinion throughout the land. All this made an urgent royal summons to one of his sons less unlikely than it might have been for many another young man of breeding.

I am a Quinton, I thought. *My king has summoned me, and that should be sufficient.* But loyalty cannot displace raw human curiosity, and I had an ample measure of that.

We were soon on the road for London, with myself mounted on Zephyr, a good black stallion who had been a favourite since my youth. We avoided the so-called Great North Road, for that would surely be clogged with all manner of traffic: slow carts, the Edinburgh coaches and mean northerners bound for London to try their fortunes. Instead we weaved our way along the lanes of that dark and mysterious land to the south, of which our less erudite Bedfordshire tenants spoke in hushed tones; a land of midnight hags and hobgoblins; or in a word, Hertfordshire. All the way, I turned over in my head increasingly fanciful reasons for the summons to Whitehall, creating elaborate secret missions to fantastical foreign courts, or to wild, rude lands such as I had heard of in the Americas. As we rode through Hampstead, a poor village with geese cackling on its street, we heard the deep-toned, distant bells of old St Paul's chime ten, and as we breasted the heath, we reined in for a moment. I had seen London by night from this spot many, many times, but some sights always have the power to stop a man in his tracks. There it lay, England's leviathan-city, lit by a cold April moon and the orange lights from a myriad fires and lanterns. We could make out the cathedral, its tall spire pointing to the moon — to think how little time it had left before the flames consumed it. Behind it, the Thames, a slim silver thread often lost to sight behind the buildings. Away to the left, the Tower, its chimneys smoky from the fires that warmed England's prisoners of state. Away to the right, Whitehall, a sea of lights revealing a royal court that never slept. Beyond, the dark bulks of the Parliament-House and the abbey church at Westminster. And up from it all, sweeping like a wave on the wind, the pungent stink of three hundred thousand souls and their communal close-stool, the River Thames.

We rode down and finally came into the sprawl of new houses encroaching ever further into the country beyond Clerkenwell. The streets were dark, with only a few lanterns showing. Laughter spilled out of the taverns, shouting and the shrieks of women and infants from many a house. Smoke from house-coal fires shrouded the narrow streets like a pall. Drunks and dogs vied with each other to get out of our way, for we were still riding hard, with no margin for delay. Despite the hour, a few beggars who had managed to evade the constables bleated their pathetic requests from the gutter: "Bless you, sirs, mercy on an old soldier for the king!" "Blinded at Cheriton fight, my lords, spare a penny, of your mercy!" "Three starving children to support, my lord, God have mercy on us!" We rode past them in silence.

At last, weary and saddle sore, we passed through the crumbling city walls and reached our journey's end. Ravensden House, my family's town residence, stood just behind the Strand. It was modest in comparison with some of its neighbours, especially the sumptuous palace that Somerset House had become. It was a prim, fading Tudor merchant's house, of a kind that had probably gone out of fashion long before my grandfather bought it; a mean dwelling far beneath the level of splendour expected from a noble family. Strange to say, for its pervasive odour of damp must have been there even in his day, it was one of the very few family possessions that the eighth Earl of Ravensden — my grandfather — had not sold off to pay for his madcap voyaging and extravagances. It was there that he had died, a long-forgotten hero of England's legend-time, surrounded by a city at war with its king and attended only by his new servant, the man now riding at my side into its stable yard, Phineas Musk.

My brother was in his study, a small, bare room with one candle, one chair, one desk and one book, the *Percivale* of Chrétien de Troyes. As I looked at him, the mystery of that most unlikely friendship between our gregarious, trivial king and my reserved, serious brother struck me anew. Charles Quinton, tenth Earl of Ravensden, sat looking out over the moonlit Thames, the candlelight playing tricks on his thin pale face and thin pale hair. He resembled neither my father nor my grandfather, or so the portraits on the walls of Ravensden Abbey proclaimed. He was dressed simply in a plain shirt and a long gown to keep him warm against the night. There was a fire in the room, but it was unlit; Charles ever eschewed what he regarded as inessential personal luxuries.

We embraced as warmly as brothers twelve years apart in age are wont to do. Charles looked me up and down as though seeing me for the first time in years, though it was but a few weeks since our last meeting. In his usual way, dragging up every word as though it were a burden, the Earl of Ravensden said, "You made good time, Matt. You did not object, then, to being taken from the exquisite company of your good-brother?"

Despite myself I laughed. "Cornelis was — just Cornelis, I suppose."

"Ah. And that, as we know, is enough for any man." Charles smiled as broadly as he ever did, which was but a slight upturning of his lip. "Cornelia and our mother are well?"

"They would both be well enough if they were not closeted so much in each other's company."

Charles nodded. He knew that I had not enough money even to rent some lowly rooms in a less fashionable part of London for Cornelia and myself;

and while the earl favoured his solitude so keenly, no invitation would be forthcoming to join him at Ravensden House — even if all but a few sparse rooms were not boarded up and infested with rats. So we stayed cooped up at the abbey, and although Cornelia and my mother could get on well enough when the mood took them, they were at once too alike and too different to make matters entirely comfortable. Certainly not comfortable enough for the husband and son who sought to keep the peace between them.

Charles turned to Phineas Musk. "Summon a boat to the stairs, Musk. We'll not take the road at this time of night, there are roaring boys and apprentices with too much ale in their bellies facing down the constables at the Charing Cross."

Musk set off, and I helped my brother with his wig, jacket, sword belt and cloak. Charles had always seemed slight and unwell, even in my few and distant recollections of him before he left for the wars. The three Roundhead musket balls that had lodged in his thin frame at Worcester fight in '51 had compounded the damage. The earl moved with difficulty, his left arm next to useless. He stood and walked as little as possible, and was out of breath within minutes. But it was just a little way to the river, and there were always watermen anxious for the honour of rowing great lords to the privy stairs of Whitehall Palace. Ours was a rude mechanic from the Hackney Marsh who wished to engage us in discourse about the iniquities of the new fashion for coffee, being convinced it was the end of beer and thus of old England; but we ignored his ranting, and eventually he fell silent. As we pulled away from the wharf, I could see light pouring from the windows of the shops and houses crowding along the length of London Bridge, just downstream. A herd of cattle was being forced, protesting, over the bridge to the south bank, bound for the slaughter-houses of Southwark, and their terrified lowing almost drowned out the laughter and screams of the people milling across the bridge.

We sat side by side in the stern of the boat, and Charles talked of family, and the state of our houses, and the tenants whose rent was in arrears. As ever, he said nothing of himself. We were those twelve years apart in age, so a certain distance between us was inevitable. But when I was only five, just before our father's death, Charles had gone off to Oxford, intending both to study and to attend the royal court, which was then encamped in the city. Within weeks, though, he was the tenth Earl of Ravensden, a man with terrible new responsibilities and a new programme for his life. Charles had joined the old king's army then, and was in time to ride out proudly at the head of his company in the Battle of Stow, in March of the year '46. It was the last battle that army ever fought: its pathetic surrender, followed shortly by that of Oxford itself, marked the inglorious end of the king's cause. At my mother's urging, Charles, then seventeen, joined the young Prince of Wales in Jersey. From there, he was to follow him on all his adventures, culminating in the desperate wounds he sustained at Worcester.

In all that time, as I grew through boyhood, I never saw my brother. We met again only in '56, ten years later, when my mother finally obtained leave from the Protector for us to go abroad. We Quintons met in a room in Bruges, among a crowd of people gathered about that lofty, impoverished, and exiled young man whom we all believed had become the rightful King of England through the fall of a headsman's axe on a bitter January day in 1649. It took me many minutes to recognize my brother. His wounds, and his travels, and much else, had made him a man old before his time. How I had longed for that moment; for Charles, in my child's mind, had become a mythic hero standing alongside our father and grandfather. He soon made it clear, however, that he had scant time for his brash young brother. We saw little of each other, and he would vanish from Flanders for weeks on end, on various unspecified journeys on behalf of his king.

Time bettered things between us, thanks chiefly to the mediating influence of our vivacious and beautiful sister Elizabeth, halfway between us in age, though in some senses far older than Charles and in others far younger than I. As our boat passed the quays at the Charing Cross, I asked Charles when he had last seen her, and if she was well. "She called by just two days ago, with young Venner and Oliver." Her sons, these, and thus our nephews, by her reptilian husband, Sir Venner Garvey; the younger named in honour of the Lord Protector and king-killer whom his father had served so notably. "She is well. She will be disappointed to miss you."

As always, what Charles did not say was more potent than any words he chose to utter. Elizabeth would miss me; so my time in London would not be sufficient even to pay the briefest of calls on my own sister.

We were passing by the riverside buildings of Whitehall Palace now. Lights shone from many windows, and we could hear the sounds of music and laughter. Although the palace was vast, stretching from Charing Cross almost to Westminster Abbey and thus bigger than many towns, the buildings were mostly low, undistinguished and of several eras. Only the great Banqueting House built for old King James, towering over the rest even in the darkness, bore any resemblance to the grandeur of the palaces we had seen in France and Spain. Our boat went past Whitehall Stairs, the public landing place, and pulled in toward a covered pier. This was the privy stairs, the king's private landing jetty, where two pikemen and two musketeers stood stiffly at attention, ready to ward off the attentions of any boat that came too close.

A small, fussy man with a great chin stood waiting on the quayside with a lantern. "My lord earl," he said. "Captain Quinton. Follow me, if you please."

Tom Chiffinch, this; keeper of His Majesty's back stairs. Chiffinch controlled most of the confidential access to the royal person, and probably knew every secret that was worth knowing in England. He led us unerringly through the warren that was Whitehall, down dimly lit galleries, up narrow staircases, through empty chambers. As always, the fragrances of Whitehall presented a grotesque and heady mix: one moment an exquisite French perfume, lingering long after its wearer had departed (doubtless to the bed of some vile rake); the next, the less pleasing odours of the palace's many cesspits, which had probably not been emptied since Lord Protector Cromwell and his swordsmen marched along these same corridors in their harsh leather boots. Finally, Chiffinch came to a closed door, knocked, entered, and bowed. We followed him into a small, dimly lit chamber, with windows that looked out over the Thames.

Three men sat in the room, laughing as a little dog with long ears shat on the floor, then looked around indignantly as though accusing one of them of having done the deed. The oldest of the three was forty or more, his face aquiline and weary. He was cursing the dog in a strong German accent. The youngest was tall and awkward; a forced smile struggled to find purchase on his long, stern face. In the middle sat a dark man, equally tall, just past his thirtieth year, with a great ugly nose, a fine black wig, and a laugh like a peal of bells. Reflexively, we Quinton brothers bowed to him. The earl my brother said, "Your Majesty."

Charles the Second, King of England, Scotland and Ireland, by the grace of God (and, more pertinently, by the grace of those politicians who had invited him back to reign over us) — this King Charles looked up and beckoned us in, gesturing towards the wine on the table.

"Charlie, Matt. You choose a damn fine moment for your audience. That's the problem with dogs. Shit everywhere. God alone knows what the new queen, my wife-to-be, will make of it when she finally arrives, for I'll wager the Portuguese don't give their dogs such latitude. Probably eat the damn things. Christ's bones, you can be king of England, God's own anointed, but can you stop dogs shitting all over your palace? Eh, Jamie?"

The young man nodded gravely but kept his counsel. Charles and I knew James Stuart, Duke of York and heir to the throne, well enough to know how uncomfortable his elder brother's easy combination of dog shit and divinity would have made him.

As nervous attendants cleared the mess, the king poured himself another glass and said, "Ah, yes, Charlie, you know our cousin well, of course, but I doubt if Matt and he have met?"

I bowed to the third man in the room, who looked me up and down and frowned. "Matthew Quinton. So. You look more like your father than the noble earl, your brother. Yes. I see him, when I look at you."

I bowed my head again in obeisance to Prince Rupert of the Rhine, the royal brothers' first cousin and once captain-general of the armies of King Charles the First in the great civil war. For one sudden moment, in my mind I was a child of five again, that day at Ravensden Abbey, barely four months after we had buried my grandfather. I saw my mother, cold, distant, pale as a shroud, as an aide to the king described her husband's death at Naseby fight. James Quinton, ninth Earl of Ravensden, my father, had ridden into battle alongside Prince Rupert on the right wing of the king's army. They drove all the cavalry on Parliament's left off the field before them. Then James Quinton, ninth Earl of Ravensden, alone of Prince Rupert's commanders, turned his company, and drove straight down on Parliament's infantry. And James Quinton, ninth Earl of Ravensden, was hacked to pieces, as Prince Rupert led the rest of his force off the field in pursuit of booty instead of following him in the manoeuvre that would surely have won the war for the king. James Quinton, poet, an earl for one hundred and eighteen days, the father that I barely knew, died a hero of the Royalist cause; but his death, and the damning reminder provided by his sons, ensured that Prince Rupert ever looked on the Quinton family as an uncomfortable indictment of what he had done, and failed to do, that day. In turn the Quinton family assuredly looked on Prince Rupert of the Rhine as the murderer of a beloved husband and father.

I said, "If I can serve the crown with just a fraction of my father's devotion to it, your highness, than I will die well content."

Rupert looked at me uncertainly, then nodded, dissembling as only the Stuarts could. "So. You will have another chance to prove this to us, Matthew Quinton."

King Charles beckoned us to sit, and we all drank. "You didn't tell him of our business here, Charlie?" asked the king at length.

"Your Majesty commanded me not to," my brother replied.

"Quite. You were ever the most discreet man on this earth, my lord earl. Which is as well, for this is not an age when discretion is honoured. Well, then, Matt, here is our problem. What do you know of the affairs of Scotland?"

The question flummoxed me. True, I had lived for some time at Veere, where for centuries the Scots had maintained their cloth staple. Despite this — and too like most of my English breed — what I knew of the affairs of Scotland could be inscribed on the nail of a swaddling babe's toe. But the Stuarts were not the only ones who could dissemble. "Sire, to the best of my knowledge, Scotland is quiet and content under Your Majesty's rule."

The king sniffed. "Quiet and content. Well, would that it were so. You'll know, for instance, that we executed that damned canting ferret-faced sanctimonious hypocrite Argyll last year?"

"Of course, Your Majesty."

Archibald Campbell, Earl of Argyll, had led the rebels called Covenanters against the first King Charles, whose attempts to impose English Church ways on those dour Presbyterians triggered war, and ultimately began the unhappy civil wars in these kingdoms. Later, this same Argyll ordered Scotland's army into England to help its treacherous Parliament defeat its sovereign lord. Then Argyll turned on his old allies, presumably affronted that the Parliament-men had executed a Dunfermline-born King of Scots without his permission. Soon after, Argyll called over young Charles the Second. Campbell of Argyll placed the crown of Scotland on his twenty-year-old head, but then proceeded to humiliate and demean the new King

Charles at every turn. The bitter truce between Charles the Second and Argyll evaporated long before the last royal army of the civil wars invaded England and was routed in battle at Worcester, where my brother received the wounds that so nearly made me an earl at the age of eleven. The king, meanwhile, after hiding in oak trees and disguising himself as the tallest, darkest and ugliest woman in England, escaped to France, where he vowed revenge against Archibald Campbell, Earl of Argyll. And revenge he had gained, ten years later; revenge both ample and full.

The Duke of York said, "There are many in Scotland who are perhaps quiet for now, Captain Quinton, but they are certainly not content. The Covenanters could still rally in their thousands, if they can but arm themselves and find a leader. Clan Campbell was ever the greatest of all the Scottish clans, and there are many men there who would seek to avenge their executed chief."

The king was absent-mindedly stroking his incontinent dog. "Quite so, Jamie. As my brother says, they need only weapons and a leader." He dropped the dog, which landed with a yelp, and leant towards me. "We suspect that they will soon have both." He was a different king, now, all business, attention and decision, the coarse humour banished.

Prince Rupert said, "We still have many friends in Holland, my lord Ravensden. A few weeks ago, we received intelligence that Scottish agents have bought a large cache of weapons from Rodrigo de Castel Nuovo, a Spanish merchant trading out of Bruges."

"I think I remember the name," said my brother slowly. "Surely he was one of those who traded arms to both sides in the late wars abroad — selling Dutch guns to the Spanish and Spanish horses to the Dutch, all while they were at war with each other. We tried to buy weapons from him ourselves, as I recall." He gave his small smile, glancing at me briefly.

Rupert nodded. "We did, but in those days, his terms were prohibitive. Now, though —"

"Now," said King Charles, "there are suddenly many parties interested in dealing with a king with a throne and an income. I find our credit in the world is so much improved compared with those days when we both slept in damp garrets in Brussels, my lord earl."

As my brother nodded acknowledgement, I ventured a question. "How large is this consignment, Your Majesty?"

"Five thousand muskets, two thousand pikes, two hundred swords, five hundred pistols, ten field cannon, sufficient shot and match to sustain a campaign for a long summer's season."

I glanced at my brother. Even the noble Lord Ravensden, normally so calm and reserved, was clearly staggered by the quantities. Entire countries could not boast such an arsenal.

"This is plainly not a supply for some skulking fanatics running through London or Edinburgh by night, gentlemen," said the Duke of York. James Stuart ever uttered such profoundly obvious sentiments with his long face set and his tone emphatic, as though he were Moses delivering the Commandments. Both this profound aura of self-importance and an unhealthy lifelong obsession with skulking fanatics, not to mention such lesser matters as attempting to turn England Catholic again, would eventually put paid to the reign of his future self, King James the Second and Seventh of distinctly less than blessed memory. On that night in Whitehall, though, the duke looked about him portentously, and resumed. "This is fit for a great army. This is fit to start a war."

"This is fit to *win* a war," said the king, who ever cut to the heart of a matter more rapidly than his brother. "There is our problem. Since we disbanded the usurper's New Model Army, we have only a few thousand troops in our service. Most of them need to stay here in London, in case the mob rises against us, as it did against our father. In Scotland, we have only some hundreds of men. An army of Campbells and Covenanters, armed with these weapons from Castel Nuovo's arsenal, could conquer Scotland in a matter of weeks."

I said, "But as Your Majesty said, they would need a leader, and Argyll is dead —"

"True, Argyll is dead. Our agents in Rotterdam and Bruges could not trace Castel Nuovo's customers back to their source. But we suspect one man above all others. Colin Campbell of Glenrannoch, Argyll's kinsman. He was once a great courtier, I'm told, at the end of my grandfather's reign and the beginning of my father's, before he went abroad. He has great lands, and good husbandry over many years may have given him the funds to afford so many weapons. Even if not, he was once General Campbell in the Dutch army, a great man of his time, so I fancy he'll have quite impeccable credit with money lenders from Antwerp to Konigsberg. Glenrannoch might see this as a chance to take control of Clan Campbell, either on behalf of Argyll's son, or for himself."

"If not control of Scotland," spluttered Rupert. "Hell's blood, sir, no man buys this many weapons to make himself leader of a mere tribe on the last edge of Europe. Campbell has commanded some of the greatest armies of our time, in battles that make Naseby seem but a skirmish in a cockpit. This man seeks to rule, as I have told you before, sire. He seeks to depose you in Scotland and to set up a Covenanter republic, with himself at its head. We must stop him — cut him off, by Christ."

"But if we are not certain it is Glenrannoch —" began my brother.

"No, Charles," said the king, "we are not certain, but we suspect strongly enough. We think there are no others in Scotland with the resources to pay for such an arsenal, and few with the experience to command the army it could equip. He has ample motive to strike now, while our rule is still relatively new and insecure." The king stood and walked to the window, where he looked out across the Thames to the dark hull of a fishing smack, just visible near the far bank. She would have been out of place there, so far from her rightful home on the Yarmouth banks, were it not for the fact that she was now a royal warship: the *Royal Escape*, the very boat in which the king had escaped to France after

Worcester fight, now moored opposite his palace as a constant reminder to Charles the Second of what had been, and what might be again. After some moments, the king turned back to us. "Fortunately, Castel Nuovo's factors have been slow in gathering the arsenal from their suppliers. He is happy to take the money for the weapons, of course, but he is also willing enough to assist the King of England at the same time." The king dropped a scrap of meat from the platter at his side. The little dog sprang forward and took it, but unaccountably gave Prince Rupert as wide a berth as possible. Just in that one moment, I recollected the old stories of the prince's diabolical reputation, of the poodle he carried with him into battle (a poodle damned as a Satanic familiar by all on Parliament's side) and wondered whether the phantom of that poodle could be at Rupert's side still, to terrify the king's dog so.

"Castel Nuovo does not know precisely where the arms will be landed," the king continued. "The agents dealing with him have kept their secrets close. We do know that they have employed a *schipper* with experience of the Western Islands. Castel Nuovo has conveniently taken many weeks to load the cargo. This has given us time to order two ships to the west coast of Scotland, there to join a regiment that will set out from Dumbarton once the ships arrive. That should be an ample force to nip this foul conspiracy in the bud, whatever its true object might be. If all goes well, our captains will intercept the arms shipment, deter Glenrannoch and any other malcontents and seek evidence against them all for high treason. There will be no rebellion in Scotland, gentlemen, be it of Campbells, Covenanters or any other variety of malcontent."

I felt a shiver that might have been fear or hope, and said, "Our captains, sire?"

James of York, the Lord High Admiral of England, said, "The senior captain is Godsgift Judge of the *Royal Martyr*, a strong frigate of forty-eight guns. A good man, highly recommended by his grace of Albemarle and my lord of Sandwich. He served in those waters in Cromwell's day."

Prince Rupert sniffed, and took a long draught of wine. "Men who served Cromwell . . . but you know my feelings on this matter, sirs." It was strange to think that in this one matter my mother was in perfect accord with the man she damned for the slaughter of her husband.

"Indeed we do, cousin," said the duke. "The second ship in the squadron is the *Jupiter*, of thirty-two guns. Her command was given to Captain James Harker, who held our commission throughout the late troubles."

I knew the name Harker, and had a sudden recollection of a big, happy Cornishman, easy in his surroundings and his skin. I said, "I met Captain Harker briefly at the Navy Office, last year. An impressive man, sober and businesslike. Common report calls him one of the best of our Cavalier captains."

Prince Rupert nodded. "A damnably good man. A captain always loyal to the crown, and to me. It makes it all the more tragic."

There was a silence before the king said, very slowly, "Captain James Harker died suddenly on the quarterdeck of the *Jupiter*, the night before last."

"The best surgeons of Portsmouth have cut open the body," added York. "It seems unlikely to be poison, but they cannot be certain. These days, the deadliest poisons can be hidden from detection."

The king looked directly at me, his dark eyes seeming to bore into mine. "So now you know why we summoned you here, Matthew Quinton. The mission of the *Jupiter* is urgent, and as important a task as can be. The ship needs a captain, and I need that captain to be a man I can trust. True, Godsgift Judge is a good man — you'll find him very different to what you might expect from his fanatical Christian name." Even the stiff and humourless Duke of York smiled a little at that, and I wondered how this Judge could possibly differ from the dozens of sanctimonious, sober Puritan captains who had served the old Commonwealth, who wore their command of the sea on their sleeves, and had changed their coats with alacrity to serve the king.

Prince Rupert seemed less than impressed with the argument. "Of course, we also need a captain for the *Jupiter* immediately, and damned few good men are available, with so many captains in the fleets to southward."

A pageboy scuttled up to the Duke of York and handed him a document, which he gave to me. I recognized the familiar text, identical but for one detail to that which had been devoured by Irish fish. It was a commission in the name of the duke, as Lord High

Admiral of England, appointing me to the command of His Majesty's ship the *Jupiter*.

I was a king's captain once more.

I barely had time to register my new circumstances before the Duke of York said, "There will be no opportunity for you to appoint your own officers, Captain Quinton. The squadron must sail as soon as the wind permits, so you will have to content yourself with Captain Harker's men. Here is a list of the officers, with my annotations for the ones I know, along with your sailing orders."

He handed me two sheets of paper, and I saw that on the first of them he had written in his own hand next to three of the names.

Lieutenant, James Vyvyan, Harker's nephew. A good man, but very young.

Purser, Stafford Peverell. Haughty and ambitious. A close, cunning fellow.

Chaplain, Francis Gale. A sot, at sea for money.

They were all looking at me. "Of course, Your Royal Highness. Thank you. If I may be permitted, though, I would request the appointment of one supernumerary master's mate."

York frowned. "Mister Pepys will upbraid me for allowing such an irregularity," he said.

Even the churlish Prince Rupert laughed a little at that, and the king smiled and said, "We all live in fear of the wrath of young Mister Pepys. The man is inexhaustible, rooting out sloth and inefficiency in everything except his own life, or so Penn and Mennes tell me. However, in the circumstances, I think we can permit you this one indulgence, Captain Quinton. Not even our esteemed Mister Pepys will quibble over one spare master's mate if it comes down to him as a command from both the Lord High Admiral and the king himself."

King Charles beckoned to a pageboy, who hurried over with pen, ink, and paper. He scribbled a note, on which I only had time to read the superscription: To Samuel Pepys, esquire, Clerk of the Acts to Our Principal Officers and Commissioners of the Navy, Seething Lane. The king said, "The name of your client, Captain Quinton?"

"Farrell, sir. Christopher Farrell."

The king nodded, and read aloud the last part of the note: ". . . to appoint the said Christopher Farrell forthwith as supernumerary master's mate aboard our ship of war the *Jupiter*, Captain Matthew Quinton." He signed, with a flourish, "Charles R". The pageboy poured a little wax onto the paper, the king dipped his ring, and James of York countersigned the document. "So be it, then, Matt Quinton. Scotland may be as wet as the Thames and full of canting hypocritical Presbyterians, but for us three Stuarts, it's our native country, God help us, and one of my three thrones. I wish still to be King of Scots on my birthday, Captain, so go to it."

Charles the Second rose to his feet, imperious, ineffably ugly, and as tall as I. He extended his hand, and I bowed to kiss it.

As my brother and I backed out of the room, still bowing, the king said, "The *Jupiter* is a damn good ship, Captain Quinton. So try not to lose this one, for God's sake."

52

CHAPTER
FOUR

I spent the night in Ravensden House, barely sleeping for the noise of the drunks rolling past the window, my excitement at the commission lodged safely in my pocket, and the thought of the princely sum of three pounds and ten shillings a month that the captaincy of a Fifth Rate frigate would bring me (and, more pertinently, Cornelia, who would immediately claim and spend a fair portion of it). Nevertheless, my pride at the trust bestowed on me by my king was tempered by disappointment that he still saw me as a sea officer, and not the commander of cavalry that I longed to be in emulation of my father.

I rose before dawn. My brother despatched Musk back to the abbey to collect my sea chest and transport it to Portsmouth, a prospect that brought forth much audible cursing from the cantankerous and saddle-sore steward. He took with him a letter from me to Cornelia, informing her in broad terms of my commission and imploring her not to be too concerned for me, advice I knew she would entirely ignore. I also wrote a note to Kit Farrell who, as far as I knew, was still at his mother's alehouse in Wapping, where he had been since our ship sank beneath us. I found a messenger who knew how to read, hoping that the few extra pence I paid him would ensure that he read out the correct message to the correct recipient. Then, borrowing sword and cloak from the earl my brother, from whose eternally preoccupied and elusive person I took an emotionless leave, I set out for Portsmouth, and my new command.

I knew it would be a long day's ride, even if I rode hard; most would have attempted the Portsmouth road in two, at a more leisurely pace, and Zephyr had already made a lengthy forced ride on the previous day. But he was a good, strong horse, and willing, and he had the prospect of some weeks of comfortable idleness in a Portsmouth stable ahead of him, so I felt no guilt at making the demand. Thus I rode over London Bridge and out into the barren heaths of Surrey, beyond Kingston, where I had ample enough time to think on all that had been said the night before.

Of course, it was obvious why they had given me the command: as Prince Rupert had so bluntly put it, if they wanted a Cavalier, there was simply no one else, not at such short notice. So the navy's youngest, least experienced, and least successful captain had been given a mission almost as much political as naval, and in waters barely known to most Englishmen. To prevent a mighty arsenal falling into the hands of this mysterious general, Campbell of Glenrabble, or whatever he was called, and forestall the rebellion that would otherwise ensue.

That much was unsurprising matter, for rebellions had been the fashion in our land for a quarter-century, and in that year 1662, when the king was but newly restored to his thrones, black rumours of new plots and rebellions were as much a part of everyday fare as bread, beer and the pisspot. But I shivered a little as I thought upon my task. It was Scotland, after all — then still an independent and a foreign land, albeit one with the same king as dear, sensible England. Even the Scots who spoke English could scarce be understood by those with the refined tones of Bedfordshire, and God knows, we saw enough of them on our county's roads, off to try their fortunes in London town. The region for which we were bound was many times more barbarous — full of men who still spoke the old tongues and wore skirts about their thighs. And it was said that the seas there contained whirlpools that could suck a hundred-gun ship to its doom, and sea caves the size of cathedrals. A captain with forty years more experience than I could own might well baulk at such a task.

Indeed, I recollected suddenly, the *Jupiter* had been given to just such a captain — and now he lay dead! At the moment Zephyr stumbled on the slippery mud. Jolted from my reflections, I looked about. It was the moment before dawn when the night seems darkest, and I shivered in my borrowed cloak. What if this was no natural death, but, as the Duke of York had so ominously implied with his talk of poisoning, a dark and foul murder — perhaps at the hands of those who plotted to raise the rebellion in Scotland? Again I looked about me, and saw the pale glimmer of dawn away to my left. *God's blood, Matthew*, I said to myself, *enough of these womanish fancies*. It was a jealous husband, or — and here I felt my equanimity return as the obvious answer laid itself before me — the apoplexy, or griping of the guts. Men die. Many men die suddenly and unexpectedly, for that can be the way of death, the thief in the night. Thus it was with my grandfather. Because some men die, other men succeed to the command of ships of war, and others succeed to crowns. Or to earldoms —

Zephyr whinnied, as if to say, "Nay, Master Matthew, neither go thee down that road!"

I bent my thoughts next upon the mysterious Captain Judge, my senior officer. I thought back to a conversation at dinner with Harris of the *Falcon*, when our ships had lain together in Bantry Bay the summer before. Judge's name was mentioned, and there was much laughter from Harris and his lieutenant, but now I could barely remember the evening, let alone the conversation. I dimly recalled falling into our boat and being rowed back to my ship as dawn broke, vomiting several times into the bay as I did so. Harris always kept a good table, and a particularly good stock of old Madeira.

Even without all of this, I faced for the second time in my life the prospect of taking command of a ship. I remembered with a shudder those moments on the quarterdeck of the doomed *Happy Restoration* at Chatham the previous summer, when my commission had been read and I could feel one hundred and thirty pairs of eyes scanning me, assessing me quite accurately as an ignorant and wildly overdressed popinjay, made captain of a ship of war on no better grounds than having the king's friend for a brother. All of them, from Aldred down to the ten-year-old cook's servant, knew full well that I had been the most junior officer in the minute Royalist army-in-exile, and had fought in precisely one battle, on the beach before Dunkirk, at which that army had been routed in no time by a lethal combination of the French and Cromwell's Ironsides. A land battle. They also knew full well that before taking command of their ship, I had served but one voyage at sea on a man-of-war, and that as a virtual passenger. To the crew of the *Happy Restoration*, I was as little qualified to command at sea as Damaris Page, the great bawd of Drury Lane, and dear Christ in Heaven, how right they had been. And how they had suffered for it, the poor wretches.

This time would be very different, I vowed to myself, and with the empty road stretching before me I began to rehearse out loud the reading of my commission, that essential and mysterious sacrament during which the command of a king's ship is assumed by her new captain. This led to embarrassment just south of Guildford when some farmhands, resting unseen behind a hedge, overheard my recitation and hooted at me as a madman, but adopting greater discretion thereafter, I quickly discovered the necessary tone. This time, I would be assured, and commanding. I would project my voice to the front of the ship, which was what I still called the bow, and I would be dressed modestly but impressively, the Earl of Ravensden's borrowed black cloak flowing at my back.

By the time I stopped to rest and water my horse, I was confident in my peroration, and confident too in the task that the king had entrusted to me. This time, I vowed, I would know my sea-trade. Aboard the *Happy Restoration*, I had believed it was beneath the honour of a ship's captain, and an earl's son to boot, to demean himself with such mechanic concerns as navigation, and a hundred men had died for it. This time, I would complete my mission, no matter how difficult it proved, and I would bring the *Jupiter* and her men safely home. There was honour and redemption in such success, but there was more, too. Succeeding in a task that the king himself regarded with such importance — preserving one of his kingdoms, no less — was bound to deserve reward, and what reward could be more appropriate, or more desirable, than a commission in the Life Guards?

The sun came out as I rode out of the bad inn at Petersfield where I had taken some bread and ale, and my soaring hopes lifted higher still. Saving the throne of Scotland was worth more than a commission; it was worth a knighthood, surely? As I had done several times a day for as long as I could recall, I could almost feel the touch of the royal sword on my shoulder, and I mouthed to myself the magical words of my lifelong dream: "Arise, Sir Matthew Quinton". I remembered sitting on my uncle Tristram's knee as he tried to mend the heart of a child broken by the death of its father with tales of gallant knights, of Hotspur and the Black Prince and Sir Philip Sidney. He told me the stories of the Round Table, of Lancelot, and Galahad, and his own Tristram, his name-knight. Before I was ten, I could recite much of old Mallory by heart, and my uncle encouraged me to think of my fallen father as a knight like those of older times, *sans peur et sans reproche*, riding to glory and immortality on Naseby field. When my twin sister lay dying of the sweating sickness at Ravensden Abbey, that bitter winter of '53, I blamed Cromwell and his New Model soldiers, who had ransacked our home days before as they searched for correspondence from my brother, thus frightening the wits out of my poor, pale, dying Henrietta. Even as we buried her beside our father and grandfather, I imagined myself a grim, armoured knight, cutting down the search party like straw, riding through the galleries of Whitehall itself, and impaling the Lord Protector on my lance like a stuck pig. *To be a knight* . . .

A sudden sharp shower put paid to my reverie. I was in the low hills that rise steadily toward the summit of the Downs. On either side of the road the stumps of fallen trees stretched away across the land, mute witnesses to the destruction of the English oaks that had built Cromwell's navy and held off his creditors. Such a landscape, and the hard spring rain stinging my face, brought home the miserable truth that knighthood now was something that fat city merchants paid for. King Charles's grandfather, James the First, had even introduced *baronets* — hereditary knighthoods, in essence, that could be sold to the highest bidder. Their scabrous sons and grandsons now strutted about court like peacocks, calling themselves Sir Vermin or Sir Arse-head. Worse, to make doubly certain that he never went on his travels again, our King Charles distributed titles like chaff to those who had so recently been his sworn enemies: men like my other brother-in-law, Sir Venner Garvey, Member of Parliament for some foul Yorkshire borough under the Rump, a regular attender at Cromwell's mock-Parliaments and a trusted advisor of the Lord Protector himself. Now he was a stalwart in the so-called Cavalier Parliament that was meant to be so loyal to its restored king, but somehow was not. Venner Garvey: an obsequious rogue who denounced the king behind his back as an atheist and a libertine while accepting largesse from the royal hand. Poor Elizabeth, for not even the title of Lady Garvey and the three thousand a year which had so attracted our mother to the match could make up for sharing her bed and body with such a loathsome travesty of knightly honour.

By the time I reached the crest of Portsdown hill, I was in bitter and downcast temper once more. My clothes were wet yet I felt overly warm and my stomach was tightening. I reined in and looked down over the great sweep of a view. The smoke of Portsmouth's chimneys rose in the middle distance, tucked into one corner of the low island which stretched away southwards from the old Roman walls of Portchester Castle just below me. A single bridge over a narrow creek separated this marshy, fetid island from the mainland. The square tower of St Thomas's Church, the best seamark for miles, rose above the mean buildings of the town. And away to the left I could make out the king's flag fluttering above the round, low bulk of Southsea Castle, the only other building of note on the island.

There were forests of masts alongside the wharves of the dockyard and filling the broad harbour, the greatest of them belonging to the unmistakeably huge bulk of the *Royal Charles*, formerly the *Naseby* — the ship that had brought our king back from exile. My eyes did not linger on these. I looked further out, beyond the narrow harbour mouth and its grey-stone forts. The Solent channel stretched from the Portsmouth shore to the Isle of Wight, the great dark blur of land beyond. There, between the two shores, several dozen ships sat at anchor. I discounted what was obviously a merchant fleet, starting to move out on a westerly wind, perhaps for the Downs and the North Sea. There were a few more ships nearer the Wight, but even in those days of my deepest nautical ignorance, I knew they were too small and broad to be king's ships. That left two, anchored close to the Gosport shore, across the harbour mouth from Portsmouth. Even without an eyeglass, I could make out the large royal ensigns playing out in the stiff west breeze. The nearer ship was the larger, so presumably the *Royal Martyr*. And beyond her . . .

I stared pessimistically for several minutes at the distant, dark hull of my new command. There she lay, His Majesty's ship the *Jupiter*, and on her, all my hopes, my whole destiny, and perhaps my very life itself, would depend.

★　★　★

I rode into Portsmouth as dusk fell. The guard on the town gate was rude and perfunctory at first, but a glance at my commission brought him stiffly to attention. During my ride, I had considered taking a room at an inn and going out to my ship in the morning, but the king's stress on urgency decided me for immediate passage out to her. For that, I would need to find one of her boats, which meant I would need to find some of her crew. I clattered through the ordered, silent streets of Portsmouth, responding to occasional challenges from watchmen or militia, then on down the High Street towards St Thomas's and past the house where the great Duke of Buckingham died. Poor Geordie Villiers, my mother always called him, but then she and my father had known the duke well. The favourite of both King James and the first King Charles, Buckingham effectively ruled England for each of them in turn, waged war impossibly and incompetently on both France and Spain at the same time and was struck down by a cheap assassin's knife as he prepared to lead yet another invasion fleet bound hopelessly for France.

There were no Jupiters on this street, and knowing the quality of our English seamen, I knew for certain that there would be none at evening prayers in the church. I stabled my poor exhausted Zephyr at the Dolphin, a reliable inn, where the power of a captain's commission and the name of the Earl of Ravensden would be more than sufficient to ensure he would not be sold to some itinerant Irish horseflesh dealer if his owner did not return to reclaim him within a week.

Then I walked out through the walls of Portsmouth by the Point Gate, whereupon I found myself suddenly conjured straight into a scene from hell.

Outside the gates of Portsmouth, on a low promontory that jutted into the harbour, had fetched up every alehouse, whorehouse and worse that wished to escape the regulation of the navy and the town's authorities. Within the space of fifty yards, I saw five heads struck, two men stabbed and one virgin deflowered, assuming, that is, that a Portsmouth maidenhead could possibly have survived intact for fourteen years. Several very drunk sailors spilled out of a rude inn, waving jugs of ale vaguely in the air and singing some obscene verse about the King of France's mistress. Tentatively, I asked, "Jupiters?", but the mob spilled away down an alley, making a poor fist of rhyming "Vallière" with "pubic hair".

A little further on, a group of six or so men stood on a corner, seemingly sober enough to stand and surprisingly uninvolved in mischief. I asked again, "Jupiters?"

The most forward of them, a bluff and tobacco-chewing crop-head, cried, "Jupiters, is it? Aye, we're Jupiters."

My heart sank like lead. If this insolent creature — as fit a man to be a captain-killer as any I ever saw — was typical of my crew, then my voyage to come would be more fraught than that of old Odysseus.

"Is there a boat for the ship?" I asked.

"Aye," said Crop-head, "there's a boat. Down this way, my lord. You follow us."

I should have stated my name and rank there and then, of course, but I was young, and my senses were being assaulted by a rare combination of smell (foreshore mud, rotting fish and the contents of several hundred pisspots emptied into the street) and sound (screaming women, drunken men, crying children, and not a few screaming, drunken, crying creatures of all ages and genders). As I followed the men into an alley that led towards the shore I did not register the fact that three more slipped in behind me.

Crop-head said, "Now, my fine lord. Let's take a look at that cloak of yours, and your purse."

Odds of nine to one gave me pause, of course, but I was a gentleman, and an officer, and there were ways to behave in front of one's inferiors — even if such behaving ended in the grave. I drew my sword. "I think not. And if you're *Jupiter*'s men, you'll pay for this with your lives."

Crop-head had drawn a dagger and was advancing upon me; the others, unarmed, were clearly less enthusiastic. A small crowd of bystanders was gathering at both ends of the alley, interested in spectating at this new sport. Crop-head, slurring slightly, cried, "Come on, brave boys. This fop wants *Jupiter*, that floating curse. Who hates the *Jupiter*? We're *Royal Martyrs*! Come for a reckoning, then, my fine lord? Come, lads!"

The mob advanced a little, but still reluctantly, all eyes on the sharp and clearly much-used blade of my brother's sword. Knowing now that they were navy men, if not from my ship, I knew I had one last card to play — my finest card of all.

Keeping the sword very firmly in my right hand, I drew out my commission with my left, unfolded it quickly with the fingers of that one hand and shouted as loudly as I could, "JAMES, DUKE OF YORK AND ALBANY, EARL OF ULSTER, LORD HIGH ADMIRAL OF ENGLAND AND IRELAND, TO CAPTAIN MATTHEW QUINTON, CAPTAIN OF HIS MAJESTY'S SHIP THE *JUPITER* FOR THIS EXPEDITION — WHEREAS I HAVE APPOINTED YOU TO BE CAPTAIN OF THE SHIP ABOVE NAMED, THESE ARE THEREFORE TO WILL AND REQUIRE YOU TO GO ABOARD THE SAID SHIP TO TAKE CHARGE AND COMMAND OF CAPTAIN IN HER —"

The mob stopped in confusion, and even Crop-head looked nonplussed, for the reading of a royal commission was as holy writ. There was whispering among the onlookers. Then the crowd parted, and a vast, ruddy man with a horribly pockmarked face stepped into the alley. He grinned insanely at the sight of bare blades, and in a strangled voice cried, "Jupiters, to me, Polzeath! For our ship, and our captain!"

A cadaverous, rake-thin man threw down a tankard and moved to the giant's side. Then a third stepped out, small, stooped and simian, making up for his stature with the two wicked curved blades that he carried. At the far end of the alley, three more men appeared. One, little older than myself, was slight and periwigged, an astonishing piece of fashion for such a neighbourhood; more appropriate for the setting was the large club that he held in his hand. The second was jet black, only a broad smile of perfect white teeth declaring his position against the black waters of Portsmouth harbour behind him. The third bore himself like a soldier. "So, Linus Brent," called he. "Attacking a king's captain, are we? Court-martial offence that, Linus Brent. You'll swing for that. There you'll be, dangling from the main yard of the *Royal Charles*, the shit pouring down your pants. That'll be you, Linus Brent."

Brent — or Crop-head — scowled and said, "Didn't know it was a captain. Didn't think they'd get you a captain so fast."

"These are the days of kings and dukes again, Brent," mocked the soldier. "They get things done. Not like your precious Noll Cromwell and your Rump Parliament, Linus Brent. And it's not just any captain, is it? It's the captain of our ship. What's the name of our ship, Linus Brent?"

Crop-head had come to a decision. "Only one ship's name counts for anything in this harbour, Lanherne, you walking piece of filth." He screamed, "ROYAL MARTYR!"

Lanherne matched it with a powerful cry of "JUPITER!", to which the giant added, "To us, boys! For God, the king, Cornwall, and our captain!"

Crop-head Linus Brent lunged at Lanherne with his blade, but my man — my man! — knocked it aside with a small Italianate dagger that he had plucked from somewhere in his clothing. Next to them, Periwig struck one of Crop-head's friends a blow so dreadful that I thought his skull must have split — though the man merely staggered forward with an aggrieved look and launched himself at Periwig in a flurry of fists. White-teeth kicked Crop-head, then grappled with an old man who was missing an ear. At the other end of the alley the giant, Polzeath, took on two more Royal Martyrs, throwing one against a wall and gripping the other in a head-lock that threatened to send him to his own imminent martyrdom. Polzeath's tall, thin friend stabbed a Royal Martyr in the hand, while beside him the monkey-like one with the two blades upended his opponent and jumped upon his stomach.

Now a mere spectator, I became aware that, beyond the alley, the same scene was being repeated ten times over. A wave of Royal Martyrs was retreating slowly up the street, throwing stones and bottles at a crowd that advanced with rhythmic chants of "Kernow! Kernow!" and "Jupiter! Jupiter!" A whore shrieked as Cornish blood splashed her face. I edged past Polzeath, who respectfully muttered, "Cap'n," as he broke a man's nose with his vicious right jab, and got back out into the main street. Suddenly Lanherne, the soldierly leader of my men, was at my side. "Captain Quinton, sir," he said, with all apparent humility and deference. "Martin Lanherne, sir, coxswain of the *Jupiter*. You'll be needing a boat out to the ship? Should be a few minutes, sir, just while we attend to the rest of this business, here. There'll be enough of us standing to form you a decent crew."

Bewildered, I glanced at the walls of Portsmouth Town and the firmly closed Point Gate. "Surely they'll be sending troops out to deal with this riot, Lanherne?"

I asked. "And shouldn't we report the causes of the affray to the deputy governor?"

Martin Lanherne grinned. "The deputy governor and the soldiers won't want to get involved in this, Captain. This is navy business, you see. They know damn well that if they open the gates and march out here in their pretty red uniforms, this won't be *Jupiter* against *Royal Martyr* any more. We'll be together in an instant, shoulder to shoulder, Jupiters and Royal Martyrs. It'd be navy against army then, sir, and we much prefer that to fighting each other."

It was almost dark when an exhausted boat's crew, commanded through a racing tide with exemplary skill by Martin Lanherne, struck out through the entrance of Portsmouth harbour, passing Henry the Eighth's stout round tower on our left. Lanherne spoke quickly in a broad Cornish accent, telling me that like James Harker he was a Padstow man, and that he had first gone to sea as servant to the then Lieutenant Harker in the great Ship Money fleet of 1637. He had been ashore when the civil war began in '42, and had gone with Grenville's Cornish infantry to Lansdowne Hill and beyond, where they had earned themselves immortality as some of the most doughty fighters in the king's doomed cause.

The men who had rescued me in the alley were among the crew, and I asked Lanherne to identify them to me. "The big man, there, he's George Polzeath, Captain, and the skinny one who fought by his side, he's Peter Trenance. Both of them Fowey men, used to fish the Newfoundland banks before Captain Harker persuaded them to take the king's shilling. Our monkey there" — broad grins from the crew — "he's John Treninnick, sir. Speaks little English, only our old Cornish, so you can call him what you like."

I took advantage of this information to satisfy my curiosity. "Was he born like that, coxswain?" I asked. "With that stoop of his, surely he's no use on a man-of-war?"

I could not make out Lanherne's face, but his answer suggested a patient teacher concealing his exasperation from a particularly backward pupil. "Oh, he wasn't born like that, sir. Treninnick, he worked in the tin mines up Zennor way since he was seven or eight, sir, until he volunteered for Captain Harker on Scilly back in '49. Seams three feet high down those mines, and those are the best. Don't let his monkey looks fool you, Captain. He's the strongest man on the ship, and the best foretopman in the navy. Swings through the rigging like an ape, and does the work of three men up aloft."

"And the black man?" The dark-skinned oarsman grinned; I was to learn this was his favoured expression whether seducing a woman (a frequent occurrence) or facing a flogging (even more frequent).

"Julian Carvell, his name is, sir, though whether it's his real one, the good God alone knows. Joined Captain Harker when we were in Virginia, back in '51 or '52, I think. Before that, servant to some old planter, who saw his neighbours making their blacks into slaves, thought he could save on Julian's wages, and tried the same.

Reckoned with the wrong man. Some said Julian there did him to death with a poker up the fundament, but Captain Harker needed every man he could get back then, and didn't ask too many questions. Learns fast, our Julian. Learned the ropes in months, got himself rated able seaman within the year. Good fighter, too — almost as strong as Treninnick, but a longer reach. Keep those two close by you, Captain, and you'll have no fear of Royal Martyrs. Or the Sultan's janissaries, or King Louis's serried regiments, or all the hordes of Tartary, come to that."

Lanherne's blood-curdling encouragement ended with a devilish chuckle and his shrewd eyes seemed to twinkle at me. I nodded, composed myself — for I felt I was looking about me too eagerly — then turned my gaze upon Periwig, a very different specimen to his fellows. He was but a few years older than me, I estimated; a long-nosed man who seemed born to wear a wig upon his head, although of course that would have been impossible for a man of his station.

"*Bonsoir, monsieur!*" he cried cheerily from his oar as he caught my eye.

Now my French was fluent, as would only be expected from the son of an earl, but I had two additional advantages above the run of most of England's gentlemen. First, I had spent many months of exile in France, and for younger sons with virtually no money, the ability to haggle successfully with Parisian butchers and vintners became a form of lifeblood; one learns not to insist upon one's honour and the deference due to one's birth when one has had no bread for three days. Second, and above all, I had grown up at Ravensden Abbey with the imperious, elegant termagant that was my grandmother, Louise-Marie de Monconseil de Bragelonne. The piratical old eighth earl discovered this beautiful, shrill and much younger creature during a court ball at Chambord about the turn of the century. Within three months, she was the Countess of Ravensden, much to the surprise and amusement of everyone from Queen Bess downward. Thus I had both the elegant court-French of *le roi* Henri le Grand's day, and the gutter-French of the Île Saint-Louis in Paris, which in translation was enough to make even a Rochester inn-keeper blush.

I asked his name — "*Roger Le Blanc, monsieur le capitaine*" — and his origin — "*je suis un tailleur de Rouen*" — and why he was serving on one of the King of England's men-of-war. Then sensing Lanherne's discomfort I added, "*En Anglais, s'il vous plais, monsieur Le Blanc.*"

"As you say, *mon capitaine*. I had reason, let us say, to be away from Rouen, and all of France. Matters of the heart, you understand. An unsympathetic judge, and a jealous husband . . ."

Lanherne snorted. "Ten jealous husbands, more like. So he came hotfoot aboard us, last year, when we lay in the Bay of Toulon. Captain Harker, he'd left enough women and cuckolds behind him in his time to recognize a kindred spirit, so he entered him on our books as a supernumerary mate to the sailmaker, who's deaf and drunk most of the time."

"*Mais oui*, Cock Swain. So I serve contentedly aboard this ship, as Jason whiled away his years in Corinth. I repair the sails and flags, and the men's clothes. Alas, sometimes they make me pull on oars, too, trying to make a seaman out of me, for the English think it a duty to interrupt the good content of the French. But it will be an honour to serve you, Captain Quinton, as I served the late and much lamented Captain Harker."

I knew two things, at that moment.

First, and above all, these men were James Harker's, as really and completely as if he still walked among them. This was his crew, virtually to a man, and no captain could possibly replace him, least of all one so young, so poorly versed in the sea and generally reputed to be so incompetent as to lose his first command with almost all hands. The Jupiters could have been forgiven for deserting en masse before such a Jonah came amongst them.

The second thing I knew was that Roger Le Blanc spoke far more elegantly than any other tailor of my acquaintance. Perhaps one might expect this in France, where clothing is a national religion; but I doubted whether even French tailors grounded themselves in the classics, or spoke such flawless English. So flawless, in fact, that he was bound to realize the different meanings in the name that he had chosen, for I was willing to swear on the souls of all the Quintons back to Adam that he had not been born with it.

Le Blanc, white, blank. A ghost.

★ ★ ★

72

So, at last, we came alongside the *Jupiter*, lying at single anchor near the Gilkicker Point. She was of the same rate, burthen and complement as the poor *Happy Restoration*, a frigate of the Fifth Rate with most of her guns on the single covered deck. She was altogether too like the doomed *Restoration* to give me comfort at my boarding of her. We came under her bow, adorned with a lion figurehead, passed down the larboard side, and made for the steps secured to the hull, halfway along. As we approached, the boat's crew shipped oars, and a rope was thrown from the deck above. I took hold of a step and pulled myself off the boat. I had to swallow hard as I stepped onto the deck of this, my new command, and doffed my hat to the royal ensign at the stern. I was whistled aboard by a swarthy, one-eyed officer, the *Jupiter*'s boatswain, whom I knew from the Duke of York's list to be a veteran of the last King Charles's navy. This was a Welshman whose family still retained their old way of patronymics, and thus went by the name of Maredudd ap Llewellyn ap Ieaun Goch ap Dafydd Brynfelin. Even all these years later, I am still not entirely certain that either the Duke of York — his late majesty King James II as he became — or I ever remembered his name correctly. I certainly never could pronounce it, and like all the rest of the crew, I was soon referring to him as Boatswain Ap.

As much of the duty watch as could be gathered was assembled on the deck on either side of the mainmast. Perhaps fifty men stood before me, less than half of the ship's complement of one hundred and thirty. All were garbed in a more or less uniform set of slopseller's wares, with blue cotton waistcoats, blue neckcloths and red Monmouth caps. Unlike the unhappy Happy Restorations, almost a year before, they were at least properly at attention, their expressions neutral and unreadable. A few broke ranks and eyed me as suspiciously as I must have eyed them. Despite myself, I could not suppress the insidious thought that accompanied the sight of each new face: *Did you kill Harker? Or you? And will you do the like to me?* Inwardly, I chided myself for such unwarranted suspicions. In truth, it would have been more justified if the sight of their new captain prompted in my men one terrible thought: *Will you kill us, Captain Matthew Quinton, as you did the men of the* Happy Restoration?

At their head was a man, even younger than me, wearing a splendid green tunic-coat and a broad-brimmed hat that was the height of fashion in London, with a great feather that reached almost to his shoulder. He was a tall lad, though not approaching my height. His face was wide and freckled but unsmiling. I marked the strength of his hostility with a sinking heart.

He doffed his hat, bowed low, and said, "Lieutenant James Vyvyan, sir. Welcome aboard his Majesty's ship the *Jupiter*. If you'll follow me to the quarterdeck, Captain, you can read your commission from there."

Harker's nephew. A good man, but very young.

"Lieutenant Vyvyan. My sympathies on the death of your uncle. By repute, he was an outstanding officer."

The young man's brow darkened. "He was outstanding, sir." He stern face worked with some intense emotion. "He was also murdered."

74

CHAPTER
FIVE

The captain's cabin of the *Jupiter* was bare but for a poorly made oak table, six chairs and two demi-culverins — cannon which were mounted rather further back on this ship than they had been on the old *Restoration*, making a large cabin uncomfortably small. The panels had evidently been painted to James Harker's specification, for in those days captains could still decorate their quarters as they saw fit, not as some faceless clerk at the Admiralty dictated. My predecessor's taste had evidently comprehended an uncomfortable mixture of the classical (the ship's divine namesake casting down thunderbolts from Olympus), the martial (King Arthur slaughtering Saxons), and the erotic (provocative nudes, one of whom bore a troubling resemblance to the Duchess of Newcastle). Otherwise, all of Harker's moveable effects had apparently been taken ashore that afternoon and stored, together with his corpse, in the house of one of the town surgeons. As I'd leant my head against the closed door of my cabin I could hear one of the crew proclaiming a little too loudly that the house in question was now besieged by a regiment of wailing women, bemoaning their lost Hercules of the oceans and fighting each other in the street over the honour of being his favourite. Evidently Captain Harker's love of the fairer sex was not confined to their painted form.

As Harker's servants had already left the ship to begin their bleak search for new employers, it was Lieutenant Vyvyan's servant, Andrewartha — a slight, dark and grubby boy with an accent almost as impenetrably Cornish as his name — who served young Vyvyan and me a light repast a half-hour later. He bustled about the table as we maintained a polite but uncomfortable silence, then retired to stand sniffing loudly outside the door. I set to with an appetite: there was some cheese, a jug of small beer, a bottle of claret, and, incongruously, a cabbage, which we both ignored.

James Vyvyan — named nineteen years ago after his gallant uncle, I supposed — sat opposite me. I sensed at once that ours would not be an easy relationship. His clouded, watchful appearance underlined his manner; he wished himself far away from this travesty of a captain, pretending a right to occupy Harker's position and his cabin. Perhaps he had believed that he could and should occupy this very place himself, for the Lord Admiral was giving ships to men who were even younger than him. At length, as Andrewartha removed the untouched cabbage and replenished our wine cups, the young lieutenant roused himself, sighed, and turned thoughtfully to face me.

"Murder, sir. It can only have been murder." Taken off guard, I experienced an unpleasant thrill at his words. How neatly they chimed with my morbid thoughts on the way down to Portsmouth. I struggled

76

to keep my expression neutral as, without waiting for a reply, he continued.

"My uncle was the healthiest man I ever knew. He'd spent years in the Indies where men die like flies, and never had a day's sickness. He'd been in twenty-six battles by sea or land, great and small, and never suffered a scratch. Not one. Only on Monday, the very day he died, we breakfasted together. He was in the best of spirits." Silence followed these words, and I tactfully busied myself with again refilling my glass. "He told me how this mission would be the making of me, a sure route to the attention of the king and the duke."

"Sir," I said, "the mission remains. You can still make your mark."

"After breakfast, he went ashore," Vyvyan said, ignoring me. "He had a meeting in Portsmouth, he said, though he never said who it was with. I went to the commissioner and the deputy governor this morning, and it was neither of them, nor any of their staffs. It wasn't with Captain Judge, either, as they always met on *Royal Martyr*, and Judge hasn't been off his ship in five days. My uncle's servants didn't know where he went, for he took none of them with him. He came back aboard about six that afternoon and took a turn about the deck, as was his wont. He knew every man by name, and took his time to talk and jest with them. He was no flogger and no tyrant, Captain Quinton. He looked after his men, and in turn, they loved him."

This was evidently just as much a model and a warning for me as it was a recollection of the methods of Captain James Harker. Still, I was grateful for the change in Vyvyan's conversation, and took advantage of it. I asked, "Most of the crew are Cornish, I take it?"

"Perhaps two dozen Devon men, whom we let sail with us out of pity and sufferance, and two dozen other stragglers, like Carvell the blackamoor and Le Blanc, the French tailor. The rest, Cornish to the bone. He had a great name in our county, Captain. Men flocked to serve under him."

The old way of the navy is much diminished in these days, where so many men are press-ganged, or turned over from ships coming in from their voyages into ships going out, keeping them from their families for years on end. Granting shore leave and other privileges to such a crew is inconceivable, for they would desert in droves, probably slaughtering their officers in the process. But once, not long ago, the navy was a different and perhaps a kinder world. Then, it was still the case that a popular captain could draw most, if not all, of his crew from volunteers, commanding the prime seamen of his native county. Men served their captain first, their king and navy second, and God a far distant third. Loyalties were more direct and more personal. There was a profound trust and respect between such captains and such crews. Coming from an inland county like Bedfordshire, and being in their eyes but a trumped-up and ignorant young courtier, I had no hope of creating such a crew of men; men who, I could see, would have followed Captain James Harker to the grave. As they had, in one sense.

"Cornwall was the truest county to the king in all of the civil wars," Vyvyan continued. "Our soldiers bled and died for both Kings Charles, the elder and the younger, from Lansdowne Hill to Worcester fight — but our sailors had no one to fight under, after the navy declared for the rebel Parliament. So the Cornish took ship in merchantmen, or privateers, or fought for France or Spain or the Dutch. Then, in the year '48, the fleet mutinied against Parliament and its preference for paying only its soldiers, and the king had a navy again. He called my uncle back from King Louis's navy, and when the men of Cornwall heard that James Harker was back at sea for his king, they came from all parts to sail under him. This isn't just a crew, Captain Quinton. This is Cornwall afloat, ready to fight and die for their proud Jimmy Harker."

It had been a long day, I was weary and saddle sore, I was still shaken by my encounter with the Royal Martyrs, and I was starting to become unconscionably irritated by the invisible, all-pervading presence of the deceased Captain James Harker. Too quickly and too peevishly, I snapped, "As they would have done, no doubt, if he hadn't gone to his grave before all of them, Lieutenant."

For the first time he looked directly at me. I saw then not a king's lieutenant, but a hurt, nineteen-year-old lad who had lost the uncle he worshipped barely two days before.

"As you say, Captain Quinton." Vyvyan placed his palms on the table, as though steadying himself to rise without my permission, but his uncle had trained him

79

well. He composed himself and continued. "He took a walk, as I said, and spoke to perhaps twenty men from the starboard watch. None of them noticed the slightest sign of sickness in him. He was himself, they said, the same as ever he was. Then he went up to the quarterdeck, leaned on the starboard rail, put his hand to his chest and fell dead on the deck. They called me from my cabin and I was there in seconds. But he was gone."

Knowing full well how unwarrantably harsh I had been to the boy, and recalling the deaths that I had witnessed, I said as gently as I could, "A tragedy, Lieutenant — for a great man to be cut down like that. But to die so quickly . . . well, there are many worse ways to die." Vyvyan, staring blankly at the deck, did not respond. "I've seen apparently healthy men drop dead in the street, or at their desks," said I, determined to quash this morbid fancy of his. "Such things happen, Lieutenant. We try to blame others, or we blame God, but most often there's some fault in the body, unknown for all a man's life, that brings about such deaths." This last was pure fraud, for although I had seen enough deaths of that sort, and more than enough of every sort, I was actually parroting one of my uncle Tristram's many discourses on the human condition, delivered long before such profound wisdom (not to mention his bibulous loquacity, generosity of purse, and blood relationship to one of the king's favourites) had won him the mastership of an impecunious Oxford college. Nevertheless, conjuring up the words that Doctor Tristram Quinton might have said had a settling effect upon my own dark fears; that and Vyvyan's own description of his uncle's death, which hardly spoke of foul murder.

Of course, a nephew in the depths of grief would think otherwise, and Vyvyan looked at me with contempt. "This was murder, Captain Quinton. Who did he meet in Portsmouth? What poisons did they give him? But above all, tell me, Captain Quinton, with all your knowledge of this world: why did my uncle have this note on him when he died?"

He took a torn and crumpled piece of paper from his sleeve and handed it to me. It read, "*Captain Harker. Fear God, sir, remember His grace. Go not ashore this day.*"

I shrugged. "Surely, Lieutenant, this is one of those notes that field-preachers and street prophets thrust into the hands of passers-by every day — the judgement of the millennium is at hand, and so forth —"

"And where would be the field-preachers and street prophets on the *Jupiter*, sir, with a crew that's good Cornish Anglicans almost to a man, and against the Ranters and Quakers and all their lunatic kin . . ."

I already sensed uneasily that this matter of the imagined murder of Captain Harker would dominate much of our voyage, but we had no more time to ponder the meaning of the note, or for me to try and repair my disastrous beginning with my young and grief-stricken second-in-command. Through one of the open windows in the stern I heard our lookout's cry: "*Jupiter*, ahoy! *Royal Martyr*, laying alongside!" There was a small commotion on the deck above as Boatswain Ap hastily assembled a side party and piped someone aboard us. Minutes later I heard firm steps on the deck of the steerage, the space between my cabin and the open deck, and then an equally firm rap on what even then I knew to call a bulkhead.

Three men stepped into my cabin. Two were seamen, their heads as shaven as the crop-head who had attacked me earlier that evening. The third was the very image of one of Cromwell's praetorian guard, the swordsmen of his New Model Army. He even resembled Cromwell, from the portraits I had seen of the old tyrant: squat, strong, his face disfigured by warts. His buff jacket and cavalryman's sword added to the unnerving effect.

Vyvyan was enough of a king's officer to remember his duty. He said, "Captain Quinton, permit me to name Captain Nathan Warrender, lieutenant of his Majesty's ship the *Royal Martyr*."

Warrender made a salute and bowed his head stiffly, as they do in Germany. "Captain Quinton," he said, "Captain Judge's compliments, sir, and he requests that you sup with him aboard *Royal Martyr*."

I was exhausted; another boat journey followed by yet another awkward encounter and a no doubt fraught discussion of the afternoon's war between our two crews, was not what I needed at that moment. But apart from a mouthful of Andrewartha's mouldy cheese, I had not eaten at all since my piece of bread at Petersfield hours before, nor had I tasted a full meal

82

since my repast with my family at Ravensden in the middle of the previous day. It was apparent that in his grief, Vyvyan could not be relied upon to attend to my comforts aboard the *Jupiter*. Most pertinently of all, though, Godsgift Judge was my senior officer, and a request from him was as good as an order. I said, "Very good, Mister Warrender. Lieutenant Vyvyan, resume command of the ship in my absence."

The boat pulled away from the side of the *Jupiter*, bound for the dark bulk of the *Royal Martyr*, which loomed between us and the lights of Portsmouth. I swiftly learned that Nathan Warrender was a man of few words; or if he could have his preference, of none at all. The two men who had accompanied him to my cabin sat behind him still, not pulling on oars, but silent and forbidding. Warrender's servants, I guessed, though they seemed rather unlikely as such.

Despite his surly demeanour, I tried to engage Warrender in conversation and prepare myself a little for the encounter ahead. He was less forthcoming than a mollusc on the topic of his captain, and on his own former captain's rank, he who now served as a lieutenant. He admitted that he himself was once of Plymouth, that bastion of Parliament's cause in the civil war, but I could glean no more than this. He seemed the very archetype of the dour Puritan that we Cavaliers at once mocked and feared. We soon fell to silence, and I had time to ponder whether this captain, Godsgift Judge, of whom the king and his family spoke so ambiguously, was cut from the same cloth. I thought, *I have a crew still loyal to a dead man, a lieutenant set to be consumed by melancholy, rumours and gossip flying amongst the men — and now, here am I, off to sup with the reincarnation of Noll Cromwell and some dull, Puritanical captain who will talk endlessly of lanyards and tackles. O God, look down on thy poor servant Matthew Quinton, for he is surely at the very gates of Hell.*

The side party provided by *Royal Martyr* was exemplary in its discipline and put the *Jupiter*'s to shame. There was no sign of my would-be nemesis, Linus Brent. Warrender and his two ever-present attendants led me below decks, to the door of Captain Judge's great cabin. He knocked, and a high, affected voice warbled, "Enter."

Timorously, I walked into the cabin, and was assailed at once by an overpowering sense that I had been transported by a sorcerer's incantation to some enchanted realm. This was no ship's cabin. Rather, it resembled the salon of one of London's more degenerate hostesses. There was no trace of the stern windows, for they were masked by great curtains of extravagant purple silk, trimmed with cloth of gold. The bulkheads at each side were adorned with cherubs and the hangings patterned with crowns. The panels above our heads were decorated with paintings of the present king enthroned in splendour, while above him his martyred father ascended into heaven, attended by the archangels. The fragrance from scented candles competed vigorously with the odours of a dozen expensive perfumes, drowning out the usual shipboard smells of wood, tar and sweat. My amazed eye took all this in, then fell upon a table groaning with sweetmeats, fruit, cold meats, and cheeses. There were silver goblets, ready to be filled with what would undoubtedly be the finest of wines in the silver jugs that stood comfortably next to the candles.

At the centre of all this astonishing luxury, so unexpected within half a mile of the swills of Gosport, stood a figure who would not have been out of place at the grandest of court balls. Captain Godsgift Judge — for it could be no one else — was of medium height, but puffed up to an unwarranted elevation by a monstrous wig, from which a little cloud of powder emanated at his every movement. His pinched, raised shoes could have been fashionable only at Fontainebleau, in the court of Louis le Grand. His remarkable grey-green frock coat was studded with jewels that glittered too much in the candlelight to be the paste substitutes favoured by the more impoverished rakes of the City. His perfectly white breeches were rounded off by delicate scarlet garters. Finally, and by far the worst of all, his long, harsh face was perfectly white, a fashion affected only by the most daring, or perhaps foolish, of London's wealthiest citizens.

As I took in the whole preposterous spectacle, a recollection crept into my mind. A supper — yet another rather drunken affair — at anchor in an Irish bay the year before. *"Judge? Oh, he's the greatest courtier of all Noll Cromwell's old captains. Desperate to stay in employment, so he seeks every means he can to endear himself with the king and duke. Runs a good ship, but looks more ridiculous by the day.*"

To my utter horror, Judge opened his arms and embraced me after the French fashion, leaving traces of powder on my face and shoulders.

"My dear, *dear* Captain Quinton!" he all but sang. "Judge, sir, Godsgift Judge. Forgive my seemingly fanatical name," here he leant in confidentially with a hint of perfumed breath, "but my mother was a great Puritan, don't you know, and bent my father to her will in this matter, as in so much else. Ah, but when I think of my poor sister, Diedforthysins Judge, I can but thank God for carrying her off when she was but four . . . If it were possible for a man to change the name he was born with, I would be a John or a Charles in the blink of an eye." He rolled his eyes. "But my dearest captain, I really must begin by apologizing for the appalling treatment you received at the hands of some of my crew. I have placed the man Brent in the bilboes, and will have him flogged in the morning. Will that suffice for your honour, Captain? We can bring him to court-martial, of course. In fact we shall, we must! Though it would take quite some time to assemble, and he is at bottom a useful man on this ship, and our orders demand urgency, so we must sail once the wind changes. But your honour, sir, shall come before all . . . No?" and here he paused expectantly.

Not knowing which part of this speech to attend to first, I murmured something about the mission not being held up on a matter of so little import.

86

"Magnanimously said, sir," and he swept me a bow. Then straightening up, he clapped his hands and four servants appeared from behind the hangings, all of whom I would have marked for certain as canting crop-headed London apprentices, were it not for their delicate pageboys' uniforms. One took my cloak, another my sword, the third bade me sit, the fourth poured wine (the finest, as I had anticipated). Nathan Warrender sat, too, his face a mask. Presumably he was inured to his captain's ways. His silent attendants stood rigidly to attention at one side of the cabin. I did my best to ignore their presence, turning to my host, who was clasping his hands together gleefully and simpering at me over the table.

"What did I tell you, Warrender? Did I not tell you that a scion of the noble house of Quinton would be at once truly honourable and truly forgiving? A pleasure to have you aboard, Captain. And, if I may say so, it will be a pleasure to sail with you. A tragedy, of course, about poor Captain Harker — a great captain, and a valiant fighter for the king's majesty."

We raised a glass to James Harker's memory. I began to relax a little, for I thought I now had the measure of this Godsgift Judge. During the last two years I had seen many other examples of the phenomenon that he represented, and not just in the navy. The king's Restoration mysteriously witnessed the disappearance overnight of those who had served the old Commonwealth and Oliver Cromwell so enthusiastically. In their place came forth a new breed of men, out-cavaliering us Cavaliers in their protestations of loyalty to the monarchy, slavishly aping whatever the court was wearing, trying desperately to find some patron among the king's friends to ensure that their past would be conveniently forgotten under our new royal dispensation. Such bewildering transformations of men had even been apparent in deepest Bedfordshire, which sent hundreds of its sons to fight for Parliament in the civil wars — yet now, strangely, it was a place where Roundheads were as rare as three-headed goats.

Our supper progressed. Whatever else he was, Godsgift Judge was a notably generous host, his table resplendent with duck, jellies, rice pudding, and tarts. Cornelia would have been furiously, unforgivingly jealous if she had known her husband was feasting on such fare while she endured the charred meats and sloppy puddings of Ravensden. Judge's wine, too, was impressive, and most efficacious at putting the captain of the *Jupiter* at his ease. I had never known a Commonwealths-man who could tell his Rhenish from his Bordeaux, but Judge was the exception. The wine was Gascon, and old, and very, very good. But as I drank, I remembered how Cromwell had entered into the unholiest of alliances with Cardinal Mazarin, then the ruler of France. The terms of his treaty had driven my brother out of comfortable quarters at Dieppe to a pestilential garret in Flanders, and led me to fight in a hopeless battle against Cromwell's and Mazarin's invincible united armies. Well, I thought, quaffing my wine, at least that same treaty had brought the finest of wines to sober, Puritanical England; as good a proof as one could seek that the Lord will always provide adequate compensation for human woes.

In conversation, Captain Godsgift Judge proved a fluent and utter embarrassment. I learned but little of the man himself. He was not a man of birth and honour, of course, and thus his lack of social grace was to be expected; he was the son of a Yarmouth shipowner, he said, and had skippered colliers between the Tyne and the Thames before the civil wars began and he entered the Parliament's service. By the time of the Commonwealth's Dutch war he was an able and experienced captain, and he distinguished himself in battle at Portland and the North Foreland. At the end of that war he was sent in command of one of the squadrons despatched to Scotland to harass the Earl of Glencairn's Royalist rising in the west — the service which made him virtually the only man suitable to command our current expedition to the same waters. I tentatively asked whom we would meet there, their amities and jealousies, and enquired about the lie of the land, but Judge stopped me abruptly.

"Time enough for such business when we're properly at sea, Captain. Tonight is for good conversation and society, and that alone!"

He refilled my silver goblet. Apart from this willingness to press upon me more and yet more refreshment, though, Judge's idea of "good conversation and society" proved very different to mine. He tried so hard to be the perfect courtier, witty and urbane, that he succeeded only in being the perfect sycophant. He proclaimed the names of all the great people that he knew, one every few minutes, as though he were announcing the guests at a grand ball. Had I so wished, I could have countered his list with my own, ten times as long and composed of people twenty times as great, but that was not the Quinton way. As it was, Judge revealed himself to be too deeply interested in my family and its ways. It soon became apparent, above all, that he was especially interested in what my family could do for him.

"I have a fighting record as good as any, Matthew — if I may? — but these days, that counts for nothing. There are men at court who scorn the likes of me, and all my kind — men who were once feared on every ocean from Jamaica to Batavia. *You served a usurper,* they say. *We served our country,* say we. Take this very ship, Matthew. She's the *Royal Martyr* now, but two years ago, she was called the *Republic.* I commanded this ship in the Dutch war, and pray to God that if we ever have another, I'll command her again. Does it matter what she's called? She's just as able to fight for old England, whatever name she bears, and the same's true of the likes of me. But no. These days, it's all to do with who you know — who you know about the king, that is. Now, your brother, for instance. My lord of Ravensden is reputed to be one of the king's oldest and closest friends, I understand."

"My brother has had the honour of serving His Majesty these fifteen years or more," I said, "since they first were in exile together."

"Quite so, my dear Matthew. And no doubt your noble brother would have considerable interest with

His Majesty, shall we say, when it comes to the weight of his recommendations?"

And so it went on, Judge trying with little subtlety to recruit the beneficence of the House of Quinton for the advancement of his career. He was interested in my brother-in-law Venner Garvey's connections with some of the great Parliament-men. He was fascinated by my anecdotes of the king (he roared at the story of the shitting dog) and the Duke of York. An hour or more passed in this way, as I tried to fend off Judge without insulting his sumptuous hospitality.

All this time, Nathan Warrender sat a little way apart, looking glum. During a momentary pause in Judge's endless stream of obsequiousness, I seized the chance to draw his lieutenant into the conversation. "You were captain of a ship before this, Mister Warrender?"

I knew that the reduction in the fleet following our peace with the Dutch and Spanish had driven many good captains to take employment in lesser ranks. Some of my fellow Cavaliers, young men like me, found themselves in command of lieutenants, masters, and boatswains twice their age; bluff old Republic-men who had captained great ships in the Dutch war. One of the stories that did the rounds of the London coffee houses held it as gospel truth that the captain who had killed the mighty Admiral Van Tromp was now the cook of a Fourth Rate, and turned out the worst beef stew in the navy.

Warrender seemed uncomfortable. "No, sir. I was a captain in the army. The New Model Army."

Judge said, "Warrender, here, was one of the army men brought into the navy by Generals Blake and Deane, to teach us sailors how to fire our guns straight. And to bring us good, tough army discipline, of course."

That would explain Warrender's attendants, I thought: former troopers, probably, taken to sea as his servants by their old officer, to give them some employment and keep them out of the gutters, where so many of them had ended up.

"So you were an artillery captain, Mister Warrender?" I asked.

"No, sir, not at first. In the early days, I commanded in the cavalry."

A chill on my neck, an instinct, call it what you will, impelled me to ask, "Were you at Naseby field, Captain Warrender?"

For the first time, Nathan Warrender looked me in the eye. "Aye, I was, Captain Quinton." He paused, seemingly wondering whether to say more. Finally, he made his decision, and went on. "I was on our left flank — on the Parliament army's left flank, that is, under General Ireton. I faced Prince Rupert's charge, sir. The finest sight I ever saw. Irresistible, they were, with great feathers in their hats all blown by the breeze. Down past Okey's dragoons they rode, ignoring the fire from that flank. When they hit us, it was like being struck by a galloping wall. We stood no chance, none at all."

As though in a waking dream, I said, "My father died in that charge, Captain Warrender."

"I know he did, sir. I saw him die."

There was a profound and awful silence. I saw Judge's face, and it was unreadable.

"He died well, your father," said Warrender, at length. "One of the bravest things I ever saw in my life. If the rest of Rupert's men had followed him, not their wastrel prince, your side would have won the war that day, Captain."

It was no longer considered seemly in polite circles to mention the war, or to talk of "your side" or "our side" — at least, not in polite circles containing a mixture of one side and the other. It was one of many topics of conversation that was now greeted at London dinner tables with the disgust once accorded to someone who had broken wind. But Nathan Warrender was plainly a man who cared not one jot for such niceties. Years later, I read that Noll Cromwell once claimed his ideal officer was "a plain, russet-coated captain, that knows what he fights for, and loves what he knows". Nathan Warrender was the model of that plain man, and he spoke with plain honesty. Of course, Judge was horrified in case his lieutenant's criticism of Prince Rupert made its way back to Whitehall through me. Little did he comprehend that I was the last man living who would betray any man to that duplicitous prince — even had Warrender not paid my father one of the noblest compliments I ever heard.

Much later, as I leaned on the ship's rail to stop myself falling into *Royal Martyr*'s boat, Judge said softly in my ear, "Good night, then, my dear Captain Quinton. God speed back to your *Jupiter*." Then, even more quietly, for Warrender was on the quarterdeck, "I do hope my lieutenant's, ah, *indiscretion* did not spoil the evening for you?"

I replied as soberly as I could. "Very far from it, Captain Judge. In fact, I valued Captain Warrender's honesty, and the honour that he paid to my father's memory. I would not wish to hear that he suffered for it in any way."

Godsgift Judge looked at me curiously, as though some mental struggle was taking place behind the ghastly white face-paint. Finally, he bowed. "You have my word on it, sir. As one king's captain to another."

CHAPTER
SIX

I woke late the next morning, not even the noisy swabbing of the decks or the ship's bell tolling for the change of watch stirring me from the insensibility brought on by Judge's liberality with his excellent wine. I reached out sleepily for Cornelia's welcoming flesh, thinking myself back in our comfortable great bed at Ravensden, but when my hand caressed instead rough wooden planks, I sat up with a start. The smell struck me at once, that unmistakeable stench of a ship of war below decks: old wood, new wood where the old could no longer serve, the oakum that stopped water pouring between the wood, the white-stuff that stopped the sea worms getting at the oakum, the gun smoke ingested from many broadsides, tobacco smoke, bilge water in all its infinite variations of stink, and most potent of all, the odour of over one hundred and thirty men, even allowing for all the dire royal injunctions against relieving oneself between the decks. A frigate of the Fifth Rate is no leviathan but a mere eighty feet long and twenty-five broad, and packing so many men within such a little frame means but little privacy or quiet for any, even her captain. I could hear snatches of talk from the decks above and below, and as I lay in the warmth and comfort of my sea-bed, I listened with amusement to the aimless gossip of the men around me.

"And your wife was on her back for old Harker, too, like half the women of Cornwall and Portsmouth town . . ."

"Why no, that were your sister and your mother, so as I heard . . ."

Then I caught some whispered words that pierced right through me and made me sweat. "Aye, the *Happy Restoration*. All hands, so they say. Gentleman captains, boys. Knows nothing of the sea, and proud of it they are, too. God curse them for their arrogance, and they'll whip the skin off your back if you so much as spit —"

"They say he shat himself with fear right there on the *Restoration*'s deck, aye, right before he gave the order that sent her the wrong way and drove her onto the rocks, just because he didn't know his starboard from his larboard —"

"Harker murdered? Never, I say. The creeping pox, he had — seen that, once, down in Alicante. Big among the Spanish it is, the creeping pox. Some old Portsmouth whore will have given it to him, mark my words —"

"Matthew Quinton, eh? Well, boys, we'll soon see if he's a hundredth part of the men his father and grandfather were —"

I turned over and groaned, then cursed at the thunder of ten regiments of horses inside my skull, regiments provided gratis by Captain Judge's liberality with his wine. As I began to stumble into my clothes, I dimly recalled my return to the *Jupiter*, and Vyvyan's grudging provision of blankets for me to lie in James Harker's surprisingly comfortable sea-bed. Praying to see the face of Phineas Musk was a new and unusual experience, but as I sat in the house of office in the quarter-gallery, the captain's exclusive place of easement, I longed for the old rogue to arrive with my belongings.

I prayed fervently for another arrival, too. For I desired, with all my heart, the presence of Kit Farrell aboard the *Jupiter*. I needed his steady advice. I desperately needed to begin the lessons he had promised me in Kinsale, all those months before. Above all, I needed on this ship one man, just one, that was my own.

For all his youth and strangeness, Vyvyan was an efficient and quietly competent lieutenant, as far as I could then judge such things; for those were the days when all ships, no matter how great, had but one lieutenant, and yet seemed to work as well as they do nowadays, when even the smallest frigates have lieutenants galore crawling out of every inch of the bilges. Nevertheless, I could have done without his bringing the ship's warrant officers to my cabin to be formally introduced to me over a prolonged breakfast of bread, veal, eggs, and small beer. I was not feeling myself, and had wished to avoid my fellow men as long as possible. As it transpired, I need not have been concerned, for rarely in my life have I encountered a more unimpressive group of men (other than when facing a committee of the House of Commons).

Boatswain Ap was the most talkative of them, though this was not much to the good for he was virtually unintelligible. I gathered that he came from some unpronounceable hole north of Cardigan, though he might just as likely have said Cardiff, or Carmarthen, or Caernarvon. It was impossible to be certain from the gabble that came from his mouth, but I quickly learned that an occasional nod and a *just so, Boatswain*, would suffice to keep him happy. Stanton, the gunner, and Penbaron, the carpenter, were devout members of Harker's Cornish coterie, too distraught at the loss of their master (and probably at their employment prospects, also) to manage much in the way of conversation. Although I had enough of a knowledge of guns to be able to find some common ground with the portly, guarded Stanton, there was none at all with the small and wiry Penbaron, for like most captains, I never could properly tell a keelson from a futtock, and to me the wooden world of the carpenter was wholly anathema. He attempted to engage me upon the subject of the mizzenmast, which was apparently held aloft only by the ministrations of the angelic host; but I had no wish to spoil my breakfast so gave him little encouragement.

Then there was Skeen, the ship's surgeon. Thin and dirty, he was a profoundly ignorant and insignificant man, a Londoner whose hearing had been shattered by too many Dutch broadsides a decade before. After James Vyvyan, he had been the first man to inspect

James Harker's body, but had done no more than eventually and solemnly to pronounce that the captain was indeed dead, a fact that Vyvyan and the whole crew had known well enough twenty minutes earlier. Skeen would have been an obvious suspect for the poisoning of Harker, but it was hard to imagine this repulsive and foul-smelling little creature being competent enough to bring off such a cunning and secretive crime. I prayed privately to Our Lord for good health through our voyage, that I would have no need of Skeen's ministrations.

The lowest of our warrant officers, in rank at least, was one William Janks, a bluff old Norfolk man and the provider of the excellent veal to which I found myself unable to do justice — a sad consequence of Captain Judge's table. Like most of the navy's cooks, he was a maimed sailor, given the post as a means of supporting himself. Janks had no left leg; it had been hacked off during the Hispaniola expedition, to save him from the gangrene. Unlike most of the navy's cooks, though, Janks could actually cook, and so well that Harker had felt no need to employ a second cook for his own table, as was usually the case. Janks was so old that he had actually sailed with my grandfather during the notorious attack on Cadiz in '25. This had been old Earl Matthew's last voyage at sea, and Janks told a good story of my grandfather stamping and raging on his quarterdeck as the invading army returned to his ship, drunk as lords after liberating several warehouses of wine, instead of pressing home their assault on Cadiz. I could imagine my grandfather's wrath at the realization that the unfailing ability of the English to get unspeakably drunk on any foreign shore had cost him a chance of gathering up all the booty of Cadiz town, thus restoring the fortunes of the House of Quinton. As the cook mumbled on toothlessly, I could see that this, my grandfather's greatest disaster, had been the apotheosis of Janks's life. For him, nothing since had matched the sheer excitement of that great adventure when he was young and whole, and nothing ever would. The ship's cook, at least, was an ally, I thought, with a disproportionate amount of pleasure.

There were two exceptions to the regiment of mediocrity that made up the ranks of my warrant officers, and I was soon to wish that they were as insipid as the rest. The first was the ship's master. Malachi Landon was a brooding great ox of a man. His salute was surly, and as he stood in front of me, lofty and arrogant, his whole body screamed its contempt for the ignorant young prig of a captain who stood before him. Even so, Landon — like all the other officers — knew well his dependence on my testimony to his good conduct at the end of our voyage, and his words, spoken in a harsh Kentish burr, were less hostile than his posture. He gave his opinion that we were wasting time, lying at an anchor waiting to sail west when we had such a fine breeze to take us east, and northabout around the top of Scotland; but our orders from the king and Duke of York were to sail west to allow us to send word to Dumbarton, and although I could not share such a confidence with Malachi Landon, I made it clear that we had no discretion in the matter. He then asked if I would be keeping my own journal, or intended to issue the sailing commands, as some of my fellow gentleman captains were already doing. I replied that, for the moment, I had no intention of doing either, and he seemed morosely content at that.

Later, James Vyvyan told me that Malachi Landon had long been master of a large merchantman trading with the Levant and was a Younger Brother of Trinity House, no less, with good connections to both courtiers and Parliament-men. Having avoided taking service under the Commonwealth (whether out of secret affection for the king, as he claimed, or a fondness for the profit to be had from Levant voyages, Vyvyan could not say), Landon now fancied himself ready to captain a king's ship. He was bitterly discontented at having been given instead a master's post on a mere Fifth Rate frigate, rather than one of the ships sent to Lisbon or the Mediterranean on their grand voyages. He and James Harker had quarrelled endlessly, it seemed; for Harker esteemed his own seamanship, and his ability to set a course. No doubt Landon was outraged to have been passed over when the command of the *Jupiter* became vacant; even more, to have been passed over in favour of the likes of Matthew Quinton. As was my new wont, I tried to cast him as a killer, and found it easy. But Malachi Landon would have killed with a blade or his fists, I thought, not with the subtlety that had done for Harker — if indeed there was any truth in my lieutenant's wild suspicions (and in the wilder fancies that roved through the far reaches of my mind).

That left Stafford Peverell, the purser. He was a perspiring man of perhaps forty years, of middling height but running now to fat. His face was florid beneath his lavish yellow wig. His breath reminded me of the stench of a decomposing dog. He glanced around my cabin with distaste, then looked me up and down in the same way.

"Peverell, sir. Stafford Peverell. Of the Peverells of Rydal. In the county of Cumberland." He paused, as though expecting to me to say that of course I had heard of his illustrious lineage. "I am glad to welcome you, Captain. I am sure that having a Quinton at our head will prove a great advantage to this vessel," and he gave a leering smile that exposed his rotten teeth. "We have been rudely governed aboard this ship, Captain. The more genteel of us have found life . . . onerous."

Vyvyan gave this slug-like creature a look of fury beyond his years. Peverell ignored him, and leant in close to me to talk malodorously of the demands of his position, for no office on the ship was as burdensome as that of purser. I must have evinced some visible sign of disbelief, for Peverell, seeing that I needed convincing, held forth at length on the manifold corruptions of the Victualling Office at Tower Hill, the endless pains necessary to keep the ship's books in good order, the importance of keeping an eye open for evil-doing and dishonour among a crew of worthless Cornishmen. A necessary sacrifice, he said, to achieve his ultimate and entirely deserved goals of a clerkship to the Exchequer or the Privy Council, followed by the secretaryship to one of the great men of the realm. Only the impoverishment of his family in the civil wars, he explained, along with Whitehall's unaccountable neglect of his obvious merits, forced him to hold such a mean position as purser on an insignificant man-of-war. And all the time he spoke, I had in mind the Duke of York's incisive assessment of him: *Purser, Stafford Peverell. Haughty and ambitious. A close, cunning fellow.*

It was evident from their faces that the other officers disliked Stafford Peverell, but there was something more in their eyes, too. Was it fear? Could this unpleasant, arrogant, toadying individual pose a threat to anyone? I thought not, although there truly was something about him that sent a chill down my spine.

Later, I asked James Vyvyan if Peverell's contempt for his uncle had been reciprocated. Vyvyan's reply was slow and careful, the response of a man who does not wish to take his enemy into his confidence, but does so despite himself. It had been reciprocated, he said, and tenfold at that. Their contempt for each other was so powerful that Vyvyan had even hysterically accused the purser of being James Harker's murderer. But when the first torrent of grief abated, Vyvyan considered the matter again, and concluded that it would have been far more likely for Harker to have killed the arrogant, overbearing Peverell, than the reverse. But my lieutenant's eyes told a different story, and I knew that one day, I would have to find the bottom of this estrangement between my purser and the rest of my officers.

One warrant officer was missing from the assembly, and at the end of breakfast, as the others trooped out to their duties, I asked Vyvyan, "So where was the chaplain, Lieutenant? The Reverend Gale, isn't it?"

Vyvyan shrugged. "Ashore, no doubt. He'll be back for the Sunday service, sir — or at least, he usually is. Much good that a service from Francis Gale will do for our immortal souls."

Ashore, I thought, *without his captain's permission?* "And what does Reverend Gale do ashore?"

"Captain Harker gave him the permission, sir. He thought it best to have him on the ship as little as possible." Then, for the first time in our acquaintance, James Vyvyan smiled a little. "As for what he's doing ashore, Captain, well, he does the rounds of the places of worship. Most mornings he's worshipping at the Red Lion. Afternoons, at the Greyhound. In the evenings, if he's still sensible by then, his devotions take him to the Dolphin."

A sot, at sea for money, the Duke of York had written.

I was sorry, but hardly surprised. The navy invariably attracted the worst sort of clerics; men who, for whatever reason, were too feeble to hold parishes ashore — or held parishes so poor that they needed to supplement their meagre tithes with almost equally meagre navy pay. My chaplain on the *Happy Restoration*, Geddes, had been past seventy and almost stone deaf. He preached on the same obscure verse of Ecclesiastes for five Sundays in succession until I received a round-robin petition from the crew and had to have an awkward, and very loud, word with him. Of all that poor, benighted ship's company, he was one whose watery death was a blessed release for all parties. A few years afterwards, the unfortunate crew of one ship found their immortal souls in the care of one Titus Oates, convicted perjurer, failed Jesuit novice, and sodomite. He later moved on to far greater notoriety as the man who lied to the king's face and almost brought down the monarchy with his fantasy of a "popish plot" to assassinate Charles the Second. In such company, a drunk like Francis Gale would be harmless enough. How little I then knew.

Gloomily, I prepared to settle down for one of the endless days of dull paperwork with which naval captains are inflicted. Some assume that command at sea is all glory and drama, sails spread, swords drawn, cannons blazing, bearing down to victory and honour. I had known such thoughts, once. Recalling Uncle Tristram's fantastically embellished tales of my grandfather's career had been one of my few ways of reconciling myself to the bitter disappointment of a commission in the navy, rather than the post in the Guards that I coveted; that, and the knowledge that accepting the commission was the only way I could prevent my loyal and livid Cornelia accosting His Majesty and His Royal Highness at the next opportunity, putting her in imminent danger of being arrested as a Dutch spy. In truth, though, very little of a naval captain's time is to do with action and glory. Instead, it is governed by the inexorable tolling of the ship's bell, every half-hour until four hours are reached, when the watch changes and every man aboard (save the captain, of course) must awake, or slumber, or move to some place else, as his particular station demands. How happy the landsman, whose only fixed points are dawn and dusk, and is free of this tyranny of time which decrees that a man must always be in a certain place at a certain moment! Then again, much of a man-of-war's service is spent at anchor in some dull roadstead, awaiting wind, or tide, or water and fresh victuals. Much of a captain's day is taken up with reading the tedious papers of his subordinates, basing upon them equally tedious reports that he then forwards to his own superiors in turn. Can it be any wonder that instead I sought the splendid uniform and glorious reputation of an officer of Horse, wishing, like my father, to charge to glory on some immortal field? As it was, I sat down at James Harker's sea table and steeled myself to pen long letters to the king, and the Duke of York, and Mr Pepys of the Navy Office (and, informally, to my wife, mother, and brother). I hardened my mind to several hours with the purser, poring over the ship's books. There were countless manifests and musters and pay books, even in those halcyon days before the same Mr Pepys and his acolytes turned the navy into a very purgatory of paper.

But as I sat before a sheet of paper on which I had portentously superscribed the words "*Your Majesty, I humbly beg to leave to report*," I noticed Lieutenant Vyvyan hovering in the doorway.

"Was there something else, Lieutenant?" I asked.

Dislike still painted the canvas of the young man's face, but he spoke, reluctantly. "Sir, the note that Captain Harker received. Did you think any further on it?"

I confessed that I had not. Then, to placate him, I took it out and laid it on the table. The words had not changed, nor had my assessment of them. "*Captain Harker. Fear God, sir, remember His grace. Go not ashore this day,*" I read aloud, my face neutral and my tone dry. "An injunction to dread the Lord and be mindful of His good grace is hardly evidence of murder, Mister Vyvyan."

He said, "Sir, look at the writing. Look at the words *Harker* and *His*. Look at the letter H."

The hand was unusual, it was true. It looked like the attempt of a schoolboy to disguise his script by using his left hand, so as to pen foul and secret notes to a young girl. I looked at the letter H. There it was. I looked blankly at Vyvyan.

Vyvyan said, "It's not a capital, sir. It's not *His grace*, it's *his grace*."

He was right. On closer inspection, the "H" in "Harker" and in "his" were quite different.

"Yes, 'his grace'. A *duke* — and a duke who was not royal, so not entitled to 'highness'? The Duke of Albemarle?"

"If I'm right, Captain, it's a duke long dead. His grace, George, Duke of Buckingham. Done to death, here — in Portsmouth town."

"Oh, come, Mister Vyvyan, that's an old story. Far too old and obscure to be a warning of murder, surely."

His face was grim. "For most men perhaps, sir. But my uncle first went to sea with Buckingham: on the La Rochelle expeditions back in the twenties. He was one of his body servants. He was one of those who held the duke as he died. My uncle told me once that Buckingham's blood ran free over his arms and shirt. 'Remember his grace.' The note means this — *Remember that your master Buckingham died in Portsmouth, James Harker, and so shall you if you go ashore.*"

During the next three days, with the wind still obdurate against us, I was engrossed in all that taking command of a new ship entailed. I entertained my officers to dinner. These were awful affairs: Stanton and Penbaron could talk of nothing beyond their own concerns, while the vile Peverell's much-vaunted gentility seemed to involve eating and drinking with great enjoyment as much of his meal spilled down his chin. Malachi Landon meanwhile took pleasure in leading me into conversations designed to expose my ignorance of sea-craft, even attempting to convince me that hogging was to do with the ritual slaughter of pigs to bless our voyage.

On one afternoon I reciprocated Captain Judge's hospitality by inviting him to the *Jupiter*, where Janks did us proud, albeit not with the scented excesses of a floating seraglio. Chicken we had in full measure, herrings galore too and a fine venison pie, followed by bread pudding and several bowls of punch, all served on pewter crockery that bore the monogram "JH".

Vyvyan proved to have excellent social graces and I came to rely more and more upon his company. I learned that he was at bottom a man of honour, whatever he might have thought of his jumped-up captain; his family were old Cornish gentry, and within living memory they had provided a Bishop of Exeter, an admiral, and several Chancery lawyers. During the repast Judge thankfully confined himself to a few ingratiating questions about my grandfather's time at sea. Instead he spent much of his time talking to Vyvyan, and their earnest conversations on obscure points of seamanship gave me cause once again to recall the depth of my own ignorance, and the death-throes of the *Happy Restoration*.

On other days, there were the inevitable duty calls on the dockyard commissioner and the deputy governor of the town, involving much lavish toasting of the king's health. Purser Peverell evidently thought that securing the recommendation of his new captain was best achieved by taking the said captain as slowly and methodically as possible through every minute entry in every single piece of paper relating to the ship. He dealt with me as I had not been treated since my schooldays, when old Mervyn had been at once wrathful and condescending towards the feeble young dullard whose utter failure to master the poetry of Vergil detained them both long after the tolling of the school bell. My dislike of the purser increased, and I began to fear he might be capable of killing a man by boring him to death, or else by breathing on him for some length of time.

Then there were musters of individual messes and watches, when I went below decks and endeavoured to look earnest as Boatswain Ap showed me defective hammocks and carelessly stowed sea chests, or else denounced a significant proportion of the crew as blasphemers, drunks, or both. One of my fixed tasks was the regular, obligatory reading of the Articles of War to the entire crew, warning them of the dire fates that awaited any who broke the navy's strict legal code. At each of these formalities, I attempted to appear at once splendid and authoritative, but probably succeeded only in resembling a leaf on a branch in an October breeze. I could not seem to avoid catching the eyes of my erstwhile saviours, Polzeath, Trenance, Treninnick, and the rest, who looked upon me with an apparent mixture of pity, contempt, and (in Treninnick's case) utter incomprehension. The black man, Carvell, had a disconcerting habit of whistling silently to himself during the reading of the Articles of War, but remembering the fate that he might or might not have bestowed upon his sometime employer in Virginia, I decided to let the matter pass. As for my mysterious French "Periwig", the self-proclaimed tailor Roger Le Blanc, he seemed to look upon every one of the ship's proceedings as a matter of considerable amusement, smiling to himself at each recitation of the ferocious litany of floggings and death sentences that formed the peroration of most of our Articles of War. My heart sank a little more at each of these occasions, for earning the respect of my men seemed as distant a prospect as the shore of old Cathay.

Even so, it was clear even to me that Boatswain Ap and Martin Lanherne had the ship's discipline well in hand, both formally and informally, so when Vyvyan requested permission to go ashore to pursue his investigation into his uncle's death, I saw no reason why he should not. This would give me some respite from his wild suspicions and — worst of all — his calm, unfussy competence, which threw my own abiding ignorance into such sharp relief.

There was no sign yet of the Reverend Gale. No sign, either, of Kit Farrell.

There was, however, one (relatively) welcome arrival. I was penning a second letter to the Duke of York when one of the boatswain's mates summoned me to the quarterdeck. A boat was pulling painfully towards us from Portsmouth, rowed by two straining oarsmen. It lay deep in the water, for it carried what I recognized as my long-expected sea chest, one of my (far larger, and thus unexpected) land chests, and a horribly uncomfortable, green-faced Phineas Musk.

Even after Musk and my belongings had been deposited in my cabin by several perspiring crewmen, it proved impossible to get a word out of him. He sat at my table, drinking only a little boiled water — itself a sign that he was truly ill — and shaking his head softly. The creaking of the ship's timbers and the gentle lapping of the waves on our hull, two of the staple sounds of life at sea, seemed to instil in Musk a terror of imminent doom. Eventually, and without a word, he reached inside his jacket and produced two letters, both addressed by familiar hands, and a third letter in an unfamiliar and shocking script, addressed to "*Capt M. Cwinton, threw care of the nobble Ld of Rivensdin at Rivvensdin House in Londun.*"

I began with my brother's letter, in which he wrote of the king and duke's satisfaction at my taking command, and which ended, "*Brother, I send you Musk. I think you will need him more than I, for they tell me good servants are rarely found at sea, and whatever his faults, Musk is good enough. Besides, I will probably kill him if he continues to lord it over me here, and a voyage by sea may teach him and his stomach a little more humility. God bless you in what you do, Matt.*"

Musk looked up miserably. "Going to sea, at my age. If Our Lord had meant Phineas Musk to go to sea, he'd have made certain I was born a herring."

I asked, "So who cares for my brother, and Ravensden House?"

"He's gone to the abbey, and your mother. Captain van der Eide has gone back to his ship, so he won't have to deal with all the boundless excitement from Veere. The earl wants to go through the estate rentals with old Barcock, too. Says he'll tolerate some of the goodwife's cooking for a fortnight or more, and in due course he'll take one of her sons back with her to train him up in the duties of the London house. Expect he thinks I'll die on this voyage, and judging by that boat out from Portsmouth, he's probably right."

I laughed, and summoned the purser. Peverell shook head and licked his lips, seeming to regard the of entering Phineas Musk as captain's servant on the ship's books as a task equal to all the labours of Hercules. If Peverell's look could have killed, I would have been as dead as James Harker. Finally, after much protest and several admonitory mentions of the names "Pepys", "the Duke of York" and "King Charles", he skulked away to begin work.

I opened the second letter, which was from Cornelia, written in the flowing, loving hand and awkward style of a Dutch woman who had not known a word of English until she was seventeen. There was more talk of my mother's waspishness, of the Barcocks, and of Cornelis, who had received urgent news which caused him to return suddenly to his ship. He had already sailed from Greenwich Reach, she wrote, on the same strong westerlies that continue to trap the *Jupiter* at Portsmouth. She eschewed platitudinous comments about missing me, though I knew she did, just as I missed her. But she could not refrain from reciting her concerns for my safety, just as she ever had. I was barely eighteen and had met her but once, at her uncle's house in Bruges (he and my mother, our matchmakers, being dimly acquainted of old), before I went off in all my finery to fight for the Duke of York and the Spanish on the dunes before Dunkirk. We were not even betrothed, but she had berated me almost from dawn to dusk until I promised not to hazard myself foolishly, and to return to her unscathed. Which I had, but for a few scratches and a slash across the ribs: no mean feat in that Battle of the Dunes, which was as one sided as any since Cannae. We had run before the incongruous alliance of the turtle-helmeted

113

fanatics of the New Model and the French Mousquetaires du Roi, crossing each other as their mass-priests paraded relics of the saints before them, to the evident distaste of their allies.

My escape satisfied Cornelia: while our tiny Royalist army disintegrated in the twin whirlpools of penury and recrimination there was no employment for my sword. I could be safely married. Yet despite being on every other count the most sensible and practical wife any husband could wish to find, Cornelia remained incorrigibly convinced that the moment I left her sight I was in mortal danger. She cried for days when I went off to command the *Happy Restoration*, believing that we were bound to encounter an Algerine corsair (which would have been preferable to our encounter with the rocks of County Cork, if truth be told). She once even pursued me all the way to a horse-fair in Royston merely because she dreamed I would be murdered there by a one-eyed Chinaman.

"*God guard and keep you dearst love,*" she concluded her letter. "*Little we know of yr voyage but Charles tells there may be some dangers. You know how fearful I am, thinking yr schip shatterd once more upon a black shore. Or pounded by the guns of mighty enemy. Cornelis told me foolish, and perhaps he has rights. So be careful at once and glorious, if it is possible to be both. Remember always that here at Ravensden, you are rememberd and loved. From my heart to yours, for ever, Cornelia.*" She had written a postscript on the reverse. "*On hearing your schip was ordered for west of Skotland, your mother seemd*

114

agitate. I asked for why, but she is telling me not. She startd a letter to you, then threw it on the fire."

This postscript perplexed me more than Cornelia's anxiety. Irascible she may have been, but my mother was rarely agitated, beyond the scope of her usual hates and an occasional oath at her inability to move as quickly and freely as once she could. As far as I knew, too, she had no particular connection with Scotland; at least, none greater than was usual for someone who had been about the Stuart court for years, and was thus bound to know many of the Scots who had come down with their king when the crowns united. I asked Musk if my mother seemed well at his going from the abbey with my belongings, and he said she seemed to him the same as she ever was. On reflection, this was little surprise. My mother was not a woman to betray such emotion before Phineas Musk, whom she had kept on at Ravensden House for years despite detesting him almost as heartily as she had Oliver Cromwell.

I opened the third, barely literate, letter. It was from Kit Farrell's mother, to whom I had addressed my letter inviting him to join the *Jupiter*, along with a copy of the royal order to Mister Pepys. In spelling so execrable that it made Cornelia's prose read like Dryden, Mistress Sarah Farrell, widow and innkeeper of Wapping, informed me that, desperate for employment and sustenance, her son Kit had taken ship for the East Indies some weeks earlier. There was a chance that his vessel had been held up in the Downs by the same strong westerlies that held us in Portsmouth, but in her opinion as the widow of a man who had served

115

at sea for *twinty ayt yers*, it was unlikely. Even so, she had forwarded the letter and the warrant to Deal, and prayed that her zeal in my cause would earn her recommendation and remuneration from both her *good Capt Cwinton* and the *most nobel Erl of Rivinsdin*.

I was even more alarmed by the contents of this third letter than by the news of my mother's behaviour. It seemed that for this most dangerous and delicate of voyages, I had exchanged the considerable nautical experience and good sense of Kit Farrell for the alternative attributes of Phineas Musk. It did not seem a good bargain.

That evening, I selfishly shunned the company of the other ship's officers and supped both wigless and alone, apart from the baleful presence of Musk, who was at least three times older than most other servants in the navy and a thousand times more miserable than any of them. I could hear the noise of the other officers dining at their table in the steerage, just outside my door, and as the wine and ale took hold, I made out Peverell's voice, raised about the others, talking loudly and indiscreetly of this arrogant young sprig of the nobility that they now had for a captain:

"Why, gentlemen, the first Quinton was but a saddler to William of Normandy! Not a respectable line, at all, despite all his airs and graces."

Landon remarked on the king's liking for gentleman captains, men ignorant of the ways of the sea and the heavens. They would soon drive out of the navy all of the honest tarpaulins — seaman officers born and bred, like himself and Godsgift Judge — who had rightly monopolized all the commands under the late republic. Then where would the country be in the coming war with the Dutch, he asked. A generation of butterfly captains going up against Lord Obdam, Evertsen, de Ruyter, and the rest, great seamen all — God help England and preserve her from conquest by strutting Dutch butterboxes!

Penbaron, the carpenter, grunted encouragement in those rare moments when he was not bemoaning the state of the mizzen or the rudder, while Boatswain Ap's eloquent speech might have represented agreement or disagreement for all anyone could tell. Finally, they mixed the toasts for all the days of the week, toasting in turn the king, sweethearts and wives, absent friends, and adding their own particularly loud toast to the memory of James Harker. I finished my own supper in even worse temper than I had begun it, glaring at Musk if he attempted to speak.

James Vyvyan came back aboard late that evening and reported to me on the quarterdeck, where I had gone in hopes that the breeze would blow away the recollection of my officers' conversation. My lieutenant was more than a little chastened; a more tired and humbler version of himself. He had little to show for his two days ashore, in quest of evidence of murder. He knew that on the day of his death, Captain Harker attended morning communion at St Thomas's church, and had later dined, seemingly alone, at the Red Lion in Portsmouth town (and if he had been poisoned there, Vyvyan observed, twenty others who ate the meat

117

of the same cow, and fifty others who drank the same beer, would also have died that night). He had briefly met Stafford Peverell, who was ashore negotiating with the victualler's agent, and had exchanged a word with some of the ship's crew at the side of the camber dock. No one saw him from two in the afternoon until about five, when he returned to the ship's boat. For those three hours, Captain James Harker's whereabouts were a mystery.

"Well, Mister Vyvyan," I said, as tactfully as I could, "surely there might be an innocent reason for his disappearance? Could he perhaps have had a friend to take leave of?"

Vyvyan thought upon the point and said, very slowly, "If you mean a woman, sir, then yes, it could be an explanation, I'll grant — but I spoke with some of those whom — well, whom he favoured, as it were — and he was with none of them. Or so they said."

"Might it not be, Lieutenant, that he had found a new object for his affections — one unknown to you and to his other . . . friends?"

James Vyvyan struggled with his own thoughts for a moment longer. But he was an intelligent young man, and ultimately, his good sense triumphed over grief and rage. "Yes, sir. It's the likeliest explanation." Then he smiled faintly. "My uncle was ever a man for conquests, sir. Ships, islands, women — they were all alike to him, and he took as many of each as he could. So . . . no murder, then. You have the right of it, Captain. Indeed, I think I am grateful."

He extended his hand, and I shook it.

118

By the time I retired to bed that night, Musk had made a tolerable job of transforming the *Jupiter*'s great cabin into a floating miniature Ravensden. Old hangings from the London house adorned my walls — or bulkheads, rather — thus obscuring some of the more dubious examples of James Harker's taste in art. Silver-plated vessels that had been the servants' pewter until my grandfather sold off all the finest Quinton ware now decorated the cabinets and table, relegating Harker's pewter to the officers' table. Pride of place went to two small copies of the portraits of my father and grandfather from the great hall of the abbey, their faces picked out unerringly by the two lanterns that swung overhead, and the somewhat larger portrait of Cornelia by Lely, painted just after the Restoration. My sword hung upon a spike: the sword that had been in my father's hand when he died, which Charles had eschewed, and which I had thus inherited. Near it lay my chief inheritance from my grandfather, an odd, gold-gilt oval box which opened up into a succession of dials: God alone knew what they all meant, or did, but I had loved playing with it as a child and its presence alongside me aboard the *Jupiter* was strangely reassuring. Surrounded by my own things, lying in my own blankets, my head on my own pillow, and despite the half-hourly clangour of the ship's bell, I gradually fell into a more comfortable sleep than any I had known since coming aboard . . .

Only to have it shattered, some time in the small hours of the morning, by a great roaring from the

119

starboard side. Sleepily convinced that we were being boarded by corsairs, I snatched sword and pistol and ran from the cabin. As I did so I trod on Musk, who, too fat for the servants' kennel-like cabins on the poop, had decided to sleep on the deck outside my door. In truth, and although I would never have admitted as much to him, I found it a powerful reassurance that anyone who wished to reach me would have to get past Phineas Musk first; whatever else he might have been, the old rogue was one of the fiercest (and dirtiest) fighters I ever saw in my life.

Vyvyan emerged from his tiny cabin, sleepy and unarmed, and called after me, "Captain, there's no alarm . . ." But I was already running for the deck.

I reached it to see our sentries holding their sides in an effort to suppress their laughter. Polzeath and Treninnick were trying to pull a struggling, roaring, kicking, swearing brute of a man onto the deck. When I reached the side, I saw Lanherne, Carvell, Le Blanc, Trenance, and two others manhandling the creature upwards from the boat below. Trying to gather as much of the dignity of command about me as my nightshift would allow, I said, "What's the meaning of this, coxswain? Who is this fellow? Boatswain, administer the appropriate punishment for disturbing the quiet of the ship —"

Le Blanc and Carvell swapped obscenities and sniggered. Lanherne looked at me, grinned, and said, "Don't think you'll want to punish this one, sir. This is the chaplain, Reverend Gale. Today's Sunday, and he's got to preach a sermon seven hours from now, so we

120

thought we'd better pull him out of the Dolphin and back on board."

By this time, the Reverend Francis Gale was approximately upright. He had several days' growth of beard, his hair was matted and he stank of drink, piss, and vomit. A man less likely to be serving our saviour, and, more immediately, the Most Reverend William, Lord Archbishop of Canterbury, was difficult to imagine. In the circumstances, it was also perfectly impossible to imagine anything appropriate to say to him.

In the event, it was Gale who spoke. He fixed me with two little red eyes and said, "The grace of our Lord Jeshush Chrisht, and the love of God, and the fellowship of the Holy Shpirit, be with you, Captain." Then he squinted at me, swayed and reached for my shoulder. "Hell's gates, you're tall. And your hair's going, already. Bald as a coot before you're thirty, I fear. For ever and ever, thy kingdom come." He gave a great belch. "Now . . . where's my cabin."

CHAPTER
SEVEN

I stood nervously on the quarterdeck of the *Jupiter*, staring out over an assembly of crewmen who shuffled apathetically on their heels. The more devout, like the giant Polzeath and the blackamoor, Carvell, were already mumbling prayers to themselves. There was a great deal of murmuring and gossiping, despite Boatswain Ap's barely intelligible imprecations to keep a godly silence. I thought I saw eyes on me hastily averted, and whispered conferences, and laughter. I imagined that in their eyes I merited as much respect as "the liar" — the man chosen each week for the exquisite punishment of swabbing the bow directly beneath the four holes of the ship's heads. Some men looked about them in that distinctive way sailors have, estimating when the wind might change and our voyage might begin. The hard westerly had moderated a little, but our ensign still streamed out strongly behind the bewigged and capped head of James Vyvyan, who stood at my side.

I could hear the church bells of Portsmouth and Gosport summoning their respectable congregations to services led by respectable, competent vicars. In contrast, the rather less respectable congregation thronging the deck of the *Jupiter* awaited one of two equally dreadful alternatives: in the first, the Reverend Francis Gale arrived in time to lead our devotions, assuming he could remain upright and deliver the words in something approximating to the right order; in the second, the Reverend Francis Gale did not appear, in which case the service would be led by an even less adequate substitute. The tradition of the navy demanded that in the absence of a chaplain, the spiritual well-being of the crew, and the task of leading their divine oblations, be taken upon the unwilling shoulders of her officers. Vyvyan had volunteered for the task (having a bishop in the family ensured that it held no terrors for him), but I could not surrender it to him without giving up the last vestige of my authority. Thus, and unlike virtually every other seaman in history, I prayed with all my soul for the arrival of a Gale.

As the sand ran from the ship's glass towards the moment when the bell would be rung, I thought ever more despairingly of the services that I had attended at our local parish church; I combed them for inspiration in case the task of leading the Jupiters in prayer should devolve upon me, but the Reverend George Jermy was hardly a shining example of Anglican eloquence. Put in as vicar of Ravensden by my grandfather fifty years before, Jermy had, with equal dexterity, survived countless changes in the official religion of the state and warded off the attentions of the grim reaper. Ordained by an ancient bishop who as a young man had been one of the chaplains attendant upon King Henry the

Eighth's Archbishop Cranmer — the very man who had created the entire Church of England on which our immortal fates depended — Jermy's Methuselah-like refusal to die did not prevent his falling victim to the meandering habits of old age. As a result, his services were invariably an opportunity for the good folk of Ravensden parish to snatch another hour's sleep of a Sunday morning, the pews rocking slightly as snoring men and women swayed back and forth to the accompaniment of his soothing whispers. Strangely, Sunday was the only day of the week when my passionately Anglophile Cornelia reverted unhesitatingly and very publicly to the dour Calvinism of her youth, giving her the ideal excuse to avoid attendance at church.

I glanced at the clumsy pendant-watch that had been a coming-of-age gift from my uncle. Despite my complete failure to recollect a single sermon of Jermy's where I had stayed awake long enough to note the subject matter, I realized that the moment for action was at hand. We could wait for the sottish Gale no longer. I had a Bible in my cabin, of course, and the good old prayer book from the days of Cranmer and Queen Elizabeth. I would send Musk below to fetch them. Perhaps I could extemporize something on the first verse of Genesis . . .

A flurry of black and white from the steerage heralded the timely and surprisingly sober arrival of the Reverend Francis Gale. In daylight, Gale was not an unimpressive man: stocky, ruddy, and aged perhaps in his mid-forties, he was clearly no milk-and-water cleric, donnish and lost in his books. Shaven and washed, his wild hair concealed — at least to some extent — beneath a modest wig, and clad in full canonicals, Gale looked the part of a man of God. At the very least, he looked the part far better than his putative substitute, Captain Matthew Quinton. He raised a comparatively steady hand in benediction, and his unlikely congregation shuffled into a variety of prayerful postures. Even our four known papists (including the enigmatic Frenchman Le Blanc), and our one Mahometan, a thin and ingenious Algerine renegade named Ali Reis, closed their eyes and bowed their heads in their position slightly apart from the rest at the starboard rail.

I expected the usual prayers and intercessions from the century-old Prayer Book; but not today. Gale looked around his congregation, then directly at me, and began with the words of Psalm 51: "I acknowledge my transgressions, and my sin is ever before me."

I had heard these words, as the prelude to a short sleep, from George Jermy many times before. But from Jermy, who had committed no sin in half a century that anyone knew of, this sentence had always been a mild rebuke to his flock for the manifold inebriation, fornication, and quarrelsomeness in Ravensden village during the course of the previous week. Not so from the lips of Francis Gale. Our chaplain continued with unfamiliar words, read from a very small and very new leather-bound book that he drew out of the sleeve of his cassock.

"O eternal Lord God, who alone spreadest out the heavens, and rulest the raging of the sea; who hast compassed the waters with bounds until day and night come to an end; be pleased to receive into thy Almighty and most gracious protection the persons of us thy servants, and the fleet in which we serve."

Vyvyan glanced at me, a quizzical frown on his young face. Down in the waist of the ship, Polzeath's features were beatific. Some around him seemed confused, others transfixed. Even our half-deaf surgeon Skeen seemed to listen intently to Gale's strange new prayer, and both Roger Le Blanc and Ali Reis seemed rapt.

"Preserve us from the dangers of the sea," continued Gale, "and from the violence of the enemy; that we may be a safeguard unto our most gracious sovereign Lord, King Charles, and his dominions, and a security for such as pass on the seas upon their lawful occasions; that the inhabitants of our Island may in peace and quietness serve thee our God; and that we may return in safety to enjoy the blessings of the land, with the fruits of our labours, and with a thankful remembrance of thy mercies to praise and glorify thy holy Name; through Jesus Christ our Lord. *Amen*."

The echoing "*Amen!*" from the crew was thunderous, and carried across the water to the *Royal Martyr*, some three hundred yards away. Judge, who had no chaplain and who had thus conducted his own service punctually and concisely, was looking across at us from his quarterdeck, no doubt wondering what strange wave of evangelical zeal had swept over the *Jupiter*'s company.

Gale took the rest of the service forward in an equally brisk and impressive manner, leading a surprisingly responsive crew in three lusty hymns, dispensing the bread and wine at Holy Communion with exemplary efficiency, praying for our new Portuguese queen and casting a brief but incisive sermon upon Psalm 107, ever a favourite in the wooden world: "They that go down to the sea in ships, that do business in great waters; these see the works of the Lord, and his wonders in the deep." This he turned into a paean to the memory of James Harker, passing over the dark rumours of murder that consumed both Vyvyan and the entire lower deck, where suspicion had taken as firm a hold as bindweed.

Following Gale's final benediction and the dismissal of his congregation, James Vyvyan murmured to me with a new and almost conspiratorial fellowship. "My God, sir, if he could speak like that every Sunday, he'd be a bishop."

This sudden confidence from my lieutenant delighted me. For a moment, I was torn between engaging Vyvyan in further discourse and seeking out the Reverend Gale. But I knew which of them would prove more elusive in the future. I went across to my chaplain to introduce myself formally.

Gale was deep in conversation with the Frenchman, Le Blanc. I caught just a snatch of his words — ". . . terrible, indeed. But rumour is truly the devil's seedbed, monsieur . . ." — as I approached. Gale halted and turned his only faintly bleary eyes upon me with a discomforting stare that both weighed and measured.

"Captain Quinton," he said at length. "Lord Ravensden's brother, then. You're very young to be taking Harker's place."

Inwardly, I raged at the impudence of the man. But the eyes and ears of the crew were all around, he was a man of God in full canonicals, and it was a Sunday. Thus, with difficulty, I confined myself to sarcasm, that last resort of a defeated protagonist.

"A pleasure to make your acquaintance, Reverend. For the *second* time, in case you have forgot the first." He glared at that and I felt a small satisfaction. "A most interesting service, if I may say so. A particularly unusual prayer at the beginning."

Gale sniffed and looked steadily at me with the wan, distant expression that I would come to know so well. "You won't find it unusual for long, Captain. It's to be said daily, on every one of His Majesty's ships, from Easter Sunday until the day of judgement. We'll be heartily sick of it within a month."

"Ah. So your prayer book —"

He nodded lightly. "The new book of Common Prayer, now being despatched to all the parishes in the land by direct command of King, Parliament, and Convocation, to be adopted in place of the old one from this Easter. The weekend after next, in other words. A sure path to salvation for a nation that lost its way, Captain Quinton."

I could not tell whether Gale's remark was spiritual or sarcastic, although I suspected the latter. "I'd heard there's to be a new book, of course — my brother attended the debates in the House of Lords. But I was not aware that the copies had already been sent out."

The chaplain smiled. "As Christians, Captain Quinton, we believe that when the last trump sounds, we shall all stand naked and equal before the judgement seat. Until that dread day, however, we all live most unequally." He turned with a gesture, and we strolled towards the poop. "You, sir, are the brother of an earl, which gives you the command of a king's man-of-war at a most tender age." I felt my face grow hot with the seeming impertinence of his observation, but he continued as if unaware. "Whereas I . . . well, Captain, for all my manifest faults and sins, nobody can take away the fact that Billy Sancroft and I are the oldest and best of friends from our Cambridge days. When we were newly matriculated at Emmanuel, we wagered that by our sixtieth birthdays he would be Archbishop of Canterbury, and I, of York. Now, with thirteen years to go, he is the personal chaplain to King Charles, and I am the chaplain of the *Jupiter* . . ." He waved vaguely towards the deck abaft the mainmast, where a clutch of men stood patiently waiting to speak to him. "We may conclude with some certainty that he will win his part of the wager, and I shall lose mine."

Gale was silent for a moment, looking intently out towards the Isle of Wight. Then he shrugged, as though he had reconciled himself to his unequal fate. "But Billy still throws his old friend some scraps, like my position on this ship and an early copy of the new prayer book. In truth, it surprises me that he doesn't think I'll sell it off to a crooked printer and make cheap copies to undercut the royal printers' monopoly. Come to that, I'm not entirely certain why I haven't."

A sot, at sea for the money. Yet there was plainly more than that to Francis Gale, and I wished to cultivate this unexpected, sober side of my chaplain. After all, he, Stafford Peverell, and Vyvyan were the only men aboard whose rank and station remotely approached my own, and I had less love for Peverell even than Vyvyan had for me. Gale was a younger son of Shropshire gentry who had been stout for the king in the civil wars, which had been particularly murderous in that county; or so the incorrigibly inquisitive Musk had established within a day of being aboard. Gale had fought with the royal armies in both England and Ireland, it was said. That alone, regardless of his connection to one of the king's favourite clerics, would have made him a fit guest at my table. And perhaps he, of all the men on board, had enough authority and common sense to lay to rest this blasted talk of murder, as unsettling to the crew as to their captain. I invited him to dine with me that same day. He smiled but momentarily, and shook his head.

"No, Captain Quinton, I think we'll not eat together, this day."

For a moment, the shock of the offence silenced me. "Sir," I said at length, "refusing your captain's invitation is —"

"Yes, unforgivable, I know, by all the laws of the navy, which have almost the same force as those of God, et cetera, et cetera. But I have a prior invitation from a bottle of crusted port wine, Captain, and by I

130

know not what means, it seems to have brought some of its friends to keep it company. And you, too, have a prior and pressing commitment, of course." I was flummoxed, but before I could speak, Francis Gale looked skyward, as though casting his eyes to the heaven he served.

"The westerly's dropped away entirely, Captain Quinton," he said quietly. "And an old boatswain of my acquaintance who shared a bottle with me at the Red Lion yesterday assures me that by dusk today, we'll have a lively southerly to carry us out of the Solent. *Royal Martyr* is just hoisting the signal to make ready to sail. You'll need to prepare your ship for the sea, Captain. As I don't doubt you already know."

The next hours resembled one of Signor Dante's circles of hell. I had myself rowed across to *Royal Martyr*, there to receive Judge's brusque command. We would sail with the afternoon's ebb, which would carry us easily out of the Solent's western mouth. Lanherne took a boat back into Portsmouth to round up the ticket-of-leave men who were still ashore. The crew's midday meal was rushed and perfunctory, despite Janks' valiant efforts, but the men still queued in orderly fashion to have small beer ladled into their tankards from an open barrel by the mainmast. Victuallers' boats thronged back and forth. We took on chickens, a dozen sheep, and three goats; only my express command prevented the acquisition of a cow, on the grounds that we were bound for Scotland, not Sumatra, and that we already stank like a farm. Other boats took off the wives and the women who perhaps were not quite wives, accompanied by much sobbing from those departing, and some relief from at least a few of those remaining. Men climbed rigging and fanned out along the footropes to ready the sails, long tied tightly to the yards. Surgeon Skeen dealt with his first casualty of the voyage, a stupid brute of a Cornish boy who dislocated two fingers when he missed his grip on the main yard and was saved from falling to his death only by Treninnick's quick reaction. Ali Reis kept up an endless concert of lively tunes on his fiddle, though I had little time to wonder how a Moor had learned such an instrument or the tune of "Loath to Depart". I hastily penned brief letters to my trinity of official correspondents — King Charles, Duke James, and Mister Pepys — and to that other trinity, my mother, brother, and wife. Between them, Musk and Janks the cook conjured for me the sustenance of some fine ham, an unusually edible biscuit, and a fine draught of Hull ale.

On deck again, and as best I could, I took the measure of my officers. Stanton, the gunner, was quietly competent, carefully checking each of the great guns, their carriages and tackle, then going below to attend to the powder room and its manifests. Boatswain Ap paced up and down the deck, issuing instructions that hardly a man could understand and waving his rattan cane vaguely in the air — yet at his approach they all sprang to and ran to attend to three or four separate tasks in quick order, perhaps in the hope that one of them might have been the object of his unintelligible command. The carpenter, Penbaron, was below, attending no doubt to the whipstaff and the rudder, about which he seemed to have an obsession equal only to his fears for the mizzen; he was convinced that when the Deptford yard refitted it a year or so before, they sold off the good new rudder intended for the ship and simply fitted back in place the original, carefully repaired and disguised to conceal the shipwrights' fraud. This was too close for comfort to my own experience of the yard's workmanship, even if it had saved my life, so I left him to his work. I saw no sign of Janks, of course, though smoke wafted continually from the pipe that led from the galley down in the hold.

Stafford Peverell the purser was, alas, all too much in evidence. He shared the quarterdeck with me, though neither of us deigned to speak to the other. He looked out over the scene with an expression of weary contempt until one of the ship's boys, careless of his footing, fell onto a marlinspike and almost lost an eye, at which he roared with laughter. Perhaps I should have upbraided him there and then, but it did not do for officers to undermine each other in public; moreover, Peverell was a man of good birth — albeit of the worst manners — and still deserving of the honour due to his rank. So I told myself, although in my heart, my dislike of this callous creature grew apace. Of the last of my officers, the Reverend Gale, there was no sign at all.

Landon, the master, had placed a table on the quarterdeck, setting it out with priggish formality. On it were arranged those strange books of sea-charts, mathematical symbols, and secret wisdom that sailors call "waggoners". At noon, Landon and his masters' mates raised strangely fashioned instruments, somewhat akin to one of my grandfather's dials, and looked towards the sun, then at the likes of St Thomas's church, Southsea Fort, and the white tower of the Gilkicker seamark. The mates chattered excitedly to each other and to London, who eventually informed me gravely that we had a true observation, and thus the new sea-day had commenced. I felt just as awkward at this ritual as I had aboard the *Happy Restoration*, when old Aldred had reported to me each noon-tide in equally solemn tones. For the mariners, this was clearly a great event, a daily papal conclave that resulted in the election of a series of meaningless numbers, written down with all due reverence in our ship's journal. As far as I was concerned, they may as well have been speaking to me in old Aramaic or Cornish.

I felt a searing pang of regret that I would spend a second commission as captain in utter ignorance of the ways of the sea. It was clear now that Kit Farrell had never received my letter and would not be joining the voyage, and I could not demean the heir to Ravensden before the likes of Landon by asking him to teach me the sea-method. As for James Vyvyan, he had plainly learned much from his uncle Harker. He knew the names of the ropes, yards, and sails, could speak confidently to the master about bearings, and moved among the crew as we made ready for sea, giving a cheerful word of encouragement here, a gentle word of admonishment there. Three years younger than I and far more complete a sea officer, he had the respect of the men, and I did not; nor would I, then or ever. Vyvyan might well have disliked me on sight for taking his uncle's place and not listening to his fool's babble about murder, I thought, but in that moment I suddenly hated James Vyvyan with a harsher passion than any he could have ever felt towards me. It was that cold, irrational, jealous hatred that comes to us when we know, in our heart of hearts, that another man is our better. Vyvyan's easy competence threw my own abiding ignorance into sharp focus. I could not ask him to teach me what he knew. I would not give him that pleasure; nor would I learn the sea indirectly from the still all-pervasive ghost of Captain James Harker.

It was nearly six when I stood once more on the quarterdeck, the ignorant gentleman captain in all his splendour, watching through the gathering gloom as the sails fell from the yards on *Royal Martyr*, and Judge's ship began to make her way very slowly on the tide. Vyvyan, Landon and Ap all watched me expectantly. After a moment, my lieutenant coughed and addressed me, no doubt mischievously but with a perfectly neutral face.

"Do you wish to give the commands to take us to sea, sir?"

I thought suddenly of the *Happy Restoration* in her dying moments in the storm at Kinsale; the last time I had been called upon to give a sea command. I saw the men falling from her doomed, upright hull . . .

"No, Lieutenant," said I. "Mister Landon, you will take us out, if you will."

I would not give James Vyvyan the satisfaction of giving the commands, though I did not have the slightest doubt that his uncle had taught him how to do so.

Landon began the strange litany with a shout. "Hale in the anchor, there!" The crew on the great spoked man-wheel called the capstan began their push, accompanied by the rhythmic stamping of Ali Reis's foot as he fiddled in time with their efforts. The anchor cable rose from the sea-bed, groaning and wailing like a hundred dying men. Once the anchor was clear of the water, Landon moved from side to side of the quarterdeck, bellowing his instructions in sequence.

"Let go the weather braces! Loose the mainsail! Cast off the weather sheet! Let fall the mainsail!"

The cries were repeated by the petty officers in charge of the various parts of the ship, Cornish throats answering Landon's Kentish voice. One by one, the great swathes of Lincolnshire canvas began to fall from their yards, and the light wind breathing across to us from the Isle of Wight began to fill them. Men raced each other up and down the great nets called shrouds that stretched up into the masts. They moved back and forth along the yards and their footropes with a disregard for the height and their own mortality that never ceased to impress and terrify me. At the top of the foremost of our three masts, the simian tin miner Treninnick scuttled about with breathtaking speed, just as Coxswain Lanherne had described. All this time, Landon kept up his ceaseless barrage of commands.

136

"Cast off the main brace! Cast off the main topsail! Hale aft the main sheet!"

At the pull of their teams, great ropes tightened, fixing the sails into place. Landon shouted commands about strange sea-beasts called clewlines, bowlines and the like, and seemed particularly exercised by the incompetence of those attending to a creature called a crojack. James Vyvyan, ten times the seaman that I was, lambasted the men on the main mast for committing the mortal sin of "luffing". And there I stood, upon the quarterdeck, watching as if I were a spectator at a play or a bear-baiting; detached, remote, uninvolved.

We were moving now, indiscernibly at first, but as old Aldred had taught me to do on the *Happy Restoration*, I lined up my eye on one rope and on the tower of the church at Gosport. Slowly, very slowly, the rope began to move away from the tower. The *Jupiter*'s timbers began to creak a little more, in a song of greeting, or perhaps of protest, to her natural home.

A ship setting her sails is a glorious sight, especially by evening's dying light. It is truly a sight to elevate even the dullest heart. As we became a proper man-of-war, rather than a great mass of idle wood swaying on an anchor with the tides, I saw the *Royal Martyr* moving out ahead of us, her sails already well set, her great red-white-red ensign spilling over her stern lanterns, newly lit. Uplifted despite myself by the entire spectacle, I turned cheerily to Phineas Musk.

"Well, Musk, you're going to sea on a king's ship. What d'you make of it, man?"

"Rather be in London town, sir, taking ale and veal stew up at the City of York," the dullest heart replied. Musk was already faintly green, even though the ship's movement was as yet barely noticeable and the wind was the lightest of sighs. But his talk of food and drink reminded me of one duty, at least, that I could perform successfully as captain.

"Musk, go round the ship and present my compliments to each of the warrant officers. I request — no, I *require* their company in my cabin at seven o'clock, there to toast success and good fortune to the voyage of the *Jupiter*."

James Vyvyan, who had come up to the quarterdeck and was in earshot, said, "Two bells of the second dog watch, sir. Not seven o'clock, with respect, when we're at sea."

At that moment, I wished the nephew dead, rather than the uncle; although of course, he was entirely right to correct me thus, for the custom of the sea must prevail over even the most ignorant who pass upon it. I corrected myself to Musk, who slouched away in evident bad odour, complaining to himself that the steward to a great noble house had been reduced to a mere messenger boy, carrying invitations to ignorant pettifogging scum like carpenters and surgeons.

A good gust of wind caught our sails at last. The *Jupiter* began to make proper headway, and I walked to the starboard rail to take my last look at old Portsmouth before it receded. As I did so, I heard the shout of a lookout — I think it was Trenance — and saw a boat with a small square sail set, tacking rapidly towards us from the Portsmouth shore. It was one of the myriad fishing craft that regularly thronged the Solent, and the boy on the tiller and the man at the sail were presumably father and son, and her regular crew. Between them sat their passenger, Kit Farrell.

CHAPTER
EIGHT

"So Rame Head bears three points away to larboard," I said uncertainly, staring hard at the headland off to our right, dark and menacing in the morning murk. A little hermit's chapel was just visible on its summit. Behind us, the sun fought a battle to break through dull clouds. It was a cold morn, the day on the cusp of glory or gloom.

"To *starboard*, sir," said Kit Farrell, with unwarranted patience. "Starboard, right. Larboard, left. We go by the sides of the ship, sir, not by our own viewpoint, so that although the Rame is to your left as you see it now, it is starboard beam of the ship herself."

"That cannot be so, I'd say," came the dry, quibbling voice of Phineas Musk. Aboard a ship for barely a week and already he fancied himself an expert on the sea, as he did on all else. "If larboard is left, Mister Farrell, why does Master Landon, there, keep telling the man on that . . . that whip-thing down below, to port the helm when he wants us to go left?"

"The custom of the sea, Mister Musk. Starboard, larboard, are words altogether too similar for commands. Imagine calling one out in a storm, say, and the helmsman at the whipstaff mishearing and setting the ship's head on the other bearing. So if we wish to steer to the larboard, we order 'Port the helm!'"

Musk grunted, evidently still convinced of his own innate superiority and half-suspecting that Kit's "custom of the sea" was in truth a deliberate ruse designed to confuse and confound Phineas Musk.

A smile on his round and ruddy face, Kit turned back to me. "So, Captain, what would you say was now the relative bearing of the ship on our other tack?"

I looked off to the left — *to larboard* — to the distant sail that one of our men aloft had first sighted almost an hour before. I was aware of Landon's inscrutable gaze upon me from his position on the far side of the quarterdeck, and was glad that James Vyvyan was asleep below, having stood his watch for most of the night. I looked down at the face of the instrument that Farrell and Landon called a meridian compass, and looked again at the far-off sail. "Five points," I said.

Kit Farrell nodded. "Five points it is, Captain. And the wind?"

I looked at the set of our sails, the way that they faced the country beyond Rame, and at our ensign, streaming hard in the strengthening breeze. I recalled how the direction of the breeze had changed the previous evening.

"The wind is east by north, Mister Farrell," I said at length.

Kit smiled. "Indeed it is, sir. Our *Jupiter* sails large, with a fair wind from east by north. Your bearings are coming to you, sir, as I knew they would. For but a very few hours' work yesterday and this morning, I'd rate that a fair outcome."

Ahead of us, and slightly to starboard, the *Royal Martyr* sailed majestically on. I had signalled Judge with my intention of intercepting the strange sail on the horizon, but he had overruled me. Through his voice-trumpet, the exquisite fellow shouted that we had already lost too much time to challenge every ship we saw, despite the Lord High Admiral's injunction to his warships to enforce the "salute to the flag" demanded of all foreign vessels passing through the king's waters.

In those times, we fondly believed that we ruled the waves — every inch of water up to the tidal mark on the beaches of France or Holland, and all the way from Norway down to Cape Finisterre. But this one, distant ship, at least, would escape having to prostrate herself before a warship of the King of England. We had already lost much time on the previous day, becalmed for hours off Portland Bill and then waiting for *Royal Martyr* to enforce the salute on a wine ship bound from La Rochelle to London, manned by drunken Frenchmen who had strayed off course and perversely refused to salute the King of England's flag. Refused, until the threat of Judge's broadside taught them the error of their Gallic ways.

The wind was now fresh and too favourable to squander, Judge shouted. We were sailing fairly close to the land; this was the custom of those days, wind and tide depending, but it was also a condition of our sailing orders. We were to hug the shore, no more than a few miles off, until we had cleared Cornwall. Landon had grumbled mightily about the folly of this course, proclaiming it too close to a lee shore if the wind shifted more southerly or westerly. Judge now shouted that we must make all haste to round the Lizard and Land's End before such a shift occurred and trapped us in Falmouth for days or even weeks. His words, carrying across the water indiscriminately to every man on our ship's rail, caused many a frown and some audible grumbling; our brave Cornish lads had, it seemed, been praying for exactly that eventuality.

Kit Farrell had supped with me two evenings before, the night we sailed from Spithead, after I had toasted our voyage in bowls of punch with the rest of the officers. All, that is, but the Reverend Gale, whose family of crusted port had seemingly propagated, and who responded to Musk's invitation with a stream of invective that would have shamed Lucifer, let alone his notional employer on high. Among the other officers, there was evident resentment at the newest and most junior of the master's mates being singled out to share the captain's table on our first evening at sea. James Vyvyan sulked like a schoolboy. Landon protested at having to accommodate yet another mate, one above his complement. Peverell barely restrained his fury, for in his view, entering a supernumerary mate in his precious muster and pay books so soon after the unexpected addition of Musk was apparently a contravention of the whole of English common law and an affront to the Lord God himself. He had burst into my cabin, without even a by-your-leave, and thrust his ugly face so close to mine that I could see the black pus that clogged the pores of his nose. Landon and Peverell were eventually cowed into submission only by the sign of the king's own seal on the order; even then, Peverell warned me that there were limits both to his exemplary patience and to the powers of captains and kings alike. I did not know whether to laugh out loud at the liberties these two wretches chose to take with their captain, or to be intimidated by their lack of regard for my office. No doubt James Harker would have rewarded such disrespect with a spell in the bilboes. In the end I did nothing, falling prey once again to my habit of indecision.

Phineas Musk, who had an infallible ear for other men's conversations, reported the immediate birth of a rumour that the captain's catamite had come aboard, and was to share his sea-bed that very night. He also reported that some of the larboard watch had woven my presence fancifully into the other conspiracy of the moment, and avowed in hushed whispers that I was some sort of all-seeing Machiavel who had sanctioned Harker's murder in order to take his place (presumably absconding with the Duchess of Newcastle in the process). But Musk had taken against Kit Farrell almost at once, and could have been as easily the originator of both rumours.

Kit Farrell seemed oblivious to such tittle-tattle. He had listened intently on that first day as I explained our mission to him, and told him of Harker's mysterious death. I did not confide in him that, for all my scepticism upon the matter of murder, I found it hard to suppress the pervasive dread that someone might seek to mete out the same to the second captain of the *Jupiter*. But Kit had glanced keenly at me for a moment, and I do not doubt he could see my thoughts writ large in my eyes. He plainly thought hard upon the matter, but for the moment, he kept his counsel.

I had seen my saviour but once since that black October day in County Cork, and that was on the occasion of my court-martial: the obligatory trial that occurs on any captain who loses his ship. This had been in the great cabin of the mighty *Agincourt*, laid up in the Medway, on a January day so cold that it was almost possible to walk out to the ship from Chatham shore. There had been no time for conversation on that occasion, beyond a rushed word of thanks for a deposition that threw all the blame for the loss of the *Happy Restoration* onto her drunken master. Despite some contradictions in the statements of other survivors, and some awkward questioning by the president of the court, old Sir John Mennes, Kit Farrell held to his story, and Captain Matthew Quinton was honourably acquitted. His debt to the young man who had now saved him twice over weighed heavily on his heart and honour.

I said nothing of this to him, for we were both entirely and silently aware of how matters stood between us, and of what each owed the other. Instead, I asked him why he had abandoned a lucrative Indies voyage for what would probably be but a short commission, with no certainty of speedy pay. "We'll hardly be back in the Thames before the ships in the

Mediterranean and Portugal come back home, Mister Farrell. They'll take precedence for payment, no doubt."

Kit nodded. "You'll be right enough, Captain. But if I'd gone to the Indies, you see, would I have been paid in three years or more, until we came back? True, I'd have made much more in the end, but at what price? The Indies does for enough men, be it through disease or the guns of the Dutch or the Portugee. Then there's the natives. And even if you keep clear of all of them, you're at the mercy of cheating Arab factors, and worse, all the way from Cochin to Melaka." He looked away, his mind bent upon distant memories. "I can be a master in the king's service in another five years or so, if I cultivate enough brethren of Trinity House and — begging your pardon, sir — get enough good certificates of recommendation from enough captains. Down in my mother's alehouse, they all say there'll be another Dutch war sooner than later, and that's always a sure way of creating vacancies for promotions. On the Indies voyages, I'd be lucky to be a master of a ship this side of my fiftieth year. No, Captain. When I got your letter, in the Downs, I looked into my soul, and it was written there as large as life. You're a navy man, Kit Farrell, it said, just like your father."

"Your mother wrote that your father had served twenty-eight years in the navy," I said.

"Twenty-eight it was, Captain. He went out first under Sir Robert Mansell against the corsairs of Algiers in the year twenty. Served with merchants a while, including that Indies voyage, but came back to the navy in thirty-seven, when the late king's Ship Money fleets were strutting the oceans. But then . . ."

For every family in England in those last twenty years, my own included, there had been a *but then* . . . It was a time that had set fathers against sons, brothers against brothers, and killed enough of all of them.

"But then, the war between king and Parliament began," I said, "and the navy declared for the Parliament. Your father stayed in the navy, ergo he was a Parliament-man."

Kit Farrell shrugged sadly. His father had told him that he and his fellows thought they were fighting for king and Parliament together — not to overthrow the king. Those who led them said it was a war against the king's evil ministers, who had misled His Majesty. They said those things year after year, until the day they cut the king's head off — or so Kit Farrell's father had claimed. Uncle Tristram, whose politics had been more inclined to Parliament than those of his brother or sister-in-law, my father and mother, had said much the same thing to me, once.

"You're fighting for a new commonwealth now, boys, they told my father and his kind. A land where we've abolished kings and Christmas alike, and you need to hear three sermons every Sunday, and you must never drink and never gamble and never whore and never sin. We were in the family alehouse one evening, Father and I alone, and there were no customers. You see, sir, all the seamen from Shadwell down to Stepney village were so afraid of the ministers and being denounced from the pulpit, and of the fanatic soldiers who stood

147

behind the ministers, that they wouldn't be seen with a drink any more. And he said to me, sir — my father said — 'Kit, boy, if I could live long enough to see just one thing more in my life, I'd want it to be the day when England has its true and rightful kings again.'"

Many were making such speeches in those days, for it did not do to admit enthusiasm for the old rule, when the godly fanatics and their turtle-helmeted agents, the swordsmen, had dictated how people should live, and lie. But as I watched Kit Farrell, I knew that he, at least, spoke the truth. It was impossible to doubt those clear blue eyes and the good soul that looked out from them. We sat in silence for some little while, and I envied Kit Farrell in that time. I envied him his command of his trade; I wished that I too could move unerringly about the ship, fixing what was wrong and improving what was right. And I envied him that time with his father in the Farrell alehouse, too. He had known his father until he was thirteen, and almost a man; I had lost mine when I was but five, and still a child.

"And then there is the rest, of course," he said suddenly.

"The rest?"

"Of why I decided to leave my Indiaman and repair here, sir, to join you on this particular expedition. It was the day the *Happy Restoration* was lost, sir. What we said to each other, in the fort of Kinsale. I made a promise to you, Captain Quinton," he said quietly. "As you did to me. And the Farrells keep their promises, too."

148

I thought on this for a moment, and said, "I fear I'll be a poor pupil, Mister Farrell. I do not know if my heart is truly in it, if truth be told, for my ambition still lies elsewhere — a commission in the Horse Guards, at the very least." I looked out at over the waters that stretched smoothly away to my left, turning pewter and violet in the evening light. It was a beautiful sight. I turned to look Kit full in the face. "And you'll face many on this ship who'll hate you for the privileged place you'll have in my company, to teach me the sea-craft."

"Only as many as you'll have for setting up a favourite, which is something all sailors hate."

I thought of Vyvyan. His demeanour, once distracted by grief, seemed to have hardened into something colder since Kit's arrival. His manners were impeccable, but the disdain in his eye was a hard thing to bear.

"But as you say, Captain, it'll be but a short commission," he went on. "And besides, the crew seem too wedded to the shade of Captain Harker to love you, whatever you do. It's more to the king's benefit, and mine, to turn you into a good seaman, and for you to make me into a man of letters, than it is for me to seek out popularity on the lower deck. Or the quarterdeck." The evening gun fired, the signal for the night watch to be set and all lanterns and candles doused. When Kit spoke again, his tone was serious but tentative. "Sir, may I speak freely?"

"I rather thought you already were, Mister Farrell," I said, laughing despite my trepidation at what might follow. "By all means. Plain-speaking is a rarity when the speaker is to be trusted."

He pondered a moment, choosing his words as carefully as a man of his breeding could. "Sir," he said at length, his tone thoughtful. "Men talk much of the matter between the gentlemen captains and the tarpaulins — which of them is better fitted to command the king's ships. I've already observed that Master Landon talks of little else when you are absent, and envies you this commission." I nodded, for that much was obvious amidst the master's grim malevolence. "I see it this way. Now, the advocates of the tarpaulin will tell you that a gentleman is ignorant of the sea, so the men will be discouraged, and he must leave the navigation to the master. They'll tell you a gentleman captain will be too harsh to his men. They'll tell you that a gentleman can't recommend good officers, because he doesn't understand their trades, and the officers can delude him and so defraud the king." This was too close for comfort, but I wished to know Kit Farrell's conclusion, so for the present I merely nodded. "On the other hand, your tarpaulins can detect embezzlements and will keep their accounts in good order, or so their advocates say. They'll take care of their ships and will know their men —"

"But," I said, impatient at being damned on so many counts, "surely, Mister Farrell, some men would say that your tarpaulin is *too* familiar with his men. Not to mention that they have no lineage or honour. How could they possibly tell the difference between the honour of a warship and a merchantman? Nor do they bear themselves well in proper society. Can you imagine Master Landon as a captain, dining with the Grand Master of the Knights of Malta or the King of Portugal, Mister Farrell? He'd disgrace himself before the end of the first course. The captain of a king's ships must be a man of honour, for it is more than a ship — it is England incarnate."

Kit Farrell nodded. "Yes, sir. I've heard all those things said, on both sides. But it seems to me, one of the failings of our English temper is our eagerness to take one side or another, simply so that we can say we belong to a side."

I had a sudden thought of Cornelia, who often declared something similar to me, but with one small difference; being that whereas the English predilection was to divide into two sides, the Dutch were never content with fewer than five or six. I said to Kit, "Your point being?"

"Well, sir. I'm an ignorant man, as you know, with no reading or writing — not until you finish teaching me, at any rate," and he smiled swiftly at me, "but it seems to me there may be grains of truth in all these points, good and bad. Now, if that be so, why should some cry up the gentlemen, and say that all the commands in the navy should be theirs? Why should others damn the gentlemen, and give those commands only to rude tarpaulins like myself or Master Landon?"

"Mister Farrell, I have heard the king and Duke of York speak on this many times, and I agree wholeheartedly with them. What they say is, commands should go to a mixture of gentlemen and tarpaulins, according to their merits. Take our own voyage. I, a gentleman, have one of the commands, and Captain Judge, a tarpaulin, the other —"

"Yes, sir," said Kit, "but my point is that the day must come when we have no distinction of gentleman and tarpaulin any longer! When we have gentlemen who know the sea and their ship so well that they are as capable of command as any tarpaulin. And our tarpaulins, in turn, become gentlemen, to give them those qualities they need to be proper when dining with the King of Malta or the knights of Portugal, sir."

The great red sun was sinking down behind the *Royal Martyr*. I watched it turn her sails to gold. "There's something in what you say, I think, Mister Farrell. The king and duke have started sending young gentlemen to sea under royal letters, some of them as young as thirteen or fourteen. Not many years from now, there'll be a whole generation of sea-officers who'll be gentlemen born and bred, but who've been at sea almost as long as any tarpaulin, and learned the trade just as well." A thought struck me. "Men not too unlike Lieutenant Vyvyan, in fact."

Kit smiled. "I forbore from mentioning him, sir, but it's true. A very fine sailor, and a good family."

Kit Farrell ever spoke with a rare clarity. Nevertheless his words angered me and I stood for a moment composing my countenance before I turned to him again. "A pity indeed that such a fine officer should be so marred by suspicion and perversity," I said, spiteful and ashamed of myself at the same time. "His tiresome obsession with his uncle's death . . ." I tailed off, aware of my companion's stillness and silence. "But perhaps I should try harder to deal with him, then, Mister Farrell, if you say he should be my model."

Farrell shrugged and smiled, and vanquished my peevishness of spirit with that one honest gesture. We feel into a sprightly conversation on the quarters of the wind and finished our meal in good humour.

As he made to leave the cabin, I detained him for a moment. "You are a plain speaker indeed, Mister Farrell," I said. "I value that. I *need* that, here on this ship, with these officers who are Harker's, not mine. You have my sanction to speak plainly to me at all times, Kit Farrell. Do not flatter me as you teach me the sea-craft. If I've been a dullard, tell me so. If I make mistakes as the captain of this ship, tell me that, too. I am determined on one thing above all, which is that I will not take another *Happy Restoration* and all its men to their graves, and face another court-martial for so doing."

Kit Farrell nodded. "I speak plainly only with men I trust, Captain." He ruffled his hair in a gesture of boyish embarrassment. "Well, sir, if it's a reminder of mortality you want, then learning the dead reckoning and some celestial navigation should do it. Shall we begin with them in the forenoon watch, Captain?"

"Not, then, the names of the ropes and the sails, or all the pieces of wood? I thought such knowledge lay at the heart of the mariners' mysteries."

He smiled. "Knowing the name of a rope won't bring you off a lee shore, Captain, nor bring you alongside an

153

enemy. My father served in the last Dutch war under Generals Blake and Monck, that's now the lord Duke of Albemarle, and they knew so little of the sea they'd shout 'Wheel to the right!' or 'Haul up that whichum there!' or the suchlike. It didn't stop them bringing down the Dutch and all their great sailor-admirals, did it now? The sea's not a mystery, Captain, though sailors are like lawyers — for both make their trades a mystery, wear peculiar garb, and gull the layman with a strange language. But using the sea is just like making a journey on land, sir. It's all about knowing where you are, where you're going, how you'll get there, and what you'll do once you're there. You don't need to know the name of a horse to make it gallop, or to carry you to the next town, Captain. And you don't need to know the name of every sail and shroud on this ship to win a battle in her."

Rame Head had fallen away well behind us, and the distant ship was out of sight up the Channel. I was still on the quarterdeck. In the continued absence of Francis Gale and his new prayer book, I had that morning taken the crew through a perfunctory reading of the daily prayer from the old, using the still pristine copy that Uncle Tristram had given me for my eighth birthday. Landon, Kit Farrell and Musk then went below, as did most of the crew, carrying their wooden plates, to receive Janks' latest offering for their midday dinner. A sullen master's mate from Rotherhithe had the watch, calling out the occasional order to the helmsman on the whipstaff in the steerage below (for these were still the times before it became the fashion for ships to be steered by a wheel, as they are today; another damnable innovation cried up and adopted on no better grounds than that Europeans favour it, and thus it must be superior to our old English ways).

Apart from the mate, the Moor Ali Reis, and two of the ship's boys, the quarterdeck was empty. With so few witnesses in sight, I returned surreptitiously to my feeble attempts to master the sea arts. On one of our starboard great guns, I balanced a blank ship's journal covered in sailcloth. Musk had grudgingly drawn columns on each page, and at Kit Farrell's prompting, I was endeavouring to fill in the entries for our voyage. Even then, all captains were meant to keep their own sea journals, but on the doomed *Happy Restoration* I had followed the example of most of my fellow gentleman captains and merely copied the entries from the master's log book. Now, Landon's journal was forbidden me by Kit Farrell. I looked out to sea, up to the rigging and scanned the coast. Then I turned my eyes downward and looked again in puzzlement at each of the columns on the page before me.

Weekday. Well, it was a Tuesday, but this would not be enough for Trinity House, Mister Pepys or Kit Farrell. In the mariners' secret knowledge, each day had its own symbol, drawn from the dark worlds of astrologers and alchemists; symbols to which Master Landon appeared to be particularly devoted. Although I had drawn all the day-symbols, the sheet bearing them was below in the great cabin. For once, Farrell and Phineas Musk were united in something; that being, their determination to keep it from me. I would leave this column blank for the time being, I decided.

Month and date. That was easy, despite the mariners' perverse insistence that each new day began at noon, not at midnight or dawn, as the rest of the world contended.

Distance run. I knew this number, and wrote it down: seventy-six. But God alone knew what it signified, for the mariners insist that their mile is different to a mile on land. Perhaps it was greater, but then, it might have been smaller. Farrell had told me, and given me the exact figure for the difference. It was but one of the many elements of this strange new science that my grandfather had once mastered, and but one of the many that seemed so unwilling to lodge in my head.

I heard a sudden snort of laughter, looked up, and saw two of our men in the mizzen rigging. The monkey-like rapscallions looked down upon me as schoolboys look down from a great height upon the spiders they seek to torment. Their faces attempted a blank innocence but bore the unmistakeable expressions of those who stifle their mirth only with the greatest expenditure of effort. I could have punished them for mocking their captain, I suppose, but that would hardly have helped my cause. *Great God*, I thought, *why do I do this?* The mastery of the sea was a hopeless task, opening me up to ridicule and humiliation. Why not merely strut my quarterdeck in arrogant splendour, as Harris, Jennens and the rest of them did? *Your destiny is in the Guards*, I reminded

156

myself, *not at sea*. But then I saw the death throes of the *Happy Restoration* in my mind's eye. I looked about me at my trim little ship that bucked along its sea path with such energy. And I called to mind Kit's patient, open face as he taught me and his scowling determination as he looked at the letters I showed him. I had my answer. I frowned in a "be about your business" fashion at the men on the mizzen and resumed my efforts with the journal.

Course. Well, we were plainly sailing west — even a Bedfordshire man knows the significance of the Sun's path through the skies — so I confidently wrote down the letter W. But then I would need to write a number, and this would be derived from the meridian compass that Landon cherished like a lover. Although I could already essay a sound guess at the bearing of a fixed point, an empty horizon was another case entirely. I decided to leave the remainder of this column blank for the moment.

Latitude by Dead Reckoning. This, of course, was the substance of the mystic ritual that Landon and his mates conducted every noon-time. I was dimly aware of what the term "latitude" signified — great circles around the globe, or at least, circles that did not exist, but which were deduced by mariners from the strange sightings that they took of the Sun or the stars by night, followed by much mumbling over books filled with impenetrable numbers. But as for "dead reckoning", what form of reckoning was this? And why was it dead? Farrell had certainly mentioned it, but then, he had told me so much, and in so short a time. I pressed my

157

quill hard against the paper, making a blot that would look as though I had accidentally obscured the correct number.

Wind. Somewhat from astern, and somewhat off the land, which lay to the north. But I knew "north" would not be good enough for Kit Farrell. No, the mariners had decreed that there were many kinds of north — "north by east", or "east by north-east", and so forth. Was it still east by north, as it had been earlier? The yards seemed to have swung a little, but we had changed course too, which confused the matter. I wrote an "N", and decided that would be sufficient.

Weather. I looked at the sky . . .

A cry came from our lookout, Treninnick, perched an improbable way up our mainmast, and although some would damn it as popery, I thanked God, the shade of my grandfather, and our family's old patron saint, Quentin, for saving me from this purgatory of the log book. Treninnick's guttural Cornish shouts would have been unintelligible to me even if he had not been dangling from the mast in excitement, but Ali Reis, seemingly master of every tongue spoken from Calicut to Carolina, had no difficulty with it.

"The port of Looe, Captain," said the swarthy rogue. "First harbour in Cornwall. Boats coming out to us."

Indeed, five or six small craft were coming out of Looe Bay, tacking rapidly to intercept us, seabirds circling in their wakes. Within minutes, almost our entire ship's company was on deck; the starboard watch, whose duty it was, jostled with all those of the larboard who had come up from below. It was the first time I had seen so many of my crew in an unguarded moment, not at a formal assembly, and great Lord, what a crew they were. Almost all were bronzed by years spent in the open, in every weather condition under heaven. Every second man, at least, bore some sort of scar, no doubt obtained in one of James Harker's many battles. I knew a few names, now — "Tre", "Pol", or "Pen", most of them, the unfamiliar surnames of this Cornish breed. God alone knew what they truly thought of me.

A brave soul called out and waved to the approaching boats. Boatswain Ap, who bestrode the deck with an expression of alarm on his angular Welsh face, glanced at me for direction, but I shook my head. Seeing the exchange, a second man called out, then a third. Within moments, the entire ship's rail was alive with leaping, shouting, laughing Jupiters.

Alerted by the commotion, Musk and Kit Farrell had returned to the quarterdeck. "So this is what they call a mutiny, I suppose," said Musk. He rubbed his white hands together and fixed a desolate eye upon the rowdy crew.

I smiled. "I think not. This is their country, Musk, so close they can almost touch it —"

"Or throw you and I to the fishes and steer for it, if they were so minded," said he.

"They have all been away from home for months, if not years. It being that we must creep along the coast, let them have joy of it while they can."

"Captain Judge seems to be taking an interest in our proceedings, sir," Kit said.

I raised my eyepiece, and saw Judge on his quarterdeck, studying the *Jupiter* through his. He had discarded his wig and face powder, revealing a shaven head crowned with grey stubble and a harsh warrior's countenance at odds with the delicate Turkish gown of yellow silk that he wore.

"I doubt if Captain Judge approves of such abandon in a ship's crew, Mister Farrell," I said. "But if he wishes to take us past Cornwall as fast as the wind will permit, I'll at least give my men the consolation of some contact with their people."

The first of the Looe boats was within hailing distance, and a shout came up from it. "John Craze of Muchlarnick!" A young bearded man of the larboard watch waved. "John Craze, your mother's dead these three weeks!" Craze turned away, his messmates comforting him.

A second boat hailed us. "Will Seaton of Looe! Your wife's left you! Aye, and for John Craze's father, too!"

Seaton, a big man in the carpenter's crew, howled in fury, sprang down from the starboard rail, and launched a furious attack with his fists against his newly bereaved shipmate. Boatswain Ap and two of his mates stepped in briskly and cudgelled Seaton about the head.

"Maybe Captain Judge had the rights of it," said Musk disapprovingly. "By the time we get to Land's End, this ship won't have a man left standing."

I was beginning to regret my decision to allow such liberty to the crew, but another boat had tacked smartly alongside us. She had three aboard her: two grinning

160

young men on her sail and tiller, and a strong young woman with long black hair that flew about her comely face in the breeze. "Hey, the *Jupiter!*" she called in a lusty voice. "Hey, husband!"

"I'll husband you, woman, whenever you want it!" cried Julian Carvell, his grinning black face and slow drawl unmistakeable. The men around him laughed.

"I've better than you any day, blackamore! Where are you, John Tremar?"

Two men hoisted a little man, half the woman's size, onto their shoulders. He waved and shouted, "I'm here, Wenna!"

"Tremar, you giant!" she cried, to laughter from every Jupiter. "Look, John Tremar, at your parting gift to me!"

She stooped to a wicker basket jammed in the bow of the boat and lifted a corner of a blanket to reveal two tiny red sleeping faces. "Holy Jesus! *Twins!*" cried John Tremar.

Wenna Tremar shouted, "You'd best take the prize of all the oceans this voyage, John. Only the Spaniards' plate fleet will keep your wife and sons content!"

Emboldened by the delight of fatherhood, John Tremar shouted to me, "Captain, sir! What chance we can take such a prize?"

Boatswain Ap moved threateningly towards him, but I raised my hand and smiled. "We may struggle to take the entire plate fleet, John Tremar. But who needs King Philip's papist silver when we have good King Charles's honest coin? I rejoice with you in your good fortune!"

161

I reached into my purse and threw a silver crown, which Tremar caught expertly. The crew cheered, the first time they had saluted me thus, and I saw my mysterious Frenchman, Roger Le Blanc, smile to himself. Tremar grinned and held up the coin for his wife and sons to see.

"Damned madness," muttered Phineas Musk. "They'll think you weak. Weak, soft in the head and rich. I'll come to wake you tomorrow and I'll find your throat slit. Then they'll come for me. And my throat'll be slit, then, and there'll be Musk blood all over the floor. Deck, I mean. Musk blood, washing away into the sea. Oh . . ."

I knew Musk was wrong in every sense, and his bile came more from jealousy that a Quinton coin had not found its way into his own capacious pockets, as they had so many times before. Rather I was pleased with myself, sure that my action had raised me in the crew's estimation. Lordly charity: I had seen my brother distribute such largesse countless times in pauper homes around Ravensden, and knew from experience the goodwill that it generated. And perhaps, if Captain Matthew Quinton could not earn the respect of this crew, then he might buy it.

James Vyvyan came on deck just then. He studied the scene with his contemptuous eye, took in the computations of wind and tide and course with an ease that shamed me, and saluted.

"Well, Captain. The wind's on its way round to head us so our passage will be somewhat harder than before." And then, unexpectedly, he broke into a smile so good-natured I could not help but return it. "And word of our coming will be well down the Lostwithiel road by now. All Cornwall will know of it by nightfall. There'll be boats coming out of every harbour between here and the Scillies, which will slow us yet further."

So it proved. Another six boats came out of Polperro and a dozen from Fowey, where my father had fought in the last great battle that King Charles the Martyr won. That had been a great fight, in the year '44: Parliament's Lord General, the mighty Earl of Essex, was forced to make a hasty escape out of the Fowey River in a pathetic row-boat. All but forgotten now, of course. There were more boats hailing us at Mevagissey, and Gorran, and Veryan, and Gerrans. Vyvyan remained on deck, rolling the names off his tongue as he marked each hamlet and fishing port like a poet reciting a sonnet.

He was a happier man now, so close to his own shore: he was almost like a proud host, showing off his home to a visiting bumpkin. And his shore it most certainly was. We could hear the mourning-bells toll for James Harker in every church along the coast. Once again I felt the most abject of outsiders; an interloper in a ship still commanded by a dead man.

We came at length by Falmouth Bay, saluting the round, brooding castle of Pendennis, confident on its high headland; the last fortress in all of England that had held out for its undoubted king in the late wars. In the roads behind it, we saw four of our East Indiamen at anchor; two great Dutchmen getting under way for the Levant; a fleet of squat, grimy Welsh colliers bringing coals to warm Cornish hearths; and some twenty small craft — all bound for the *Jupiter*. At every port, and at Falmouth above all, there was more news of births, and deaths, and cuckoldry, so that every man on the ship seemed to have word of his family's doings. Even James Vyvyan's brother came out from the Helford River in a small boat of his own, and came aboard us for an hour or so with the news that their sister was to be married to the scrofulous and allegedly impotent heir of an Irish viscount. I saw my lieutenant in a different light, laughing and exuberant in a brother's company.

It was after the elder Vyvyan had disembarked, and our ship was rounding the headland that Kit Farrell named to me as Manacle Point, that Vyvyan came to see me in my cabin. My Frenchman, the mysterious Roger Le Blanc, was there already, come to repair a gash in one of the damask drapes. I had hoped to engage him in a conversation, for I wished to look further into this man whom I thought to be neither tailor nor sailor; but then came a second rap at the door and Vyvyan entered the now crowded little cabin.

"Congratulations, sir," I said. "The news of your sister — a notable match, Mister Vyvyan." But James Vyvyan's thoughts did not seem focused on his brother's tidings. Instead, he turned his countenance to me with a dark and puzzled air. "Sir, one of the men has had some strange news. It may bear on the murder of my uncle."

Since we sailed from Spithead, Vyvyan had been silent on the matter of James Harker's death. His own

164

researches at Portsmouth had seemingly undermined his conviction that it was foul murder. Moreover, he had been absorbed in the work of the ship, and in proving to his captain that he was by far the better seaman out of us two.

I said, "Which of the men?"

"Alan Tregerthen, sir. He's of St Just in Roseland. As was Pengelley, one of my uncle's servants, who acted as his clerk."

"And?"

"Tregerthen's wife sent word to him, sir. Seems that a justice of the county came down to see Pengelley's wife. The justice told her that Pengelley's corpse was found at the side of the road from Portsmouth to Southampton, near to old Titchfield Abbey. Stabbed to death, sir. But the Hampshire justices think he'd been bound and tortured first."

CHAPTER
NINE

We rounded the Lizard slowly and with difficulty, beating a jagged path into the wind, then turned up to sail directly for the Land's End — much to the disappointment of the men from Penzance, Porthleven and the other places on Mount's Bay, for we were too far off for their families and friends to come out to them. Kit Farrell had me taking bearings on distant church towers and recording the results dutifully in my journal, which was beginning to fill out with more and longer entries. Malachi Landon looked on all this with contempt, but he was too much a navy man, and far too much of a hypocrite, to say anything to his captain's face.

Phineas Musk had no such constraints. He prowled around the quarterdeck, complaining audibly that this was no work for the heir to Ravensden, and that he knew full well that the good wife of the heir to Ravensden would second him emphatically were she present. At least these grumbles provided a welcome interruption of his ongoing tirade against what he supposed to be the slowness of travel by sea, with its inexplicable reliance on such trivial concerns as tides and winds, and his consequent astonishment that we were still nowhere near a landfall in Scotland.

Nominally, James Vyvyan had the watch, but he kept apart, morose and uninterested in the ship's progress, muttering occasional vague words of command. Since his revelation of this second death — the cruel torture and murder of the man Pengelley — my lieutenant had become obsessed once more with the notion that his uncle had been murdered; and if truth be told, this new killing had given me pause. I kept a primed pistol at my belt. Vyvyan had gone below at once and questioned all those on board who had known the dead man, but as was so often the way, it seemed that the captain's servants mingled but little with the rest of the crew. Pengelley may as well have been a phantom, or a fiction.

As we cleared the Land's End, the wind blew ever more strongly from the south-west, forcing us further and further out to avoid the deadly cliffs on the lee shore of Cornwall. As the first star glimmered out, I thought I saw the low, dark land of the Scillies, far off to larboard. At length, I retired to my cabin and invited Vyvyan to sup with me.

In part, this was because my ambition to dine with the Reverend Francis Gale was relentlessly thwarted by substantial quantities of port wine, which may have been responsible for the frequent screaming nightmares that Musk reported to me. I had thought of physically entering the man's cabin and ordering him to leave it, but God alone knew what a strong man like Francis Gale — a veteran of the civil wars — would do, even to

167

his captain, if in drink or otherwise deranged. In part, too, the invitation was an attempt to mollify Vyvyan. I thought my favour to Kit Farrell, though necessary, must be hard for a lieutenant, almost my equal in honour and rank, to take; I should be confiding in him by rights, and not in a supernumerary master's mate. Finally, I meant to offer Vyvyan the chance to disburden himself of his thoughts relating to Pengelley's murder. He was becoming too quiet and distracted. The men had noticed, and it would do the feeling aboard the ship no good. I had done my own thinking upon the matter, and hoped that I could talk young Vyvyan out of his state of deep and uneasy suspicion.

So it was that we came together to eat and discuss the question of Pengelley. I filled his cup and bade him drink, thinking to win some confidence and restore his composure. There were footpads enough on any major road in the kingdom, said I; bold highwaymen, too, and roving gangs of rough, masterless men, discharged from the old Republic's army, and who belonged to no parish. Any or all of them would have been attracted to a road out of Portsmouth and the prospect of waylaying mariners newly paid off from the sea, with ample coin in their pockets or saddlebags. The likes of Pengelley could easily have fallen prey to one of their kind. As we chewed on Janks's offering of chicken, I suggested all of this to James Vyvyan, but he was beyond such reasoning. He spoke with blind passion, his eyes wide with excitement and vengeful fury. Pengelley must have been killed, he said, because he knew the truth of his uncle's murder. Pengelley must have been the man who brought the mysterious note, with its precognition of death, into James Harker's cabin. I admitted this could be true; but why, I asked, would a faithful body servant have written a note in the first place — and an anonymous one at that? Why couch his suspicions in such ambiguous terms? And how could he have learned of a plot, if such there was? And why not speak up after his master's death? No, I said firmly. It was queer indeed, but to make any more out of the coincidence was fanciful.

Vyvyan made no answer to any of this. Instead he turned his venom quite unexpectedly upon Stafford Peverell, the purser. It seemed Pengelley served informally as captain's clerk, and in that office he would have been well placed to discover corruption by the purser. Harker and Peverell had often quarrelled fiercely, he said. Peverell was the only officer who was also ashore on the day that Harker died. Peverell was a haughty and insolent man, but he was worse, far worse . . . James Vyvyan trailed off, looking meaningfully into his goblet. This was all supposition, I said. Men had been hanged at Tyburn on less evidence than such suppositions, Vyvyan countered, for that was the way of English law.

"Lieutenant, that men argue does not mean that they murder. Besides, Peverell was aboard this ship, at sea, when Pengelley was killed." Although privately I thought my purser a foul specimen of humankind, I could not countenance such an accusation against one of my officers.

Vyvyan glared at me. "True," he said angrily, "but like the devil, he may have agents elsewhere."

Against such casuistry there could be no reasoning, and as Vyvyan helped himself to more wine I changed tack and asked him why it was he disliked Peverell so.

"Ha . . ." he said, and sat swaying on his chair, leering at me.

The wind was strengthening; we already had to brace ourselves at times as my cabin rocked with the motion of the sea. I was uncomfortably aware that Vyvyan had taken more wine than I realized — perhaps he had been drunk when he came to supper — and that he was due to stand a watch not many hours hence.

When speech came, it was sudden and unexpected. "Sodomite," he hissed.

This was a weighty charge indeed, for the thirty-second naval Article of War, enacted by Parliament but the previous year, specified that "the unnatural and detestable sin of buggery or sodomy with man or beast" was to be punished by death. Such rigour applied ashore would have decimated the ranks of the clergy and the court, if not the navy too; and I was not a little mindful of my own brother's inclinations in such matters. But as it related to my immediate question, all of that was academic. A vague suspicion of sodomy was hardly something that would make tough men like Vyvyan, Stanton and Landon fearful of a vain, puffed-up landsman like Stafford Peverell.

"Lieutenant," I said sternly. "You forget yourself, I think."

170

"Papist," he slurred, "and alchemist. A warlock. He has a crucifix and a rosary in his cabin. Andrewartha has seen them. And potions. He knows more of potions than Skeen."

That an educated man like Stafford Peverell should know more than our profoundly ignorant surgeon was hardly the basis of a charge, I thought. I briefly wondered how young Andrewartha, Vyvyan's servant, knew so much about the purser's cabin, but then realized that this was probably also how his master knew of Peverell's other proclivities. We continued our meal in an uncomfortable silence, with Vyvyan glaring drunkenly into his goblet, or at me. The lanterns swung from the beams to which they were fastened, casting fantastical shadows upon Harker's eccentric panelling. I wondered briefly whether, after all, there might be something in Vyvyan's drunken ramblings. If James Harker really had been poisoned, and Peverell knew how to blend alchemical potions —

I chided myself for falling prey so easily to the predilection of seamen to believe superstitions, and of all humanity to believe the darkest of conspiracies. I thought of Uncle Tristram, contentedly mixing elements in his shambolic Oxford lodgings or at Ravensden, forever hoping to find the philosopher's stone. A different age, and men like James Vyvyan would have had him burned as a warlock. Even my mother had once been denounced as a witch in the market square of Bedford, albeit by a lunatic who thought he was John the Baptist, and on no better ground than her liking for cats. Scratch the surface of men of reason like James Vyvyan (or, God knows, perhaps Matthew Quinton too), and a suspicious bigot often lurks just beneath.

We ended the meal in an ill temper, for Vyvyan was young and convinced of the rightness of his theory. He fell heavily against the bulkhead as he left, and I wondered how he could possibly be fit to stand his watch. For the first time in my life I — still but twenty-two — felt impossibly old and dull, the voice of age and authority calming the hot, irrational passions of youth. Yet for all that, I could not quite forget what he had said of my purser.

After Vyvyan had gone I went up on deck, for I was in need of air and solitude. It was late in the evening, and we were well into St George's Channel, that busy crossroads at the confluence of the Irish Sea and the Bristol Channel. The wind had strengthened and rounded again into a stout westerly gale bearing sharp flurries of rain. For a horrible moment I felt the chill of the *Happy Restoration*, but even I could gauge the forces of different winds against my face and knew at once that this was not cast from the same ship-breaking mould; but it was strong enough, and I had to move from rope to rope, bracing myself and waiting for each roll of the hull. Lanherne, part of the watch on deck, saluted perfunctorily and in apparent unconcern at both the wind and his saturated, amphibian condition as he turned the glass and rang the ship's bell to mark the passage of another half-hour. Our hull and masts creaked in a loud song of protest against the winds and seas that assaulted them. We had but a few men aloft: I thought I glimpsed the unmistakeable form of John Treninnick, far above me on the main yard. In the furrows between the great waves, I could sometimes just make out the *Royal Martyr*, to windward of us and well ahead, sailing steadily northward. Like us, she bore only hitched half-sails at her lower yards: reefed courses, the seamen called them, though God alone knew how I had remembered that piece of information. She bore away from us no more than three points, I reckoned. Away to starboard, I could see the distant masts of some half-dozen large merchant hulls, no doubt coming down from Bristol, probably bound for Africa or the Americas. They would have to tack often, I speculated, for their course would be almost directly into the wind. Far off to larboard, riding on the great waves like ducks upon a weir, lay a smattering of tiny sails, Cornish fishing craft plying their trade on the shoals that must lie in that direction. Brave souls, to be out in such feeble craft in such a mighty sea; no doubt the kin of some in my crew, many of whom had known that life.

I stood on the starboard side of the quarterdeck, gripping a rope — a *shroud*, yes, that was it — and swaying with the ship's motion. Despite the effort and the wet and the noise, I found myself almost ready to laugh out loud — for I had needed no reminders of what to look for, or what to sense. It was as though I was new born, and seeing the world around me for the first time, drinking in its wonders and mysteries with the wind and the salt spray.

It is strange the way such things happen in life. We learn, and the lessons pass over us as the waves over a shore, leaving no mark. But when enough tides have ebbed and flowed, the shore is reshaped, and thus it is with mastering a new skill. There is a moment when the matter is too difficult, and we cannot master it. Then, without warning or seeming reason, there is a moment when we have it. The pedagogues will doubtless call this the moment of understanding, or such like. Whatever it was, I felt it and knew it, that dusk-tide on the quarterdeck of the *Jupiter*. I still feel its thrill in my bones, all these years later; aye, despite all the horrors that it foreshadowed.

I surveyed the scene again with a peculiar sense of contentment: a scene so similar to my nightmare on the *Happy Restoration*, yet so different. I thought of the kind face of my grandfather on its canvas high on the wall of Ravensden Abbey. This had been his domain, the sea. As I felt the wind suddenly gust a little more southerly, and watched the effect it had on our reefed sails, I finally believed I understood what had drawn him to this sphere. For man to move on the sea at all flies in the face of logic. Any voyage on water, even the transit of a punt across a river, is a miracle, the triumph of man's ingenuity over the most alien environ imaginable, and over his own darkest fears. To be a master of this watery realm must have given my grandfather more pride, and more delight, than all his titles, and lands, and the adoration of a queen. Godsgift Judge and good-brother Cornelis, too, though they were both born to the sea, and thus perhaps took it for granted. But we, the two Matthew Quintons, were landsmen, who had come to the sea as ignorant supplicants to a most demanding mistress. I would not speak for Judge, but I was willing to wager that Cornelis had never experienced the satisfaction that I felt then, as I heard our hull creak and felt our rigging strain in response to the strengthening wind, and watched the grey-clouded April dusk darken to the west, over the grave of the *Happy Restoration*.

My moment of satisfaction, such as it was, proved short-lived.

Malachi Landon had the watch. I had been dimly aware of his presence on the other side of the quarterdeck. Now I noticed that he seemed agitated. He paced the deck, looked across at me, then at the heavens, then at me again, and so he continued for almost a turn of the glass. Finally, he approached me, doffing his plain woollen cap in salute.

"Captain, this voyage," he said, far more deferential than was his wont, "it's gone well, thus far. We've had God's grace with the winds. Even this gale — abeam, almost from the quarter, the ideal wind to speed us to Scotland." I acknowledged it, but Landon seemed morose. "Sir, I've been casting our charts. They're ominous, some of the worst I've known."

"What charts, Master?"

The only charts I had seen bore lines that took us west from Portsmouth, around Cornwall, then due north through the Irish Sea to the west coast of Scotland, according to the sailing orders given me by the Lord High Admiral. This, I suddenly recalled, was the "dead reckoning" that had perplexed me but so short a time before.

"Why, our heavenly charts, sir. The auguries for this voyage, based on the alignment of the heavens at the moment of our sailing from Portsmouth." Any confidence in my supposed new-found mastery of the sailor's arts evaporated, and witty Poseidon saw fit to increase my discomfort by sending a great wave to soak me with a measure of Atlantic water. Shaking himself and shouting above the gale, Landon continued. "It's Mars, sir. Mars, the lord of the ninth house. He's retrograde on the cusp of the eighth, sir, thence casting a malicious quadrate to the Lord of the Ascendant. Worse, the lady of the eighth, the *domus mortis*, is on the very degree ascending!"

I listened to the words much as I would to a speech babbled in Hebrew. "And this all means, Mister Landon?"

"Why, this all foreshadows great difficulty, Captain. Obstructions and danger lie in our way, sir." He was wringing water from his cap and looking earnestly at me. "Death itself, in truth."

I was shaken by his words; not many can hear a presentiment of death without reacting so. But I took hold of myself and said with some impatience, "Then what would you have me do, Master? You know our orders. You know that I can answer only to the king and the Lord Admiral. Can I turn this ship round, or put us into port, on a suspicion you may have formed from star-gazing?"

Landon's expression twisted as if with pain but his voice was angry. "Never seen charts this bad. No captain who knows the sea would ignore an omen this clear . . ." He must have sensed he had strayed too far, for he became quieter, almost imploring. "Sir, there are countless ways to delay or prevent a voyage — a leak could be discovered — Penbaron's precious rudder cannot hold forever . . ."

He stopped quite suddenly, looked at me as though anew, and shook his head. He must have known that, ignoramus though I be, I could not in all honour sanction such a gross deceit on our king. Then he scowled, saluted loosely, and returned in bad grace to the other side of the quarterdeck, bracing himself against a cannon as another wave broke over our side. As I mused on the strange scene, I realized that for Malachi Landon to have approached me in this manner, to have confided in me thus, and to have even dared suggest the desperate stratagem of ignoring the king's express order, was proof of the dark, Hades-like depths of his concern. These charts of his had alarmed him beyond measure; so powerfully, indeed, that his fear of them had even briefly displaced his hatred of me, and his duty to the king. Landon and Harker argued often, Vyvyan had told me, and now that I had seen the quality of Landon's rage, and his servitude to this mysterious knowledge of the old necromancers, I found I could cast him quite easily in the part of Harker's murderer. Or, indeed, of my own —

There was a sudden noise, like the felling of a great tree. I heard Lanherne's desperate shout — "Mizzen's sprung!" — and looked across to see a great crack near the base of the mast.

That slightest of movements saved me. I saw the block from the corner of the eye, felt it graze my hair as it passed my temple at skull-breaking speed. I looked up, and saw ropes strain and break as the mizzenmast trembled in the gale. More blocks flew off crazily into the air. Lanherne screamed orders to Treninnick and his companions on the main yard, while the men on deck laboured to secure the great rope called the mizzen-stay. Then I looked across the quarterdeck and saw Malachi Landon's face; it was twisted in what might have been a smile.

As I stood, paralysed by horror, one of the mates ran forward across the main deck to the belfry on the forecastle and began to ring the ship's bell with a vigour that could have summoned the dead at doomsday. Kit Farrell and Musk were on the quarterdeck within moments, but of my lieutenant there was no sign: presumably the drink had consigned him to oblivion along with my chaplain. As each man emerged from below, summoned by the bell and the quartermasters' desperate cries of "All hands!", he made for the shrouds or his work station. Even a land-captain could see that all now hinged on keeping the mainmast safe, for if that sprang as well, pulled out of alignment by the rope — or rather, *stay* — that secured it to the mizzen, the wind would push us up the Bristol Channel and onto the lee shore. I had no desire to relive the wreck of the *Happy Restoration* on some cliff of Gower or Lundy Isle, so I urged them aloft with the sort of bellowed imprecations that I felt my grandfather might have used — "God speed, my brave lads! Climb as though the devil's on your tail!" Musk gave me the look he normally reserved for madmen, beggars and Members of Parliament. As it was, my encouragement was superfluous, for each man went aloft faster than a squirrel escaping a fox. They knew all too well what they had to do, and were about their business with no need of urging.

Of no man was that more true than John Treninnick. Quite suddenly, with the ship rolling and pitching, with the gale screaming through our rigging, Treninnick took hold of the mizzen stay and stepped out into space. Lanherne had told me of this skill of his at our first meeting, but Lord, what a sight it was! Arm over arm, he hauled himself at speed from main to mizzen, his short legs kicking wildly in the air.

"Thank the great God that you have him, sir," said Kit Farrell by my side, as Treninnick reached the mizzen and began to attend feverishly to the binding of ropes at the topmast head. "He'll make sure the backstays hold, now. The mizzen should be secure, and the main with it."

Penbaron, the carpenter, appeared before me and saluted gravely. "Permission to fish, Captain?" he said.

At first, I thought I had misheard; next, I thought that the block had actually struck me, and that I was senseless, dreaming all that had passed since it struck. Here we were in a gale, with the mizzen useless, and the officer responsible for its repair was seeking my

179

permission to cast lines for herring. "What in Jesu's name —" I began.

Kit Farrell stepped closer to my side and whispered, "Fishing, Captain. It's the method of repairing a sprung mast."

"Ah. Of course." I nodded with as much gravity as I could muster, feeling Cornish eyes upon me. "Permission granted, Mister Penbaron. Go to it at once, for God's sake, man."

And go to it Penbaron did. He may have been a prince among dullards, but he knew his job. Barely a minute had passed before his crew brought up from below two long pieces of wood, somewhat akin to river punts with their ends cut away. They lifted one into place at the front of the mast, over the great crack, and matched it with the other at the back. The cooper brought up spare hoops, and within but a few minutes more Penbaron's men were bolting the hoops onto both the wooden supports and the mast itself. There was a cry for woolding, and great coils of rope were wound around the mast, pulled taut by a crew of some of the strongest men on the ship — among them, strangely, the minute father of twins, John Tremar. The whole matter took less time than the turn of a glass.

"Great difficulties, Captain," said a voice by my ear. It was Landon. His voice was quiet but his look contained more than a challenge. "Obstructions and danger. The charts never speak falsely."

There was that twisted grimace again. A smile — just as he had smiled moments after the swinging block very nearly killed me. Pleasure born of satisfaction when one

180

is proved right. No doubt my death would have been an even more conclusive proof of the perils of Mars' malicious quadrate, and a satisfactory conclusion to the business.

"Hardly great difficulties, surely, Mister Landon?" I said, as lightly as I could. "Penbaron and his crew seem to have fished the mizzen quite easily."

"Fished the mizzen" — O Grandfather, sailing the eternal ocean above (or, more likely, below), art thou not proud?

Landon's look was wild and cruel. "Aye, the mizzen is well fished indeed, Captain. But it's the whipstaff, sir. It's jammed. See how our head turns eastward? Polzeath's the strongest helmsman on the ship, but not even he could keep hold of it when the mizzen sprang, and now it's jammed. If it can't be freed, we'll drive up the Channel on the gale, sir." His eyes bulged as he turned from me. "Doom, as the charts foretold. The *domus mortis* itself, that's where we are!"

Landon's unshakeable faith in his celestial charts tested my own belief in their worthlessness. The horror of another wreck swept over me — but only for the briefest moment. My mind found its antidote in a strange place: in the image of an ineffably ugly creature, far away in a warm and comfortable Oxford study. This was my Uncle Tristram, he who had spent so much of his life dabbling in the practices of astrologers and alchemists. He would have had no difficulty with Landon's talk of the *domus mortis*, and of malicious quadrates. No difficulty at all, for I remembered the conclusion to a conversation that he, Charles and I had at Ravensden Abbey, not long after the Restoration, when the court was much consumed by talk of comets, and the happy auguries that had made the king's return inevitable. "*Near forty years I've searched the heavens and plotted the stars,*" said Tristram Quinton. "*Your grandfather laid great store by such things, and would never set out on a voyage without casting his charts, so I was bred up reckoning there must be truth in them. Forty years, then, of drawing up charts, and measuring them against the realities of this world. And you know the conclusion I've come to? After all that work, and all those charts? It's all naught, boys. There's nothing in the heavens. You may as well cast about in Ravensden pond to learn your futures, for you won't find the answers in the stars.*"

No. I would not follow Landon down the road to despair. I would take the more practical course. Leaving Kit on the quarterdeck, I went to examine the matter for myself. Quite what good I could do, Heaven alone knew, but after my folly over the mast-fishing, I sought both redemption and a refuge from the contemptuous stares of my crew.

Below, the steerage resembled a funeral party; the sort of funeral party that takes place on a seesaw, with its members flung from one side to the other at frequent intervals, all of them shouting and cursing. Penbaron and two of his mates were circling the whipstaff, which was fixed at a sharp angle to starboard. Every so often, one of them would attempt delicately to push it to larboard.

I called to Penbaron for his verdict. He explained that he had a man down below, on the orlop, who was attempting to free the rowle and goose-neck mechanism directly beneath the deck on which we stood. This connected the whipstaff to the tiller which, in turn, controlled the troublesome rudder at our stern. My first thought was that Penbaron was a ship's carpenter of many years' standing and knew his trade. I stepped back a moment — but then I recalled the closeness of the lee shore. I remembered also that I had bestowed similar deference upon John Aldred. That diffidence had cost the lives of several score. Then I remembered Cornelia's favourite maxim, that experience was merely the accumulation of a lifetime's mistakes. And lastly I thought that perhaps I was not entirely ignorant in this matter. This mechanism did not sound too different in principle to that which drove Ravensden Mill, and as a child I had watched Hillard, the miller, carry out frequent impromptu repairs. Moreover, during my exile I had whiled away many days inspecting van der Eide windmills and their machinery on behalf of my father-in-law. It did not seem to me then that much of this sort of gentle pushing and pulling went on. It was more a question of applying as much force as possible to rid the mechanism of its blockage.

"With your permission, Mister Penbaron," I called out. He turned to me and fixed me with a look of amazement. "We have no time for this. Please alert your man below to stay clear of the tiller. Carvell, Polzeath, Monsieur Le Blanc — to me, if you will."

I grasped the whipstaff and heaved on it, as hard as I could. Musk went to the other side, and pushed. Le Blanc, Polzeath and Carvell looked at each other in confusion, then stepped to the whipstaff.

"All of us, together, on my count of three. One — two — *three!*"

Despite an ominous grinding sound from below, the ash-wood whipstaff remained obdurate. Musk swore.

"Christ, Captain, I'm too old for such games! And your brother won't thank you if you kill off his steward. Damn, think it's already given me a hernia."

Penbaron clasped his hands in agony and implored me to desist. From above came the cries and shouts of the men on deck. I felt my tenuous authority waning, but would not give up. I called in two more men from the main deck just beyond the opening of the steerage. One was a brutish Devonian whose name I did not know, the other the tiny John Tremar. On a second count of three, we seven men heaved for all we were worth . . .

. . . and flew headlong into the larboard cabins as the whipstaff freed itself.

I was the first to recover my balance, and as the men cried out to each other and set at once about their business I took hold of the whipstaff, pulling it back until it was almost vertical. Polzeath staggered up and stretched his hand to take it from me, but I waved him away. For the first time in my life, I felt the thrill of the ship itself in my hands. Through the small windows in the bulkhead that separated the steerage from the deck, I could see our main and fore courses swing as they responded to the righting of the whipstaff. I could feel the motion of the sea against the rudder at the stern, and felt the force of the gale itself, pushing the ship toward the east; a motion Polzeath quietly told me to resist by moving the whipstaff to point the *Jupiter*'s head in the opposite direction. It was hard work, and work that was below an earl's brother, as Musk proclaimed to all and sundry. I knew myself a spectacle there, as the men looked on, some in approval and some in confusion. But rarely have I felt such a strange exhilaration as I did on that stormy April evening in the year of grace 1662, when the Honourable Matthew Quinton first took the helm of a vessel upon the waters.

Kit Farrell came down to the steerage at that moment, then stopped, his face a picture of astonishment.

"Mister Farrell," I shouted, "please inform Mister Landon that the whipstaff is obedient once more, and that the helmsman requests a course to steer."

Kit smiled. "Sir, I was bringing that very order down, but did not expect to find at the helm the one man on this ship who can receive no orders! Our course is north-north-west. Port the helm, sir!"

I studied the compass in its binnacle, and hauled on the great wooden pole. The needle swung at once far too far to the left. "A little strong, sir," said Polzeath. "Make it gentle. Slow and gentle, as much as possible."

Julian Carvell laughed. "Like taking a woman, Cap'n. Slow and gentle is best, I've always found. At any rate, until you feel the need for fast and rough!"

It was at that moment that Lieutenant James Vyvyan emerged from his cabin. He took in the scene in the steerage without his usual cold and contemptuous glance. For the first time in our acquaintance, he looked like what he truly was: a confused young lad with too much drink in his belly.

"Mister Vyvyan!" I called. "Good evening to you, sir. Please take over the watch. Our bearing is north-north-west. Three bells of the second dog and all's well, Lieutenant!"

CHAPTER
TEN

My exertions at the whipstaff induced a sound slumber, unaffected by the endless pitching and rolling, Landon's forebodings of doom, or my very narrow escape from doom's airborne wooden manifestation. My sleep was just beginning to be made memorable by a particularly energetic dream of my Cornelia when I was woken by cries of murder. I was already perched on the side of my sea-bed, reaching for my sword, when a bedraggled Musk burst in.

"Lieutenant's servant's tried to kill the purser," he said excitedly. "Should have helped him, I suppose. Any rate, they're all setting up for a hanging court."

Outside was dimly lit by just two lanterns swinging from hooks on the bulkhead, but I hardly needed to see my way for I could easily follow the sound of the rumpus to its source. The steerage on a Fifth Rate is but a murky, low place, with the tiny makeshift cabins of the officers, six feet by five, at either side. The whipstaff lay at its forward end, with its own lantern to light the compass in its binnacle.

I found young Andrewartha struggling against the restraint of Monkley, a haggard, one-eyed boatswain's mate. Monkley had the terrified lad in an armlock, while Stafford Peverell, ruddy and hysterical, was screaming abuse into the crying child's face. James Vyvyan, who should have been on watch, was in turn screaming at Peverell, and only Boatswain Ap's firm grip prevented him from drawing his sword. Ahead of them stood the helmsman, mute but clearly all agog, moving the great lever of the whipstaff every now and then to keep us on our course. My heat sank, and I prayed for just a little of my brother's unfailing composure in times of crisis; either that or another storm to divert us all to our duties. But although the wind was still strong enough to make balance difficult in that dark, confined space, it was abating slowly, and only one duty lay before me.

At my appearance, Vyvyan and the boatswain stiffened into salute, but the purser was oblivious, continuing his ferocious tirade against the barefooted boy.

"Mister Peverell!" I shouted. "You are disturbing the peace of my ship, sir!"

He turned toward me and blinked, aware of me for the first time. He was breathless and sweating, and it was a struggle for him to get out a coherent sentence.

"Quinton," he stuttered, quite forgetting himself. "This boy attacked me. With a knife. Intent on murder, he was, nothing less." The spittle flew from his snarling lips and he turned and stabbed the boy in the chest with his bony finger. "I demand justice, sir. I demand summary judgement. I demand he be flogged raw, sir. I demand a court martial on that little —"

James Vyvyan interrupted vehemently, his face as red as a cannon-of-seven at the moment of firing. "Sir, Andrewartha was only defending himself against the attentions of this — this *creature*."

"He killed Captain Harker!" piped up young Andrewartha, swallowing his sobs and pointing at Peverell. "Mister Vyvyan says so!"

"What a deplorable rogue you are, sir," said the purser, turning furiously upon Vyvyan who had the good grace to flush. "A fantasy, in God's name! What would I gain by Harker's death, when that might have brought the abandonment of our voyage and the end of my employment? Answer me that, Lieutenant!"

The wind howled, and a great wave drove us all to starboard. Vyvyan twisted himself free of the boatswain's grasp and stepped menacingly towards the purser. I reached out and held his arm.

"Now, gentlemen," I said. "First, keep your voices low. I'll not have my ship's officers bawling like Billingsgate fishwives. I will not tolerate that on my ship. Second, Mister Peverell, no man *demands* anything in the presence of a king's captain." The purser scowled at me, and he and Vyvyan glowered at each other, but both seemed to accept the point. The helmsman's presence guaranteed that tales of the scandal would fly like swifts through the lower deck the moment he went off watch; in the meantime I had no desire to attract a larger audience and the sleeping men's hammocks were but inches away beneath our feet. I relieved the helm, and ordered Monkley to release the boy and take the whipstaff.

189

"Now," I said calmly, "before there's any talk of judgements or floggings, we need evidence, and we need witnesses. So now, gentlemen, calmly and openly if you will, answer me this question. Who witnessed the lad attack the purser?"

"I did," said Musk, reluctantly, for he had come to hate Peverell with the passion that he normally reserved for London lawyers.

"I too," said Monkley, turning briefly from his new duty at the whipstaff.

"And I, God help me," admitted Vyvyan. "But it's true what he says — I'd gone from your table, sir, and as you know, I continued in drink, to my shame. Thus I missed the call for all hands, and that drove me into a darker temper still. I drank more, and thought more, and then I raged more. I denounced the purser as a murderer, before the boy. I passed into sleep once more, and he must have taken my knife, and made for the purser's cabin. When I woke, I went after him, and saw him lunge for Peverell."

I contemplated my penitent lieutenant with fury. I saw nothing but nightmares ahead, for thanks to his lack of self-control I could envisage three courts-martial: one for Andrewartha, one for Peverell, and one for Vyvyan himself. Christ alone knew what the king and the Duke of York would make of a captain who permitted such riot and ill discipline among his own officers. Perhaps there would be room for a fourth court-martial: my own, the second of my career, and no officer's reputation could survive two. God, how I prayed in that moment to wake and find that this entire

190

voyage had been but a nightmare, and that in truth I was safe with my Cornelia and a commission in the Guards! But no waking came, and I still stood on that rocking deck.

Of them all, Andrewartha's case was by far the worst. Three eyewitnesses, including his own master, had testified against him for attempting to murder one of his superior officers, a man of breeding who held the Navy Board's warrant for his place on the ship. Despite his youth, that would suffice to condemn Andrewartha to enough lashes to rip all the flesh from his back, followed by a hanging from the yardarm.

I turned to him, and said as gently as I could manage, "What have you to say for yourself, lad?"

Andrewartha was shivering. How many times in his short life had he stood in line with his fellows to hear the Articles of War read aloud by their captain? He would have thought on the thirty-second, perhaps; but he was certainly now thinking on the twenty-first, which specified that assaulting a superior officer, like so many other crimes, was punishable by death.

"G-got to his cabin, sir," he stammered. "He . . . he thought I'd come for the same reason as before. Came at me, he did."

Peverell began to protest but I silenced him with a look. As captain of a king's ship, duly commissioned by the Lord High Admiral, I was judge and jury in one at that moment.

"Are there any witnesses to this?" I asked the company, in a low voice. "Did anyone see an assault by the purser upon the boy, at any time?"

The silence that followed my words was interrupted only by Peverell, protesting his innocence in a low, vicious voice. He warned that even the imputation of this was an almighty slur on his reputation, and on the honour and good name of the Peverells, and that his unnamed mighty friends would make us all regret this indignity. The boy should pay the highest price for his insolence and abominable falsehoods. So he continued as the ship rolled and pitched and the steerage lanterns swung manically upon their hooks. And as Peverell spat and hissed his venom, the rest of us in that crowded space looked at one another. None spoke; none had witnessed an assault by the purser on the boy, even though none doubted the man's cruelty. It was Andrewartha's word against Peverell's. The purser would survive, and by the full force of the state, the lad would be put to an agonizing death.

"Perhaps someone did," said a new voice. The Reverend Francis Gale had emerged from his cabin. The chaplain was barefoot, and wore only a stained shirt and breeches. Even from a distance of some yards, I could smell the stench of drink on his breath and in his sweat. Yet his speech was sober enough, and his cold eyes were clear.

Peverell snorted. He, too, had recognized the strength of his position and had regained his customary arrogance. "You, Gale? Belike you were insensible, as always." He turned his malevolent gaze to me. "Captain, I was merely attempting to instruct the lad in the ancient truths of the Roman Church. He's an

192

inquisitive boy, quick to learn. Almost as quick as he is to show violence to an officer."

Andrewartha shook his head miserably, but in such a way that I suspected there was some half-truth to the purser's story. Gale, though, simply stared at Peverell with unconcealed contempt.

"Who knows what I've seen when the rest of you have been looking the other way?" he said, in a steady, terrible voice. "That's the thing with my discourses with my friends, the bottles. I can be asleep all through a storm, yet awake and roam the decks when all the rest of you are asleep." He took a step closer. "Who knows how many times I may have witnessed you buggering that boy, Peverell, when you assumed I was far gone in drink?"

I glanced at the faces of Phineas Musk and James Vyvyan, both ghostly in the dancing lantern-light. All the men in that circle of misery and accusation looked grim; all of them feared the public exposure of this most awful and intimate of acts. Peverell's face was a mask of horror. "You *lie* —"

"Ah, Purser, Purser . . ." said Gale, moving closer still. "Would any court in the land take your word over mine? Now who would dare think that a man of God would lie on oath, and testify that he had witnessed things he had never truly seen? And me the firmest friend of the king's own chaplain, too. Any judge, or jury, or court-martial that you know of, Purser?"

"Let me see if I have the right of what you say, Reverend Gale," I interrupted. I understood my chaplain's intent, discomforting though it was. "You

193

claim to have witnessed the purser, Mr Peverell, and the boy, Andrewartha, perform acts in direct contravention of the thirty-second Article of War? Which article prescribes death as the automatic punishment for such a heinous sin? And you are sure of what you've seen, Reverend, and would testify to it?"

Gale shrugged. "Who's to say what I've seen and haven't seen, Captain? My recollections come and go, these days." His face hardened as he turned back to Peverell. "But be assured of one thing. If this worm presses any charge against the boy" — he stared intently at the cringing man — "then the recollections I put before a court martial will be as clear as day."

"The injustice . . ." Peverell could hardly speak. "You're a creature of the devil, not of God. I have friends and I will have vengeance on you, you drunken pisspot."

"You'll not be avenged on anyone or anything, Stafford Peverell," said Gale savagely. "In the old times, the Church gave sanctuary to those who sought it, with God's holy wrath as their defence against pursuit by their enemies. Well, so do I. If Lieutenant Vyvyan concurs, I'll take the lad for my own servant." Vyvyan nodded. "In all official senses he now serves me, and thus the Lord Archbishop, and thus God Almighty. So mark this, Peverell. My sword hasn't tasted blood these twelve years, but if you stray anywhere near that lad now he's under my protection, whether it's to convert him to Rome or to do whatever else you might have in mind, then I'll stick you on the end of it like the overripe pig you are."

The purser's face was twisted, and I could see veins pulsing on his neck and forehead. For a moment he stood torn between his fear and his anger. Then he turned furiously on his heel and retired to his cabin. Andrewartha looked confusedly between James Vyvyan and the Reverend Gale. The chaplain inclined his head toward the lieutenant, and the boy went to his accustomed master, who saluted me before returning to his place of duty on the quarterdeck. Boatswain Ap, satisfied that murder and equally gross disorder had been prevented on his ship, saluted in his turn, and left the steerage.

I began to say something in thanks to Francis Gale, but he raised a hand. "Forgive me, Captain. I have a conversation to resume, and this bottle is proving particularly loquacious."

As he turned toward his cabin, I called after him. "We *will* talk, Chaplain. You'll not avoid me this entire voyage!"

"Ah, my dear captain," he said, "you'd be surprised how long my avoidances can last."

CHAPTER
ELEVEN

Kit Farrell scraped the quill across the paper, spilling ink to left and right. Slowly, he completed his unsteady downstroke and turned the pen to the left, drawing something like a hook, as he had been told. He lifted the pen and moved it a little way to the right, where he scratched a shape that vaguely resembled a horseshoe. Further to the right again, he essayed a small circle with a downstroke coming from its left, then a bold single stroke, then a Christian cross. He stopped, looked at the paper, and frowned. With his face a mask of concentration, he drew a horseshoe on its side, and closed it off at the top. Finally he scratched another hook, the mirror image of his first, upright and pointing off to the right of the paper.

He looked at the finished effort, and said with a little pride, "Jupiter."

"*Jupiter* indeed," I said. "You can write your ship's name, Kit Farrell. Be thankful you're not serving on the *Constant Reformation*."

We were a day beyond the confrontation with Stafford Peverell. The *Jupiter* was sailing northward through the Irish Sea in fine and clear weather. The mood on board had improved with the weather, and there was no further word of Malachi Landon's grim prognostications of doom.

That morning, I had sat in my cabin with my grandfather's compendium dial in my hand, and looked upon the inscription on the outer face: *MQBC 1585*. Matthew Quinton, Baron Caldecote. My grandfather. The year before he inherited the earldom. I opened up the device and looked upon its many pages. When I played with it as a child, these were all meaningless to me, and so I thought it would be now, for I had not opened the device properly in ten years. But strange to say, the pages now made a certain sense. That one was evidently a calendar, and that — why, a miniature sundial, surely. One was plainly a compass for taking bearings; Landon and Kit Farrell had larger versions of the same instrument, and called it a circumferentor. I went to the stern window, lined up the device on a distant Irish horse-boat and took a bearing. Another dial resembled the compass, but was scaled in the named months, and twelfths, and thirtieths. A nocturnal, then — the instrument used by the master and his mates to take bearings on the Great Bear! Then there was a table by which a man could tell the time of the tide anywhere on earth. No, not such a mystery, after all! My grandfather had mastered this device, and so would I: MQ 1662.

The bell had rung then for the change of watch, Kit Farrell came below, and in the blinking of an eye, I turned from student to teacher.

I had begun instructing Kit in the lexical mysteries by giving him an alphabet on a copy-tablet, and suggesting he recite the sounds of the letters over to himself. Then I had shown him the method of holding a pen properly, and taught him to sign his name — or at least, to write the word *Kit*, as to a man of no learning, both *Christopher* and *Farrell* would be as daunting as a poem by Milton. His second word was *ship*, though the *s* and the *p* took a while to march across the paper in the right direction. *Jupiter* was his third word. Phineas Musk, who had always been suspiciously literate for a rogue of such dubious birth, had watched my teaching with amusement until he became bored; whereupon he went up on deck to shout insults at the distant coast of Wales. I trusted that the target of his bile would not be mistaken aboard the *Royal Martyr*, which was sailing parallel to us a few hundred yards to starboard.

"Well, Captain," Kit Farrell said, shaking me out of my reverie, "if seamanship is as hard for you as this of writing is for me, then I think we should . . ." He stopped, gazing over my shoulder out of my quarter-gallery window.

"Mister Farrell?"

"*Royal Martyr* . . ." he said, and said no more, for suddenly there was a flash and in the same instant a mighty thunder deafened us both. I turned, and saw the side of Judge's ship engulfed in smoke. She had fired her full broadside. She had fired it at us.

Men scattered from our path as we ran to the quarterdeck. They seemed startled, but none displayed the panic I would have expected under fire. *Why had*

Vyvyan not ordered our decks cleared? And why had Judge fired at us?

A second broadside roared out from *Royal Martyr's* larboard battery. We reached the quarterdeck to find James Vyvyan, hands braced on the rail, looking over to Judge's ship with his face set. Musk had backed against the larboard rail, his face as white as a shroud and his breeches suspiciously damp. It was only in that moment that I realized we had not been hit. Our rigging still stood, our sails were intact, our hull unscathed.

Royal Martyr's guns were not shotted.

"Lieutenant Vyvyan," I said, joining him at the rail. "What in Christ's name —"

The foremost gun of *Royal Martyr's* larboard battery finished my sentence for me. Even it had not, the task would have been accomplished by the next gun behind her, which fired barely moments afterward. Then her next, and the next, and the next after that. And then I knew.

"She's firing a salute," said Kit Farrell at that instant. "She's even hoisting all her ensigns and bunting. A royal salute, Captain."

"There's no anniversary today — no cause at all for this," said Vyvyan.

"Unless the cause is to impress us with her broadsides, sir," suggested Kit. "I make that two full broadsides in less than a fifth of a glass, and this rolling fire not long after. There won't be many ships in our navy that can match such a rate of fire. Not many ships in *any* navy, come to that."

I promised myself that I would order a drill of the great guns as soon as it was fitting — which would be a time when the *Royal Martyr* was out of sight and therefore unable to gloat over our inadequacies — for if Judge's intention was to impress, he had succeeded all too amply. He had told me that almost all his men were veterans who had sailed with him before, learning their trade in the great war with the Dutch. Their excellence explained in no little measure why not even the great butterbox sailors, my own good-brother amongst them, could stand against these ironsides afloat.

"*Martyr*'s hoisting the signal for captains in company to repair aboard, sir," said Kit.

I nodded. "Well, then. Perhaps Captain Judge will be kind enough to explain exactly why he chooses to waste so much of the king's powder."

Boatswain Ap and his crew hauled in our longboat — in these light seas we had been towing it in our wake — and Martin Lanherne assembled his oarsmen. They rowed me over to *Royal Martyr*, where I was greeted by a full side party, her boatswain's pipe, and the sullen Lieutenant Warrender. Lanherne, Le Blanc and Polzeath stood at my back, dressed as smartly as Le Blanc's hasty efforts would permit; a not unsuitable escort for the heir to Ravensden. I raised my hat to the stern and the royal ensign streaming out in the breeze. As I did so, I noticed with a shock a man that I had not seen since my first night at Portsmouth. My brutal old crop-headed adversary Linus Brent looked me up and down, then turned his back on me and stooped to attend a sailor who lay unconscious upon the deck in a pool of his own blood.

Leading me to the quarterdeck, his servants close behind, Warrender explained. "Accident with the recoil, sir. Should have known better than to be standing there, a man with fifteen years' service. He'll only be good for a cook now, if he can get a warrant, or else an almsman's place. May God have mercy on those whose day is done. Those like poor Captain Harker."

Warrender spoke these words in a quiet, detached voice that puzzled me. There was no opportunity to dwell on his strange mien, however, for we were already at the quarterdeck stair. Godsgift Judge looked almost military, at least by his own, entirely unique, standards. He wore a red jacket after the Persian fashion, which could have been mistaken from a distance for a Guardsman's tunic. His sword hung by his side, his great wig was capped incongruously by a black turban, and he held a large goblet of wine in his hand.

"Captain Quinton!" he trilled. "A very good day, my dear sir. I trust our little salute did not startle you?" With a coy smirk he tapped me on the shoulder. "I should have forewarned you, perhaps, but I was so impatient to hail the happy news."

"News, Captain?"

"A princess, sir! A new daughter to the Duke and Duchess of York! A cock-boat out of Cardigan Bay brought us the news but half an hour ago. You'll join me to toast the glorious event, I trust?"

Now, my love of my country and my king was as strong as any man's, but I felt not a little embarrassed as I stood once more in Judge's aromatic great cabin, toasting an infant girl in far-off Whitehall. Surely, I reasoned, this child was hardly worthy of such attention. She would either die in infancy, or she would be supplanted by all the sons the duke would have, and even more by all those that King Charles would have with his new Portuguese queen. It seemed to me that, once more, the exquisite Judge was attempting to prove himself a true Cavalier, the staunchest Royalist. It turned my stomach. His chosen way of marking the royal birth, demonstrating in the process the very real superiority of his ship and crew over my own, doubtless did its part to shape my feelings.

Such were my thoughts, for we cannot read the future. Neither Godsgift Judge nor I knew that on that day in April 1662 we were toasting the birth of Her Most Gracious Majesty, Mary the Second, who would one day, by the grace both of God and several unlikely turns of fate, find herself Queen Regnant of England and the wife of William of Orange, our late and unlamented Dutch King. A queen twenty-two years younger than myself, yet I saw her buried, and that long, long ago.

After we had drunk what Judge considered to be an appropriately loyal amount of wine, and he had again nakedly solicited the good offices of the House of Quinton on his behalf, he sat me down at his table and unrolled a sea-chart of the west coast of Scotland. Like our sovereign lord the king, when he turned to matters of life and death Godsgift Judge put aside his outward appearance and superficial mannerisms, and became a very different man, decisive and clear. In truth, he became precisely the sort of man to whom Oliver Cromwell would have given the command of a great man-of-war.

"So, Captain Quinton," he said, "this is what I propose. When we come off the head of Kintyre, we'll send word to Dumbarton for the king's regiment to begin its march toward the coast. You'll take on your pilot for Scottish waters thereabouts — I can manage without any such, of course. Then, we'll make for the Sound of Jura, here, pass into the Firth of Lorne, here, and show ourselves around Mull, Lismore, and the coasts up to Skye." He pointed at inlets and islands on a coastline that even on a chart looked to be strange and remote. I saw fingers of sea that stretched far into a land of mountains, and marked the many rocks and shoals scattered along our course. "That should alert Glenrannoch to our coming, and perhaps be sufficient to change his mind before the soldiers reach Oban. We'll call on him, of course, and on some of the other chiefs in those lands. Maclean, certainly, Macdougall of Dunollie too, and some of the Macdonald septs: Clanranald, Glengarry, Lochiel . . ." He stopped and thought for a moment, drumming absently on the chart with his manicured fingertips. "And perhaps Ardverran too. Yes, Ardverran, I think. They'll all benefit from a gentle reminder that the king's writ runs even in their black fastnesses."

I was guarded, and feeling not a little resentful of Judge that day. Not at all put out, he leaned back on a chair that would not have been out of place in a salon, and shook his head slowly.

"Blood feuds, Captain Quinton. Endless blood feuds, these clansmen indulge themselves in. Generation after generation, century after century. God knows, when I was there last, I came to feel that many of them looked on our great civil wars as but a trivial and annoying diversion from their business of avenging themselves on each other for all eternity."

"So what should I know of these lands and these people, Captain," I asked, "before we reach our destination?"

He smiled. "More than I have time to tell you, Matthew, and more than you want to learn. Trust me in that. I was in those waters a whole year, and learned but a fraction of it. These people are a century or more behind us in manners and warfare alike, and their feuding makes the Italians look like saints. But it will work for us. For instance, if we but hint to the Macdonalds that the Campbells are rising under Glenrannoch, they'll likely do our work for us, at no expense to the king. Campbell against Macdonald, Captain Quinton. Forget all the lesser names, and the lesser feuds. Once, the Macdonalds had a kingdom in those lands, the Lordship of the Isles as they called it, but then the Kings of Scots and the Campbells brought them down. So in the late wars, when Campbell sided with Parliament, Macdonald fought for the king. They suffered harshly in those times, of course, but now, with the king restored and the Campbell Earls of Argyll brought low, the Macdonalds have risen again in the world. They'll not want to see Glenrannoch with an army, Captain Quinton, for though his aim is to conquer Scotland, you can be certain that somewhere along that road he'll use it to slaughter every last Macdonald."

I asked, "You knew Glenrannoch, when you were there before?"

"No, he was still abroad then. But I dealt with all the rest of the Campbells — and old Argyll, of course, Glenrannoch's cousin and chief, in name at any rate. He was still holed up at Inveraray after betraying every side he ever joined. Glenrannoch's name was everywhere, though, from Galloway up to Shetland. 'When Glenrannoch comes back to his own,' they'd say, as if he was some sort of Arthur returning from Avalon. They made him out to be the greatest general that ever lived: a cross between Gustavus Adolphus and Noll Cromwell. 'Clan Campbell wouldn't be brought so low,' one told me, 'if Glenrannoch was here, and in Argyll's stead.' All so much vainglorious Scots bluster, of course. We'll bring him low in his turn, Captain Quinton."

Judge raised his cup to me. His rings sparkled in the sun, and I saw he was his simpering self once more. "So, sir, I give you a swift and prosperous outcome to our mission." He sipped his wine and dabbed delicately at his lips, all trace of the warrior gone. "And then, who knows what beneficence we might expect from His Majesty, eh?"

★ ★ ★

My boat's crew was sullen as they rowed me back across the calm Irish Sea towards the *Jupiter*. It was Le Blanc, with that unfailing capacity of the French to disregard the moods of the English, who finally broke the silence.

"So, *monsieur le capitaine*, shall we, too, salute *l'enfant royale*?"

Lanherne glared at him for his impertinence and I made no answer, but Le Blanc's question reflected my own thoughts. We would have to fire a salute, of course, but I knew full well that we could not hope to match the speed or immaculate coordination of the *Royal Martyr*'s broadside. Judge and his men might laugh our efforts to the skies, and that would be a humiliation too far for these proud Cornish lads and their captain.

Out of the corner of my eye I saw Le Blanc engage in a whispered conference with Polzeath and Lanherne. With a dismissive gesture at the *Royal Martyr*, Polzeath then turned to Treninnick. The simian oarsman's face broke into perhaps the most terrifying grin I ever saw and then, quite suddenly, he began to sing. For such an ugly creature, his voice was soft, almost feminine. I had encountered good singing many times, of course — only the previous winter, my brother Charles and I had encountered Desgranges, the great French bass, sing in London — but I never heard any, no matter how cried up, who could frame a tune as John Treninnick did in the *Jupiter*'s longboat that day. It was an old, old song, Lanherne said, of King Mark of Cornwall and the loves of the fair Isolde, and it was in the Cornish tongue. Treninnick finished the last verse just as we came alongside the starboard side of the *Jupiter*, and as he shipped his oar, Roger Le Blanc turned to me.

"Since I have been on this ship, *mon capitaine*, I have observed two things about these Cornish." He looked at me, a strange smile playing about his lips. "Yes, they can fight. But they can also sing."

Thus it was that several hours later, His Majesty's ship the *Jupiter* fired precisely one gun to mark the birth of Her Royal Highness, the Princess Mary. But no man of the *Royal Martyr*, or of any other ship in the navy, could have saluted her so well. For as the echo of that single gun died away over the Irish Sea, John Treninnick sang a note, and one hundred and thirty-five Cornishmen, by birth or adoption, starboard and larboard watches together, with the Mahometan Ali Reis on his violin and our trumpeters matching the harmony, sang the great coronation anthem of Mr Lawes — "Zadok the Priest" — in which they had been hastily coached by Le Blanc and me. I had heard the same words sung almost exactly a year before, in Westminster Abbey, when King Charles was crowned. They tell me that German Handel made a new setting of it for his present majesty, German George, no doubt sung by his legion of Italian sopranos — great God, the country is overrun with foreigners — and though I have not heard it, I'll wager it is inferior to our good old English Lawes. But no matter. For I will swear on the graves of every Quinton in the vaults of Ravensden that whichever Zadok suits your preference, neither the choristers of the Chapel Royal nor Mr Handel's swarthy divas were even the slightest match for the men of the *Jupiter* on that April day so very long ago.

"God Save the King!" they sang. "Long Live the King! May the King Live For Ever!" As they reached the final crescendo, Phineas Musk drew my attention to the *Royal Martyr*. Many of her crew were lining her larboard rail, watching and listening. I saw Godsgift Judge on his quarterdeck, and when he saw me, he smiled and raised his turban in salute. Then the *Royal Martyr* bore away, put on sail, and took up station well ahead of us once more.

I dined all the officers that afternoon, determined to make amends for my lack of attention to them since we had sailed from Spithead. Moreover they would all be well aware of the altercation over the boy Andrewartha, for no doubt most of them had been listening avidly in their cabins throughout. I wished to shore up the frail sense of unity and solidarity that existed between us before we sailed into what might prove to be enemy waters. Thus it was that at my order, Janks provided a meal fit for visiting royalty to delight the dullards of the *Jupiter*'s officers: boiled pork; a gigget of excellent mutton and turnips; a piece of beef, well seasoned and roasted; a green goose; and best of all, a great fresh Cheshire cheese. I commanded our fullest range of liquor and my board fairly groaned with bottles of Canary, sherry, Rhenish, claret, white wine, cider, ale and beer, and punch like dishwater for the toasts.

The wind had died almost to nothing as we came to the table. We were somewhere in the middle of the Irish

Sea, making barely any headway at all: no danger, then, of our lavish feast being tipped off the tables by an April storm, a fate that befell many a meal afloat; no danger, either, of our table being blighted by Malachi Landon's sourness, for he had the watch on deck where, no doubt, he was still brooding over his premonitions. Even the malevolence of Stafford Peverell seemed to have been put aside for once. He was still evidently abashed from the events of the previous day; as a result his society proved almost tolerable, for he said not a word. Those same events also seemed to have served as a catharsis for James Vyvyan. To my relief he kept his thoughts on his uncle's "murder" to himself and acted the lieutenant's part admirably, serving as co-host at the far end of the table. The mood of my other officers was tentative; they were hardly exponents of courtly repartee at the best of times, but in the circumstances no man (their captain included) seemed quite to know which conversations were safe, and which were bound inexorably for the rocks of embarrassment.

We were seated, with Musk standing glumly behind my chair as my attendant, when the door opened to admit the Reverend Francis Gale. I noted with relief that he was attired rather more fully than on the occasion of our previous meeting.

"I heard there was finally a meal worth eating on this ship," he said without ceremony.

Suppressing a smile I ordered a place to be laid for him alongside my own, and all the officers moved down, which caused a moment of pandemonium in the cramped cabin. Peverell, who had paled and turned away, his fist clenching upon the tablecloth, suddenly exclaimed that he felt quite ill, and with the captain's permission, he would retire to his cabin. That permission was immediately and unreservedly granted, and as the door closed upon him, the chaplain took his seat beside me.

Gale had been absent yet again from the day's prayers, conducted by the captain with his customary lack of enthusiasm, but he seemed sober enough now. A state that was unlikely to last, I thought wryly, as Musk, at an impatient signal from Gale, poured both Canary and then a cup of claret which was drained in two draughts. My opportunity to learn something of the chaplain would plainly be brief.

At the far end of the table, Penbaron over knocked a flagon of wine. Amid the laughter and chaos that followed, I turned to Gale and began, quietly, "I must thank you for your timely intervention last night, Reverend." Gale's grunt made it clear that to him the matter was closed. I tried another tack. "We have missed you at our daily prayers since Sunday, though."

He chewed a mouthful of mutton and washed it down with wine. "I'll lend you Billy Sancroft's prayer book, Captain," he said at length. "Then you'll be legal, at least, when you lead the men's devotions. Good mutton, this."

I knew from Janks that Gale had dined only on ship's biscuit, ale and port wine since we sailed, and marvelled at his seeming determination to make up for all the meals he had missed. He ate with silent purpose,

210

calling frequently for Musk to replenish his cup, while the rest of us attempted to converse politely on the topics of the day. I found I wished to know this man, but could not think how to engage him in conversation. Cornelia would have known the right words instinctively: in her brief time in England I had witnessed her put down bishops, beer-sodden roaring boys and royal mistresses alike. I had no such gift for the apt phrase, however, and could resort only to the authority of my rank. Vyvyan had led the table through a particularly arduous discussion of the theatrical troupes he had encountered in Penzance before I had the chance to address the chaplain once again.

"With due respect to your divine office, Reverend Gale," I said quietly, "we are both paid, and honour bound, to play our parts on this ship. You and I, we are Church and state, as indivisible at sea as they are on land. The king and Lord Archbishop Juxon pay you to minister to my men's souls, and the king pays me to preserve their bodies and this ship in which we sail."

He tasted the Canary. "Indeed, Captain," he said. "Just as you did on the *Happy Restoration*."

I was silent for a while, paying close attention to my platter. I noted with relief that the conversation of my fellows had become a little louder. Vyvyan, Boatswain Ap and Gunner Stanton, contrary to all the rules of the table, were now engaged in some argument about clewlines, whatever they might be. Skeen, the surgeon, more than a little deaf, was nodding along to the general discourse with a frown of concentration. None had heard. But such an intolerable impertinence could not be allowed to stand. I thought nothing, then, of Gale's age and calling, nor of my youth. I did not care that the man himself intrigued me, nor that his jibe was well merited. I turned on him, mastering the shame and anger he had provoked in me with an immense effort.

"Sir, I am the captain of this ship. A captain has the powers of God and King in one." I took a breath, controlling my countenance and my voice with determination. "I will not tolerate insolence from you, and I will not tolerate you demeaning this ship by your drunkenness, regardless of the gallant part you played over the boy Andrewartha. You may be a man of the cloth, sir, but it's as one to me whether I call you out or have the boatswain flog you at the railings."

For the first time, then, Francis Gale turned and looked me directly in the eyes. He put down his glass. "My God," he said. "I do believe you would."

I looked into those steady grey eyes for a while. Then his gaze passed beyond me, out through the window of the gallery. He stared into the distance for a minute or more. I waited, listening idly to the conversation of my officers. Then Gale seemed to make a decision.

"Can you smell that, Captain?" he asked, once again turning to me. I could smell only Janks's meal, and shook my head questioningly. "I can smell it, still, after thirteen years. It is there, due west of us, well over the horizon. But I can smell it. I can smell the blood on the wind, and the rotting stench of the grave-pits. I can smell it all as though it was yesterday, and I can hear

212

the screams still, to this very day. There it lies, Captain Quinton. Drogheda."

With that, and without my permission, Francis Gale stood, and left the cabin. The babble of argument among my officers died away and they looked at me with anxious faces, for all were aware of the dreadful incivility of our chaplain's departure. I wrestled with a dilemma: to go after him, or to act as though nothing untoward had happened? It was a minute or more before I left the table, bidding them finish the repast at their leisure. They scraped their chairs back and made hasty bows as I departed, and I heard the murmur of voices rising behind the closed door. I strode to the upper deck and went in search of Gale.

I found him in the forecastle, gazing out to larboard, towards the land just out of sight in the west. I knew as I looked on him that upbraiding him for his disrespect would have been folly; this was a man far beyond the niceties of civility. I had seen it but a moment ago, etched in his features; I had seen despair looking back at me through his eyes. He seemed not to have noticed my approach, but then, and without turning towards me, he began to speak, slowly and deliberately.

"You expect an apology, Captain. A gentleman and a man of honour would grant you one, or else accept your challenge, or take the flogging. A gentleman and a man of honour. I was both of those things, once. But Drogheda, there, put paid to such fine notions."

Then Francis Gale told me his story, talking as dispassionately as if he was reading a tradesman's bill.

He had begun the Civil War comfortably, he said, as one of the chaplains to the royal court at Oxford, but he had fretted after action, and soon went off to minister to the king's armies in the field.

"I became the personal chaplain to Colonel Sir Peter Willoughby, an old friend and neighbour. An able soldier was Peter, and a just man. When the king's last English armies were defeated in the year '46, we went together into Ireland. But after they had executed King Charles, Cromwell and his time-servers in the Rump Parliament decided it was time for a final reckoning; time to deal with the Irish, and with the Cavaliers who fought on there in a cause now hopeless." He paused, gathering his thoughts of that grim time. Above us, the foresail flapped its forlorn demand for a better breeze, but the light gusts, playing across the calm sea below, were evidently in no hurry to strengthen.

"In September 1649 they came. Peter and I were within the walls of Drogheda, where he served as deputy governor, when Lord General Cromwell and his cursed Ironsides came before the town. We had some three thousand men, a mixture of Irish and English. Cromwell summoned the town to surrender, but Aston, the governor, was determined to make a stand — God knows why, for it was madness. It was the morning of 10 September that the lord general's army began their assault on the town. That is when it all ended for me."

All this time, I, his sole listener, stood by him in rapt attention. Of course, I knew the story of what had passed at Drogheda. During the past four or five years, I had spent enough winter days at Brussels, Veere and

214

Ravensden with nothing else to do but read the accounts of the late wars, and I thought I knew what was to come. The lord general's men, crazed with blood lust, had annihilated not only the garrison of Drogheda, but also the men, women and children of the town, to the number of several thousands of innocent souls. "The righteous judgement of God on these barbarous wretches," was Cromwell's justification. The sons, grandsons and countrymen of those "barbarous wretches" nurse this story, and their hatred of Cromwell, in their hearts to this day. That is what I had read in exile, and even now I know Irishmen who will swear to the truth of it all. That is what I expected Francis Gale, who had been there, to repeat to me. Such was my presumption.

"They will tell you that Cromwell and his men slaughtered women and children alike in Drogheda town," he said. "But they did not. War breeds lies, and Irish wars breed more than most. Aston had refused the terms, so Cromwell was perfectly entitled to unleash the sword of wrath against our men. That much I can accept. I saw them beat Aston's brains out with his wooden leg and then hack him to pieces, and that, too, I can accept, for it was his obstinacy and stupidity that brought calamity down upon us that day." Gale paused and screwed up his eyes, as though hoping to see the towers of Drogheda once more, too far distant though they were.

"But I saw Peter Willoughby, my friend, walk out with his sword presented in surrender, and I saw four Ironsides cut him down. They called him Irish filth and papist dog." Gale's voice shook though he remained perfectly still, leaning upon the rail. "Willoughby, with not a drop of Irish blood in his body, and his family the most loyal sons of the Church of England you'd find in Shropshire. And when he had fallen, they carried on hacking at his corpse, and fed his parts to the dogs of Drogheda town, while their soldiers and officers alike stood around, and laughed. And they did this, when the battle was all but won."

Gale stopped, struggling to compose himself. Now I thought I understood. From childhood, I had known the depth of my mother's bitterness at the death of her husband — and that was an honourable death in a fair fight. For Gale, the wretched and ignoble death of his friend must have left a wound such as I could scarce imagine.

"Women and children were not slaughtered out of hand, as I have said," he went on. "But enough of them fell, that day. There was one . . . Catherine Slaney, her name was. Of a good Dublin family." His eyes were bright and his mouth drawn, and though the last rays of the sun burnished his features I saw pain imprinted everywhere.

"Once they had finished their sport with Peter Willoughby, they came into the tower. I was lying there. I had been wounded as my friend was being . . . mutilated. I did not even have my sword. The battle was long over, but the first man into the room, he came for me with a half-pike. I could do nothing. And she . . ." I saw his hands grip tight around the wooden rail. "She threw herself in front of him. She took the point intended for me. She took it in her belly. We had been lovers for two years, and she was carrying my child."

Nearly becalmed as we were, there still came the usual sounds of a ship at sea — the lightest of breezes in the rigging, the water lapping against the hull. Yet even these could not break the utter and complete silence that prevailed on our forecastle, as the sun finally set over Drogheda. I think I shall only know that silence again when they place me in my grave.

At last, Gale looked at me. When he spoke, he was calm once more. "His Majesty and the archbishop tell us that we must be reconciled, Captain. We must forgive and forget what passed in the late wars. We must be good neighbours again, Roundheads and Cavaliers. Our Lord Jesus Christ tells us the same thing, and I am His servant. But I defy them all, here again tonight, as I have these thirteen long years. God and the king and the archbishop and Billy Sancroft can preach at me all they want, Captain Quinton, but I will not be reconciled to the men who shared a cause with those who slaughtered Peter Willoughby, Catherine Slaney . . . and my child."

At that moment the bright stern lanterns of the *Royal Martyr* twinkled out, illuminating the dark hull of the ship. Beneath them, light poured from the windows of Godsgift Judge's great cabin. Judge, who had fought for the same man who ordered that final assault on Drogheda.

"I will not forgive," said Gale in a low voice, "and I will never forget. But at least, in my cups, I can find oblivion."

I struggled to think of words that I could say to him, but there were none. Only one I knew might have found those words, but he had died on a cross long ago. Francis Gale spared me the ignominy of specious platitudes.

"Captain Quinton, you are only the second man in thirteen years who has heard that story. Telling it to Billy was one thing, but telling it to you, an utter stranger, is another." The ship's bell tolled, and he nodded, as though agreeing with a friend's sage observation. "You know, perhaps the papists have the right of it. Perhaps confession truly is good for the soul. I feel somewhat lighter in the heart than I have felt in some time."

A strange thought came to me, in the way that such thoughts sometimes do, unsought and unheralded. "The boy, Andrewartha. He'd be about the age a son of yours would have been by now, wouldn't he?"

Francis Gale looked at me curiously for a while. "You're a man of surprises, Captain Quinton. God knows, you are too young to bear that rank, despite your name and your lineage. But there's something to you, after all." He nodded slowly, and essayed the ghost of a smile. "Yes, Captain. He's about the age my child would be."

We stood for a minute, looking at the bright lights of the *Royal Martyr*. Then Gale stirred, and laid his hand upon my arm. "Time for us to return to the table, I think, with your permission? We have a good meal to finish, and a new princess to toast, after all. And you have my apology for my unspeakable conduct, sir."

CHAPTER
TWELVE

The breeze came up again in the middle of the night. I was awake in my sea-bed as the last of my candles died, thinking on Francis Gale's story and the ruin of his life, when I felt the motion of the ship begin again. It must have lulled me to sleep, for some time beyond dawn I heard the distant tolling of our bell and woke to see from my cabin windows the coast of Antrim to larboard, that of Kintyre to starboard. Ireland and Scotland, but a few miles apart and clearly visible. Musk arrived to shave me, and said that our pilot had come aboard in the night, and had taken on his duty of advising Landon in our navigation. After narrowly avoiding having my throat slit by Musk's efforts with the razor, I dressed and climbed impatiently up on deck.

I scanned the sea around us and saw *Royal Martyr*, in the distance, steering for the cape of Kintyre. Judge was following our orders to the letter. He would go under the walls of Dunaverty Castle, where the king maintained a signal station, and there hoist a flag: this was the prearranged signal for a regiment to be dispatched from the royal fortress at Dumbarton. There was no need for us to anchor or back our sails, Judge had told me; the *Jupiter* was to sail on and begin the task of showing herself and the king's ensign along the shores of Kintyre, Islay and Jura. We had a rendezvous appointed at Craignish, at the head of the Sound of Jura, and Malachi Landon was dismissively confident, declaring it an easy course in all but the strongest northerlies or southerlies. Our pilot concurred. He was a little, pungent man with a lazy right eyelid, who spelled his name Ruthven and yet pronounced it Rivven, if for no reason other than to confuse the English it seemed to me. But he knew his trade, and agreed that in the light westerlies that now prevailed, our passage to Craignish would be the easiest of sails.

It was a glorious morning. To the north, I could see mountains shrouded in low cloud, and Ruthven announced these to be the heights of Islay, beyond Ardbeg and Ardmore. I stood at the rail taking in the view and filling my chest with the uncommonly fresh air, then went over to the master's open waggoner and studied the chart. I now knew what many of the numbers scattered across the sea meant; they were soundings, and they told me we had ample deep water, almost up to all the shores we could see.

Kit Farrell came on deck at that moment, to Malachi Landon's evident annoyance. Just then some whim, some strange conceit, took hold of me. I still remember the feeling: it was like the need to impress old Mervyn, my schoolmaster, with a correct answer; or to please Uncle Tristram by demonstrating that I had listened properly to his latest tale. Cornelia would have chided me for my foolishness and presumption, quite rightly, but she was far away, probably seeking excuses to avoid another awkward morning of needlework in the brooding company of my mother. Untrammelled, I looked around once more, saw only the tiny shapes of Kintyre fishing boats and a few small vessels of the Antrim shore, and decided that surely, there would never be a better moment.

"Master Landon, Master Ruthven," I said. "We need not steer directly for the rendezvous, for we would be there early. You will please set our course for this headland on Islay, called the Oa. You will inform me when we are within five miles of land, when I would have you alter course to the north-east, towards the rendezvous."

Kit Farrell looked at me with astonishment, but that was as nothing to the dumbstruck horror that contorted the face of Malachi Landon.

"Captain," he spluttered at length, "would that be by way of *an order?*"

I smiled. "Yes, Mister Landon. That is my order." *The first true sea-command of my life.*

Landon was a poor dissembler; his features betrayed every jot of the hatred that he felt towards me. He stepped close and said, barely able to shape the words, "And after the warning I gave ye from the charts? To what purpose should I take this ship out of our way, Captain?"

I could have been conciliatory to him, but in that instant his arrogance and presumption decided me to bring this to a reckoning. "As for your charts, Master Landon, I care not for Mars ascendant or descendant, only for *Jupiter* transient and *Jupiter* preserved. As for my reasons, a captain of a king's ship needs give reason to two authorities alone on this earth, namely the king and the Lord Admiral. And I see neither on this deck, Mister Landon. It is for me to decide what is and is not out of our way, and I have a purpose in taking us toward that shore. My purpose, and mine alone."

With that, I left the quarterdeck. The miserable rogue was forced to salute me at my going.

I went below and fell heartily upon the breakfast of fish, eggs and bread that Janks had sent to my cabin. As I ate, I felt the ship begin her slow and gentle turn, a few degrees of the compass towards the north-west. With the turn came doubt, and I began to half-regret my impetuous order. What if I had misread the charts and missed the presence of some great rock, toward which we were now inexorably bound? It was with great relief that I was interrupted by a knock at the cabin door. Musk went to open it and announced waspishly that "school had begun", whereupon Kit Farrell bounced cheerfully into the room.

"You have made Mister Landon more than a little irate, sir," he said happily.

"Good. Ships have but one captain, Mister Farrell," said I between mouthfuls, concealing my self-doubt. Then added, "Even if they are wholly ignorant of the sea-trade."

"With respect, sir," he said mildly, "I think you do yourself an injustice. The captain I knew on the *Happy Restoration*, and at the start of this voyage, may have been that. But even these few days have changed you.

222

Why, I think you learn the sea faster than I learn word-craft, Captain."

Musk grunted. "Not surprising, that, is it? Captain Quinton here's an educated man — his uncle's master of an Oxford college, just mark that — and he's got the natural authority that he was born with, the blood of all the Quintons back to the start of time. Not like you or me, Mister Farrell. Out of the gutter came the likes of us."

I smiled, then turned to Kit. "I was not wrong to speak in such a peremptory way to Master Landon?"

Musk spluttered something about the rancid paganistic hypocritical old bugger deserving everything he got, but Kit was more measured. "You gave a command, sir. It was clear, and left no room for doubt. That is all."

The opposite of the order I failed to give on the *Happy Restoration*, I thought, and perhaps Kit Farrell did too.

I waved Kit to a seat and set him to copying the superscription of the letter I was writing to the Duke of York. This occupied some twenty minutes, with Kit fretting over how the "high" in "highness" could be pronounced exactly the same as "eye" and yet be spelt so differently. We talked for a while, then I sent Musk to bring Lieutenant Vyvyan and Gunner Stanton to me.

They had evidently both heard of my command. Vyvyan, in particular, studied me more curiously than usual. Like all of my officers, he undoubtedly felt that Kit Farrell was my evil familiar, a black cat to my crone. No doubt he saw this attempt to turn Matthew

Quinton into a seaman as doomed, but he was too much of a gentleman to show it, while the squat, beetle-browed Stanton seemed too ineffably stupid to form an opinion. I shared my purpose with them, knowing that Landon would be even more offended by this. Looking back, I see my action for the childish pettiness that it was; but even now, there are few things more pleasurable than deliberately offending those who dislike you. Indeed, I have found myself doing it more often of late, for mankind excuses such behaviour in the very old.

My purpose was simple, and I had settled on it the day before, when the *Royal Martyr* had startled us so with the speed and ferocity of the salute from her broadside. We would come five miles off Islay, I told them, far away from the derisive gaze of Godsgift Judge and his crew, and there we would exercise our own great guns. I wished to see if the *Jupiter* was as much a man-of-war as our vaunted consort.

Malachi Landon was not a man to disobey a direct order, and he duly sent one of his mates with word when we were exactly five miles from the point of Oa. Then he executed the change of course to the north-east, as I had commanded. Vyvyan and Stanton were waiting expectantly for me on deck. I looked around, and saw only an empty sea, a blue sky with low, scudding clouds, and the grey-green land of Islay, with Kintyre's shore well off to the east. Of *Royal Martyr*, there was no sign.

224

"Very well. Mister Vyvyan, Mister Stanton," I said. "We shall proceed as we discussed, in exactly the same manner as *Royal Martyr*'s salute. Larboard battery first, then starboard. On my command."

They saluted. Vyvyan went to take up his position in the forecastle, while Stanton went below to exercise command over the guns of the main deck. The *Jupiter* carried a total of thirty-two great guns. Eighteen of these were demi-culverins, including the two that crowded my cabin: nine feet long, they fired a nine-pound shot. We mounted ten light sakers, which fired five-pound balls, and four minions at the bow and stern, firing four-pound shot. I watched the crews of the guns on the upper deck, especially those on the quarterdeck nearest to me, load their weapons with much bustle and some confidence. The canvas-covered charges of gunpowder were placed carefully into the gun barrels on long ladles, then rammed home and secured against the end of the breech with a wad, rammed home in like manner. If we had been firing in earnest, the shot itself would now have gone into the barrel, but this was to be a mere dumb show. Finally, the captain of each gun crew stuck an iron spike down the vent to puncture the cartridge, poured powder into the vent, and awaited my order.

These commands, at least, I already knew, for this truly was work for warriors. Indeed, I had first learned the sequence at the knee of Uncle Tristram, who in turn had learned it at the knee of his father. Earl Matthew was ever fond of recounting the orders he gave on that fateful July day in 1588, when the

Constant Esperance sailed into the impregnable crescent of the Spanish Armada.

Thus I cried, "Loose the gun tackles! Beat open the ports! Thrust out the guns!"

All along the larboard side of the ship, gun ports swung open, and our cannon protruded beyond the ship's side. I watched the gun crews, waited, judged my moment, and finally cried, "Gunners, prepare to give fire!" The call was repeated along the decks.

"Give fire!"

My intention and hope was that the larboard broadside would fire simultaneously, one great blaze of flame and smoke, just as *Royal Martyr*'s had the previous morning. Instead, a few of the guns on the upper deck, and perhaps three on the main, went off at approximately the same time. Thereafter came a ragged series of firings, rather like an inept fireworks show, followed by the scream of each gun's recoil. One gun on the upper deck did not fire at all, and one on the main deck broke its carriage during the recoil, or so I was told. A great pall of gun smoke drifted over the quarterdeck, its acrid stench tearing at my nose and throat. When it cleared, I looked upon the faces of those around me, and wondered if my own expression was such an unguarded mixture of horror and embarrassment.

"Dear Christ in Heaven," said Phineas Musk, now fancying himself an authority on gunnery, "the Dutch fleet will be shitting itself all the way to Amsterdam. Shitting itself with laughter."

A calm and relatively sober Francis Gale advanced along the quarterdeck to my side. "Captain," he said sadly, "I know gunnery. I faced the guns of General Deane himself, so I've seen the best. With all due respect, sir, I have now also seen the worst."

I stood stock-still, looking out over this calamity. The Jupiters were nervous now, even of the reaction of their ignorant captain, and were reloading the guns with as much alacrity as they could muster, their countenances serious. The barrels were scoured with prongs and then cooled with sponges before the business of replacing the cartridges began. When the gun captains seemed ready, I gave the order to fire once more. This time, a few more guns fired on my word of command, but the interval before the last went off was even longer. Another gun on the main deck misfired. The guns that remained were reloaded once more, and this time we attempted to fire in sequence, as *Royal Martyr* had done, bow to stern. The ensuing cacophony of incompetence echoed accusingly around the Scottish sea. Several guns on both decks fired out of turn, and two did not fire at all. Smoke drifted away from the *Jupiter*, accusing wisps upon the wind.

Kit Farrell had been keeping the time. "Almost half a glass, sir," he said in hushed tones. "Three broadsides, of a sort, in twenty-five minutes or so."

"Christ God," I exclaimed, "even the French can do better than that." Roger Le Blanc, who stood in the ship's waist attending vaguely to some torn canvas, raised an amused eyebrow. I thought for a moment. We had several hours until the rendezvous. I made some

227

quick calculations, then called to Vyvyan and sent an order below for Stanton. We would attempt the task thrice more, once on the larboard side and twice to starboard.

The dispiriting display that followed confirmed what was abundantly obvious to all. We would have difficulty holding our own against a hulk drifting on the tide, let alone against a Dutch man-of-war commanded by a competent captain like my good-brother Cornelis. It was with relief that I at last gave the order to desist and returned the men to their watches.

I summoned Vyvyan and Stanton to my cabin. I wanted keenly to know how this calamity could have been allowed under such a renowned and capable captain as James Harker. The two officers looked at each other nervously, and Stanton began to explain that Harker had never set much store by exercising the great guns. James Vyvyan listened for a few seconds, then leapt to the defence of his uncle.

"Captain Harker believed in the old ways, sir. Fire your battery by all means, but bring your ship in fast, lay her thwart the hawse if you can, and board your enemy. It's the way the Cornish like to fight. Hand to hand."

Like the pirates you all are beneath the skin, I thought. I had seen the Cornish in action that night in Portsmouth when I first joined the *Jupiter*. I had no doubt they could board and fight with aplomb. Yet in modern warfare, the fashion called for enemy fleets to approach each other in long lines of battle, lay up parallel at the closest range possible, and blast each other to hell. The old method that Harker had favoured still had its advocates — notably his patron, Prince Rupert — but the new, scientific reliance on weight of gunnery had proved its worth in the Dutch war, when the smaller enemy vessels had been pounded to pieces by the heavy broadsides of our stronger-built English ships. Godsgift Judge — who had held a command in many of those battles — and his men were adept in this new kind of war, and its endurance to this day is proof of its superiority. The Jupiters and their late captain were throwbacks to an older time, my grandfather's time; and that day was done, it seemed.

I dismissed Vyvyan and Stanton, and, in bad temper, sank down upon a chair and held my hands over my face. *Thank God for one small mercy*, I thought. *At least we will not need to fight another ship.*

Late in the afternoon, we were off a village that Ruthven named as Crinan. Ahead of us lay Craignish Point and its sea-inlet, a maze of pleasant-looking islets guarded by a small castle. I was stood on the quarterdeck, listening to a passionate lecture from Penbaron on the damage the broadsides had supposedly done to our fragile rudder; *about the only thing we were likely to damage*, I thought, as I set about trying to mollify my ardent interlocutor.

As he talked on, my attention drifted to the *Royal Martyr*, now dead astern. She had steadily made up ground since we first sighted her off the Isle of Gigha. Her new figurehead came on proudly toward us: the Blessed King Charles the First carved from oak, a wreath about his brow and a sword in his hand. For this one ship alone, Vyvyan told me, the king and his brother had made an exception to the rule that figureheads should depict crowned lions, as was the case with ours. I waved to Godsgift Judge, who was attired in a strange confection of furs, a poor imitation of everything I had ever heard of Russian dress and thoroughly inappropriate for the mild spring weather. He raised his voice trumpet and ordered me to sail into Craignish, where we would anchor for the night, and invited me to dine again on *Royal Martyr*.

The fare, as ever, was excellent. We dined on a good steak of boar — a delicacy that had been brought out as a gift from the Governor of Dunaverty — along with venison and some excellent puddings. Judge brought out his charts once more, and explained that the loch of Craignish was surrounded on three sides by Campbell land — the small castle guarding the headland was theirs, too — and that we were about as close as it was possible to come to the Campbell seat at Inveraray, where Lord Lorne brooded on his father's destruction. There was, crucially, a narrow strip of land here, said Judge, between the sea and the great stretch of Loch Awe, along which all travellers going north or east must pass; it was certain that by anchoring here, news of our coming would swiftly pass to Inveraray and Glenrannoch, if it had not already done so.

Judge was less effusive than usual and seemed somehow preoccupied, lost at times in his own thoughts. I asked him if anything was amiss, but he waved an elegant hand in denial. His lieutenant was ill, he said, and he was standing extra watches. Such burdens had been nothing when he was my age — at that a glimmer of the old, obsequious Judge — but he was no longer the brash young captain he had been when last in these waters. I had not known Godsgift Judge so contemplative before; all the concern to impress, to solicit the Quinton family's influence for his advancement, had been put to one side. He still dressed and decorated his person as though for a court masque, but it seemed more a shell than the man's true identity. He reminded me, once again, of the king — another who could at will put on garments and expressions to mask his true feelings. I knew several different versions of Charles Stuart, just as I now felt that I knew several different versions of Godsgift Judge. With both men, I began to sense, their true and ruthless selves remained firmly hidden away in some unreachable place.

As I left the ship, I asked Judge to pass on my wishes for a speedy recovery to Nathan Warrender. He looked at me curiously, but promised me that his lieutenant would soon be a man reborn.

The next morning the wind was still light and westerly. We used our boats to warp out to Craignish Point, then tacked for a northbound course. Judge had told me to look to the west, at the channel between the north end of Jura and the small isle of Scarba, for there, he said, lay the whirlpool of Corryvreckan. This was the most remarkable and feared sea-feature of these parts: vicious spirals of water that had done for many an unsuspecting ship. I asked our pilot about it as we sailed swiftly past, and in his unintelligible, mumbled reply sensed a real dread of the strange phenomenon. Musk, unimpressed, suggested that perhaps the Hag of Winter, queen of the witches, was using the whirlpool as her laundry. The eclectic breadth of Musk's knowledge was always as unexpected as its rare manifestations.

We sailed out into the broad Firth of Lorne, with the large and rolling Isle of Mull ahead of us, and turned downwind to show ourselves off Oban — a rude fishing town dominated by the Macdougalls — and nearby Dunstaffnage, where the wind-torn standard of the red lion rampant was a solitary but welcome sign of our king's authority. This, the royal castle of Dunstaffnage, was our one gateway to the world we had left behind: letters to and from the *Jupiter* could pass through the ancient castle gates in the Mail Royal, which maintained teams of riders down the long road to England.

A clamour of shouted instructions punctuated the afternoon as we tacked to and fro in a westerly direction. We passed the Isle of Lismore. The Jupiters scuttled aloft and down again, rushing hither and thither with a noticeable new enthusiasm — perhaps trying to redeem themselves after the gunnery drill. We showed ourselves next in the Sound of Mull, where gaunt, grey-green hills stretched away on either side of the sea-channel. Duart Castle, at its entrance, stood proud upon a great rock and was the seat of the Macleans, who had been loyal to the king in the late wars. The castle saluted us by dipping her flag. I have no doubt that Maclean had cannon from the wars hidden unlawfully in his cellars, as did all the chiefs of those parts. Of course he did not reveal his hand to the king's ships by firing in salute.

So we came to Tobermory, a small fishing village at the end of the island of Mull. A great galleon of the Spanish Armada had come to grief here, in Queen Bess's day, as she struggled past this dreadful coast in the forlorn hope of returning to old Galicia. Uncle Tristram insisted that she was one of the very ships my grandfather had attacked back in July 1588. As we passed, so I nodded a salute to the old warrior and those of his honourable enemies who had died in this sea.

Beyond Tobermory, the wind fell right away again. Within the hour a dense fog had come down, shrouding us so deeply that we could not see *Royal Martyr* a few chains ahead of us. Only her bell and trumpets told us where she was. Judge shouted that we should warp towards where he believed a safe anchorage to be. Boatswain Ap dropped our boats, and Lanherne's craft took position at the head of the tow. After every few yards the sounding-lead was slung over the side, and shortly afterwards came a shout telling us of the depth of water beneath our keel. "Four fathoms!" carried eerily through the dank greyness as I huddled in my coat upon the quarterdeck. We spent perhaps an hour in this fashion, inching to safety, as I hoped, and not to oblivion on an unseen shore. Then I heard a sound like the wailing of a hundred dead men.

"*Royal Martyr*'s," said Kit Farrell, appearing out of the gloom. "She's dropping anchor."

Martin Lanherne's shout followed almost immediately. "Ho, the *Jupiter*! Captain Judge's order! Drop anchor!"

This time, Landon looked at me before he gave the order. I nodded. The cable was released and our bower anchor slipped into the dark waters. His work done, Landon went below, leaving me to contemplate the strange scene. It was early in the evening, but it may as well have been the depths of night, for there was no sight of anything, beyond the three dim glimpses of light that were *Royal Martyr*'s stern lanterns. There was no sound, once our ship was secure and the men had stood down. No sound at all.

James Vyvyan heard it first. He was younger than any of us, true, though not by many years; but Vyvyan had never fought in a battle and had his hearing assaulted by the blast of gunfire.

"Sir," he said, in the hushed tone that mankind reserves for being in churches or thick fogs, "I swear I can hear a drum . . ."

Then I heard it too. A single drum, beating time, drawing closer.

My grandfather, who had been there when they slipped Drake's lead coffin into the waters of Nombre de Dios bay, claimed to have created the legend of Drake's Drum: the phantom beat that would rouse the old pirate's ghost from its infernal slumber. For a moment, just one fleeting moment, I thought that here in these waters, where the Armada they fought had come to grief, Drake and the last Matthew Quinton

234

had returned to resume their battle against the great popish crusade.

The drum grew louder, but now there were two other sounds that accompanied it: water parting rhythmically, and the unmistakeable creak of wood on wood. It was a sound I knew well, from the barges that plied the Ouse and the Ivel as they meandered across Bedfordshire.

"Oars," I said.

The fog lifted for just a moment and I saw them. First three, then six, then ten: long, low craft, built high at bow and stern, with a single mast and yard, bearing no sail. Instead, they were driven forward by rowers, sweeping their oars in time with the drum on the lead vessel.

I had called up the wrong ghosts: I had been dreaming that my grandfather and his old friend had come again. These ghosts were just as familiar, though, and should have been more expected in these waters. I had seen them in drawings in some of Uncle Tristram's books, and I knew them for what they were.

They were the longships of the Vikings, returned from Hell to drag down the souls of us poor mariners of the *Jupiter*.

CHAPTER
THIRTEEN

I have lived long enough now to know that there are no ghosts, other than the phantoms of our own pasts. There are no ghost fleets, either, and the shades of the Norsemen had not come again in their longships to drag the *Jupiter* down to fiery oblivion. But I was a young man then, my head still full of the legends from history that Uncle Tristram had drummed into me as a child: of the fury of the Vikings, terrifying all the lands of antiquity from Greenland to Byzantium; of abbeys ablaze, from Lindisfarne round to St David's; of women ravished and men slaughtered. So I stood like a statue, watching the long, low shapes come towards us out of the fog, oars keeping time with the single drum that beat from the leading craft. A giant stood in the bow of the first boat, a bearded giant wrapped in black furs, and I thought of Odin and Thor, of Skjold and Sweyn Forkbeard. My head swam across centuries, and time as I knew it faded away into the fog.

Then Ruthven the pilot came up on deck, an older man and a Scot. He laughed heartily at the sight of the Jupiters, their captain included, rooted to the deck, staring at a spectacle that had struck terror into our ancestors a millennium ago. These craft, he said, were merely *birlinns*, the ancient war galleys of Clan Campbell. Frightening they may have been in a fog, but one blast of even our feeble broadside would have smashed them all to driftwood. They were the last relics of a past long dead.

The first boat came alongside, and the fur-clad giant climbed aboard. Close to, it was plain to see that he was a very modern kind of warrior. Two pistols protruded from his belt, and they seemed to be flintlocks, perhaps even French ones — the best. The giant's left hand was mangled and lacked the middle two fingers. He was Zoltan Simic, he said, attendant upon his excellency General Campbell, who invited us to call upon him at his Tower of Rannoch. Simic's English was immaculate, but tinged with unexpected Gaelic inflections that betrayed a man who had spent years fighting alongside Scots and Irish soldiers of fortune. I pointed out that he was in error in boarding my ship first; he should have paid his respects to Captain Judge, the senior officer, who was bellowing at me across the water in the hope of learning what transpired. But Simic just shrugged, and I had to send Lanherne over to the *Royal Martyr* to convey the invitation.

Within an hour, Simic, a soberly dressed Judge, and I were ashore and mounted on the squat, long-haired horses of those parts called garrons. Perhaps thirty Highlanders ran alongside us, bare-legged and clad in swathes of rough cloth; they seemed capable of keeping up with us indefinitely. The fog disappeared as we moved further inland, revealing a dull, cold sky. There were no roads, only harsh, treeless hills and bare moor.

The soil seemed to spring beneath our horses' hooves. Every few miles, we saw the smoke or smelled the fragrance of peat fires from cottages that appeared almost to grow out of the land, but no man or woman came out to view us. The light began to fade sooner than it did at Ravensden or Portsmouth, and there was no sign of our reaching our destination. I asked Simic, who had been silent throughout our journey, how much further it would be, for I did not relish the thought of returning this way in the depths of the night.

"Beyond the ridge ahead," he said. "There lies the Tower of Rannoch."

Moments later we breasted the ridge and looked down into the broad valley beyond. I expected to see a gaunt tower-house, very much still the fashion in Scotland in those times, like those that stood sentinel along the shores we had passed. But the Tower of Rannoch confounded me utterly. At the head of a long lake — or loch as the Scots call them — a formal garden had been laid out that would not have disgraced the valley of the Loire. Hedges and bushes that had been set in neat geometric patterns surrounded a low white palace, exactly modelled upon the French style. Torches lined the immaculate avenues, their flames fanned by a breeze that — I noticed just then — was becoming steadily stronger. I could have been looking down on a miniature Chenonceaux, transplanted by some alchemical trick from its warm habitat to this strange, blasted land at the edge of the world.

We rode down, dismounted at the foot of a grand sweep of steps, and were led inside by Simic. A fine

238

hallway, furnished with classical statues and vases, gave no sign of the military inclinations of its owner. There were no racks of swords or pikes, no carefully mounted muskets. Instead, the walls were papered in the very way the fashionable of Whitehall adorned theirs. There was a fireplace on the right, and above it hung a picture of a handsome young gallant in the court garb of King James's time. At the end of the hallway, two servants opened a pair of imposing doors with a great flourish. We stepped over the threshold and entered an astonishing room that seemed to be walled entirely with glass.

Judge and I paused and looked around in silent amazement. Great windows stretched from floor to ceiling on three sides; the fourth was taken up with mirrors and two small fireplaces. Flames danced from glass to glass, window to window, creating nothing like enough heat to warm the room. It was only then that I noticed the figure sitting on a high-backed chair at the centre of the room. He was a little man — barely taller than John Treninnick — grey-haired, thin, perhaps of sixty years or so, with a small pointed beard that had been the fashion at the start of the last king's reign. An old but still livid scar ran down his left cheek to his jaw, and had evidently almost cost him his eye. His clothes were plain, and they too were of an older, altogether different time. He seemed utterly insignificant, and but for that great scar, the image of a dull market-town notary.

He rose and extended his hand to both of us. We approached and I found myself towering over him.

"I am Glenrannoch," he said simply, his eyes holding ours fleetingly as is the way with timid men. "Welcome to Scotland, gentlemen, and welcome to this, the Tower of Rannoch." Judge shook first, then I. Like his gaze, the great general's grip was weak, like a young girl's. "Captain Judge. Captain Quinton." He held my hand for a moment, and his eyes seemed to search my face intently. Then he turned away and signalled for chairs. Two boys, dressed incongruously in the height of London fashion, scurried forward and positioned them before the general.

Judge looked about him in ostentatious admiration. "A most impressive home you have, sir," he enthused. "I had heard of it, of course, during my last commission in these waters, but the opportunity to visit never arose — you were abroad at the time, and I had other matters in hand."

Glenrannoch shrugged, and said but one word. "Madness." In the pause that followed I pondered the ambiguity of this remark. Then he waved his hand at the glass that surrounded us. "Utter folly, Captain Judge," he continued. "There was a strong old castle on this site. The true Tower of Rannoch, where I grew up. It was centuries old with thick walls that made it warm in winter and cool in summer. But my father served thirty years with the King of France's *Garde Écossaise*, escorting the late King Louis from one splendid fantasy in the Loire to another, and he took a fancy to having a chateau of his own. So down came the old tower, and up went this in its stead. In winter you can scrape the ice off those mirrors, and in summer I could put an egg on this chair and fry it. I was campaigning somewhere in Brabant at the time, and could not stop him. He died a week before the infernal place was finished. As the preachers tell us, the Lord moves in mysterious ways, but few are as mysterious as the ways by which those of us who reside here stay alive."

Glenrannoch's conversation was so soft that I had to strain to follow his words. There was almost no trace of the Scots in his voice, but an occasional vowel betrayed the long years that he had spent in the Dutch service. The longer he spoke, though, the more the initial impression of smallness and weakness dissipated. Some say that the greatest generals fight as sparingly as they can, kill as sparingly as they can, and speak as sparingly as they can. But when they have to fight or kill or speak, they do it ruthlessly, and with clear intent. I wondered whether this was the case with Colin Campbell of Glenrannoch. The simplicity of his demeanour discomforted me, for something seemed to lurk beneath it.

The general nodded to Simic and spoke some words of a harsh and guttural language. This must be the language of Simic's people, from far to the east of the Rhine. The huge mercenary brought forward three goblets of wine and I thought how strange it was to see the great giant dancing attendance upon the tiny general. When he had retired I sipped my wine, which proved to be a more than acceptable claret, and turned back to Glenrannoch, who was speaking.

"Well, gentlemen. Much as it delights me to have such rare guests, I have to ask what it can be that brings

241

two of His Majesty's men-of-war, and two such illustrious captains, to such an obscure quarter of his dominions?"

"Sir, His Majesty ever has a care for all of his dominions," Judge replied smoothly.

"That may well be. But he has been happily restored to his thrones these two years, Captain Judge, and in all that time we have seen not even a ketch of the king's in these waters. Nor have we seen a single soldier west of Inveraray, where, it must be said, they pester my kinsman Lorne quite mercilessly."

Judge sipped his wine and nodded. "His Majesty is concerned to protect these waters from any mischief the Dutch might attempt, sir. He also seeks to ensure that the very absence of his forces from these lands does not encourage malcontents to stir up trouble." Judge was looking at Glenrannoch impassively. "Then again, I suppose there may even be some discontent amongst your own clan, following the execution of your late chief, Argyll."

Glenrannoch smiled politely at that. "Not from me. Archie was that most dangerous of combinations, Captain: a man at once utterly devious and exceptionally stupid. He could have ruined Clan Campbell with his absurd posturing. None of my sept shed a tear for him when his head came off, me least of all." Glenrannoch had not drunk from his wine. Now he placed the goblet carefully on a table beside him. "But another Dutch war would be a different matter, as you say. I know more than a little of the Dutch, of course, having served their high mightinesses of the

States-General for a quarter-century." He looked steadily at us. "Pray tell me, gentlemen. Why do you suppose His Majesty expects the Dutch to come vapouring on these coasts? If I was Grand Pensionary de Witt or Lieutenant-Admiral Lord Obdam, gentlemen, I would aim straight for the Thames, hard and fast, and starve London into surrender while you have no defences. I would not worry myself with such godforsaken wilds as these."

Campbell's manner indeed belied an unexpected sagacity. "Sir," I said, leaning earnestly towards him, "in the last war, the Dutch sent many ships around Scotland to avoid our fleet in the Channel. They regularly use the harbours on this coast to shelter their fishing fleets. These waters are important to them, sir, so they may seek to secure them ahead of another war." Judge looked at me curiously, perhaps surprised that such an insight could come from such an ignoramus. In truth, it came from an unimpeachable Dutch source. My good-brother Cornelis seemed to have spent most of his career fretting after the return of fat Amsterdam fly-boats sailing around Scotland — *achteroom*, as he called it — and protecting the fishermen who pursued the herring shoals wherever they migrated. "We are but a deterrent, sir, to remind the Dutch — and anyone else — that the King of England's writ runs in these parts."

Glenrannoch smiled tightly. "The only writ that runs in these parts, Captain Quinton, is that of the King of Scots. Even if he chooses to spend all his life south of the Fens and treats his native kingdom worse than the meanest of his English counties." I shifted uncomfortably on my chair, embarrassed by my schoolboy error. "But I wonder," Glenrannoch went on musingly, "whether two ships alone would be a sufficient deterrent for anything? Even with the help of the brave regiment that set out from Dumbarton yesterday. Four hundred men and four cannon, I'm told, under Colonel Will Douglas of St Bride's. A man, incidentally, I dismissed for incompetence at Breda back in '37." I glanced at Judge, but his gaze was fixed steadily on Glenrannoch's face. *He knows of the regiment? And news of it has come to this fastness in just a day?*

"A deterrent, gentlemen," said Glenrannoch, "must be strong enough to make an enemy think again, for otherwise, why should he be deterred? But just two ships, in these fatal waters? Just one regiment, commanded by an ignorant old buffoon like Will Douglas, travelling many miles over land it does not know, through glens where it would be so easy for a knowing commander to lay an ambush? Does Charles Stuart really call that a deterrent? But then, I'm told King Charles has precious little money, so perhaps empty gestures are all he can afford."

I struggled to think of a loyal riposte, but was too appalled by the implications of Glenrannoch's words. *He knows. He has made his plans. He will ambush and destroy the regiment. We are on a fool's errand, and our mission is doomed.*

Judge, though, seemed unperturbed. He said blandly, "All hypotheses, with respect, sir. We expect no trouble, and seek none. For my part, I look forward to renewing old acquaintances."

"Ah, yes. I heard much of your times in these parts, Captain Judge." Glenrannoch raised his goblet in salute. "But now tell me, Captain Quinton" — and he looked at me with that same slightly quizzical frown — "how is your mother?"

My mother? "She . . . why, she was quite well, sir, when I left for this voyage. But how . . .?"

"Ah. That is a story of another time, Captain. And to be told *at* another time, I think. But come, gentlemen. You must see my father's preposterous French garden while we still have some light. Then you will take some supper with me. Simic will lead you back to your ships before the blackest part of the night."

I half expected that we would die on the moors that night, hacked to pieces by Simic and his running men, our parts fed to the wolves. But Campbell of Glenrannoch seemingly felt no need to invite greater royal forces to his lands, having made plain his contempt for those already present. As we rode, I had no opportunity for a private word with Godsgift Judge, and when we reached the shore Simic escorted us directly to his birlinn. The little longboat rowed out to our two ships, illuminated only by their stern lanterns. They swung at anchor in the blackness of a bay from which the fog had cleared to reveal a star-bright night. We came to *Royal Martyr* first, and I asked Judge if he wished me to come aboard. No, he said, there was no need, and wished me a good night. The birlinn took me on to the *Jupiter*, where the voice of Trenance, the lookout, alerted Kit Farrell, who had the watch, and I boarded to a perfunctory greeting from a small side party. I acknowledged Farrell, established from him that there were no matters requiring my attention, and went below to my cabin.

I kicked off my boots and sat on my sea-bed, turning over in my mind the events of the night. I recalled also Cornelia's letter to me at Spithead, in which she spoke of my mother's agitation on learning that I was bound for the Western Isles. Phineas Musk appeared, complaining vehemently of the lateness of the hour but bearing a welcome tankard of small beer. He lit a candle or two and muttered as he unearthed my nightshirt from its stowage.

"Musk," I asked at length, "have you ever heard my mother or my brother speak of a man named Campbell? Colin Campbell, of Glenrannoch? A general in the Dutch service?"

Musk paused in his rummaging and turned a truculent face to me. "We're in the back end of the worst country in the world, forsaken by God and our king, I'm a thousand miles from my hearth and a goodly wench in London town, and you want to know if I've heard one name spoken in all my days?" My look at him must have been murderous, for in haste he added, "No, Captain. Campbell of Glenrannoch. Never heard the name spoken."

I ate a mouthful of rough ship's biscuit, drank, and pondered how, in our saviour's name, this great general

246

— one who looked and sounded so unlike any general I had ever seen — could possibly have known my mother, hidden so far away behind the walls of Ravensden Abbey.

Musk fidgeted impatiently and wandered around the cabin. As he did so, he regaled me with his own version of the latest news. "Invitations galore you've had today, sir, you and Captain Judge. Every mean chief of these parts wants to entertain you. Must be the most excitement they've had here this century, at least. Unearthly names, all of them, but I wrote them down." He produced a list with a flourish, and proceeded to read it. "Macdonald of Lochiel, tomorrow afternoon, for hunting. Maclean of Duart, tomorrow evening, for supper. Macdougall of Dunollie, tomorrow evening again. And then . . ." He paused dramatically. I looked up to see one beady eye squinting at me over the paper. "And then there's the lady."

"Lady?"

"Cuts quite a figure in these parts, it seems. Surprised Captain Judge hasn't mentioned her to you. We've had Scots of all shapes and sizes aboard us today, and very talkative about these things they are, once you pick up their outlandish way of speaking. Yes, quite a lady, they say. The Lady Macdonald of Ardverran, she is. But she goes by another name, too. The Countess of Connaught, no less, and in her own right, too. Wants you both to attend an *audience*, of all things, tomorrow night, just like the king holds at Whitehall, with herself and

247

Sir Ian Macdonald, eighth of Ardverran, baronet. All very puffed up and grand with their titles, the people hereabouts. Still, think I'd know which invitation to take up, Captain."

CHAPTER
FOURTEEN

At precisely four the following afternoon, the *Jupiter*'s boat brought me alongside the jetty beneath the high walls of Ardverran Castle, a great tower jutting out over the sea with a strong curtain wall to its landward side. This was a place of strength built in the usual fashion of the country, a far cry from the fantastical Tower of Rannoch. Campbell of Glenrannoch's father must indeed have been a confident and powerful man to have abandoned this form of protection from the raiding parties of his enemies. The fact that its walls remained high and intact when only the earthworks of, say, Bedford Castle were left to mark where it had stood, bore silent witness to what Judge had told me of the constant blood feuds of these people. The writ of successive Kings of Scots must have run but weakly for such fortresses to survive; most of England's had fallen to neglect or royal edict long before the guns of civil war brought down the rest.

It was one of those dull and dismal days where the combined greyness of sea and sky seem to penetrate the very spirit of a man. As my eyes roamed over the inscrutable fastness of the castle, I thought I could have been transported back two hundred years and not have noticed. Ardverran's gaunt, grey walls spoke of other days, of the knights and longships of which I had dreamed as a child. There was, however, one visible concession to modernity: three cannon protruding through holes in the base of the walls. But even they were old and small, perhaps sakers salvaged from the Armada wrecks. They would frighten off a few clansmen, no doubt, but they would be good for little else. The artillery train that the king's regiment was bringing from Dumbarton could, in fact, make short work of Ardverran's walls, so imposing and yet so desperately fragile. The world had left them well behind.

Judge was already ashore, wearing an astonishing gown that looked from a distance like cloth-of-gold, and a periwig even larger than his usual fashion. I was attired more modestly, in a black tunic coat that Cornelia had chosen for me. An elaborately skirted and swathed old man with a vast beard came down from the castle's postern gate and announced himself in perfect, heavily accented English as Macdonald of Kilreen, kinsman and steward to the noble Macdonald of Ardverran and the Countess of Connaught, who would welcome us shortly in the castle hall. Then he turned and bounded back to the gate. I confess I found myself startled at the sight of the man's wiry, thickly muscled legs. I would surely grow used to the outlandish costume of the Scots in time, but still, it was a queer thing for a courtier to behold.

We strode up to the gate and entered the courtyard. A few rough herdsmen and their hirsute cattle eyed us curiously. Steps led to the first floor of the huge tower-house, and Kilreen indicated that another flight led from that to the hall. We climbed up and came to a barrel-vaulted space filled with Highlanders, who fell silent at our coming. The room was warmed by a great fire of peat which spread its pungent smoke generously over the assembled company. Light came from four small, high slit-windows, two on each side, and blazing torches were mounted at intervals along the walls. Those walls were largely bare and austere, but at the far end, either side of the great fire and the dais that stood in front of it, grand tapestries hung in splendour. I knew a little of such things; it was difficult not to, living in Flanders, where tapestry is both one of the greatest industries and also the chief topic of conversation among an ineffably dull population. These hangings were very fine and fit for the palace of a great court. How they came to be hanging on the walls of this hole on the edge of oblivion, I could not help but wonder.

Kilreen led us through this chamber to a small staircase and up to a gallery. We took our places where minstrels and pipers must once have played for the favoured ones below, and perhaps still did. From here, we could look out over the entire scene. As soon as we had passed, excited talk began again, as though we had never been, and there was undisguised mockery both of Judge's appearance and my height. Serving boys clad all in tartan brought us silver plates laden with carved meats and cakes, and cups that contained the fearsome drink of the Scots which they call the "water of life". As we supped and looked upon the throng, a grey, wasted creature in Ardverran tartan stepped out into the middle of the hall. The effort seemed too great, and he struggled for breath. All the same, the crowd of befeathered clansmen turned towards him. Their talk ceased. There were moments, perhaps a whole minute, of utter silence. Then the old man looked up, seeming to stare directly at me in the gallery. His eyes were damp with tears. I knew those eyes were not looking at me. Their gaze penetrated right through me, out beyond the windows and walls of Ardverran Castle, to some place and time beyond the reckoning of everyone else in that hall.

And then the man spoke. It was not the voice that I had expected, the reedy, broken whisper that such an ancient one should possess. It was perhaps the deepest and loudest voice I ever heard.

"Behold, all you who come to Ardverran of the ages! Behold, all you of lesser humanity! Behold, I proclaim to you the mighty Ian! Bow, and acknowledge your lord, Macdonald of Ardeverran! For this is Sir Ian, the son of Sir Callum, the son of Sir Ian Mor, the son of James, the son of Alastair, the son of Callum . . ." The recitation of names went on, song-like, back through the generations. The dozens of men in the hall listened intently, some of them speaking the names with the old man. *Or not speaking them* — for when the old man spoke the words *son of*, his listeners mouthed the word *mac*. This was a ritual usually conducted in the Gaelic tongue, I realized. This English was for our benefit, but surely there was little point in that?

252

". . . the son of Donald, the son of that illustrious prince Alexander, Earl of Ross, last true Lord of the Isles! Hail Ardverran, descended of kings! All hail Ardverran, of the truest royal blood in all the land! Tremble, you rulers of the world, for Ardverran comes! All hail Ardverran! Ardverran! Hail Macdonald! All hail Macdonald!"

And now his audience joined him, their acclamations building to a crescendo that seemed to shake the old walls of Ardverran — "Macdonald! Macdonald! Macdonald!" My heart raced, for it was impossible not to be swept into that whirlpool of emotion. The door at the end of the hall opened. The entrance of Macdonald of Ardverran was at hand, the entrance of this awesome, all-powerful prince . . .

A very small, pale boy, perhaps eight or nine years old, stood in the door. He was dressed in a simple clan tartan and a cap from which three feathers protruded. My astonishment died away, and I almost laughed. *We had come to this God-abandoned hole for an audience with a mere runt?*

As the boy moved nervously to the dais the shouts of acclamation died away. In the hush that followed, the aged herald spoke once more. "And hail to the Lady Niamh, Countess of Connaught *suo jure*, daughter of the noblest blood of old Ireland, mother to Ardverran."

A woman followed the boy into the hall. All eyes fell upon her greedily, my own among them. She was very tall, this Countess of Connaught, clad in a shimmering white gown that would not have been out of place at a court ball in Fontainebleau. Her hair was of a red that could only be seen in a fire, or in the defiant, blazing hues of the setting sun. It framed a face that outdid any other that I had ever seen — even the beauties who thronged Whitehall hoping to win a place in the king's bed. Her skin was smooth and unadorned; it was of such a lustre she had no need of jewels or pearls. A delicate mouth and sad green eyes should have given her a look of weakness, but instead they somehow composed a face that seemed at once infinitely vulnerable and infinitely strong. I was a married man, and true to my dear wife. But I knew then, in all certainty, that surely here, in the cold hall of this castle set between a bleak ocean and a barren headland, I was looking at the most beautiful woman that lived.

Like all men, even men in the contentment of the warmest marriage, I have had that same thought of a woman many hundreds of times in my life. But perhaps once in every man's lifetime he meets a woman for whom, he knows in his heart, the thought is true.

Lady Macdonald took her place slightly behind her son. She raised a hand and the audience hushed in expectation. She and the ancient nodded as one to the boy. The child took his cue and began speaking, stumbling almost inaudibly over the words.

"I, Ardverran, give you greeting, my lords and friends."

Then Lady Macdonald spoke. Her voice, accented with the lilt of the Irish and strangely harsh, broke through my reverie at once. "You of the Clan Macdonald, we bid you welcome once again to Ardverran, and to the hospitality of this, our humble house. Especially, we greet our guests, the officers of our sovereign lord Charles, King of Scots and his other territories. We invite them now to join us, to greet the Macdonald in person and to discuss with us those matters which bring them to this *brutish edge* of their world."

There was some murmuring at that, but some mocking laughter too. Dismissing the kingdom of England as too insignificant to name would be well received even by those incapable of realizing the irony that lay behind her choice of words.

At that moment the burly, bearded Kilreen came forward to beckon us down the stairs. Judge nudged my arm and, as we descended, murmured, "All show and flummery, sir. I have witnessed it before, of course. Clinging to their dead history . . ."

We strode across the hall, between the ranks of the clansmen. The stares of the hostile easily outnumbered the gazes of the merely curious. I had a disquieting image of the mob closing round us, cutting us to pieces with their dirks, but we passed through unscathed and came before the dais. Judge bowed his head very slightly to the child and the countess, and I followed suit. The tiny Macdonald nodded uncertainly, his mother gravely.

"So, Captain Judge," she said. "We had not expected to see you return to Ardverran after all these years." She studied him silently a moment. I had almost thought her my own age, but at close quarters the slightest of lines about her eyes betrayed the ten years or more between us. "You have changed greatly since your last visit to us. A most fascinating wig, I must say. Would your Lord Protector Cromwell have entirely approved?"

Judge essayed a smile and inclined his head. "As you say, my lady. I delight that I can continue to serve my country in a small way, and delight even more that this service brings me once more into your presence."

She raised an eyebrow at that. "You have become a flatterer, Captain. The perfect courtier, no less. You were not so genteel when you were here before. The king is indeed a forgiving man."

"Time changes much, my lady, and we are all its slaves. As was the case even for the late Lord Protector, for time brought the malaria to cut him down. But now, may I name to you Captain Matthew Quinton, of His Majesty's ship the *Jupiter*, brother to that most noble and illustrious lord, the Earl of Ravensden."

Lady Macdonald inclined her head towards me. "Brother to an English earl, no less. The king does choose his sea captains from a mixed basket, does he not? And who did you sail with, Captain Quinton? You were surely too young for Prince Rupert's fleet? Or were you with the Dutch, and the mighty Van Tromp?"

Her knowledge of naval matters was unexpected and disconcerting. "This is but my second commission at sea, my lady —"

"Your second commission? And our esteemed monarch and his royal brother send you among the islands and waters of Scotland! Some of the worst seas in the world, Captain Quinton, yet they send a novice, and an *English* novice at that! And where, pray, did you serve in your first commission, Captain?"

My eyes had been fixed so intently on the face of the countess that I had not noticed Kilreen still at my side. Now he spoke.

"My lady, the good captain had the misfortune to lose his first ship. She was the *Happy Restoration*, an inappropriately named vessel. That would have been at Kinsale in the County of Cork, the twenty-first day of October, last past. One hundred and seven men drowned, so they say."

Kilreen's precision was as unsettling as it was obviously rehearsed. Lady Macdonald raised a mocking eyebrow and turned to the men of the hall.

"Indeed. How unfortunate. Yet the king is doubly forgiving, for he employs Captain Quinton again, who sinks his ships by accident, just as he employs Captain Judge who once sunk 'em on purpose. We do live in such a forgiving age, do we not?" There was some laughter in the hall at that, presumably from those who could understand the English tongue. "So, Captains. What can we in these savage lands possibly have done to persuade the mighty king, Charles Stuart, to send two of his great ships to overawe us?"

Judge ignored her goading, made a preposterous courtly bow, and proceeded to deliver the same tale we had told the night before to Campbell of Glenrannoch. As he spoke, we stood like supplicants before a throne, with no chairs offered. But the countess stood too, and young Macdonald her son stood before her, listening with seeming intent to the words the adults spoke. The countess made but little comment on our mission, unlike her neighbour Glenrannoch. Finally, she laid a hand upon her son's shoulder and stepped forward.

"Well then, Captains," she said, "if you must remain in these waters to deter the wicked Dutch, or perhaps the even more wicked Campbells," again that mocking raise of an eyebrow, "then we must entertain you once again, severally or individually. The Scots and Irish alike have ever taken their duties of hospitality with a seriousness that you English seem to forget, upon occasion." She nodded regally to us, and Kilreen moved forward to indicate that this strangest of audiences was over.

"A great beauty, isn't she, to be hidden away in this remote corner?" said Judge, as we walked back down to the jetty.

I asked him to tell me more about this startling enigma, Lady Macdonald, Countess of Connaught. He knew her story well enough, and related it to me. It seemed that her title of countess was not recognized by the king and his heralds. Her grandfather was one of the old Gaelic earls who fled Ireland at the end of Queen Elizabeth's reign, abandoning their inheritances and their people when the old harridan's armies got too close. Judge had been told that the lady's father died in a hovel in Spain, leaving his young daughter an empty title — for it was one of the few Irish earldoms that could descend through the female line, or so Judge thought. In due course her uncle was able to arrange a good match for her: Sir Callum Macdonald, seventh of

Ardverran, baronet; a wealthy man, and a strong Royalist.

"Callum Macdonald," repeated Judge. "He died fighting in Lord Glencairn's rebellion, which I was sent here by Cromwell to crush, the last time I was in these waters. A big man, but ever too quick to anger."

"You knew him?" I asked. "Her husband, Sir Callum?"

Judge's face was set, his expression harder and darker than I had ever witnessed. "Oh yes. Much more than that, my dear Matthew. I killed him."

CHAPTER
FIFTEEN

I turned and looked out over the bay where *Jupiter* and *Royal Martyr* lay at anchor. It was a rare day, with bright sunlight reflecting off land and sea. Empty moorland almost surrounded our roadstead, and beyond, miles to the east, I could see hills far taller than anything I had ever seen in England. Indeed, even the lowest ridges would have been esteemed mountains in Bedfordshire. Somewhere between them and the shore, hidden behind the dark ridges, would be the Tower of Rannoch, and the dangerous, quiet presence of its owner. Above me, clouds scudded across a perfectly blue sky, blown by the fair westerly breeze. I looked away from the splendid view, and continued my climb.

I had seen the broken ramparts of an old fort through my telescope that morning, and as Judge and I had no invitations to attend upon any of the local chiefs or lairds that afternoon, I decided to investigate it. It would be good to escape the confines of the ship, I reasoned, and to have some time almost alone. We had been at anchor now for four days; the previous three had been an endless round of accepting and returning invitations, visiting draughty tower-house castles, chasing the deer, and eating the singular food of those parts. Some mail had come to the ship on a boat from Dunstaffnage, but none of it was addressed to me — not for any want of letter-writing on Cornelia's part, I knew, for in my last command, I had been lucky to escape with fewer than four missives from her each day, and as was the way of the Mail Royal, they often arrived in batches, several weeks' worth at a time.

It had rained unremittingly for the whole three days. Kit Farrell, worthy and good man though he was, took up my spare hours as both pupil and teacher. Meanwhile, the Reverend Gale had gone ashore accompanied by his newly acquired attendant, Andrewartha. Shortly after my return from Ardverran Castle, Gale discovered an urgent need to locate a particular book in a famous library that he assured me was kept somewhere in this land by a Covenanting minister. *Naught but an elaborate euphemism for a distillery*, snickered Musk; but I had found the chaplain remarkably abstemious since the night he told me his story of Drogheda, and he had delivered an exemplary Sunday service. With Gale gone, Purser Peverell emerged from his self-imposed exile of the previous few days. Fully recovered from his ordeal, he was apparently convinced that a sustained period at anchor gave him a divine right to impose upon me his odious self and his endless paperwork. This was the final straw. With the sun shining at last, and Lieutenant Vyvyan and Master Landon more than capable of watching over my command, I saw no reason to deny myself a brief period of shore leave.

I had a guide: a young, red-haired fisherman named Macferran who had come aboard on our second day and at once appointed himself our intermediary with the local people. He spoke good English, unlike most others along this coast, tolerable Dutch, and even a little French, in which Le Blanc quickly set out to improve him. Many great ships passed this way or sheltered in these waters, Macferran said, and learning their tongues gave him a path to trade, coin and betterment. He immediately won favour with the crew (and especially with Musk) by providing a seemingly inexhaustible supply of good fish and, better, many bottles of the water of life. Macferran, who seemed to have no other name that he cared to reveal, attached himself to me with an eagerness that betrayed his intent. He had no little intelligence, and had grown bored with the relentless hardship and isolation of his life. He sought a place on a king's ship, and a chance to see the world, and I would have obliged him if I could have found him a berth; but James Harker had ensured we were fully manned, and manned above our complement at that; and unusually, none of the crew had yet died of disease or accident. I promised him that if a vacancy arose before we left, I would enter him in the king's service, but I was not sanguine about his prospects.

Macferran was ahead of me and already at the rampart. I climbed up to join him and stopped to draw breath. Here at the summit, of course, I could see far to the west as well. There was Ardverran Castle, in the middle distance, smoke rising from its chimneys and a pair of Macdonald birlinns alongside its jetty. The sea lay beyond, and I could make out fishing craft, strung across the water between the mainland and the islands that lay further out. The land was largely empty — so different to the flat, busy farmland around Ravensden — though here and there a great herd of deer or of long-haired, horned cattle, or else the occasional solitary Highlander, could be seen. It was a glorious prospect, and I sat down with pleasure upon the old rampart. Macferran offered me a flagon of the water of life or *whisky*, as he called it, and although it was too fiery for my taste, as I had found it at Ardverran Castle, I took a long measure. I asked him how old the fort was, and he said the storytellers of his village maintained it was a stronghold of the Picts, thrown up here long before St Columba brought Christianity to these parts. This was a new history to me, and a confusing one, for it seemed the Scots had once been Irish, and had warred with the Picts, who had been the original Scots. I did not doubt that Uncle Tristram had a book somewhere that could enlighten me, and I resolved that when I returned to the south, I would ride over to Oxford to search his library; and thereby, no doubt, to experience yet again the liberal hospitality of his high table and college cellar.

I lay back, felt the sun on my face and breathed the sharp, clear air of that sea-girt land. I thought of Cornelia, and how I missed her. I thought of Glenrannoch, and of ways in which Judge and I might halt his desperate schemes. I thought of Lady Macdonald, Countess of Connaught. I thought of my brother, and wondered if he had died, and whether I was now Earl of Ravensden, with all the manifold horrors that would entail. I thought of Lady Macdonald again. I thought of the death throes of the *Happy Restoration*. I thought of the slaughter of my father on Naseby field. I thought of the sudden end of James Harker, and for the hundredth time or more, I dismissed the possibility that his death could have been murder; and then wondered, if it had been, whether it were not possible that I might be despatched in similar fashion? I thought upon my ambition for a commission in the Horse Guards, and realized with a little surprise that it was the first time my thoughts had turned that way for many days. I thought of Lady Macdonald. I remembered Judge's explanation to me, as we were rowed back to our ships from Ardverran, of the manner of his killing her husband. Sir Callum Macdonald, it seemed, had been wounded while serving in Lord Glencairn's Royalist army and had retired to his castle to recover. When the Lord Protector's squadron approached the same seas that I now surveyed from the fort, he hurriedly threw up a gun battery to delay its passage, but Judge led a shore party which came upon that battery from behind. Sir Callum fought bravely, he said, but his wounds slowed him, and then they burst, rendering him defenceless to Judge's fatal stroke. I wondered at Lady Macdonald's inviting her husband's killer back to her castle, but had already learned enough of this land to see that they prized their laws of hospitality very highly indeed. It seemed that not even murder could diminish that imperative.

264

I must have fallen asleep soon afterwards, for I remember being woken by Macferran's prodding. He pointed down into the bay, toward the two ships. The *Jupiter* was as I had left her, at anchor and with her sails furled, a few of her crew fishing from the deck. But on the *Royal Martyr*, all was activity. Men were in her rigging, and her sails were falling. She was getting under way.

I ran to the beach where I had to leave Macferran behind. Lanherne's longboat took me back out to my ship, where Lieutenant Vyvyan had the watch. By now, *Royal Martyr* had hoisted her anchor and was turning with the favourable westerly to head into the deep sea-channel that led away to the north. Vyvyan presented me with a note which, he said, Captain Judge's coxswain had delivered to him some half an hour earlier.

To Captain Quinton of His Majesty's Ship the Jupiter.

Sir, I have received intelligence that a ship believed to be that which we seek was seen passing Stornoway the evening before last. I intend to sail north, to look into the anchorages between here and that town, to intercept her before she can come within the territories of General Glenrannoch. My orders to you are that His Majesty's ship under your command should remain at its present anchorage and in a state of immediate readiness for sea, in case this ship should succeed in evading capture. In that event, sir, we ought to be able to entrap her between us, and bring our mission here to a happy conclusion. You have, Captain Quinton, my most profound and enduring respect,

Godsgift Judge

I summoned most of my officers to my cabin and informed them of Captain Judge's orders. Ruthven, who knew these waters, damned it for a goose-chase, saying that the multitude of islands and channels would make finding this one ship a miracle to rival the loaves and the fishes. I reminded him that Judge, too, knew this place, and was in any case the senior captain, so we were bound by his commands.

I dismissed the officers and sent for Kit Farrell. "Well, Mister Farrell," I said, "what shall it be today? Sea-craft for me, or word-craft for you?"

Farrell hesitated for a moment, but then smiled. "Sea-craft, I think, sir. Of a sort, at any rate, with your permission."

I nodded my agreement and he led the way out into the steerage. From one of the tiny wooden cabins wherein my officers slept emerged a loud, decisive fart. Probably Gunner Stanton, I thought, and that snoring must be coming from the carpenter's cabin. Invariably I left the upper deck at this point, passing out beyond the steerage bulkhead and the life-sized, carved Jovian gods that adorned it, before turning to climb the curved stairway to my accustomed place on the quarterdeck. But now Kit Farrell led me instead down the steep ladder from the steerage into the body of the main deck.

I came this way at times, but only for the captain's formal inspections with James Vyvyan and Boatswain

266

Ap at my back and every mess rigidly at attention. Now, though, the deck was at ease. Men sat at their mess tables between the great guns, playing dice or talking. Some had rigged hammocks or laid out mattresses on the deck and were managing to sleep through the constant chatter and laughter, snatching their four hours at most before the watch changed again, for we maintained the system even at anchor. In the middle of the deck, perhaps a dozen men were sitting around a large water tub placed beneath the ventilation gratings, smoking contentedly on their clay pipes; this habit had not yet been banished to the forecastle or the upper deck, as would soon be the case.

The nearest messes noticed my coming and jumped to attention, and a whisper ran along the deck from man to man: "The captain! The captain's on deck!" I gestured for them to be at ease, and slowly the peaceful hubbub returned. I did not know, then, that the atmosphere on that deck spoke of a happy ship. I had never gone below informally in this way on the doomed *Happy Restoration*, so I had no point of comparison. As well that I had not, perhaps, for the Restorations had been a surly, dangerous crew, most of them the scrapings of the London foreshore, and they included a fair share of thieves, broken men and killers. There had been floggings almost daily, and only a boatswain's crew of quite exceptional brutality maintained anything like discipline on that benighted vessel. Of course, the Jupiters were volunteers to a man, for it was peacetime and they were mainly James Harker's men, loyal to him and old Cornwall, mostly easy in each other's company (and, by now, seemingly tolerant of the young captain who walked among them). Nowadays, there are king's ships where Norfolk and Suffolk men, or Irishmen and English, are at each other's throats every watch. There are ships in wartime where two-thirds or more of the men are pressed, and looking for any opportunity to desert. There are ships where the captains flog and brutalize their men and take pride in it. But for my part, I have never forgotten that afternoon on the main deck of the *Jupiter*, where I beheld the model of what a contented man-of-war's crew could be like.

Halfway down the deck on the larboard side, between the two demiculverins nicknamed Lucifer and Lord Berkeley's Revenge, was the mess that contained John Treninnick and Ali Reis. These two seemed to be having an animated argument in Cornish, egged on by their messmates. In the next I came upon Polzeath and Trenance playing cards against a couple of Devon men. There was county pride at stake here — each man stared so intently at the hand he was dealt they never realized their captain was by. Further forward, Julian Carvell was engaged in arm wrestling against all comers. He had gone unbeaten until he came to the tiny new father of twins, John Tremar, who brought the black man's forearm crashing onto the mess table.

"Damn us all, Tremar," cried Kit. "What do they feed you on? Or are you old Samson reborn?" Carvell, grinning in defeat, slapped Tremar's back to roars of laughter from his messmates.

Everywhere, it was plain to see that Kit Farrell was at ease with the men, and they with him. The crew's early suspicions of him had evaporated once we were at sea and they had seen that he was a fine seaman, not a worthless favourite puffed up by a boy-loving gentleman captain. His acceptance was made easier by the behaviour of his superior officer. Landon, the master, may have detested me, but he was far worse with his crew. They in turn despised him for his haughty arrogance, the superstitious dreads that threatened the ship's equanimity, and the violent unpredictability that would see him laugh uproariously before handing out the severest punishment for the smallest offence. Landon's other mates were too good at playing the sycophant, and too bad as seamen, to win much love among the messes. It was no surprise that Kit Farrell had earned respect so soon and so completely.

We made our way back down the deck — toward the stern, that is — and when we reached the ladder by which we had descended, Farrell said, "So, Captain, will you take a turn about the orlop too?"

Now, I had never gone down beneath the waterline to the half-deck known as the orlop, or its neighbouring hold. It was an unknown land of store rooms, barrels of victuals and strange, dark recesses; the domain of my standing officers and them alone. But I was in the mood for exploration, and with my expedition to the fort curtailed, I resolved to inspect every inch of my command instead.

We descended the ladder that led from the main deck. I reached the bottom and found myself stooped at an odd angle; this was a world where only the likes of

John Treninnick could stand fully upright, and my height was such that I had to bow my head whenever I was belowdecks. My forehead already bore several bruises which testified to my failure wholly to master this necessity. Scots waters lapped hard against the hull, the ship's timbers creaked and groaned like a regiment of the dead, and the stench of the bilges rose to salute me. My eyes began to adjust to the darkness. Only a few small lanterns lit the crowded space; the powder room was very near, and many great ships have been blown to oblivion by fumbled candles or lanterns, so naked flames were unwelcome in these lower regions of the hull.

We went forward on the larboard side, negotiating with difficulty the cable tiers — where the ship's cables were laid out across the deck — and the great knees that supported the deck above. We negotiated our way round the galley, a brick structure surrounding great copper pots; Janks and his assistant tugged their forelocks in salute and returned to breaking open a barrel of salt pork. There were gunner's, boatswain's, and carpenter's storerooms on either side of the deck, looking much like the officers' cabins on the decks above, but larger. Farrell opened the door of each store in turn, and it struck me in that moment that any man on the ship could do the same. True, my officers were meant to keep an exact tally of all their stores, but did they? If something went missing, how would they ever know, given the great jumbles of stores that lay before me, stacked high from deck to deck? And if they did not record any loss, so that their papers remained serene and correct, how would any captain ever know? I resolved then that I would order locks on each storeroom forthwith.

We turned to walk back down the starboard side. Farrell paused at one of the sail stores and opened the door. There, perched high on the folded spare sails, was my enigmatic Frenchman, Roger Le Blanc, reading by the light of that lantern. He looked at me in amazement, then smiled.

"Well, *mon capitaine. Un visiteur* — an unexpected visitor, indeed!" He got to his feet and essayed a touch of the forelock in a salute that lacked even the faintest whiff of deference.

"You choose strange quarters for a library, Monsieur Le Blanc," I said questioningly.

"Ah, *Capitaine*, reading on the decks above, it is not possible. The men talk and shout, and the English ever look on reading with suspicion. So I avoid their insults, and when I have repaired a sail or two, they are transformed into my couch, and so I read."

I was intrigued despite myself. "And what is your choice of reading, Monsieur?"

He handed me the book. It was in French, of course, but thanks to my grandmother, I had no trouble with scholarly writing in that tongue. *Discours de la méthode*, it was called, but as I turned the pages, and although I could understand the words, I could follow almost nothing of the sense. I turned another page. There seemed to be deductions drawn from a piece of wax. "*Je pense, donc je suis,*" I read aloud. And what the blazes was that supposed to mean? Shaking my head, I handed the book back to Le Blanc.

"So, *Capitaine*, I cannot then convert you to the thinking of Monsieur Descartes? As well, perhaps, that I do not introduce you to his Cartesian geometry, for that is a mystery even to me."

I looked into the amused, dark eyes of the Frenchmen, and momentarily thought of clapping him in irons. He was not who he claimed to be, and here he was mocking me. I could interrogate the truth of his identity out of him for was I not the captain? But we are all entitled to our secrets. James Harker had evidently left Roger Le Blanc's well alone, and so, I decided, would I.

Nevertheless, I said flatly, "Monsieur Le Blanc, if you are truly a runaway tailor, then I am the Sultan of Turkey."

Le Blanc bowed his head and smiled. "As you say, *monsieur le capitaine*. But you are a man who knows your history, I think, even if you do not know your natural philosophy. Remember, then, the history of the reign of *le Roi François Premier*, and the times since. France was ever the best friend to the Grand Turk, and he to him."

We left Le Blanc to his strange book and continued our way towards the stern. Past the cable tiers once more and we came to the starboard side of the cockpit, the confined but essentially open space where Surgeon Skeen was tending to a patient on a bier that had been erected on the deck. I stood a little way from this scene, for Skeen's usual odour was complemented by a

272

deathly stench of decay from the patient who lolled there, insensible with drink.

"Gangrene, sir," Skeen said. "Will have to take the leg off shortly." I looked at the patient, but his face was unfamiliar. "One of *Royal Martyr*'s men, sir," said Skeen, in answer to my look, "sent over to us while you were ashore yesterday. They have no surgeon, only an ill-natured surgeon's mate with strange ideas of treatment."

I felt a faint remembrance stirring in my mind; something I felt sure was important, if I could but take hold of the memory and see it clearly. I had no wish to smell any more of that unwholesome stink, let alone witness Skeen sawing off a man's leg. We turned away in relief and continued astern.

At the very back, Farrell opened a scuttle, pointing out the bread room that lay below, with the fish room next to it. I looked down into the little holds, and by the light of a lantern I could see a pile of loaves stacked against one corner of the room, coming perhaps halfway up to the deck on which we stood. I did not need the mathematics of Le Blanc's Monsieur Descartes to estimate the number of loaves in that space; nor to comprehend the difference between that number and another figure I had been shown but recently.

There was a commotion on the ladder from the main deck, and Purser Peverell appeared before me, red-faced and breathless.

"Captain, I had no idea you were making an inspection —"

"Not a formal inspection, Mister Peverell. Far from it. Merely taking a stroll around my ship, in fact. But now you mention it, Purser, I think that a formal inspection is long overdue. Tomorrow, let's say, at four bells of the forenoon watch. Ten o'clock, if you're not certain of sea-methods, sir. Just after the prayer of *terce*, if you prefer the watch-keeping of your Roman Church." That struck home, for like all Catholics who clung on to public office in those days, Peverell was not keen to have the fact trumpeted. I went on, keeping my tone light and enjoying myself immensely, "You can bring all your papers, and we shall go down to the hold, Mister Peverell. Naturally, the figures that you have shown me so often in my cabin will tally exactly with what we shall find in the stores, but when I next report that fact to Mister Pepys and His Royal Highness the Lord High Admiral, both my conscience and yours will be so much clearer if we have properly compared the one with the other. Don't you think that's so, Purser?"

To my dying day, I will remember and relish the expression that had come over Peverell's complacent, condescending face. The previous triumph over the loathsome purser had been Francis Gale's. This was mine, and I cherished it.

"Thank you, Mister Farrell," I said, when we had returned to my cabin. "As you predicted, that was a most instructive lesson. Perhaps more for the purser than me, though."

Kit smiled merrily at me. "I had my suspicions, sir, but then, all seamen have suspicions of all pursers.

Rogues to a man, thieving from the king and the common sailor alike. But this one is altogether the worst I've ever come across. I began to make it my business to enquire into Peverell's. Not that I had the grasp of numbers and manifests to do so to any great purpose. But another did."

The door flew open as though someone had kicked it. Musk appeared, glowered at Farrell, and said sourly to me, "You're dining the Provost of Oban, remember. Need to get the table ready."

Musk set about his task with his usual infinite bad grace. As I watched him, it dawned on me that somehow the hatred he had displayed toward Kit Farrell since his first day on the *Jupiter* had been replaced by something else, something that I could not quite grasp. Understanding, when it came, was as welcome as it was unexpected.

"Well, Musk," I said, "I think you have been assisting Mister Farrell? Investigating our purser's frauds against the king?"

Musk grunted. "Someone had to," he said, "and most seamen can't count."

I remembered my brother's comment on sending Musk to me, that the old rogue was "good enough". In truth, he was much more than that. His immaculate command of the domestic and estate accounts of the London house was the reason why my mother, and now my brother, had kept him on all these years. It seemed out of character in one so churlish, so villainous in appearance. But perhaps it was *not* so out of character. For who better to keep a set of accounts than the man who understood every fraud that could possibly be committed against them?

Farrell and I sat in my stern gallery, talking of the means by which a captain could check the activities of his warrant officers without causing them to take umbrage. I heard the bell toll seven times; but half an hour to the changing of the watch. As we talked, Musk went grumblingly about his business, preparing a lavish reception for this Provost of Oban, protesting now and again at the workload that, in truth, he imposed upon himself. The tide was ebbing and our ship had swung on its single anchor, its bow to the shore. I knew such things, now; felt them, rather. From my windows we looked out onto the bleak shore and, through the channel behind us, a glimpse of open sea.

I could see a small boat coming out from the shore of Ardverran. I thought nothing of it, for we were visited daily by at least a dozen such craft, most of them manned by curious Scots or cunning rogues come to peddle their wares — say, overpriced whisky — to the king's gullible mariners. But as I idly looked upon it, I noticed with a start that this boat's passenger had an unmistakeable and vast beard.

Minutes later, Macdonald of Kilreen came aboard and was shown to my cabin. There, he delivered an invitation to the esteemed Captain Quinton to join the Lady Macdonald the next day, for a short cruise. My acceptance may have been a little too rapid. When I turned I caught, for just a moment, the trace of a knowing smirk upon the countenance of that old rogue, Phineas Musk.

276

CHAPTER
SIXTEEN

The Macdonald birlinn came alongside us just before noon, shortly after I had concluded a revealing and (from his viewpoint) acutely discomfiting inspection of Peverell's accounts. There were twelve rowers, six on each side, all in extravagant tartan finery and plumage; a servant girl and a helmsman completed the entourage. Close to the stern, cushions had been heaped into a comfortable divan, and on them reclined the Countess of Connaught. She was dressed soberly and practically in a masculine jacket, cloak and long, encompassing skirts, for although the sun was shining, the wind was still from the west and fresh enough to be counted cold.

A disconcertingly large number of my crew had found an excuse to come to the starboard side to observe the spectacle, and to offer advice in tones quite clearly audible to their captain on courses of action to take with his visitor. Boatswain Ap circled menacingly with his cudgel and growled something about being more respectful to the captain and lady, but his heart seemed not to be in it. Perhaps he had abandoned me as a lost cause of undue leniency.

Ignoring the ribaldry I climbed down into the galley. The countess smiled, raised her hand to be kissed, and bade me sit down alongside her. The craft pulled away from the *Jupiter*'s side moving with easy strokes right into the wind, a course that no sailing ship could take.

"So, Captain Quinton," she said, and I was struck anew by the flinty tones of a voice so at odds with her beauty. "Here you are, after all. Kilreen reckoned you wouldn't have the wit for it, in full sight of your crew."

I rejoined that I was a married man merely accepting the generous invitation of a noble lady — one whose rank made refusal impossible. She asked, half-mockingly, if that meant I was there only out of duty rather than pleasure, and I made some silly, gallant remark about how the two could coincide quite happily. She smiled at that, and fed me some small, flat Scottish cakes that she claimed were of her own making. The servant girl, a young islander who spoke no English, poured us some passable wine.

The birlinn took us close among the islands, through channels that would have been impassable for a ship. This was Ardverran land, she said, what was left of it. She proudly pointed out this farmstead and that fisherman's cottage, taking pleasure in reciting the names of places and people in the singsong Scots tongue, so like her native Irish, she said.

She asked me of my family, and within an hour she had it all: my comely wife, my embittered mother, my heroic father, my elusive brother, my piratical grandfather, my French grandmother, my dead sister and my living one; the whole Quinton history. She learned of the death of Captain Harker, of my sudden appointment as his replacement, and of my tortuous dealings with the *Jupiter*'s officers. Of her own history, she said not a word.

In my turn I asked of her late husband, seeking to learn more of Godsgift Judge's part in his death. She would say only that her husband had been a strong man and loyal to his king. She spoke animatedly only of her son, and of how she would see him enter into his inheritance. Then, perhaps, she would retire to her native Ireland; though she was told it was much changed, with many of her people thrown off their lands by Cromwell's men and the speculators who came in their wake. "Hell or Connaught", the saying went; thus her own title had become an abomination, though the lands of Connaught were none so bad, she claimed. It was clear from her passionate way of speaking that the distance between the Connaught lands and their countess, whose family had lost them, made them all the more desirable.

We came by a ruined fortress on the shore. This was not as ancient as the one I had explored with young Macferran the day before; it seemed to date from the days when England and Scotland fought for possession of this entire land. I asked her if this was so, and her eyes flashed — though whether in disgust at my ignorance, or something quite other, I could not tell.

Not so, she told me. "This was a seat of the Lords of the Isles, my son's ancestors. It was a great sea-kingdom over all these islands, the Inner and Outer Hebrides, and the mainland fringing this sea:

Ardnamurchan and Kintyre, and such places. Their chief palace was at Finlaggan on Islay, but they sometimes came down to these waters for calmer weather and the hunting."

This was a history of which I knew nothing. I asked her to tell me more of it. For a moment she ran her fingertips through her long red hair, seeming lost in thought. Then she turned to me.

"This is no ancient history, Captain. The last Macdonald Lord of the Isles was illegally deprived of his lands and titles by King James the Fourth of Scots in 1493, less than one hundred and seventy years ago. When I first came to Ardverran, as my husband's child-bride, there was an old retainer, long past his ninetieth year. His own father had married late in life, when he was almost at his three score and ten, to a wife half a century his junior. As a boy, Captain Quinton, the father was a scullion to Alexander, the last Lord of the Isles. He witnessed the fall of the lordship. He saw the soldiers of King James ride up to that tower, there, and burn it. He relayed the story to his son, who relayed at to me, as vividly as if I were witnessing the event myself. Two lives back, Captain, and you and I are here, on the edge of living memory."

Aye, as am I, now. Here I sit, in the London of the second George and that scabrous thief Walpole, and yet in my mind's eye I can conjure up the image of an old man I once knew; an old man who sailed against the Invincible Armada and danced with Queen Bess. An old man whose own venerable childhood attendant hacked that same King James of Scots to death at

280

Flodden Field. Such are the tricks and mysteries that time perplexes us with. And the older a man gets the more he is drawn to his memories, and the more of a fool he finds himself to be.

This lost heritage evidently mattered deeply to the countess. She turned her long neck and hid her face in contemplation of the ruins while the serving girl refilled our goblets. I sat in silence, watching the hundreds of gulls that wheeled around the great crags of the headland, calling out in their wild, harsh voices. Suddenly my lady bestirred herself, bending close with a smile to ask whether my wife and I had children. When I answered none, and that after three years of marriage, she frowned a little.

"But matters between you, Matthew — yes, I shall call you Matthew, I think — matters are as you would wish them to be?" She paused, as though choosing her words with care. "You are close to your wife, Matthew?"

There, on a warm afternoon, with good wine inside me and this beauty of all the world only inches from me, it was easy to imagine the matters to which she referred. Too easy. I felt my neck grow warm as I looked at her face, at the mocking smile on those perfect lips. I answered awkwardly, a little breathlessly, that "matters" between Cornelia and me were satisfactory — and so they were. So satisfactory, indeed, and so frequent, that our failure to conceive a child was a mystery to us both. It was less of a concern to Cornelia, whose parents had produced children but twice, ten years apart, in forty years of marriage. But I was the heir to Ravensden and in danger of becoming the *last* heir; the last of the Quintons. My brother Charles, the earl, was hardly likely to marry and even less likely to be a father, for such of his inclinations that had not been shot to pieces in the Worcester fight lay elsewhere. That left Uncle Tristram, over thirty years my senior. Although he, like our king, had sons enough around the kingdom, he had never married any of their mothers, again like our king. Every other Quinton line had ended in daughters or still-borns or impotent lunatics. My mother was tactful enough not to remind Cornelia or me of this appalling fact, or of the responsibility upon us to produce a new heir — or not more than three or four times a week, at any rate.

It took my lady of Connaught but a short while to prise my fears and hopes from me. She, whose own marriage of some ten years had produced only one child, was sympathetic, and plied me with more cakes and wine. Emboldened by good Rhenish, the dazzling sun upon the water, and my proximity to those half-laughing, half-serious green eyes, I asked whether she had not been tempted to remarry. Widowhood in these parts, especially in the winter, must have been an ordeal of solitude.

She could and perhaps should have damned me for my impertinence. Instead, she said equably, "Oh, I have had proposals, Captain. A title, even one with attainted lands and no royal patent, draws a certain kind of man like a moth to a flame. Macdonald of Glenverran, my late husband's kinsman, proposes to me annually, every Christmas Day, but he is a man who has never known soap. Even Campbell of Glenrannoch proposed to me, when he first came back from the wars." This was news indeed. The countess noticed my look of surprise. "His own German wife died many years ago, and his son prefers the fleshpots of Amsterdam to estate husbandry, they tell me. His is an isolated existence. But for a Macdonald to marry a Campbell — even if she is only a Macdonald by marriage — why, Captain, that would be like France marrying England, but with less chance of success." She looked out over her waters. "Besides, I think I scare men away. I believe I speak too plainly for most. A failing both of my family and my race. But I am well content alone, with my son."

She asked me of my own plans for the future, and I found I could not answer with any certainty. "As an heir, I suppose all my plans must be tentative . . ." I faltered. "They all depend — that is to say, they all suppose —"

"That your brother does not die? And is he like to die, Matthew Quinton?"

"Charles — the earl — he was wounded, in the wars —"

"Ah. As the cynics in my old country say, Captain, we are all dying, even babes in arms. The only issue is how long we take over it. Your brother has perhaps taken long enough?"

Her suggestion startled me. It was not the coarseness of it. I had encountered enough plain-speaking amongst the whores who thronged the court of Whitehall, and Jane Barcock of Ravensden could be as direct as the plainest dealer when suggesting what she would like to do with the Honourable Matthew. But the falseness, the presumption of her suggestion —

"I do not wish my brother to die, my lady. I do not wish to be an earl."

She smiled, raised an eyebrow. "Ah, Matthew. Poor, poor Matthew. I did not wish to be the titular Countess of Connaught, but somehow my father died. I did not wish to be mistress of Ardverran, but somehow my husband died." A strange expression I could not read passed over her face. "Sometimes, in the winter, when we know it is day only because the rainclouds become a little lighter for a few hours, I find myself with little to do but read. A while ago, I read a canting, ugly book which states that life is but solitary, poor, nasty, brutish and short. I have thought much on that phrase, Matthew. *Solitary, poor, nasty, brutish and short.* The truth of it is what has brought me here, and who knows where it will take you?"

Our craft rowed along an empty shore. Here and there, a ruined tower or cottage stood forlornly. My lady was silent, looking out to the sunlit lands beyond the foreshore. At length, she gestured towards them with a slender arm.

"Lost Macdonald lands, Captain," she said. "All this, as far as you can see, once belonged to my husband's sept. Ardverran's lands stretched almost to Kintyre. Now all is Campbell property. To the north, there, is Glenrannoch's soil, all of it once Macdonald territory. Everything south and east is Campbell of Argyll's, though Argyll be dead. Tell me, Captain Quinton. You know the king, I take it? Your brother is one of his oldest friends, I've heard?" I admitted it. She said, "Then explain this to me, Captain. The Macdonalds, my husband among them, fought for this king. The Lord Argyll humiliated him and betrayed him, and the king has rightly stuck his head on a pole at the Edinburgh tollbooth. Now, would not natural justice suggest that the lands of the traitor, Campbell of Argyll, should go to the loyal, to the Macdonalds, whose soil after all it rightly is from time immemorial?" Her eyes locked on mine, her expression hard to read. "So where is your king's justice, Captain Quinton?"

I was silent, thinking hard upon a reply. My honour demanded that I defend the king, my monarch and my brother's friend. But there was much in what she said; and, in truth, I had heard arguments like hers many times since the Restoration. Many Cavaliers came flooding back from exile to find their lands long sold to speculators or swordsmen, and perhaps sold on again to perfectly innocent third parties who had entirely legal title to them. What to do? To keep his truest supporters content, and declare invalid all land transactions since his royal father's execution? That would almost certainly begin another civil war out of the howls of the dispossessed. Or to confirm the title of all those in actual possession, thereby rewarding men who had been vehement against the crown for decades, and forcing his truest supporters to shift for themselves?

Typically, King Charles the Second had chosen a course that he often took in such cases, when the choice before him was as between Scylla and Charybdis.

He did nothing.

Returning Cavaliers and incumbent Roundheads had been left to reach individual accommodation where they could, and families had often been forced to pay again for lands that had been theirs for centuries. Although my mother had somehow kept most of the Quinton estate together through the worst of times, even she had been forced to sell some of our subsidiary lands in Huntingdonshire to a venal old civil lawyer; a Parliament-man, from Chancery Lane. He enjoyed them still.

I began awkwardly to explain the thorny difficulties surrounding the king to Lady Macdonald, but she swiftly grew impatient.

"Enough, Captain. You confirm what I already know. Argyll's lands will not be attainted and restored to their rightful owners, but will pass to his worthless son Lorne, who also stands accused of treason. And if not to Lorne, then doubtless to Glenrannoch. Yes, I'm sure the general will happily extend his boundaries yet again, as he has done at the expense of Macdonalds more than once. Why should General Campbell gain such power at my son's expense? Glenrannoch, a man of no proven loyalty to our king, and kinsman to such great traitors?"

Her cheeks were flushed with passion but she held her head proudly. I concurred with her sentiments about the general, and as she turned toward the shore, her fire-red hair brushing my cheek as she did so, I saw myself once more as the grim, armoured knight, despatching the enemies of a wronged woman.

For a moment our cruise seemed threatened to end on this sorrowful and bitter note, but I have observed that all mothers, including my own, can be diverted safely from any difficult matter by asking them about their sons, and so it proved once more. At my turning our talk back to the subject of the young Sir Ian Macdonald of Ardverran, my lady's face brightened. She began a lengthy discourse on the various childhood illnesses he had overcome, his moods and qualities, and her hopes for his future.

"He will be a great man, Matthew," she said, eyes aglow with pride. "Greater than his father. Maybe, under him, Ardverran will be mighty again."

At our audience in Ardverran the child had seemed to me but a feeble wretch with no qualities above the ordinary, but I praised him as a new Achilles, Aristotle and Solomon all in one. This pleased her and she patted my arm in gratitude.

"You must dine with us, Captain. It will be good for Ian to talk with a man like you — a king's captain, and from such a bloodline of great warriors and noble earls! Yes, you must dine at Ardverran. I insist on it." She held my gaze a fraction longer than necessary then turned away, a half-smile playing about the corners of her mouth.

We had rowed to the tip of a short headland and our oarsmen were pulling against a sharp current. The wind had dropped and the afternoon was as idyllic as any I had ever known. The sun was bright on the water, sparkling through the drops splashed up by the oars. We were close enough to shore to smell the sweetness of the heather. A tiny ruined chapel stood on the headland, and I wondered if it had stood there since Columba's time. My lady, the countess, was content beside me, her eyes closed, letting the sun warm her face, her hair. Her cloak had slipped and my eyes followed the line of her jaw down her long neck to the white skin that curved away beneath her jacket. I had thoughts that a married man should not have, to my eternal shame. Cornelia was in my heart, but my mind, my eyes, belonged only to this woman. I wondered what might happen, should she and I be alone together at Ardverran. I remember thinking, *No afternoon could be more perfect . . .*

Suddenly, as we cleared the headland and turned into the next bay, the helmsman gave a strange cry. Lady Macdonald opened her eyes and sat forward, startled. There, anchored in the middle of the bay, lay a great man-of-war.

I was still no seaman, but I knew enough to give a rapid judgement on this ship. Forty guns, by my reckoning, perhaps a couple more; almost as powerful as *Royal Martyr* and outmatching *Jupiter*. Not English built, for certain. Flemish or Dutch, perhaps, though they built ships for all of Northern Europe. Her hull was dark hued, almost black. She flew no ensigns that could identify her, her sails were hanging loose, and she swung at a single anchor. She was not idle, as my *Jupiter* was at that moment. She had men aloft and the lookouts had already seen us. On her upper and main decks the guns were being run out.

On her command, Lady Macdonald's helmsman brought his tiller hard to larboard and we turned to fall back behind the headland, our oarsmen doubling their strokes. The ship could not follow us, even if her captain was minded so to do; the channel was too shallow, and the winds too light in any case. It must have taken less than a minute for us to be safe and out of sight of those mighty guns.

"We will for Ardverran directly," the lady said with grim determination. "I'll send word along the coast to see what we can learn of that ship. It may be a Dutchman, of course, or a Dane. They often anchor and victual in these waters . . ."

I was silent a moment. "My lady, do they ever anchor and victual with their main guns run out, and no ensigns flying?" She held my eye, searching my face for meaning. "Whatever ship that is, they don't want to be known."

I could not tell her the suspicion I had formed. Everyone from the king down to his humble captain, Matthew Quinton, had assumed that the ship carrying the arms to Campbell of Glenrannoch would be an ordinary merchantman out of Bruges or Ostend. That had been the intelligence from the merchant, Castel Nuovo. But what if Glenrannoch had raised enough money to buy not just a mighty arsenal for an army, but a man-of-war more powerful than anything in the western seas? Or at least more powerful than anything that was *usually* to be found in these waters, with the present exception only of Judge's *Royal Martyr*. Glenrannoch could not have known, when he bought such a ship, that the king would learn of his plans and send a squadron against him. All of Europe's wars were over, in that year 1662, and weapons and warships were as easy to buy as roasted chestnuts, and almost as cheap. Never had there been such a glut on the market of killing.

The birlinn swiftly won back to the *Jupiter* where the countess and I parted with chaste, courtly acknowledgements. As I watched the little craft row back towards Ardverran, I wondered how different things might have been if a strange ship had not been awaiting us, around that last headland.

CHAPTER
SEVENTEEN

I despatched Martin Lanherne and Julian Carvell to find *Royal Martyr* and warn Captain Judge of the dark ship. Macferran, eager to be of service, offered to take them in his boat, which could cut through channels that the *Jupiter* could never navigate, and I gladly accepted. We spent the next few hours ensuring the ship was ready to sail or fight if necessary, even against such mighty odds. Several balls of roundshot were laid alongside each of our cannon, and the ship's corporal broke out the small arms, distributing a ferocious array of halberds, half-pikes, muskets and swords to each mess. The full naval discipline of our ship, somewhat half-hearted of late, was sternly reinstated by James Vyvyan and Boatswain Ap. Feeling as ever that I served no purpose on deck but to impede the hurrying sailors, I took myself to my cabin. There I studied the charts, trying to conjure the depths, shoals, tides and winds into some kind of strategy; a strategy to overcome I knew not what.

As evening came on, a strange calm settled upon me. In my presence, the Countess had ordered Macdonalds to all the summits around the bay in which we lay at anchor, including the old fort I had visited; at least, such was her translation of the orders she had issued in Gaelic to her clansmen at the oars. I knew that these lookouts would see an approaching ship long before it could come within any distance of us, and that we would thus have ample time to prepare for battle or to run out to sea. And then, Landon and Ruthven were both of the opinion that no ship, no matter how knowledgeable of these seas, would dare try to approach us by night, for the channels were narrow and the rocks that lined them forbidding. The mainland was Glenrannoch's territory and therefore hostile, it was true, but no phantom man-of-war was going to attack from that direction. I posted additional lookouts lest any attempt be made overland or in small craft, but the consensus of my officers was that we could not be more secure if we lay in the heart of Chatham Dockyard.

James Vyvyan was more inclined to make an attack on the mysterious ship, but the consensus of my officers was that she was too large and, indeed, that we had no conclusive proof she was hostile — God forbid that I should be responsible for a war with Sweden, perhaps, or worse, the Dutch, by making an unprovoked attack on a ship of theirs! Even if she was truly Glenrannoch's ship, simple common sense dictated that we should remain where we were, lying at anchor between it and the general's lands, its likely destination; and, after all, remaining in this anchorage was what my senior officer had explicitly ordered me to do. Vyvyan conceded the point with reasonably good grace, the seaman in him winning out over the glory-hunting youth.

292

We dined together, later than was our custom, with my cabin lit by lanterns and candles. As ever, Janks had wrought a comforting miracle: excellent beef from a cow bought from a Macdonald and slaughtered on the shore, with ample fish and cheese. We were merry and, for once, we were almost as one. Only the dark silence coupled with the unpleasantly noisy eating habits of Stafford Peverell marred the table's spirits. James Vyvyan soon became more than a little drunk. I was relieved his talk did not turn to his murdered uncle. He sang happily of a girl in Truro that he loved, and I reminded him that some days before, he had sung the same song, and that of a girl in Bodmin. Even Malachi Landon was amiability itself, his tarpaulin rage at gentleman captains briefly forgotten. Perhaps his spirits were perversely elevated by the prospect of all the dire foretelling contained in his heavenly charts finally coming to pass. I looked around the assembly and thought that, truly, there is nothing so good at uniting men who live by the sword as the prospect of battle.

Yet through it all, as we caroused and laughed, I thought of our gun drill, and I thought of the broadside of that mysterious ship, and of what it would do to us if it ever came within range.

The officers had all gone and I had removed my boots, yet still Musk lingered on, shuffling round the cabin in the performance of some imagined task. Unaffected by the war-fever of my officers, he was, it seemed, much more interested in discovering whether or not I had seduced the countess. "Or she you," he cackled. I suspected that he shared my mother's

293

concerns about my lack of an heir and had weighed up the widowed lady of Ardverran as good breeding stock. No doubt a grand Irish title would also befit the heir to Ravensden. I could well imagine the pestilential old rogue devising several ways of disposing of Cornelia, some of which doubtless entailed absconding with her himself (for I never doubted that he lusted after her mightily). Musk had many strange traits, but perhaps the most unexpected was the extent of the unswerving loyalty he had always demonstrated, albeit in the most complaining way, to the noble house of Quinton.

As he probed and pried, Musk finished off the half-empty flagons of ale and wine around the table, grumbling about how poorly he ate and drank in the king's navy compared to Ravensden House. The good captain would not feel the same, he observed sourly, because the good captain was being entertained so liberally ashore and afloat, by everyone from countesses downwards.

"Do these Scots do anything but eat, and drink, and hunt?" he asked, indignantly, gulping from a flagon and wiping his mouth upon his sleeve. "Reminds me. You've got yet another invitation, for tomorrow afternoon. A country ride, it seems. You'll have some of those running men of theirs laden down with hams and whisky, I don't doubt. Pah. And me, I'll be on hard cheese and ship's biscuit. Again."

I could hardly accept an invitation to a hunt with a strange and probably hostile ship in the same waters, and told Musk so.

"Can't turn this one down, Captain," he said slyly. "Not as it's by way of an order."

An order? Who could give me orders, other than Captain Judge? With him gone, I stood there in my cabin as the supreme authority in that sea, under God and the king. With the king hundreds of miles away in Whitehall, and God presumably engaged elsewhere, I was safe from any order.

Musk struck an attitude of recollection. "Now, what did that huge old Turk say? Or is he a Pole? That Simic, anyway, ugly ferocious brute." His beady eye upon me as I waited. "Ah yes. *The Vice-Admiral of the coast of Argyll, Kintyre and Moidart*, that's what he said. General Campbell of Glenrannoch, in other words."

I could easily have rejected this so-called order had I seen fit; indeed I told Musk so in terms that set him scuttling around in some dudgeon. Vice-admirals of the coast had vague powers over wreck in their counties, but no authority over the captains of the king's ships. Glenrannoch could not give me an order, and he knew it. But he was evidently a master of strategy, in all senses, and he would have known that inviting me in such a peremptory way would give me pause. I dismissed Musk and, alone, I sat in my chair, looking out over the waters, considering the matter at some length. Finally I decided that if by noon there was no report of the mysterious ship, then I would take up Glenrannoch's invitation. For, as he must have guessed, I was full of curiosity to learn what lay between Colin Campbell and the Dowager Countess of Ravensden, my mother.

★ ★ ★

It was very early in the morning, not far past seven bells of the middle watch, as I was now learning to call half-past three o'clock. I was already about in my cabin, though, for my dreams had been too full of battle and countesses on cushions for my sleep to be entirely serene. I heard a lookout's cry, and went up on deck. James Vyvyan had the watch. He was standing at the starboard rail, looking out towards the mainland, at a small fishing boat that was making its way out to us. To my delight his boyish face broke into an easy smile at my approach, and he saluted me before launching into a laughing explanation.

"Well, sir, I do believe I'm witnessing a minor miracle. I didn't think we'd see the Reverend Gale again this side of the king's birthday."

We stood in companionable silence, watching the boat tack out towards us. In due course it came alongside and Francis Gale climbed aboard with young Andrewartha. To my surprise he was perfectly sober. He asked to see me alone in my cabin, and I immediately invited him to breakfast with me. Gale was unusually clerical, even saying grace over Janks's crisp bacon. He talked equably of the weather, and the empty beauty of the land. Then, quite suddenly, he turned the conversation to the very thing that had been preoccupying my thoughts all morning.

"Your countess, Captain," he began. "You don't know her name before she married, I suppose?"

This was unexpected. As equably as I could, I confessed that I did not, and Gale chewed on more bacon before continuing. "When I heard who'd been entertaining you, that first time at her castle, I thought upon the title Countess of Connaught, and I thought, I have heard that before." He paused, helped himself to more food and went on. "But y'see, Captain Quinton, I don't trust my memory after all these years of port wine and bad dreams. I needed a book of pedigrees, and from the lad Macferran I'd heard of a decent library hereabouts, although that prospect seemed as likely as Moses finding a banquet in Sinai."

He explained that some twenty miles inland, in a perfectly ordinary, mean Highland village, was a remarkable treasure: a low church, in appearance little more than a barn; in its loft, a free library generously endowed by an enlightened lord of those parts and maintained by a minister a little too zealous for Gale's liking, but knowledgeable. There, he said, he found the book that he sought.

Francis Gale's sober breakfast was evidently over, for he took out a flask of animal hide and, as he uncorked it, I recognized the powerful smell of the water of life. He drank, straight from the flask, but less than had once been his wont, and smacked his lips.

"O'Daragh, your lady's name was, before she came here as but a slip of a girl. Niamh O'Daragh then, the Lady Niamh Macdonald of Ardverran now. And O'Daragh was a name I had heard often, back in Ireland, in the time before Drogheda."

I had long lost interest in my breakfast. I pushed the platter to one side and nodded for Gale to continue.

"The Catholic rebels had their own state then, independent in all but name — the Confederation, they

297

called it. For a few years, while England tore herself apart in civil war, they sent ambassadors all over Europe, and received some in return. Even a papal nuncio was sent to meddle. I met him once, at Kilkenny, in '46 or '47." Gale paused. I wondered if he were recalling that different time, when he had been young, sober and in love. I hesitated to interrupt, for like most Englishmen, my knowledge of Ireland and its tortured history amounted to little more than a flea's fart.

The moment passed. Gale ate a little more bacon and drank a little more whisky. I took a long draught from a flagon of small beer.

"Attending on the nuncio was one of their own," he said at length. "An Irish bishop who had been selected as a promising young postulant, and trained up by the Vatican and the Inquisition. He had a fierce reputation even then as the best politician amongst the Irish papists. Some said, though, that he followed the teachings of Signor Machiavelli rather better than those of Our Lord. I met him too, that same time in Kilkenny town, and I'd concur with them. Shocking red hair, though it must be grey now, I should think. He had probably the sharpest mind I've ever met. His name," Gale paused, looked at me, "was O'Daragh. Ardal O'Daragh. Younger brother to the titular Earl of Connaught of that time, and so uncle to your lady."

I listened with a mounting sense of unease. I had known that the lady was popish, of course; most of the people thereabouts were, but then, so was half of King Charles's court. Furthermore, even in those early days of his reign, there were already rumours concerning the king's own true faith. My own feelings on the matter were relaxed. To my mother, popery had always been more acceptable than the king-killing hydra of dissent, the multitude of strange Protestant sects that flourished under Cromwell and the Commonwealth, and I had inherited her beliefs. Even if I had not, there was my grandmother; the former Louise-Marie de Monconseil de Bragelonne, Dowager Countess of Ravensden, had died with the rosary in her hands, having spent much time in her last years trying fruitlessly to convert her favourite grandson to her faith. No, I had none of the hysterical fear of Rome that drove so many of my countrymen. My dislike of the purser Stafford Peverell had been driven not by his faith, but by his very being. But what Francis Gale was telling me was of a very different order, and I feared his peroration.

He took some more bread to soak up the whisky and said, "He's far grander these days, the man I knew as Bishop Ardal O'Daragh of Rathmullen. A red-robed prince of the Church, indeed. The Cardinal-Archbishop of Frascona, he is called now. That's a fine archdiocese in Sicily, rich with crops and wine and a good trade by sea, or so the books in the library at Inverlarich tell me. He must be a very rich man, the Cardinal O'Daragh. Not as rich as his closest friend, though." Gale pushed his plate away and sat back, hands resting on his round stomach. "You'll have heard of Fabio Chigi, of course." I shook my head and stiffened to interrupt, but he must have sensed that he had savoured his moment for long enough, that my patience with Irish and prelatical history was not limitless, and raised a hand to halt me.

"The House of Chigi, Captain, is one of the greatest banking houses in Europe, and has been for many centuries. Which, along with the machinations in conclave of his dear friend Cardinal Ardal O'Daragh, no doubt explains why His Eminence Cardinal Fabio Chigi is now His Holiness Pope Alexander the Seventh."

After Gale left the cabin I sat alone for perhaps an hour. I even turned Musk away. My head spun with thoughts of popes, cardinals, armies, and the very bowels of Hell. Above my head, I could hear the larboard watch bringing the ship to life, busy with cleaning, attending to ropes and blocks, and the myriad tasks aboard a man-of-war. I was vaguely aware of the smell of tar, for it is holy writ to seamen that each day there is something aboard that demands the application of tar, whether it requires it or not. I could concentrate on none of it. I stared at the pages of my captain's journal, still awaiting my entry for the previous day; I could not even read the words already written. I picked up my waggoner, looked at the chart, and recalled as much as I could of my voyages in the Lady Macdonald's birlinn and young Macferran's fishing boat. I went to my larboard stern window, opened my grandfather's compendium dial, took bearings with it and made a series of calculations. I studied the tide table and measured distances upon the chart. Perhaps I concentrated more intently than I had on anything since I memorized, years ago, old Mervyn's Latin primer from beginning to end out of fear of the birch. For the first time in my life, I studied the business of the waters as if my very life depended on it.

Then I sent for Kit Farrell.

At first, I did not truly know why. I could not share with him the new direction of the thoughts that raced through my head. He was not my equal, and I could not confide in him about the Countess of Connaught, or her uncle, or the dread that began to stir in my mind. I could not share with him the fear that tightened my stomach and brought bile to my throat: the fear that another crew of mine would die, that another ship of mine would finish on the floor of the sea. And at bottom, gnawing away beneath it all, was the darkest fear of all: the fear of my own death without honour, and with it the extinction of the House of Quinton. I wished that Cornelia or Charles, my brother, could be spirited magically across the hundreds of miles to listen to my anguish. I even wished for the return of Godsgift Judge, puzzling though I found his character to be. In them at least I could confide.

Instead, I had only Kit Farrell. But he, at least, had skills that my wife and brother did not possess, and could offer advice that they could not. I wished to conceal my mood and intentions from him, and yet to gain this advice. I thought for a minute, then turned to him with as clear an expression as I could muster.

"Mister Farrell," I said lightly, "today, if you allow, I would turn from the theory of navigation and ship handling to a hypothesis." Kit's bemused expression prompted my first genuine smile. "What I mean is, imagine a ship of war with the same number of guns as, say, the *Jupiter* here. Now, let us suppose such a ship faces a much larger ship of force, in confined waters full of islands such as these, and that the enemy ship has the weather gage. Let us also suppose that the larger ship has a superior captain, a stronger crew and a greater weight of broadside. Let us further suppose that this enemy has allies ashore, so striking the colours, abandoning your ship and fleeing overland is impossible: your men would be cut to pieces. So what would you do, Mister Farrell? What would you do to survive, and get your ship and crew clear?"

Farrell was not a man of letters but his wits were quick enough for all that. Despite my conceit, he plainly understood at least a little of my purpose. He sat down without my permission, and thought hard on the matter, his face grave and attentive.

"Could not," he said at length, "the lesser ship attempt to seek out a channel deep enough for her to navigate, but too shallow for the greater ship?"

I told him peremptorily that such a course did not exist; I knew from my waggoner, and from observation, that it did not.

He considered the matter for a few moments further. "In such a case, Captain," he said, "your position appears impossible. It would seem that you are doomed." This was not the counsel I wished for, but before I could interrupt Kit continued. "My father's ship was in almost such a position, once, back in '52, in the winter battle where we lost to the Dutch off

Dungeness. Bad shoals and sandbanks in those waters, Captain, hemming them in just as you describe." He stopped, seemed to search his memory. "He was on one of the old Whelps, as top heavy and awkward as an elephant on a footstool. They were trapped between sands by a nimble Frieslander with double their broadside. The last night Father and I spent together in our alehouse, Captain — the night that I told you of once before — he told me of that fight, and he taught me this." Kit looked up, held my eye. "In such a situation, Captain Quinton, there is one thing, just one thing alone, that you can do."

When Kit had gone, I settled down and began another round of letter-writing. Even in those days, many of my fellow captains were employing clerks to do this for them. However the only candidate available for the role would have been Phineas Musk, and though he was probably amply qualified, he ruled enough of my life as it was.

To Mister Pepys and his colleagues of the Navy Board, I wrote of the state of the ship and in praise of the willingness of the Scots to supply us with good victuals, albeit not necessarily at the cheapest of prices. To the Duke of York, I wrote of Captain Judge's voyage to intercept the arms ship, of my fear that it had slipped by him and of my suspicion that it was the same mysterious vessel I had seen from the Lady Macdonald's birlinn. To the king, I could write nothing beyond *Your Majesty*. What could I say of the thoughts that had raced through my head since Francis Gale informed me of his genealogical discoveries? As it was, I included all my worries and thoughts in the letters that I eventually wrote to Cornelia and my brother, though I guiltily refrained from all but the most cursory descriptions of the Countess of Connaught.

I was visited at regular intervals. This was part of command, I realized; others reckon that they always have a right to one's time, never seeing that the sum of all their calls leaves their captain with little time for himself. The odious Peverell was at my door once more, keen to prove that there were no errors or manipulations in the ship's books. I had no time for his desperate half-truths and sent him away. Stanton, the gunner, was next, reporting that damp had got into two barrels of powder. I was too distracted to do more than nod sympathetically which, judging from Stanton's sidelong glances, was not quite the proper response.

James Vyvyan afforded the next interruption. To my dismay he was once again on the trail of his uncle's murderer. He stammered that one of our men had received a letter in the last mail from Dunstaffnage from his mother, who happened to know the mother of Pengelley, Captain Harker's murdered clerk. The men had been talking of it, and James had overheard. The man in question — Berry, I think his name was — was currently ashore, one of a party fetching broom to replenish the carpenter's stores. Vyvyan intended to interview him on his return. I humoured my young lieutenant in his quest to make sense of his uncle's death, yet it was but an old story and this new tale was as like to be a goose-chase as any of the others. Thankfully the interview was brought to a close by the arrival of Penbaron. I smiled reassuringly at Vyvyan then turned with relief to the carpenter. Penbaron had come to report on the dire state of the whipstaff, or perhaps the rudder, or possibly both. I duly added it as a postscript to my letter to Mister Pepys, and then returned in some perplexity to my letter to the king. So my afternoon passed, and through it all I remained preoccupied and anxious.

It was a little after eight bells in the afternoon, or four o'clock. The crew had just begun the first dog watch: one of two short, two-hour watches that break up the regular pattern, ensuring that each man aboard gets his fair distribution of duties in the morning, afternoon and night. There came a routine call from one of our lookouts, telling of yet another small boat approaching us. I ignored it. A few minutes later, though, one of Landon's mates came to report that the boat was young Macferran's, and it was bearing Lanherne, Carvell and a cargo of some sort. This was strange: I hardly thought that they would have caught up with the *Royal Martyr* and made their return so quickly. I went out on deck and watched as the boat manoeuvred skilfully alongside. Coxswain Lanherne came on deck and saluted me, while Macferran and Carvell struggled to haul up their cargo, wrapped in one of the boat's sails.

"Captain, sir," said Laherne, and took a deep breath. "We never found the *Martyr*, but we found this." He gestured to the bundle without looking at it.

"Macferran, there, he's good eyes. He saw it washed up on a beach in . . ."

"Moidart," Macferran said, after a pause.

Lanherne nodded. "Thought it best to bring it back right away, sir."

The bundle was lying on the deck. Julian Carvell undid the knots that tied it together and pushed the sailcloth apart. I could not refrain from a gasp of horror, for there lay a corpse. It was bloated from the sea, and the fish had been feasting upon it. But I recognized the buff tunic, and there was enough of the dour face left for the identity to be beyond doubt. I was looking down upon the mortal remains of Nathan Warrender, lieutenant of the *Royal Martyr*.

We took the body below to the orlop deck where Surgeon Skeen attended to it. One of the men went to fetch the Reverend Gale. There was no need for me to ask Skeen how Warrender had died, even if the surgeon's judgement was worth a whit. This was not the result of some great sea-fight between *Royal Martyr* and the mysterious dark ship; that much was clear. I had seen enough drowned men to know the signs well enough; but what made the crew recoil in horror, and my mind race, and Skeen falter over his inspection, were the cords that bound his wrists and ankles. It was not the end that should have befallen this man who had fought honourably against my father at Naseby, and who had behaved with equal honour towards me, the son. I shuddered as I thought upon his last words to me: *May God have mercy on those whose day is done.*

It was in a mood of bleak melancholy that I retired to my cabin to add postscripts to all my letters, informing the recipients of this new development. I did so with a heavy heart, for I was convinced that if Cornelia ever read my words I would already be long dead, feeding the fish as Nathan Warrender had done. I sealed the letters and gave them to Macferran, who was to sail them down to Dunstaffnage Castle where they would join the Mail Royal.

Not long after, James Vyvyan knocked at my cabin door. In truth, I had forgotten all about my lieutenant and his latest line of enquiry. Reluctantly, I called on him to enter. The face that he displayed when he entered my cabin was etched with fear and uncertainty. He suddenly seemed but a child, far younger than his eighteen years.

"Sir, this of Captain Warrender's death . . ." He came to a whispering halt, then began again, but was little better. I poured him some small beer, which he took.

"Captain Warrender was a staunch man, Mister Vyvyan," I said. "The manner of his dying is a shock to us all."

"No, sir — not that — sir, it was him . . ." and again he faltered, fell silent.

I waited patiently, painting an encouraging expression upon my face, but in reality I was more than frustrated by this ongoing obsession. I had almost reached the end of my ability to tolerate it. Finally he took a shuddering breath and managed to describe, in coherent fashion, how he had passed his afternoon. The man he wished to examine over Pengelley's death had returned from the shore party, he said. This was one of our few Devon men, William Berry by name, a close and sly rogue unpopular on the lower deck. He had exhibited profound and uncharacteristic shock when he heard of Warrender's dire fate, and had apparently asked to speak to James Vyvyan before his lieutenant even had a chance to seek him out on his own account.

Vyvyan was shaking so much and his tale so broken and incoherent that my patience was wearing thin. I was sharp with him, telling him to speak more directly. He looked up at me, and I saw the confusion shrouding his face. Without saying anything he held out his hand. In it was a crumpled letter. I looked at him, questioningly. He nodded, still holding the letter out to me, and I took it.

Beloved son. The words were written in a crabbed, stunted hand.

Forgive your Ma this letter, writ for me by the constable, but the terrible matter is all around the village and I could not but send you word. It concerns Goodwife Rose, as came up as a widow from Cornwall to marry old Isaac Rose that farmed Calhele, if you recall, though you were but a buye then to be sure. It is dreadful doings concerning her son, who is called Pengelley, who was apprenticed to a merchant of Truro when she came here. May God have mercy on his soul, she has heard of his most terrible end, cut up like a gelt pig upon the roadside in Hamptonshire. And she speaks too of his last master, who was your own captain Harker. Another murder, says she. I am so affeard, you must forgive your old Ma, but in our dearest saviour's

308

*name, write to me son, for these grave events do weigh
mightily upon my heart and I must know you are safe.
Goodwife Rose is overcome with grief and cries out in
her troubles for her brother, aboard the other ship that
sails with ye. An officer, she says, one Warrender by
name, though mayhap she is distracted, for I had heard
he was of Chudleigh's cavalry in the wars . . .*

"Sir, it was Pengelley's mother," said Vyvyan, unable
to contain himself as I read. "Her name at birth was
Warrender."

The secrets of men are fallible, for our names are
immutable, but the secrets of women can lurk forever
behind the names they assume with each new marriage.
I learned that lesson twice in one day, there in the far
western fastnesses of Scotland, and since have had
ample cause to affirm its worth. MacDonald and
O'Daragh, Pengelley, Rose, Warrender; the truths long
concealed. I stood facing James Vyvyan, the names
repeating themselves over and again in my head.

Then, and only then, did the scales fall at last from
my eyes.

CHAPTER
EIGHTEEN

We buried Nathan Warrender very early the next morning, Good Friday, in the churchyard of an ancient, dilapidated kirk — the Scots word for church — that stood on one of the headlands overlooking our anchorage. Macferran had located its minister, a senile old man who seemed convinced that I was the Marquis of Montrose resurrected and who had no objection to the service being conducted by the Reverend Francis Gale. Indeed, it was Gale himself who offered objections. Warrender had been a rebel, he said, and no doubt a dissenter, violent against king and Church. He had fought in arms against the Lord's Anointed. True, said I. But whatever else he had been in life, Nathan Warrender died holding the King of England's commission as an officer in his navy and was entitled to the honours due his rank. Moreover, he had not fought only against his king, for he had also been present at my father's death and had done honour to his memory. Francis Gale may not wish to forgive or forget, I told him, but Matthew Quinton could.

Warrender's body, shrouded in canvas, was brought up from the beach by an honour guard of seamen headed by James Vyvyan. Martin Lanherne followed the corpse and Carvell, Le Blanc, Polzeath and Treninnick were the four pallbearers. They placed the body at the side of the grave and Gale took out his new prayer book, reading aloud from the service for the dead. He spoke the words of Psalm 90, the glorious *Domine Refugium*, with passion, but I knew he thought of his own life rather than that of Nathan Warrender.

"A thousand years in thy sight are but as yesterday; seeing that is past as a watch in the night. As soon as thou scatterest them, they are even as a sleep; and fade away suddenly like the grass. In the morning it is green, and groweth up; but in the evening it is cut down, dried up, and withered. Comfort us again now after the time that thou hast plagued us: and for the years wherein we have suffered adversity . . ."

I stood in the pale and watery sunlight of that Good Friday and thought of other deaths, past, present and future. It was profoundly still in that quiet, ruined churchyard on the hill. The wind was gentle and carried the scent of spring inside it, and the murmur of the sea filled the air. I felt overwhelmingly alive, but full of sorrow. I turned my thoughts back to the lonely soldier we were burying so far from his home, and tried to concentrate on the words of the service.

"Man that is born of a woman," Gale was intoning, "hath but a short time to live, and is full of misery. He cometh up, and is cut down, like a flower; he fleeth as it were a shadow, and never continueth in one stay. In the midst of life we are in death . . ."

Though the words were altered, I remembered suddenly the first time I had heard them read from the old and now abandoned prayer book of Queen Elizabeth. It was at the burial of my grandfather in Ravensden Abbey. Even as a child of five I had thought how false it sounded: *but a short time to live, and is full of misery*, when it seemed to me that my grandfather had lived for ever, and been full of careless joy until his dying day. But when I heard those words again just a few weeks later at the funeral of my father, I thought upon them differently. Perhaps I grew up more in the course of those two burial services, so short a time apart, than most children of five years are wont to do.

James Vyvyan, Warrender's fellow lieutenant, cast earth onto the canvas, and as it was lowered into the hard Scottish earth Gale continued to deliver the order of service. "Forasmuch as it hath pleased Almighty God of his great mercy to take unto himself the soul of our dear brother here departed, we therefore commit his body to the ground; earth to earth, ashes to ashes, dust to dust . . ."

I looked out over the waters beyond the churchyard, and thought of those whom I had loved who were now of that dust, my grandparents, my father and my sister. *Soon they shall be saying those words over me, for I shall not be leaving these waters alive.*

The service was over. Lanherne brought his honour guard to attention. Muskets ever sit uneasily in the hands of seamen, but several of the guard were veterans of Grenville's Cornish infantry. There had been none

312

finer, and they knew their drill. On the coxswain's command, they fired a smart volley in salute as the mortal remains of Nathan Warrender disappeared forever beneath the ground. Down in the roadstead, the *Jupiter* fired a mourning-salute of five guns, the muffled cannonade echoing off the Scottish hills.

It was James Vyvyan who pointed out the small party of horsemen riding towards the church. There were six of them, with two spare mounts running behind. One rider was taller than the rest, sitting easy and confident on a horse that seemed far too small for him; I recognized him as Simic the Croat. He rode behind a horse that, conversely, seemed unduly large for the little man that it bore. Glenrannoch.

The party reined in at the kirk's boundary wall. The general dismounted, walked over to us and paid his respects at the graveside, saluting sombrely with his sword.

"I heard of the death," he said quietly to me. "I presumed you would be loath to stray too far from your ship, so I suggest we ride hereabouts. I have something I would show you, but a few miles hence."

I was reluctant. The dark vessel might still be lurking nearby, Judge and the *Royal Martyr* had vanished and the nature of Warrender's death had sounded an alarum through my ship. What business had the *Jupiter's* captain ashore in the company of a man like Glenrannoch? And yet . . . I found it was impossible to deny the force of this man's presence. I hesitated but a moment, then called James Vyvyan to me, and told him in a low voice that if there appeared any threat to the ship, he was to fire one gun. Glenrannoch, standing close by and overhearing my words and Vyvyan's surprised reply, said that one of his riders would lead me quickly back to the ship on such a signal. The winds were light, we would not go far, and with the warning that our lookouts would give us, no attack could come against the *Jupiter* before I was back on board.

Then Glenrannoch asked who I wished to accompany me on the second horse. I considered this. Vyvyan could not be spared from the ship. Musk and Kit Farrell were still aboard, and it would take too long to send for them; besides, it was unlikely that Kit could ride well — certainly not on such rough terrain as this — and Musk was but an indifferent horseman for all his bluster. Of all my men at the old kirk, only one could ride for certain: Francis Gale, a gentleman's son and a soldierly priest.

But perhaps there was one other there who could ride. In fact, I was certain of it.

I called out, "Monsieur Le Blanc!" He looked around, a little startled. "You can ride, I take it?"

"*Mais non, monsieur le capitaine.* A tailor of Rouen, what would I have to do with riding?"

"I would have you accompany me on this expedition with the general, Monsieur Le Blanc. As my personal attendant, if you will."

Le Blanc's face fell. "But, Captain —"

Matters were truly serious for Roger Le Blanc to give my rank in English. It amused me even as I ignored his objections, saying airily, "It is an order, Monsieur Le Blanc. I would have you ride with me."

314

"Very well, *mon capitaine*. But I will bring my *knapsack*." He gave the word a preposterous English ring. "I do not trust any of these Cornish."

Lanherne and Polzeath laughed at that and slapped him rudely on the back. The Frenchman picked up the largest knapsack I had ever seen, and moved reluctantly towards one of the general's spare horses. As I had suspected, he mounted with the easy movements of a man born to horseback, and reined in his steed with assurance. I smiled at him but he merely shrugged, as the French do. Thus mounted we moved off, and I rode up to the shoulder of Colin Campbell of Glenrannoch.

We rode across a wild, bleak land of rough hills and moorland. Glenrannoch was a good horseman, as I might have expected from one who had ridden the length and breadth of war-torn Europe. Le Blanc, too, rode exceedingly well, despite his protestations to the contrary. For my part, I could not help but revel in the freedom of being on horseback once again. My mount was an excellent one, albeit not the equal of my Zephyr, and as we cantered along I felt the accumulated hours of anxiety and sea-discipline slough away. Indeed I almost felt, for a moment, like any young man of twenty and two, out for an exhilarating ride on a spring day. I urged my horse faster and gave myself up to the vigorous pleasure of being alive.

We reached the top of a steep slope and I reined in my mount, pausing to admire the sweeping bleakness and beauty of the land. Glenrannoch stopped beside me. "So, Captain Quinton," he said easily, "I gather that the lieutenant of *Royal Martyr* was murdered?"

It was hardly a surprise that he knew. This was his land, as far as the eye could see, and little would happen here without him knowing of it. Perhaps young Macferran reported to him. I told him how Warrender's body had been found. He asked if I had any suspects for the murder, and I answered neutrally. It would not do to share my suspicions with this man.

We rode on further up the hill a little way, and then he said quite suddenly to me, "I am not your enemy, Matthew." His directness unnerved me, and I made no reply. "I had to be discreet when you and Captain Judge were at my tower. I had to be discreet until I was certain of . . . well, no matter. Let us say, of a number of things."

"I have not looked on you as my enemy, sir," said I, dissembling with some awkwardness.

Glenrannoch smiled. "Perhaps not, Captain, though I have little doubt that the king has. But there are many matters of which Charles Stuart is unaware. Of these lands he has always been profoundly ignorant, for his northern kingdom is of but small concern to him as he sits in his Palace of Whitehall, surrounded by sycophants and mistresses. I can understand this in some part, for my cousin of Argyll treated him abominably while he was here. Perhaps our sovereign lord can be forgiven for remembering Scotland with detestation. But there are other matters that he should know better." He looked away from me, gazing out over his territory. "In my experience, Captain," he said

316

quietly, "wars are made when clever men act stupidly, or when stupid men think they are clever. They tell me King Charles is a clever man." He turned and looked intently into my eyes. "But believe me, Matthew, in the business that you are now about, he has acted more stupidly than I would have imagined possible."

Nowadays, every street urchin speaks of our illustrious German George in such terms, or worse. Thus far has the divine mystery of royalty departed from Britain. Back then, though, I was not accustomed to hearing the king spoken of in this way, even by those who, like my brother-in-law Sir Venner Garvey, privately despised him.

I was still groping for the right words to defend His Majesty against Glenrannoch's unforgivable words as we breasted the hill; a second later, all was forgotten. I reined my horse to a halt, astonished at the sight that lay before me. There, on the level ground below, stood an army. Two, perhaps three thousand men, all at attention, all armed. Many had the great basket-hilted swords of those parts, but whole regiments bore pikes, others muskets. All wore Highland garb, and most were in colours that I recognized from Glenrannoch's retainers. The same colours adorned the black-and-yellow flags that flew proudly before them.

The general looked at me. "The host of Clan Campbell, Captain," he said, and turning his horse he began to pick his way down the slope towards his remarkable private army.

I sat for a moment, my heart hammering in my chest. I could hear the others clattering up the track, then a sharp intake of breath from Le Blanc. With mounting trepidation, I urged my horse on down the steep track towards Glenrannoch, a slight figure dismounting before his men. There were no cheers, no movement. This was not a rabble of wild clansmen; this was an army, trained and disciplined.

The general was waiting for me. I dismounted, and we turned to walk in review along each line.

"As you see, Captain, I have no need to wait for an arsenal from Flanders." *Then he does know.* "If I so ordered, this army could be in Edinburgh in days. Nothing under Charles Stuart's control could stand against me. Certainly not poor old Willie Douglas and his regiment — who spent last night under the walls of Kilchurn Castle, incidentally. I pray they didn't suffer more desertions overnight. Twenty-three since setting out," said Glenrannoch, and frowned. "But, Matthew, you must understand one thing: that whatever His Majesty may think of my loyalty, he has it; without precondition, and in full degree."

I wished to believe this quiet, plausible man. I wished to trust him. But the silent army seemed menacing and unnatural. And, too, I recalled how quiet and plausible Lucifer had seemed to Eve when he took the form of the serpent in Eden.

We moved to the head of the second line. Glenrannoch straightened one man's pike and spoke to another about the state of his sheiling. As we walked on, he turned to me once more.

"I've witnessed enough of war, Matthew Quinton. I have seen horrors that would turn the stomach of any man. I witnessed the Sack of Magdeburg, and in my day I have ordered atrocities that were almost its equal." He looked away, over the hills to the east, as though seeking a glimpse of the blood-drenched graves of Germany. In that quiet, almost timid voice, he continued. "I vowed that I would never lead another army, nor order more young men to their deaths in pointless wars decreed by idiots. But fate forces me to march one last time, to fight one last battle."

We reached the end of the second line and turned to review the third. I now knew, or thought I knew, the enemy against whom Glenrannoch would fight. But if I was to believe this man, and trust him, I had at last to know the answer to the question that had haunted me since our first meeting in his Tower of Rannoch.

"How is it, General, that you know my mother?"

He stopped to chide the next soldier in line. Only then did he turn his scarred face directly toward me. "Your mother, and her mother, and your father, and his father and mother. I knew them all. It was a different age, Matthew. A better age. We old people are too prone to say such things, I know. But perhaps few young men would dispute my case, after all these years of war and death." He smiled faintly. "And there are others of your family that I have come to know, that would surprise you."

As we walked, Glenrannoch began to speak of himself and I listened with equal measures of apprehension and anticipation. He had come to England, he said, in the winter of the year '24, when he was the same age that I was. A faction at court wished to set up a new favourite to bring down the king's great love, and the young Colin Campbell was to play the part.

"But although I looked comely enough in those days, as most young Scots do before the whisky takes hold, old King James favoured a different breed. Long legs, above all. How height and looks can change history, Matthew." *The portrait in the hall of the Tower of Rannoch*: the handsome young courtier, unscarred and bright of countenance, would be the young Colin Campbell himself. "My rival remained unassailable, although he soon became a good friend to me. He had the height and the legs, did Geordie Villiers, the Duke of Buckingham."

A faint memory stirred. *Remember his grace . . .* the mysterious note found upon the dead Harker. Vyvyan had been convinced that it referred to the Duke of Buckingham — himself most foully murdered in a Portsmouth tavern — and that it served as a warning. A warning Harker ignored with fatal consequences. Or was there more to it? Could there have been a link between Harker's death and Buckingham's? They had known each other, once — and Glenrannoch, too . . . I thrust the thought away impatiently. This was neither the time nor the place to dwell on Vyvyan's mad delusions, nor on deaths long ago. I had fresher prospects of death before me, my own among them.

The general was oblivious to my thoughts and continued the story of his youth. The young Colin Campbell stayed on at the English court, he said, even after the old king died. Buckingham, at once royal favourite, chief minister and Lord High Admiral, identified a military streak in him that he had never known existed, and found him a useful adjutant in the campaigns he was planning against France and Spain. It was in this way that Campbell came to know my grandfather, almost a demigod to the military men of those days, as were all those who had fought with Drake and against the Armada. I eagerly asked him for his memories of the grand old earl. He smiled then, and told me he remembered a large, lusty man, always quick to laugh off the pomposities of the court.

Glenrannoch had also come to know my father. They were of the same age. My father had been about to fight his first campaign on the disastrous Cadiz expedition. A good man, Glenrannoch said: firm and steady, less extravagant in all things than my grandfather; a man who favoured the book and the sonnet over the sword.

And my mother? I asked then. Yes, he said, he did indeed become acquainted with the woman my father was courting: the Lady Anne Longhurst, one of the many daughters of the Dowager Lady Thornavon. I asked him to describe her to me as she was in those days, but Glenrannoch would say only that she was a paragon of that court, an intelligent beauty who attracted the ardour of any man with blood in his veins.

"Your father was away for some months. I had few other friends at Whitehall, so many hundreds of miles from this, my home. Your mother was . . . she was good. Sympathetic. Do not misunderstand me, Matthew," he said, carefully. "Nothing on which the scriptures frown passed between us. But if on the day of judgement, when the last trump sounds and the dead rise to face the east . . ." He paused, closed his eyes. "If on that day the archangels asked me to name one person on this earth whom I trust and love, I would name your mother."

Then everything changed, he said. My father came back from the war and married my mother. But that brief and hopeless campaign, the fiasco that was Cadiz, had changed the then Lord Caldecote, my father. He had seen enough good men die and enough incompetent men in government order yet more war; and so he vowed never to take up the sword again. My mother, who even then believed that those who fought and died for their king were exalted for all eternity, found this a strange and alienating belief, and for a time, Glenrannoch said, there was an estrangement between them.

Meanwhile the new king, Charles Stuart, who was only a little older than my father and Glenrannoch, was also newly married — to the French princess, Henrietta Maria. Theirs, too, was a cold and uncertain union in those days, for Charles was still too much in awe — or more, perhaps — of his father's late favourite and his own closest friend, the Duke of Buckingham.

"All men err, Matthew Quinton, and I erred more than most. The new queen was frightened and alone, in a strange country. I understood more than a little of that. We became close companions, she and I, for a time. But at a court, nothing is private. There are eyes and ears everywhere, and mouths that are incapable of staying closed, and soon our friendship was laid before the king. I was banished the court. Many spoke up for me, your grandfather and your mother at the head of them, for their word counted mightily with that king in those days. But nothing availed." He turned to me, at last. "All Europe was at war, Matthew. I had Buckingham's recommendation to get me a commission in any army I chose, and I had learned during my work for him that I possessed a certain aptitude for war. The next spring, I was campaigning as a raw captain in the Rhineland, and my course was set. Soon Buckingham himself was dead at an assassin's knife, and my only patrons were the Dutchmen and Germans who paid me to do their killing for them. I have not seen your mother since those days. I often think how, if fate had taken a different turn, I could so easily have been . . ."

At that, the general fell silent. He said no more as we started back toward our small mounted party. Le Blanc was slumped in his saddle looking ineffably bored. Simic, the giant Croat, was receiving a message from a Highland man mounted on a garron. Just before we reached them, Glenrannoch turned to me. His eyes, always cold and impassive, were alive for once, and full of emotion.

"Matthew," he said, and his tone was imploring, "for all that passed between myself and those whom you love, and who have loved you, I ask you, once again, to trust me in this one thing. I am not your enemy."

He wanted an answer, that much was apparent; but my heart was a labyrinth of confusions, and I could not speak. I turned away.

We began the ride back to the *Jupiter*. There were only four of us, for the two Campbells who had accompanied us on the outward journey had stayed behind. I was sombre, playing over the general's words in my head and setting them against what I knew — or thought I knew. Glenrannoch, too, seemed preoccupied, his eyes turned inwards. Le Blanc rode at our rear, idly studying the rough country around us. Simic, the Croat, was a little way ahead.

We were making our way through a narrow defile when Le Blanc rode up to my side and bent close to my ear. "We are being followed, Captain," he said, very quietly. "Five men, maybe six. I think some of them have ridden round to our right —"

Just then, Glenrannoch called out. "Simic, why this route, man? We would have been better taking the Kilverran road —"

The Croat turned. He had a dagger in his hand. Without a word, he raised it back over his shoulder and then hurled it at the general.

Glenrannoch's horse reared and that saved him. The blade struck his left shoulder. I wheeled around, came to his side, and reached for his horse's reins. He clutched the dagger with his right hand and pulled it from his flesh. "A scratch, man, no more," he said. "Look to our flank!"

324

Three men were scrambling down the side of the defile. They were armed with dirks, the deadly short sword of the Highlands. Two others, mounted and armed with claymores, entered the defile behind us. Up ahead, Simic was drawing his sword. *They could finish us more easily with muskets*, I thought, though of course the roar of flintlocks would have brought half the Campbell host down on them in minutes. They needed a swift, silent killing, the traitor Simic and his men. I unsheathed my own blade, the sword that my father had wielded at Naseby. With blood-soaked fingers, Glenrannoch drew his. Two blades against six . . .

Le Blanc reached inside his large knapsack. He pulled out a glorious jewelled épée, and grinned at me. Then he turned to face the two riders behind us, brandishing the blade with a wicked laugh.

I turned to the men scrambling down the steep bank. Before they could reach the floor of the defile, I charged. There was little space, and they could only leap aside to avoid the crushing weight of my horse. But now they were free to attack, while in so confined a space my beast was slow to turn. I lashed out, down and to the shoulder, but struck nothing. Then one seized my reins from the left. He tried to unhorse me, but I elbowed him in the nose. The one to the right stabbed at me, but he was wary of my whirling sword arm and missed. I had my horse fully around now and slashed at him again. He ducked away from my blade and ran behind to join his fellow. *They would attack together on my weak flank.*

I glimpsed Glenrannoch unhorsed. He was trying to keep his sword arm up as blood oozed from his left shoulder. His opponent had a dirk in each hand and was circling, waiting for his moment, waiting for the wound to weaken him. To my left I could see Le Blanc fighting a cavalry battle in miniature, his blade swinging and his horse moving in unison. Only a man born to the saddle and the sword could fight thus.

Then my opponents attacked again, rushing at my left side. There was no room and no time to turn. I felt a dirk sink into my horse's withers, an inch from my own thigh. The second man stabbed at the beast's neck, but it avoided the blow as it reared in agony. They backed away, ready for their final attack. Then they came again.

I passed my sword into my left hand and swung down, then up.

The first man took the edge of my blade under his right armpit. I felt flesh, and bone, and muscle. I heard his scream as he grasped his half-severed arm. In the same moment, I spurred my horse forward and drove my father's sword hard into the gut of his astonished companion. He sank onto the ground, sliding from my blade, blood and guts falling over his fingers as he tried vainly to close the wound.

I transferred the sword back to my right hand and thanked God yet again that I had first been taught swordsmanship by my uncle, Doctor Tristram Quinton, a left-handed man. Then I looked around for Glenrannoch.

He was still fending off the feints of his opponent, but it was clear he was weakening. My horse was crazed from its wound and would answer the reins no more. I slid from its back and rushed the general's adversary. He turned to meet me, parried with the dirk in his right hand, and thrust with his left. So I faced an equal; another who could fight from either hand. Behind him, I saw Glenrannoch sink to his knees, drop his sword, and grip his bleeding shoulder.

My opponent kept himself between the general and me. He drew back from my every thrust, read every feint. He was good, this one, far better than the filth that I had just despatched. They were rude Scots, but this man had the bearing and the method of a soldier.

I heard hooves behind me, and cursed myself. My opponent had kept my eyes on him, absorbed all my attention. I had forgotten to look behind me where Simic, the traitor, with his sword drawn, must be spurring his horse forward to ride me down —

I dared not turn to face him, for that would put two dirks in my back —

The hooves were almost on me, I could feel the earth shake under my feet. Trampled to death or stabbed to death, only that one choice left —

The roar of the shot drove birds out of the sparse bushes. Simic's horse brushed my left arm as it carried on down the defile, riderless. My opponent stood in front of me, transfixed. He never saw General Colin Campbell of Glenrannoch rise unsteadily from his knees behind him. He would have known of it only in that brief, final moment after the general drove his sword hard into his would-be assassin's back.

I turned, and saw Zoltan Simic lying dead on the floor of the defile, no more than ten feet behind me. The pistol ball had hit him on the upper lip, flattening out as it ripped through his brain and the back of his skull.

I looked for Le Blanc, and there he was, at the rear of the defile. He sat perfectly upright on his horse, his arm raised from the recoil, the pistol still smoking in his hand. I thanked God for the contents of that blessed knapsack. Two bodies lay by him, their blood discolouring the heather, displaying the work that his blade had done.

I raised my father's sword and saluted the man who had saved my life, my fellow warrior.

CHAPTER
NINETEEN

Le Blanc's shot echoed around the glens and hills and brought a mounted and armed party of Campbells to us within minutes. After a few words of explanation from Glenrannoch, some dispersed to set a guard around us; the rest hovered anxiously about their general, and though they murmured in their lilting Gaelic tongue the concern in their voices was unmistakeable.

Glenrannoch himself was clearly weak, but he gave short shrift to our concerns. He had seen enough wounds, he said, to know this one was but a small matter. Once the bleeding was properly stopped it would be of no consequence beyond some days of pain and yet another scar, to add to the two dozen or so that he already bore. Before we could persuade the general to lie down and rest, he insisted on looking upon the body of Zoltan Simic. Glenrannoch seemed little surprised by the Croat's treachery. A soldier of fortune, he said, is loyal only until someone makes him a better offer, and then his loyalty moves seamlessly elsewhere. Le Blanc asked who could have suborned Simic, but Glenrannoch shrugged in the way that men do when they know the answer to a question perfectly well, but do not intend to give it.

As he turned away, Glenrannoch staggered and seemed about to fall. To a man, the Campbells moved towards him, concern softening each warrior's countenance. However it was I who stood nearest; and as I stepped forward, Glenrannoch all but fell into my arms. I helped him to the primitive couch that had been hastily prepared for him from grass, sprigs of heather and the cloaks of almost all his followers. It was not long before he began slipping in and out of consciousness. I sat down on the heather beside him and looked into his ashen face, drawn with pain and etched with something else. Regret, perhaps? The Campbells milled around, watching their leader with anxious faces. He noticed me and pulled me close, out of the hearing of the others.

"Matthew, you must know of the ship . . ." he began, but the effort exhausted him and he closed his eyes. Ten minutes or so passed. I loosened his clothing a little and placed my cloak under his head. When next he stirred, he rambled of secrets and of the king. Then his eyes were focused again, and fixed on me.

"The secrets your mother and I share, Matthew . . ."

The struggle was too much and I hastily told him to rest, to quiet, that we would talk soon, but not now. His hand reach for me and closed around my arm, the grip weak but urgent.

"I tell you, Matthew. It is important." He drew a gasping breath, turned his head away. "The civil war

330

was fought for less . . . *for less* . . ." But he could say no more. His eyes glazed over and he fainted once again.

The general was finally borne away on a litter toward the Tower of Rannoch under a heavy escort of his Campbells. There, he would be attended by his personal physician, a Swede whose life he had saved, and whose loyalty was presumably more assured than that of Zoltan Simic.

As the litter disappeared from sight, I wondered what great secrets Glenrannoch could possibly have shared with my mother. I knew him only a very little, but I was already sure and certain that he was not a man to exaggerate. If he said that the secrets they shared were so dreadful, then that was exactly what they were; and I learned in the fullness of time that he had spoken only the truth. I vowed that I would talk to him of it when this business was done, and I would see to it that he and my mother met once again. Such things were for the future, though, and more immediately, there was a debt of honour to be repaid.

It was with a great sense of foreboding and a sadness I could not quite understand that I turned, at last, to the man whom I had known until recently as Roger Le Blanc: competent tailor, barely competent seaman, abiding enigma. He raised his sword in salute then swept it down and to the right in the French fashion.

I replied in kind. "Monsieur Le Blanc," I said, "My friend. I think it is time to end these charades."

He smiled. "Well, *mon capitaine*, all things end." He rubbed his eyes and face as though wiping away a painted mask. Then he looked at me; his shoulders

331

straightened and his head tilted with pride. "The name I was given at my christening, in the cathedral church of Rouen, was Roger-Louis de la Gaillard-Herblay. I am better known in my lands as the comte d'Andelys."

I bowed deeply, both in deference and in gratitude.

We walked out of the defile and down to the water's edge, not far beyond. There, in the bleak, splendid emptiness that only a Scottish beach can provide, he told me his story.

It was true, he said, that a jealous husband forced him out of France and to his berth on the *Jupiter*. But what he had not said to James Harker, nor to his messmates, nor to me, was that the jealous husband was none other than Nicholas Fouquet, finance minister to the Most Christian King, Louis XIV of France. The gossip at Whitehall held that Monsieur Fouquet was avaricious, jealous and powerful beyond his station. It was hardly a surprise that he should have relentlessly persecuted and pursued the ardent lover of his beautiful but wanton young wife.

Le Blanc — or, as I had now to call him, the comte d'Andelys — slashed at a clump of seaweed with the sword he still held. "I had Fouquet's paid killers in hot pursuit, so I rode hard for the south, the longest route away from my lands, and the one that they might think me least likely to take. I hoped to find a ship for Sicily or Malta. To reach some remote hold where the very name of France was but a dim rumour. But when I reached Toulon, what should I see at anchor but a ship bearing the King of England's flag? And I thought, how perfect! I always had a conceit to see something more of the world than the valley of the Seine, and my king and Monsieur Fouquet would never imagine that a nobleman of France would take to the sea as a common sailor." He laughed. "And on an English ship at that. I don't doubt Captain Harker suspected my motives and my rank, but he was a close man, and forgiving. Once I proved that I could be of use repairing flags, sails and clothes, he questioned me no more."

His talent struck me as extraordinary, and I asked how a great lord of France could possibly have become skilful in such menial work — the work of a woman, if truth be told. The comte replied that his father, too, had been forced into exile, for opposing the mighty Cardinal Richelieu. He had been scratching a living out of a garret in Luxemburg when his eye had fallen on a seamstress in the street below. She proved to be delightful, strong, plain-spoken and astonishingly fertile, and soon she was comtesse d'Andelys. Five years later Richelieu was dead; the old king followed him to the tomb soon afterwards, a general pardon was issued and that poor seamstress of Luxemburg was suddenly installed in the vast, crumbling chateau of Andelys. No part of her good fortune turned her head one whit. For there, she proceeded to teach all of her children, including her husband's heir, how to sew and mend; for as she always said, it would take but a turn of fate to send her progeny back whence she came.

I had enough knowledge of exile, and the extremities to which it forces men of good birth, to sympathize with his tale. But my exile had ended, and I wondered why that of Le Blanc — *le comte* — had not. I asked him whether he had heard the news that came out of France the previous autumn. Fouquet, puffed up in his vanity, had invited the young King Louis to his glorious new chateau of Vaux-le-Viscomte. Louis XIV had looked around the magnificent gardens, marvelled at the splendours of the house — and wondered where, exactly, his finance minister had found the money to create such a paradise. Within weeks, Fouquet was cast into the first of a series of dreary prisons; and twenty years later — long after that day when the comte d'Andelys and I walked along that bleak Scottish beach — King Louis was finally to complete a chateau to surpass Fouquet's. It stands to this day, and remains a wonder of royal magnificence. It is called Versailles.

"Oh, indeed, I knew of Fouquet's disgrace, and raised more than several tankards of your excellent Hull ale to toast it," said my new friend. "I know also that his successor is a certain Monsieur Colbert, who was always a good friend to my father. But the court of France is a viper's nest, Captain, and I am still unsure of the reception I would receive there." He looked out to sea, toward the mastheads of the *Jupiter*, just visible over a low peninsula. "And, if truth be told, I have been reluctant to part with my new life. There are no comforts, no servants to tend my every whim; but there is something beyond all that. I have come to know a bond with my fellow men that few of our rank ever experience, I think. These last months, I have borne no responsibilities, had no troubles with tenants and harvests, felt no concern for the doings of kings or courts or great ladies. I have sung and laughed, worked hard and got drunk. I have played dice with the bastard sons of farmhands. What is more, I have come to love the sea. I have taken something of a fancy to the notion of captaining a man-of-war, in fact." Then he turned, clapped me on the back and laughed. "So who knows? One day we may sail together, *mon ami*."

I laughed too, but was mindful of the long and torturous history between England and France. "Or, of course, we may fight against each other too, my lord."

"Let us pray not, Matthew Quinton," said Roger, comte d'Andelys. "Let us pray not." We walked on, and were both silent for a minute or more. Then Roger, comte d'Andelys, turned to me, and said gravely, "We are men of lineage and honour, Captain Quinton. But there is something beyond those things, powerful though they are. There is contentment. Here, on the *Jupiter*, I have been content." He looked out, beyond the beach, to the islands and the distant ocean. "But I think that contentment is ended now, Matthew."

Back aboard there was much talk and not a little amusement at the sudden transformation of our French sailmaker's mate into a fully-fledged nobleman. Lanherne, Polzeath and the rest of his friends made much of carrying his sea chest and knapsack in some state from his mess on the main deck to Purser Peverell's cabin, now that of the comte d'Andelys. Whatever he thought in private of his enforced move — and I have no doubt that it was murderous — Peverell could hardly challenge the will of a captain who had ample evidence to bring him to a court-martial, should he choose; nor could he quite refrain from an unseemly obsequiousness when dealing with the suddenly ennobled sailmaker. With bad grace and peremptory rudeness, he ejected his mates from their pestilential cabin on the orlop deck and retreated in silent indignation into his new abode.

Le Blanc was greeted by a marked new deference from my officers. It is strange how this putting on of a title changes the way men see other men. Malachi Landon bowed and scraped as though he was in the presence of royalty; James Vyvyan was positively in awe, and even Phineas Musk became ten times more deferential than I had ever seen him before, despite the fact that *le comte* was actually my brother's equal in rank. Only the Reverend Gale treated him the same, but perhaps this should have been expected from a man who referred to His Grace the Archbishop of Canterbury as Old Bill Juxon.

I summoned a council of my officers to discuss the death of Nathan Warrender, the attack on Campbell of Glenrannoch, the whereabouts of the mystery man-of-war and the continued absence of Captain Judge and the *Royal Martyr*. I had suspicions and theories of my own to put to them, and although I valued the judgement of some of them not a jot, I hoped to hear something worthwhile from Vyvyan, Gale, Farrell and the comte d'Andelys, who would now automatically join our council by virtue of his honour and rank.

An hour before we were due to convene, there was a knock at my cabin door. I had been staring out the

336

window, watching the gulls in the distance and thinking over the events of the day, but at the knock I turned swiftly to my chart table, took up a quill, and only then called "enter". Kit Farrell had brought young Macferran to me. There was a ship, he said, lying off Ardverran Castle, unloading a great cargo. I asked him if this was a man-of-war, slightly larger than the *Jupiter*, built high at the stern after the Dutch fashion and painted a dark colour. No, he said. He had seen enough ships of different sorts pass through these seas, or take shelter in these roadsteads. The ship off Ardverran was but an ordinary fly-boat, the common sort of vessel used by the Dutch in the northern seas: wide, full in the hull, and carrying as small a crew as possible to undercut their rivals' costs and elevate the owners' profits. I wished to see for myself, so Kit and I climbed down into Macferran's boat, pulled over to the beach, and climbed up to the old Pictish fort.

There it was, at double anchor off the jetty at Ardverran. The young Scot had made no mistake. It was not the ship I had seen from Lady Macdonald's birlinn. I squinted my eyes against the sun, which was already well to the west, and scanned the waters and the islands for as far as I could see. Of *Royal Martyr* and the mystery ship, there was no sign at all.

But at Ardverran Castle, all was bustle. Three birlinns kept up a continuous ferry to and from the jetty, where a chain of men unloaded large sacks and bundles, passing them from man to man up to the castle gate. There could be no doubt. These were the arms bought in Flanders, supposedly for the cause of

Campbell of Glenrannoch. A false intelligence — one fit to bring about a war. For my eyes told me what my heart had known for the past day. The arms were bound for Macdonald, and my lady of Connaught.

Yet I did not want it to be true.

"Macferran," I said, "did not the countess order a Macdonald guard up here, and on all the other heights round about?"

He looked puzzled and shook his tousled head. "No, sir, Captain. All day I have sat here, and in that time I've seen nor hide nor hair of any dampnit Macdonald." He spat. "Begging your pardon, sir, Captain."

"But the other heights, Macferran. What of them?" I asked.

"Well, sir, Captain, I can't speak for them all, seeing as I was sat here. My cousin was up Ben Britheamh this morning, though," and he pointed away to the greater hill to the north, "and it was bare."

As it would be. Protecting the *Jupiter* was hardly what the countess was about.

Kit Farrell said, "If we stay at anchor where we are, Captain, we're in a killing ground. If your mystery ship comes down that channel with the wind in her favour, the *Jupiter* will be good only for stoking Satan's fires."

Back aboard the *Jupiter* I gave my orders in swift succession, with as confident a demeanour as I could muster. It was not a confidence that I felt within, however. Indeed my stomach seemed to be playing leap-frog with my heart. The pieces were falling into

338

place, but too late; I had not been prepared for this and I was angry with myself.

I beckoned to James Vyvyan. "Mister Vyvyan, you will please go down to Ardverran Castle in Lanherne's boat, flying a flag of truce. You will present my compliments to the Countess of Connaught and inform her that Captain Quinton of the *Jupiter* is pleased to accept her invitation to sup at Ardverran. Immediately."

The ship's boat delivered me to the jetty at Ardverran just as the sun began to sink toward the islands to the west. All was quiet. I could hear the gulls, and the splash of the oars. Nothing more. Where I had observed fevered activity when I looked from the old fort, now there was none. The fly-boat lay at double anchor a few hundred yards away, but there was no man to be seen on her. The jetty itself was deserted, as was the path up to the castle. I left my boat crew there, giving Lanherne orders that they should shift for themselves at the slightest sign of danger.

I felt a strange mixture of fear and determination. Several on the *Jupiter* had felt compelled to remonstrate with me. Francis Gale and James Vyvyan described my scheme as madness. Kit Farrell begged me to think again. Phineas Musk bemoaned the fact that the imminent slaughter of Captain Quinton would leave him unemployed and prey to the whims of the dreadful Scots. Even the comte d'Andelys urged me to take a stout party of armed seamen for protection.

I will have protection enough, I told them, and hoped in my heart that I was right.

I strode into the courtyard of Ardverran Castle and once again took the steps up to the hall. In contrast to my previous visit it was silent and empty. Empty, but for the great table, laid for two; empty, but for the Lady Niamh, Countess of Connaught, who sat at one end.

I bowed. "My lady."

She wore a gown of imperial purple, cut low in the bosom, with a gold crucifix on a long chain around her white neck. She seemed regal and yet incredibly delicate — as though at one careless gesture she might vanish. She was even more splendid than at my first sight of her, here in the hall of Ardverran. I thought to myself then that perhaps the greatest beauty is always the handmaiden of the greatest danger.

Even as I looked at her she studied me with her green eyes; eyes as cold now as they had been bright, penetrating and playful during our last afternoon together. After a long, silent moment she bade me sit, and two attendants emerged from the curtains at the end of the hall to serve us.

"Captain Quinton. Your belated acceptance of my invitation was unexpected, if I may say so. And on Good Friday. I would have expected you to be busy with the offices of the cross, sir."

"A thousand pardons. I trust that I have not torn you from your devotions?" She smiled coldly at that but said nothing. Her servant laid the choicest morsels on her plate with tortuous circumspection, then retired, bowing.

I looked around the hall, at the old armour, swords and pikes that adorned the wall. My attendant laid a dish of rabbit before me and filled my glass with wine. If she wanted me dead, I thought, this was the moment for poison. But I had come too far to baulk now, and I still believed my reading of this woman.

"A fine display of arms, my lady. But I see your latest weapons are not for public display."

I drank, took a mouthful of meat. The rabbit was well cooked and in no way lethal, the wine tolerable and not fatal.

"You are speaking in riddles, Captain," she said, guardedly, "and I have no time —"

"Enough, my lady."

To interrupt was an unforgivable rudeness back then, though it is common enough these days. The countess did not betray the slightest discomfort, however. She merely drank from her goblet then laid it back upon the table, watching me.

"It is time for plain-speaking between us, and you have deluded me long enough, I think. I shall be your fool no more, my Lady Niamh." It was the first time I had used her true name, and she startled. I pressed on. "I know about the cargo that ship at your jetty has brought you. Five thousand muskets, two thousand pikes, swords and cannon. Enough for an army. For your Macdonald army, my lady. Paid for by your uncle, Cardinal O'Daragh, and his close friend, the pope."

She seemed to look at me anew, then. Her radiant face was impassive and calculating. "You are better informed than I had expected, Matthew."

"Not informed enough, my lady. You sought to kill me, along with Campbell of Glenrannoch, this morning —"

"That was not done by my order!" and she brought her fist down hard, striking a platter which skittered loudly across the table. Her retainer stepped forward nervously at that, but she waved him away without turning her head.

"And to what purpose? To bring down Clan Campbell, and take back all the lands they once took from you? Do you really think the king will allow you to do that? Oh, it will take him time, my lady. But he will call up the militia, and send a far greater fleet than just these two ships. You will be brought low —"

She laughed in scorn, shook that flame-red hair of hers, and cried mockingly, "No, not informed at all, Matthew Quinton! Mary, Mother of Heaven, forgive me! Do you truly believe I would risk so much just to overthrow the Campbells? Do you truly believe I would risk so much if I thought that Charles Stuart could snap his fingers and bring us low as you say?" She stood up and grasped the edge of the table, then leaned towards me, knuckles whitening. "There are far greater things afoot here than Macdonald against Campbell, Captain. Far greater things than Charles Stuart knows, or can prevent."

Then she began to walk slowly down the hall towards me. I watched her, trying hard not to be touched by her beauty. That calm face, the proud bearing, the hair touched by gold in the firelight. It was a bewitching sight.

"The Lordship of the Isles will be restored, Captain. My son's inheritance, confirmed as an independent state by the pope, under the protection of the Dutch."

I stared at her. The Lordship of the Isles? The pope and the Dutch? This was impossible. Her words had no meaning. She was mad, or I was mad, or else I had dreamt the entire voyage of the *Jupiter*. Yes. I would awake in my bed in Ravensden Abbey, with the rain leaking through the ceiling as it always did, and Cornelia lying by my side as she always did, and all would be well again.

I shook my head. Thoughts raced against others, thoughts that proclaimed me awake, and sane. The pope and the Dutch, Catholic and Protestant, would never combine to put a new state here, on the edge of Europe, I thought. I tried to comprehend the enormity of her words, her ambition. The Lordship of the Isles was long dead, a corpse in its grave, far beyond resurrection, and for most of the last one hundred years the Dutch had fought for their very survival against Catholic armies that sought to annihilate them; armies sanctioned, and sometimes paid for, by the pope. No. *No*, my sense argued, looking at the impassive, beautiful face drawing closer and closer, this was not merely impossible, it was an affront to everything I knew to be true: *the pope and the Dutch*.

Then I recalled my own years as a guest of Holland. I thought about what I had learned from the van der Eide family and their neighbours. The Dutch saw no dilemma in tolerating Catholics within their borders, or in forming an alliance with the pope himself, as long as those actions brought them profit. For with the Dutch, business was all; and with all its wealth, the Church of Rome was an attractive business partner. His Holiness Pope Alexander the Seventh, of the great banking house of Chigi, would be doubly so, perhaps. That being the case . . .

"The Dutch would gain havens for their trade and fisheries, safe harbours in the event of another war with England," I said slowly, thinking aloud. "A base from which to attack deep into the king's lands in any future war between us. And if they gain all that, the Dutch will not care a jot whether their puppet Lords of the Isles are Catholic, Protestant, or Mahometan."

My lady nodded and smiled, as a teacher does when a particularly backward pupil has finally grasped a fundamental notion.

The Lords of the Isles restored. It seemed madness — but then, that truly was an age where madness was in vogue and where new states were being born every day. I thought of Portugal, the newest kingdom in Europe, a folly that would nevertheless shortly give England its new queen. Back then, I remember now, Brandenburg was a mere swamp amid the dank forests in the east of Germany; today they call it the Kingdom of Prussia, and our present fat King George fears its armies more than he fears the horsemen of the Apocalypse. Even then, as a young man, the map of Europe had been drawn and redrawn several times over in my short lifetime, in treaty after treaty. New kings had risen up, old lands had vanished, and new states had been born — all because the likes of the pope and

344

the Dutch willed it so. Just as they now willed a kingdom for the Lady Niamh's son, it seemed. No . . . it was not total madness.

"But the king will not stand for such an affront," I said, for I had to speak, to say something. "You could hardly give him better cause to start the war against the Dutch that he seeks —"

She was standing by me now, only inches away; I could smell the scent of her body, sweet like gorse, salty and fresh. I looked up, and in the flickering light of that hall she seemed two different people. One was imperious and magnificent, every inch the future Queen Regent of this new land. Then the shadows would pass over her firegold hair and pale, smooth skin and she would seem, all at once, a creature fey and unnatural.

"Let me offer you an alternative history, Captain," she said, her voice as harsh as the gulls that wheeled and called outside her castle. "Your King Charles is already weak. A foolish man, he has alienated his own supporters, the Macdonalds among them." She paused, raised her hands angrily and then dropped them, sighing. "It is so much more than a matter of who has or has not got back their land, Matthew. Many compare your king with the great days of Cromwell, and find him wanting. You know this. Cromwell made Europe tremble. Charles Stuart is its laughing stock." Her words were hideous, unbearable; doubly so, that I knew them to be true.

"Can you imagine what they will do in Whitehall and London when our little scheme comes to pass,

Matthew Quinton? You know the politics there better than I. We succeed, and a Catholic state, protected by the guns of the Dutch, is carved out of the west of Scotland." She bent close to me and I felt her breath against my ear. "Think of the humiliation, the disgrace. A Stuart king who cannot even preserve intact the Scottish kingdom that he inherited? The old Puritans, those who served Cromwell — many others will rise up. There will be a great host, Matthew. All those who look on your king as a whoring incompetent, and I'm told that's most of the people of England. They will throw him back across the sea, Matthew, or send him to the block, as they did his father."

I knew there was truth in what she said. I knew it in my heart as well as my head. But my father had fought and died for a Stuart king; a man who was weak, inept, but still the king. Perhaps it was my turn to do the same. Yes. I knew in that moment that I would fight for my king until my dying breath, just as my father had. What else could I do? It was my duty, my being, and my God-given honour. It was my family and it was my life. I had no choice. And yet, at that instant, I chose.

I took a draught of the wine and looked hard into Niamh Campbell's blazing green eyes. Time to begin that fight; time, at last, to confront her, and the full depth of her dread conspiracy.

"Is that what Captain Judge has led you to believe, my lady?"

She stepped back, her eyes wide and her lips parted.

"Is that informed enough for you, Lady Niamh?" I stood and drew myself up to the considerable height that came with the Quinton blood. "Oh yes, I know Godsgift Judge is a traitor. But there's one thing that stopped me believing it, and not even your tale of the Lordship of the Isles reborn explains it. Whatever kind of foul turncoat Godsgift Judge may be, my lady, he's no papist. If he's still a Commonwealth's-man at heart, and a fanatic, who fooled us all with his clothes and his flattery, then so be it. But a man like that will not aid your cardinal uncle, nor truck with the pope, his friend, to set up a papist state in these parts."

There was a moment of utter silence. Then she looked at me levelly, calmly. When she spoke, her voice was quiet but strong.

"What man would not seek a kingdom for his own son?"

CHAPTER
TWENTY

His own son.

A wave of nausea drove my senses into the pit of my stomach. I reached for the arm of my chair, found it at the second attempt, and sat down. Lady Macdonald stood in front of me, at once more desirable than any being I had ever known and more treacherous. And she spoke.

I heard her words, not hostile, not triumphant, as she told briefly of her hopeless marriage. Sir Callum Macdonald of Ardverran had brutalized her. At first it had been occasional, almost accidental. But as time passed, it seemed to become his means of raging against her failure to give him an heir. The oldest and proudest bloodline in all of Scotland would die because of her, he claimed. His anguished revenge took many forms, and she endured them all, whether mental or physical. She had been so very young — so full of hope and life — when she arrived at Ardverran. She thought she would change her husband, or that she would get with child and become, suddenly, the cherished mother of the Macdonald heir. But after many years darkened by barrenness, cruelty and violence she came to

348

understand that life as Macdonald's wife would forever be unendurable.

Then Glencairn's rebellion against Cromwell began, and Macdonald went away to fight in the south of Scotland. Only days later, an English naval squadron sailed into the sea off Ardverran to act against that same rebellion, and an English naval captain came to pay his compliments at the castle. Godsgift Judge, without his false trappings of foppery, was strong, attentive and kind. He warded off a raid by the vengeful Campbells and protected and comforted the Lady Niamh. A bond grew between them, the Puritanical sea captain and the papist countess, thrown together by fate in a castle at the edge of the world. Whether that bond was ever love, she was not certain; or so she said. But for two people far from their own homes, in a place where hostile forces ranged against both of them, it was sufficient. And before long there was conclusive proof that the Lady Niamh's failure to conceive an heir to Ardverran was entirely the fault of her husband.

Judge's ship was cruising some miles to the south when Sir Callum Macdonald returned to Ardverran. He had been wounded as Glencairn's forlorn cause collapsed against the invincible armies of the Lord Protector. Too weak to beat his wife as his healthy self might have done, Ardverran raged impotently against her. Only the discreet loyalty of Macdonald of Kilreen, the only man who knew what had passed, kept her safe. Fearing for her unborn child when her condition became clear, she got word to Judge. He decided, in the name of Cromwell and with his heart bent upon the preservation of his woman and child, to deal once and for all with that known malignant, Sir Callum Macdonald. Judge's story of the fight at the gun battery was true enough, she said, except for one vital detail.

"Callum's death was no honourable death. His battery had already surrendered, expecting quarter. But Godsgift Judge was determined that Macdonald of Ardverran would die that day. He executed him, Captain. In the name of the Republic. But in truth, it was a punishment for the wrongs done to me, and to protect our unborn child." Her eyes were deadly cold yet I saw tears there. Tears that remained unshed. "I forgave what he had done, Captain," she said. "And I have thanked him silently for it every day that has passed."

Judge's ship stayed long enough for him to see his son born, she said, and the child was accepted without question by that part of Clan Donald as their new chief, Sir Ian, baronet of Ardverran. For Judge, it must have seemed a fair consolation for a man who knew he would never see his son grow up.

A fair consolation, perhaps, until a far greater one came within view.

A kingdom for his own son.

It was an unreal time, that hour in the great hall of Ardverran Castle. I sat unmoving in my chair, for if my mind could not cope with the enormity of her words, what chance had my limbs? All that time, she paced the hall, sometimes circling me, sometimes stopping so close that I could study the rosary that nestled upon her bosom. There was nothing to do but talk. I wanted the truth, so my questions were unvarnished. But I sensed that she needed to explain, to justify it all to herself as much as to me. Perhaps she, too, felt that in another time, when such a mighty scheme had not already been in train, matters might have stood differently between the heir of Ravensden and the Countess Niamh. So we talked with the openness and honesty of those who know that they have not known each other well enough, and will have no other chance, for they will never know each other again.

I asked when the conspiracy had first formed, and at whose hand. "Like most of his kind, the Puritan swordsmen, my Captain Judge saw the return of your king as the end all of his hopes for a better world, of all that he had fought for. Like so many of them, he admitted defeat and surrendered himself to your new royal order, swearing the Oaths of Allegiance and Supremacy with bile in his throat."

I had witnessed it myself: the lackeys, the time-servers and the fanatics, all competing with each other to find a tame lawyer or cleric to testify to their undying loyalty to king and Church. It was strange to think of Godsgift Judge among that unholy rabble.

"At first, his attempts to ingratiate himself with you Cavaliers were real enough. Then, when he saw how readily Charles Stuart trusted those who had so recently fought against him and how blindly intent he was on reconciliation, he began to conceive a great scheme. He wrote to me secretly, and I in turn wrote to my uncle. All this is Judge's doing, Matthew, even if the money comes from Rome and Amsterdam. And now we even have the tacit support of Spain, thanks to your king's idiotic choice of a Portuguese bride — the one marriage above all that could give mortal offence to the court of King Philip. Yes, Matthew. The Lordship of the Isles for the son of Godsgift Judge, triggering a revolution in England to bring down your feeble king. That is how it will be."

I resisted her still, though I felt the cold grip of fear in my bones. It seemed both preposterous and yet perfectly likely to succeed. "Glenrannoch will stand against you," I said. "I will stand against you."

"Not even the good general and his Campbells will be able to withstand the army we will shortly put into the field. And, dear Matthew, there will soon be a Dutch army to uphold our new independence. So you see, I am not afraid of you, either." And with that, she stooped and kissed me.

The Dutch? It all hinged on them. And I knew the Dutch. Something in what she was saying was not right, but I could not place it. I knew the Dutch, I knew their country and the perverse way in which they organized it. My wife was Dutch, her brother commanded a ship for the Dutch, Glenrannoch had been a general for the Dutch, I had lived among the Dutch . . .

Of course. Yes, I was informed enough, at last.

I found my strength again and stood. I looked down at her, so tall and slender in the firelight; then I made my best bow, a courtier's flourish at the end. "I must congratulate you, my lady. What you have achieved — gaining the support of the whole of the States-General

— I had thought impossible. All of their high mightinesses together? Truly, this is so unlike the Dutch way, where one province seems always driven to spite another, that I am amazed." Her face, the way she clasped her hands together, told me that I had hit home. I stood looking at her and my smile fell away. "I know the Dutch, my lady. Give them any proposition, and they will divide, as sure as the sun rises and sets. They are not a state, they are a confusion, and you have the support of only a fraction."

Every plot, every great conspiracy in history, has some flaw, some fatal weakness; its success or failure depends on whether that flaw reveals itself in a timely fashion. This was their flaw, my countess and her lover, for their whole scheme depended on a state that was not a state, but a hydra. Even so, she recovered herself quickly.

"Our support is sufficient, Captain. The plot is secret enough, and will be executed swiftly. More swiftly than you realize."

She beckoned to me and led me up the spiral staircase, until at last we emerged onto the roof of Ardverran's ancient tower.

There was the *Jupiter*, off to the east, bearing down slowly and according to my orders. Her quarry, the arms ship, lay silent and empty off the jetty of Ardverran. And now, too late, I saw her for what she truly was. Bait.

For there, behind the *Jupiter*, emerging from the channel and edging round the headland, was the unmistakeable shape of the *Royal Martyr*. Unmistakeable but for two stark alterations: her royal figurehead had been decapitated, just as its mortal namesake — the late King Charles the First — had been. And the flags that she flew were at once strange and dreadfully familiar. Two of the four quarters bore the red cross against a white background, the sign of St George; the other two the white cross on blue of St Andrew. They were the colours of an older and deadlier Britain, when England and Scotland had been brought together as one by the force of Oliver Cromwell's arms.

I knew her for what she was. She was the *Royal Martyr* no more. At last, she bore the name, and the flags, of her true master.

She was the *Republic* again.

The lady moved to my side. My treacherous countess rested her fingers on my arm, but I stepped abruptly away from her.

"You are still my guest, Matthew," she said gently. "The old way and the old laws abide here at Ardverran of the ages. You knew that when you came here tonight; knew that you were safe under the roof of one who had invited you. And you were right. I will not see my guest harmed. You may remain here, or I will see to it that you are taken in safety to England."

"And what will safety be, without honour?" I could not help the bitterness in my voice. "I am the captain of that ship. I am responsible for the one hundred and thirty souls on her. I must account for them to God, and to the king that your precious Captain Judge has forsaken."

She looked at me then with sadness. "Your *Jupiter* is doomed, Matthew. Judge tells me that you have fewer guns than he, and lesser men manning them. You are no match for him. His ship will destroy yours." Her hand reached out, her fingers found mine. "Go back to her, and you are killing yourself."

I hated her, then, for the first time. "We Quintons know how to fight and die in doomed causes. I will put my trust in God and my men. With your leave, my lady?"

I stepped back and then bowed, more in mockery than courtesy. I could see the tears in her eyes, but I think she had long practice in preventing their further passage.

"Take your leave, then, Matthew. Take your leave, and die."

I stood still a while longer, though. I looked at her without modesty or decorum, for I knew I would never see her again. I studied that face, so pale, and her hair, blowing in the wind toward the sun that claimed it for its own. I looked at her, all the way to her feet, and wished in that moment that fate had not driven us to this. She was the most beautiful woman I ever met in my whole life.

I bowed my head, as one does at the graveside of a loved one. And then I turned, and left her.

Lanherne and his crew were still loyally at the jetty, though all of them were looking eastward toward the two ships. They rowed me back to the *Jupiter*, where silent sailors lined the deck, looking for direction from their captain. I climbed the steps up the ship's side and moved through them to the quarterdeck, where Vyvyan, Landon, Gale, Stanton and Kit Farrell awaited me. The *Royal Martyr* — the *Republic* — was perhaps still half a mile away and closing only slowly on the light south-westerly winds. But there was no time for a council of war, and no time for an explanation.

I told them briefly that judge was our enemy now, his ship flying Cromwell's flags and intent on our destruction. I ordered our decks cleared and could soon hear the hammering and clattering beneath as the partitions of the cabins, my own included, were dismantled to give us an unimpeded gun deck for the whole length of the ship. Next, I would order the larboard guns manned.

Then Kit Farrell came to find me. Very quietly so no others could hear, he admonished me.

"The men will need an explanation, sir. You can't order them into battle against their own people and not tell them why."

He was right. Many of the crew were still milling around on the main deck, talking quietly among themselves, glancing up at the quarterdeck. Boatswain Ap and his mates moved among them, but they, too, were at a loss. I drew a breath, then climbed onto the quarterdeck rail, clinging to a shroud for balance.

To a man, the crew crowded up before the bulkhead and looked towards me, expectation and fear rivalling each other in their eyes. I tried to imagine the words that my grandfather must have said, as he ordered his own crew against the impregnable crescent formation of the great Armada. I tried to imagine my father's words on Naseby field, as he prepared his troopers to charge against the distant line of Parliament's cavalry. Then, by what means I knew not, I needed to imagine no more. I looked out, over my crew, and spoke to them.

"Men, the ship we knew as *Royal Martyr* is lost to us. She's the *Republic* again, and we face her in what, God willing, will be the last battle of our country's civil wars. At the end of this battle, I would see that ship bearing her name of honour again, the name of the blessed King Charles the First." Some of the officers nodded gravely. "I am not a man who knows the sea well. You all know that. But I come from a bloodline that knows how to fight, and the king himself entrusted me with this ship. I intend to do my duty to him, and to my name. So, boys, do your duty too, and even if you don't do it for me, then do it for these others." I drew my sword, and brought it up to my face in salute to these, my men. I shouted, "For God, for the King, and for Cornwall!"

The crew took up my cry, repeating it five or six times. I saw even Ali Reis, the Mahometan, screaming his loyalty to a God he did not serve, and Carvell, the blackamoor, in tears as he pledged himself to Cornwall, a land three thousand miles from his home.

Then young James Vyvyan stepped up to me and drew his own sword to return my salute. "Captain," he said, too quietly for any apart from the others on the quarterdeck to hear, "we have not always concurred, but from the moment you came aboard this ship — and contrary to what you might have believed — you have had the loyalty and respect of every man on the lower deck." Then Vyvyan turned, flung up his sword arm and cried loudly, "Cornwall was true to the last king and to this one, sir, and every Cornishman knows that no man died better in the late king's cause than your father. It is an honour, and a privilege, for us to serve and die alongside the heir to Ravensden."

He turned to the assembled crew and gave them the cry.

"For Captain Quinton, and Ravensden!"

And they cheered.

Then Francis Gale stepped forward, for it was time now to address ourselves to the only authority that could save us. I went to the larboard side, hoping they would think I had gone to study the approaching *Republic* once more. In truth, I hoped that by turning away, I would hide the tears that ran down my face.

"O most powerful and glorious Lord God, that rulest and commandest all things," Gale began, his voice carrying over our silent and respectful crew to the waters beyond. "Thou sittest in the throne judging right, and therefore we make our address to Thy Divine Majesty in this our necessity, that Thou wouldest take the cause into Thine own hand, and judge between us and our enemies. Stir up Thy strength, O Lord, and come and help us; for Thou givest not away the battle to the strong, but canst save by many or by few." He glanced toward the oncoming *Republic*, and I saw not a few of our men raise their eyes from their prayers and do the same. "O let not our sins now cry against us for vengeance; but hear us Thy poor servants begging mercy, and imploring Thy help, and that Thou wouldest be a defence unto us against the face of the enemy." Gale paused, and lifted his eyes from the text of the prayer book, extemporizing as he did so. "Lord God, grant us peace from the merciless rage of civil war, and bring us safe in the fullness of time to thy heavenly harbour. O Lord in Thy mercy, bring us the victory. Amen."

The crew echoed the *amen* lustily, not a few of them suddenly discovering a need to cross themselves after the popish fashion. At that moment, James Vyvyan stepped forward once more, offered me his hand, and saluted.

"Your commands, Captain Quinton?"

I bowed. Then I straightened and held out my hand. He did not pause, but reached out and shook it.

"I think I have little need to give commands this day, Mister Vyvyan," I said. "All men know their stations, and know their duty. The rest is with God. May He be with you today, James."

He smiled. "And with you, Matthew."

And then Vyvyan turned and simply nodded to the assembled company below us. The warrant and petty officers, in their turns, did the same. At those silent commands, all became commotion, but now it was commotion with a purpose. Our trumpeters and drummer roared out the music of defiance. The guns on the upper deck were manned, and I could hear the shutters of the gunports on the main deck swing open as the larboard guns ran out. Men climbed into the rigging to take in all but our fighting sails: the main, fore and foretop. Others played out the waist-cloth — the yard-wide red cloth fastened around the whole of the ship's rail to conceal our men from the enemy's small arms.

I turned back to James Vyvyan; he, Malachi Landon, and Kit Farrell were the only officers left on the quarterdeck.

"Mister Vyvyan," I said, "we will hoist our ensign and pendants, if you please. The king's ensign."

"By your leave, sir, Captain Harker also brought aboard a flag for which he had a particular affection, as do I and most of the crew. Saint Piran's cross. The flag of Cornwall. Do I have your permission to hoist it at the mizzen, Captain?"

"By all means, Mister Vyvyan. Let Judge and his traitors know exactly who it is that they fight."

Our ensign raced aloft, and at the mizzenmast head the white cross on black broke out proudly, to a great cheer from the men on the upper deck. Thus we waited for the *Republic* to come down to us. We could have tried to escape, but that would have driven us under the guns of Ardverran and the arms ship, and Lady Macdonald's hospitality did not extend to unmanning them. Rather than be trapped in a crossfire, I preferred to wait, and take my chances against Godsgift Judge, ship to ship.

Musk appeared at my side, carrying the body armour that my father had worn to his death at Naseby and which (since Charles shunned the inheritance) had become my own. He fastened it around my chest, then stepped back and contemplated me.

360

"Well, Captain, it's come to this, then. I saw your grandfather buried, and your father. Not that I'll see you join them, for today the reaper comes for old Musk, I fear."

Reaper or no, Musk took his place at my side then, for whatever else he was, he was no coward. He carried two pistols and a dagger in his belt, and I knew that he would use them to protect me before himself.

I looked out over the deck. My men were ready at their guns, the barrels shotted and awaiting only the gun captains' linstocks to fire the charge. James Vyvyan moved between the gun crews in his station forward of the mainmast, uttering words of encouragement. There was our unofficial new recruit, Macferran, who had somehow not gone ashore when he should, standing instead among the lads who ran powder and shot from the magazine up to the guns. There were Polzeath, Trenance and Treninnick, all manning one gun in the middle of the ship. Carvell in the gun crew next to them turned and smiled, for he had caught sight of their old messmate, the comte d'Andelys. The Frenchman had climbed up to the quarterdeck, his sword drawn and ready, eager to write another bloody chapter in the illustrious annals of his ancient line. Kit Farrell was by my side, as he had been at the death of the *Happy Restoration* — and since. His eyes moved constantly between our sails, the shore and the *Republic*, calculating wind, tide, and distance. *As was I.*

Suddenly, John Treninnick began to sing. His words were English, learned by rote. His gun crew joined in, then the rest of the upper deck. I could hear the refrain taken up on the deck below. This singing was low, almost mournful. It was the sailor's ancient song of leave-taking, "Loth to Depart".

The bow guns of the *Republic* fired.

The sound of glass and wood shattering told me that Judge's guns had found their mark. Musk hurried below to examine the damage. Before he could return, our enemy's bow guns fired again. Two balls smashed into our hull, a little ahead of the quarter gallery. I heard a scream, and knew that we had our first casualty. I hoped it was not Musk.

"Mister Stanton!" I cried. "Stern chasers will fire, if you please. Chainshot, high for his rigging!"

"Aye, aye, Captain!"

Judge had no interest in firing at our masts and rigging, ever the tactic of the weaker ship trying to disable her opponent so she could escape. Judge had learned his warfare in the floating slaughters that were the English battles with the Dutch: fire straight into the hulls of the weaker, lighter Dutch ships. As were we, now, weaker and lighter against his weight of broadside. The *Republic* could send over five hundred pounds of shot at us a time. We could fire less than half that, even if we could fire it all at once and in the right direction.

Jupiter's two stern guns fired. One shot missed the *Republic* entirely, the other passed harmlessly through her foresail. I ordered a reload, to fire again when ready. *Republic* fired again first, long before we were ready. Two more shots struck us somewhere in the stern. Stanton sent word that one of the stern chasers was blown off its carriage. Our second gun fired. A second hole appeared in Judge's foresail, but the *Republic* sailed relentlessly on. Within minutes, she would be alongside us and able to bring almost her whole starboard battery to bear.

I shouted to our crew, "Hold fire, lads! Once she's up with us, we'll give her a good Cornish broadside!"

The men on the larboard guns cheered feebly. They all knew this bravado for what it was. They all knew what they could do with a broadside. They all knew what the *Republic*'s gun crews could do with theirs.

As her bow came by our stern, *Republic*'s foremost starboard guns fired, wreaking further havoc in the remains of my cabin. We were shrouded in smoke now, the acrid fog that obscures all naval battles. Our trumpeters and drummer kept up their warlike symphony, but there was fear in their eyes. One of Skeen's mates came up with reports that we already had three men dead. Three more were mutilated, one by a great splinter of oak in his guts. One of Penbaron's crew reported that the rudder was damaged, but would still answer the whipstaff. As the smoke swirled, I looked, down on the upper deck, and saw Vyvyan. He was tireless, shouting at the gun crews, encouraging the men, bending to assist. As he worked forward, his companion worked aft. It took me a moment to recognize him. Sword in hand, encouraging the crews and swearing defiance with the foulest of oaths, was the Reverend Francis Gale.

We had to fire first. We had the smallest of hopes against a greater ship and a better crew. If we fired first, and high, with a mix of round and chain shot, we might just bring down one of her masts. Better, a lucky shot might take the head off Godsgift Judge.

I could see him, at last, on his quarterdeck. The fine clothes and the face paint were gone now. He stood there, dark and impassive, in a plain tunic, his head bare. He seemed to be giving no orders, but then I supposed he had no need to. The *Republic*'s men had been well trained for this moment. Judge knew what was to come.

He saw me at that moment, and seemed to smile. I lifted my voice trumpet, and shouted, "Give fire!"

The after half of our larboard battery fired. It was better than our dumb-show practice off Islay. Our fire was almost together, and a grey cloud of smoke drifted back over us. The shroud parted a little, and Roger d'Andelys called out eagerly.

"You have hit her, Captain! Bravo, *mes braves!*"

But Kit Farrell was studying the *Republic* too. "A little damage to her rigging. Some shot through her mainsail. A couple of balls in the hull. She's hardly scratched, Captain."

I could see Godsgift Judge with his sword raised. I looked down at my deck, at the men of my ship. They, and I, were about to die. Judge's sword arm fell, and with one almighty roar, the gates of Hell opened.

CHAPTER
TWENTY-ONE

I was blind a moment before I was deaf, and that a moment before I was dead.

The *Republic*'s starboard broadside, fired all in unison, was truly a thing from Hell. Flame and smoke bellowed from twenty-two great guns. The roar of their fire outdid any thunderclap I have ever known. I felt the breath of God, rushing past my face. There was pain as my ears perished, sending their death throes burning down my throat. My senses fled. I could see nothing, hear nothing, feel nothing. This was death, and I was gone. The arms of two angels were bearing me to heaven.

A bald, familiar angel said, "He's not hit."

A French angel said, "Stunned by the ball, Monsieur Musk. Missed him by a breath."

The angels carefully lifted me and leaned me against a saker. Slowly, my vision cleared. Musk stood over me, *le comte* beside him. Behind them, I saw nothing but carnage. Our maintopmast leaned at an impossible angle. Much of our rigging was torn. I looked down, and through the smoke I could see our larboard rail broken. There were great holes in the upper deck. At least three guns were gone. The deck was red with fresh, thick blood. Polzeath and Treninnick were attending to Trenance, or what was left of him, for I recognized only the head and torso of the tall, thin man who had once helped save my life. James Vyvyan stood amidst it all, bloodied from a great gash in his head, giving orders.

I propped myself up a little higher, and through the largest gash in the decking peered down into the steerage. Half the whipstaff was gone, and the helmsman with it. Kit Farrell held what remained of the whipstaff, and cried that despite all, including Penbaron's forebodings, our rudder still answered. I saw an arm lying in its own blood, a little way from a severed leg.

Musk noticed my gaze. His voice was muffled — for my ears refused to hear as they had — but I could make out the words. "All that's left of Master Landon, God rest his canting soul." Thus were realized Malachi Landon's dire forebodings from his reading of the heavenly charts.

I stood, staggered a little as my balance returned, and called out to my lieutenant, who was ordering men to clear fallen rigging and thus free our battery.

"Mister Vyvyan! Return their fire, each gun as it bears!"

Julian Carvell's gun crew responded to the command at once, along with two guns on the deck below. I heard Stanton screaming exhortations to the men and thanked God that my officers proved themselves better in a fight than they did over the dinner table. But they were the only guns that fired from the *Jupiter*, and

Godsgift Judge had his sword raised once more. We could not bear another broadside, not so soon . . .

Republic fired again.

There was the same stench of gunpowder, the same great flash, the same thunderous noise. But no shot came close to me. The *Republic* had made a little headway since her previous broadside, and this next was fired on her downroll as she rocked a little in the breeze. The best part of twenty-two cannon balls struck our hull lower down, at the main deck.

I sent a boy to report on the damage, but he did not return. I cried my next set of orders to Vyvyan, then ran down to the main ladder from the steerage to the main deck.

If my immortal fate is to spend all eternity there, then I have no fears of Hell. For I have seen worse.

The main deck of the *Jupiter* was a world torn asunder. Four or five great holes had been smashed through the hull, and the wood thus displaced had turned into the most hellish of weapons. A man staggered toward me, a great shard of oak protruding from his throat. He fell, and blood gushed at my feet. Beyond him, I could see only dimly through the smoke, but I could hear the groans of the dying and the wounded. Men called for help, for their mothers and sweethearts. Cannon lay across the deck at unnatural angles. Trapped beneath the nearest one I could see three men; or parts of them, anyway. Hands and heads lay in pools of blood. Entrails spread across the deck. One of Stanton's mates came to me, saluted properly, reported that the entrails belonged to the gunner, and burst into tears.

I vomited onto the deck.

A carpenter's mate came up, saluted, and reported that we were holed more than once between wind and water. Penbaron had men at the pumps, but someone would have to go overboard to stop the leaks with a plug doused in oakum and tar. I recovered myself and sent the man back with his captain's word that when the fight was done, and a man could be spared, the leak could be plugged. Inwardly, I was not confident that in an hour there would be any men left to spare, nor any ship to mend.

Francis Gale appeared at my side, I know not whence. He was streaked with blood and dirt, but his bearing gave off strength and purpose and I was glad to see him. "We have still enough men standing to fight this deck, Captain. But another broadside or two, and we'll be finished." He was all warrior now, sword in hand; Gale was fighting his enemy once again, and glad he was of it.

I nodded and tried to summon the breath to say something, but he was already gone from me, barking commands at our gunners as though he had been born to the task. Just then, one of Malachi Landon's servants ran up to me, gave me Mister Farrell's compliments, and passed on his suggestion that I should return to the quarterdeck.

I climbed back into daylight. *Republic* was alongside us, perhaps fifty yards away. She had backed her sails and dropped her anchor. Her guns were still inboard for reloading, but when they ran out again, she would surely fire until there was nothing left of the *Jupiter* or her men. At any moment, we would face another of her murderous broadsides. *Only one thing you can do*, Kit Farrell had said to me, when we had talked of this situation — but it was already too late for that . . .

I looked around the quarterdeck. For some reason, Farrell, d'Andelys and Phineas Musk were all looking astern, not at the *Republic*. I joined them at the remains of our stern rail, above which our ragged ensign still flew. The smoke from the *Republic*'s last broadside was still thick, for in light winds and in that sheltered channel it lingered about us like a shroud. I could not see what it was that they stared at.

Then the smoke parted a little. There, turning into the channel on the same course that the *Republic* had taken, was my mystery ship. Black-hulled and tall, the great vessel tacked towards us. Men sheeted home her sails with a speed and precision that not even Judge's crew had managed. Only the Dutch could do such a thing. The Dutch, our enemies, as my treacherous lady, the Countess of Connaught, had told me. So a second ship in her cause, bearing down to join Godsgift Judge and finish us off . . .

But she had been as shocked as I when we sighted the black ship.

Not all of the Dutch were our enemies. That had been my argument to the Lady Niamh, and now it was the final, best argument to her lover, the father of the child that was meant to be a king. *Thou givest not away the battle to the strong . . .*

An ensign ran up the staff of the black ship. They were colours I knew well, for I had lived under them for long enough. They were the colours I had seen when Cornelia and I came out of church after our wedding. There they flew, the red, white, blue of the province of Zeeland. At the mizzen flew the black-white-black flag of a town I knew so well, the town that had once been my home.

She was the *Wapen van Veere*.

It was Cornelis.

On the deck of the *Republic* I could see Judge, watching and weighing up this new opponent. His men were already moving to run out the larboard guns. Why should he concern himself with the shattered and dying *Jupiter*? Dispose of Cornelis first, then finish us off at leisure. He would have known of the other ship, of course; his lady would have told him of it. I thought of Judge's words to me, the first time I dined with him. He had faced the Dutch before, and beaten them. The *Wapen van Veere* would hold no terrors for him. Perhaps, safe in his fanatical arrogance, he would look on her as a worthy opponent. A better enemy by far than the poor, feeble Cavaliers on the *Jupiter* and their raw, ignorant young captain.

Four guns of the *Republic*'s starboard battery fired at us, and did some damage to the forecastle. Enough to keep us entertained, Judge would assume, while he tackled his true enemy. I turned to Kit and James Vyvyan, whose head wound had been staunched with a bandage. Musk, ever at my side with his pistols, drew closer to listen.

"Well, Mister Farrell," I said, almost light-heartedly, "you remember what we discussed yesterday? How the captain of an inferior ship can turn this situation around? And Mister Vyvyan — you remember what you told me of the fighting method that your uncle and his men preferred? Gentlemen, I take the advice of you both. It's time to chastise Captain Judge for betraying his king and murdering Captain Harker."

James Vyvyan nodded at my acknowledgement of his uncle's fate. "But, sir," he said, "are we certain that the Zeeland ship is with us? And even if she is, will she have enough searoom to engage *Royal Martyr*?"

"As for that, Lieutenant, I leave it to her captain. But yes, he's with us, or else he'll have to answer the lash of his sister's tongue. His sister, my wife."

For the first time in all the years that I knew him, Phineas Musk looked at me in utter astonishment.

Wapen van Veere came on. Cornelis's course seemed to be set for the other shore, opposite Ardverran. If he had enough depth of water there, he could come up on *Republic*'s larboard side and fight it out broadside to broadside.

"Captain! They're loosing their sails!" cried Kit, then. I saw it. The men in the *Veere*'s yards were letting her sails flap free. Even I could see that she would lose momentum long before she came up alongside the *Republic*. "No. No, no ship would do that," continued Kit, looking on with an anguished expression. "No captain would order that — he doesn't have the sea room for it, the channel's too tight. It's the blackest madness. She'll run onto the lee shore . . ."

Despite the chaos and pain, it seemed that everyone on board the *Jupiter* stopped to watch, holding their breaths. Slowly, slowly, the bow of the *Veere* began to point towards the Ardverran shore. Like all large ships, she took an age to turn. Like all large ships, she was vulnerable as she did so. The *Veere* was doubly vulnerable, for with her sails loose Cornelis could steer only by his rudder. His ship would be out of control. She would come up short of the *Republic* and run aground, or else her vulnerable bow, swinging round so painfully slowly, would be exposed to the full force of Judge's larboard broadside.

The four guns of Judge's starboard battery fired on us again, and shattered our bowsprit. Whatever Cornelis intended, or whatever mistake he had made, we had to make our move. We still had a little headway, and it was time to give orders.

"Mister Vyvyan!" I cried. "Arm the men for boarding! Mister Farrell! Port the helm!"

Slowly, slowly, the *Jupiter* began to answer the remnant of her whipstaff. Judge's murderous fire into our hull had at least spared enough of our sails and rigging to keep our momentum. Slowly, we closed the gap to the *Republic*. Judge must have realized our intent, for his four starboard guns began to fire more briskly. Two more guns joined in. As I watched our men on the upper deck take up cutlasses, half-pikes and knives, a shot took the head clean off the last of the

372

master's mates. His body stayed upright for a moment, then fell to the deck.

We inched closer to the *Republic*. Judge had put his helm to larboard, too, and she was starting to move away.

Too late. The *Veere* had completed her turn. Cornelis had judged his distances, the wind and the tide, with greater science than ever old Newton employed. The Dutch ship came in hard and close behind the *Republic*, full across her stern, forming a "T". No, Cornelis had made no mistake. He was running out his double anchors. His own sails were turned as far as they could go to starboard, backing him down even closer towards the *Republic*.

"He's taken the wind from *Republic*'s sails!" cried Kit, jubilant now. "Oh, God in heaven, I've never seen the like! To bring her up so exactly, in so little water — and now he'll rake her, by God!"

The *Veere*'s first broadside was as mighty as that of the *Republic*. If they had been side by side, it would have been a fair and equal fight. But raking is neither fair nor equal. The broadside tore into the weakest part of Judge's ship — of *any* ship: her stern. The gallery and windows of the captain's cabin shattered like matchwood. The two stern chasers, the only guns on the ship bearing in that direction, must have been destroyed at once. With the *Republic*'s main deck cleared for action, there was no obstacle to the *Veere*'s cannonade passing the entire length of the ship. It was slaughter.

Republic's fire against us fell away. We were close now, just yards away. Leaving Kit Farrell on the quarterdeck in effective command of the *Jupiter*, D'Andelys and I ran down to the forecastle where my crew was massed. The *Republic*'s starboard side loomed above us. I could smell the stench of death on her main deck, where the *Veere* had done her work. Above me, half of a man's head was lodged in one of her gunports, one eye staring blankly into oblivion.

Then the remains of our bowsprit crashed into the *Republic*'s forecastle. The two ships locked together in a morass of tangled rigging and broken wood. Each vessel seemed, to my exhausted mind, to scream in agony as wood sheared against wood. I raised my sword, climbed on our rail, and cried out, "With me, Jupiters!"

A hellish roar told me that Cornelis had raked the *Republic* once again. I seized the moment, grabbed a rope, and pulled myself up the ship's side. Jupiters swarmed after me, shrieking for blood and revenge. Lanherne, Polzeath, Treninnick and Carvell were at my back. Francis Gale was at my side, a long cavalry sword in his hand. Heads appeared at the ship's rail above us. I heard Vyvyan command a volley of musket fire and cried for my vanguard to crouch down. The heads above us disappeared, and I led my men over the rail and onto the upper deck of the *Republic*.

Judge's men were massed in the middle of the ship. Our fire had not touched them. They were drawn up in the three lines of the New Model Army, front rank kneeling, second rank stooping, third rank standing.

Each rank levelled a row of thirty or more muskets toward us. They would fire by rotation, each rank in turn, until they had swept our bodies back into the sea.

One thing to do, boy, an almost familiar but impossible voice in my ear seemed to say. I levelled my sword at the enemy lines, and charged.

The first rank fired and I felt a searing pain in my thigh. I stumbled but caught myself and ran on into the smoke of the muskets, wielding my sword right and left. I felt the blade strike flesh, and knew I had reached the first rank. I looked down the musket barrel of a man in the second rank. Gale knocked it aside with his sword, and I stabbed the man with mine. Our lads were up with us, and the line of musketeers broke. They looked like the New Model, but at bottom they were simply sailors with guns. Judge must have thought that the mere sight and prospect of rotation fire would have been enough to cow the Jupiters. He had to despatch us quickly if he was to stand any chance of manoeuvring away from the murderous fire from Cornelis's guns. But we were too close to them, and if we held our nerve and charged before the reload, we could prevail. As, it seemed, we had, for no men were better to rush into point-blank fire than a hundred or so blood-crazed Cornishmen.

It was ugly, close fighting now. *Wapen van Veere* fired another raking broadside into the deck below — had she seen the Jupiters on board? — and I heard the screams of the dying. Smoke clouded our business of murder on the upper deck. Judge's men had their dirks and cutlasses drawn, and Cavalier fought Roundhead with undiminished passion. I slashed at men, left and right, seeking to cut my way through to the quarterdeck. I saw Francis Gale, ordained of God, slice the head off a man with one stroke of his sword. Through the pungent cloud of powder-smoke, I caught a glimpse of Treninnick and Polzeath stabbing a man time after time in the guts. There was young Macferran, wielding a fearsome dirk with a viciousness that belayed his years. Warm blood splashed onto my face and shirt, I knew not whence, I knew not whose. It could have been mine. I heard scream succeed scream, and the distinctive sounds of metal striking metal or carving into flesh. The deck was slippery from blood and the very air seemed to glow red. The stench was like that of an abattoir.

Our men were falling, too. I saw Seaton, the cuckold of Looe, fall to a shot in the stomach from an officer's pistol. I came up with James Vyvyan, covered all over with the blood of others — or so I hoped — grinning hideously as he fought his first battle and slew his first men. We were friends at last, he and I; friends in blood. The throng pushed us apart then and I felt the blow of a half-pike on my breastplate, then the excruciating pain of a deep, bloody graze on my thigh. I killed my man. I killed the next. Then I turned to seek out Vyvyan again.

I saw him through the haze, a few yards away. It was a vision that will never leave me. He was staring at me, blue eyes wide, fair hair spattered with gore. He was still grinning. There was more blood on his face, and I knew with, awful certainty it was his own. And then he fell forward, and I saw the dagger in his back.

Behind him, a man that I recognized all too well sneered defiantly. It was my assailant on the night I had taken command of the *Jupiter* at Portsmouth. It was Linus Brent.

The Jupiters had been barely holding their own until that moment. At the sight of his dead lieutenant, John Treninnick howled like a wolf, crying out in Cornish. Above all the screams, all the death throes and the cacophony of blade on blade, Treninnick's voice carried. My men stopped. Their lament began as a low growl, then turned in an instant into a ferocious howl of rage. James Vyvyan, their lieutenant, was dead. James Vyvyan, a Cornishman and one of their own. James Vyvyan, the murdered nephew of the murdered Captain James Harker.

Enraged, the Jupiters pressed home with a new vigour. I saw Ali Reis swing his vicious Turkish scimitar about his head, flaying limbs as he went. There was John Tremar, the tiny father of twins, cutting his way through a man twice his size. Behind him, Julian Carvell used his half-pike to stick a man like a pig.

There was a new sound. I heard it first after another broadside came from the *Veere*. There was a sudden brief lull in our fight, as sometimes happens in battle, when both sides almost consciously decide to draw breath, before resuming the slaughter anew. This new sound was distant, but even in that hell of battle, there was no mistaking it. Somewhere on the Ardverran shore, the pipes were skirling. Roger d'Andelys made his way to my side, a great bloody gash disfiguring his cheek, his sword blade red with the blood of English traitors. He pointed towards the shore, his eyes alight.

"Look there, Matthew. Our general rides."

Over the hill above Ardverran came the Campbell host, their pipers to the fore. At their side marched a regiment of men in the king's red uniform, and at the head of all rode Colin Campbell of Glenrannoch. He was dressed in full cavalry armour and a glorious helmet of black and gold; a great cloak fell in folds at his back, an orange sash crossed his chest. He had been right about his wound, or else he had the strength of will and of body to ride out in spite of it. Above him flew the flags of Clan Campbell and the United Provinces of the Netherlands, and the red lion rampant standard of the King of Scots. As he had predicted, the mighty general was leading his last army.

I looked over toward Ardverran Castle and saw the Macdonald birlinn pulling away from the jetty, its prow toward the open sea. I could just see my lady Niamh, Countess of Connaught, standing at its stern with her little son, looking back at the ruin of their dreams. For a moment, I thought she was looking directly at me. Then a gun fired close to me, and the smoke took them from my sight.

D'Andelys and I were almost at the quarterdeck stair. We fought our way past two soldiers in New Model uniforms. Up, and onto the deck . . .

One man alone was left on the quarterdeck of the *Republic*. And there, at last, I looked upon the true face of Captain Godsgift Judge.

378

CHAPTER
TWENTY-TWO

There were no other men around us now, and no other ships. Judge stared intently into my face, and I into his. The fop was dead. Without all the face paint and the wigs and beauty spots, Godsgift Judge's gaunt features were those of a warrior. Here stood a killer: for his God, his woman and his son. He held a bloodied cutlass. A deep slash across his chest seemed not to trouble him. His eyes were tired, though, and his voice, when it spoke, was weary and harsh.

"Ship to ship, Quinton, I'd have you beaten. You know that. The Dutchman, there — now that was weighting the odds, my noble captain."

I circled him, watchful, trying to contain my anger, to gain control of myself. "You and your countess first brought the Dutch into this, Captain Judge. To give your son a kingdom, she said. But perhaps some know the Dutch better than you do. The noble general, there, for one."

Glenrannoch's army was spreading out to surround Ardverran. In the second I spared to look, I thought how it seemed but a ghost of a castle. Behind Judge, the *Wapen van Veere* lay still and silent, her guns manned and pointed into the broken hull of the *Republic*. I could see Cornelis plain on her quarterdeck, no more than a hundred or so yards away. I raised my left hand in greeting, and he raised his right, stiffly, aware that to move it too rapidly would bring a broadside down on us all and probably tear my flesh to pieces.

I looked back at Judge. "And my good-brother, Captain van der Eide there, for another."

For the first and only time in our acquaintance, Godsgift Judge appeared genuinely surprised. "Your good-brother?" he asked. Then he smiled. "Yes, it had to be, of course. Popes and cardinals and countesses, they can plot all they like. As the good Lord knows, I plotted all I liked. But God disposes." He sighed. "Divine justice, then." His eyes narrowed and his lips twisted into a cruel sneer. "What an unfortunate fool I am. I order the killing of James Harker so the whoremaster Charles Stuart will replace him with a lesser man. And I am delighted with the result." He gave me a mocking salute. "But God disposes that this lesser man is the brother-in-law of the best captain the Dutch have. And from a faction that hates our cause. Now, is that divine justice or divine irony, Captain?"

I thought of James Vyvyan. I felt a pain somewhere inside me. I had known this, but to hear it from those venomous lips was awful.

"You killed Harker?"

Judge's eyes showed no remorse. "Ordered him killed, yes — of course. Who else, Quinton? And his servant. And that miserable turncoat Warrender, who sought to betray our cause to Harker. It matters little now, for we both know I'll not leave this ship alive.

Either you kill me in single combat, or your men tear me to pieces if I kill you. That's what Charles Stuart's demented notion of reconciling us old enemies means at the end of the day. The only truthful reconciliation is found in the grave." He gave a pale, venomous smile. "And that, Captain, is where we are headed."

"But how . . .?" I said, and stopped.

"How, Captain?" Judge raised an eyebrow, then looked across to the main deck and nodded towards a man all too familiar to me. "See Linus Brent, there, my surgeon's mate? A useful man. Apprentice in his youth to an old surgeon of Cheapside who dabbled much in alchemy. Not many potions he doesn't know, my Linus. A pity his blade didn't do for you in Portsmouth town, Matthew Quinton, as his poisons had done for Harker."

At that, Judge raised his cutlass in salute. Enraged as I was, I assumed the pose of warrior-ready. I would not salute this man, this murderer and traitor. This was meat to be carved, and with that, I would avenge James Vyvyan, James Harker and Nathan Warrender together. I looked on Judge, and my anger streamed out of me.

"In the name of God and of the king, this is your reckoning, Godsgift Judge."

"I care not for your king, Matthew Quinton. Mine was the good old cause of the Republic of England. And yet more than that, too — for my cause was the love of my life, and the future of my son."

His lips drew back over his teeth and he stepped forward, raised the blade above his head and slashed for my shoulder. I was ready, my father's cavalry sword blocking the cutlass well short of its target. I thrust for

381

Judge's side, but for a mere mariner he was sharp on his feet. He swung again, for the same shoulder, and I parried again. I lunged for his chest, but he swept his blade down instinctively and forced my sword away. Our swords clashed again and we fell into each other, steel screaming, as blade ran against blade. Again I could find no way through. The cutlass is a good weapon aboard a ship and in a melee. It cuts and carves through massed flesh like a butcher's cleaver. And Judge was a master of it — that much was clear.

But one on one, afloat or ashore, two swordsmen are only as good as their blades and their training. Godsgift Judge knew the swordsmanship of the sea. I had learned mine from Uncle Tristram, and he had learned his craft from his brother and father. I was no great swordsman, not yet, just as I was no sea officer. But I was the son, nephew and grandson of great swordsmen. Cornelis and Kit Farrell could keep their mysteries of the sea. In that instant, my ignorance and my doubts were gone. I had a sword in my hand, and did what generations of Quintons, back through the centuries, were born to do.

I cut hard at Judge's waist, and he parried but clumsily. He would be used to despatching his opponent with one swing of the blade, perhaps two. He was tiring, and we both knew it. I stabbed directly at his chest, but somehow he brought the cutlass back up to deflect me. I cut at his shoulder, but again his blade came up in time to stop me.

Switch to the left hand, I heard Uncle Tristram cry, when I was but a boy. *No man expects that.*

But Godsgift Judge did. He was tiring, but his reactions were remarkable, his anticipation unexcelled. As I switched hands, he swung at my right side, cutting me deeply across the forearm. I cried out, and saw the blood begin to flow down across my hand and fingers. I backed away to gain breath but he came on, swinging and cursing like a Barbary corsair. I blocked him with the sword in my left hand, but now I was the one weakening. The hand was less familiar and I felt, suddenly, light in the head.

I could hear voices calling out — there was Musk screaming obscenities, and Roger d'Andelys urging me to counter-thrust for Judge's groin. I parried more swinging cuts from Judge's cutlass. I was giddy, and could see the shattered mizzenmast of the *Republic* swaying alarmingly, though I knew it stood stock-still. But there was one more voice. *Best hand, boy. Ignore young Tris. Best hand, and lunge.*

Judge raised the cutlass and swung for my head. In one movement I switched my sword back to my right hand, and for a moment, just that one moment, the pain in my forearm was gone. I brought the sword up into Judge's side, felt it jar on his ribs, and pass through.

We locked together, and I smelled his sweat, and his dying. His eyes were only inches from mine, staring directly into my soul. I saw them start to swim away from me, and from the world.

"She was worth it." His voice was fading but I heard him yet. He clung on to my arm and I felt an unbearable pain. "You know that. She, and my son."

One moment I looked into the eyes of a living man. Then next, I looked into the eyes of the dead.

I pushed the corpse of Godsgift Judge away from me. I was dimly aware of a great cheer, Cornish and Dutch throats as one in salute to the heir of Ravensden. I tried to stay upright, felt a hand at my elbow and someone beside me gesturing upwards. I looked toward the ensign staff, where Martin Lanherne was exultantly breaking out the king's colours once more on the *Royal Martyr*.

I watched the great red flag unfurl in the breeze, and merge into the red that swam across my eyes.

I awoke to Musk and Surgeon Skeen, evidently in competition to revive me. Pain screamed from my arm and my thigh. I seemed to be lying on sacks under some sort of an awning, stretched across what I dimly recognized as the quarterdeck of the *Jupiter*. Lanterns had been brought up and hung from the rigging, their flickering flames still complemented by the very last of the evening's light. Musk said something about my cabin being too shattered to lay me in, at the same time that Skeen was saying the orlop was too full of the dead and dying of the *Jupiter* and *Royal Martyr* to lay me there. I became aware of two other voices behind them, and presently saw the concerned faces of Kit Farrell, red with the blood of others, and my brother-in-law. Cornelis looked down at me impassively. I attempted a smile and tried to raise my arm, then groaned with the pain.

Cornelis's face was still as granite. He looked at me gravely, then he tilted his head. "So, brother Matthias. The God of the Sea preserves you a second time."

Kit bent forward, brought some water to my lips. "It's over, sir," he said kindly. "The rest of Judge's crew surrendered when they saw him fall. General Campbell's army has taken possession of the castle."

I smiled into his honest, good face. Then I tried to raise myself a little but could not do it. I looked down at the bloodied bandages and realized that Judge's cut had torn deep into my arm. Skeen leaned over me and said that if Judge's sword had been just a fraction deeper, all the fabric of the arm, all that made it live and move, would have been severed beyond repair. Where, then, had I found the strength for the thrust that despatched him? I recalled a voice, but my head swam, and I knew not whether it had been a voice of this world, or the next, or of none.

Musk and Kit Farrell both stooped forward and helped raise me a little on my makeshift bed. I could see beyond our shattered ship's rail, across to the shore and to Ardverran Castle, its walls lit by the fires of the Campbell host that surrounded and occupied it. The movement seemed to give me strength, and I asked for our butcher's bill.

"Forty-four men dead, sir," said Kit, glancing away. Almost a third of the crew, then. "Another fifty-four wounded, some dozen of those not like to live."

Skeen nodded silently. Christ in Heaven, I thought, barely forty men left unscathed. No ship in any battle of the last Dutch war had suffered so terribly.

"And my officers?" I asked at last.

There was silence from all on that quarterdeck. Even Cornelis, my bold brother-in-law, looked away.

"Reverend Gale. Penbaron, the carpenter," said Skeen after a long moment.

"What?" I said, trying to raise myself on my left arm. "The only ones dead?" But even as I spoke, a wave of remembrance came back to me: I recalled Malachi Landon blown apart before my eyes, and poor James Vyvyan stabbed to death by Linus Brent.

"They are the only ones left alive, sir," said Skeen, bowing his head. "Beyond a few of the boatswain's and carpenter's mates. Penbaron himself suffers with a great splinter between his ribs. He'll live, though, God willing."

Cornelis took a step forward and bent over me. I took his hand, tried to press it. "Your chaplain, Matthias. I have never seen a man of the cloth to equal him. He acts as your lieutenant even now, rallying the men and ordering repairs. Then he says his prayers over the dead and dying."

"Boatswain Ap?" I asked.

"Gone, sir." Farrell's eyes were downcast and he laid a hand upon my shoulder. "One of the *Martyr*'s musket balls did for him."

"And Janks?"

Musk's face loomed over me, the lantern-light making him look even more malevolent than usual. "Tried to charge their forecastle," he said. "Fell over his own crutch, straight onto a blade." He sniffed, wiped his eyes. "I was by him, and held him as he died. He was ranting when he went, sir. Quite confused. Saying how he was happy to die alongside the Earl of Ravensden."

I smiled, for I knew that the man who had once fought alongside my grandfather had died with the memory of those great days foremost in his mind. He had died as he had lived: loyal and brave.

"Peverell?" I asked at length. "The purser — what of him?" The men around me shuffled their feet and looked at one another. "Well?" I said.

"Seems he tried to hide through the battle in his own bread store, sir," said Kit, reluctantly. "But one of the last shots from *Royal Martyr* struck below the waterline, and holed it. The sacks of bread blocked his way to the hatch, and he drowned. His body's laid out on the orlop deck, sir. We gave him his crucifix."

There was one face missing, then. "The comte d'Andelys? Monsieur le Blanc?" I dreaded the reply.

Cornelis smiled. He must have heard the story of my sailmaker's ennoblement. "He is unharmed, brother. He commands your prize, for now. We have had some difficulty dissuading him from hoisting King Louis's fleur-de-lis ensign at her staff."

"Look, sir," said Kit, and pointed.

I glanced away to my left. There was the *Royal Martyr*, a floating wreck. Despondent men attended to her rigging and the dire holes in her hull. And there, on the quarterdeck, I saw a smiling Roger d'Andelys, unmistakeable even in the fading light. He turned, then, and raised in salute a preposterously large brown feathered hat that he must have purloined from

Godsgift Judge's wardrobe. He looked every inch a fitting captain for a man-of-war.

My memories were returning rapidly. I asked, "Then what of Judge's men? What of Linus Brent, the murderer?"

As I spoke, I noticed that beyond my immediate attendants stood an outer ring of concerned men. I saw Martin Lanherne, George Polzeath, Julian Carvell, Ali Reis and John Treninnick. By their side was their new messmate and comrade-in-arms, young Macferran. At the mention of Brent, they looked nervously at each other, and at me.

It was Kit Farrell who broke the silence. "Brent is dead, sir. Killed in the fight."

Kit was ever a bad liar, as I already knew. Phineas Musk, on the other hand, was equally bad at allowing others to lie in his presence. His face twisted into a grimace and he made a scornful noise.

"When you fell, the men thought you were dead. Word was that Brent was the one who'd killed Captain Harker, as well as poor Lieutenant Vyvyan. So they did for him."

Then, only then, did I notice that my Cornishmen seemed to have an unexpected amount of blood on them, and that an equally unexpected amount of it was literally on their hands. Thus were James Harker and James Vyvyan avenged.

I felt stronger by the minute. I asked for some *whisky*, and took a mouthful of the awful oat patties the Scots are so fond of. With my senses regained, I ordered my surviving officers to return to their duties, sending Skeen to attend to the wounded on the orlop deck below. Reassured that I lived, and would continue to do so, my little circle of followers melted away. The deaths of so many had levelled all ranks and created a kind of democracy on my quarterdeck. Kit Farrell, Francis Gale, and Lanherne shared between them the roles of lieutenant, master, boatswain and gunner, ordering men to the most urgent repairs. Already they had cleared the remnants of the dead. Soon I heard Ali Reis's fiddle accompany the unmistakeable voice of John Treninnick in a medley to rouse the hearts of the surviving men of the *Jupiter*.

Musk and Cornelis stayed by my side. My good-brother had no need to attend to his own ship. I could see her out of the corner of my eye, lying at an easy double anchor, pristine and almost undamaged.

"Brother," I said. It was hard to know what to say to my dour relative, but I had to try. "You saved us. You saved me."

Cornelis smiled again and patted my arm. I tried not to wince with the pain. "I had my orders, brother Matthias. The saving of you was incidental, though when I first met the general and I found an opportunity to talk —" he noted my surprise and nodded — "yes, Matthias. Glenrannoch was my ally. It was but a few days ago, not long after my arrival in these waters, that he gave me the name of the second king's captain. I have thought much on the will of God and the predestination of souls ever since."

Even in victory, and even when receiving my gratitude for saving my command, Cornelis could turn

389

it all into a dull Calvinistic sermon. Yet I thanked him again, and pressed his hand, and meant it.

"I must write to your sister," I said, pleased with my diversion, "but I think my writing hand will be of little use for a good while. If I dictate the words, brother, will you write them? She'll believe what we both put down." Cornelis nodded. "Musk," I called, "I'll need to write to my mother, too."

"She won't believe a word of what you tell her, if it's in my hand," said my faithful retainer, shuffling away.

I thought of General Glenrannoch, and of the truths at which I could hint. "Oh, they'll be words she'll believe, Musk, have no fear. But stay," for he was slinking off, "I'll also need a scribe for the letters I must write to the Duke of York and to the king. Lowly work for the acting purser of a king's ship, but perhaps you'll permit the imposition just this once?"

Musk's eyes widened. As I had calculated, the old rogue was overwhelmed in equal measure at the prospect of his writings lying in the hands of the king, and his sudden and unexpected promotion to the exalted rank of an officer of the navy. But he managed a gracious nod, and then the acting purser of the *Jupiter* strutted away proudly to fetch pen, ink and paper.

I looked over to Ardverran Castle. Lady Niamh's fortress swarmed with Campbells, while the king's regiment held the jetty and guarded the bedraggled prisoners from Judge's *Republic*. I could see the general on the roof of the great tower, that same vantage point from which, so few hours before, the countess and I had watched Judge's ship bear down

390

upon my own. He was illuminated by the firelight of the beacon that served as the castle's night-time seamark. He seemed to be looking directly at me and for a moment I was tempted to raise my hand in greeting. But then he turned to watch as the black-and-gold clan banner was raised proudly over this new Campbell fortress.

It was the last sight he saw. At that moment, a great explosion tore the tower apart. I saw, first, its walls vanish, replaced in an instant by a vast column of smoke. In the next second came the sound of a blast as loud as any of our recent broadsides. Huge stones from the castle broke the surface of the water like a hail of cannon balls, and fragments even struck our shattered hull. Flames roared up into the gap where the walls, the floors and the roof had stood.

A long, slow fuse, concealed deep in the bowels of the castle, had finally detonated. Ardverran of the ages was gone. General Colin Campbell of Glenrannoch was gone, and with him, whatever mysterious secrets of state he shared with my mother. My Lady Niamh, my beautiful, treacherous countess, had taken her revenge, and taken it in full measure.

CHAPTER
TWENTY-THREE

We lay under the shattered, smouldering ruins of Ardverran for over a fortnight. The first task, of course, was to bury our dead. Francis Gale took upon himself the task of organizing the burial up at the tiny chapel upon the headland. Our remaining able men were sent up to dig a mass grave. They toiled through the next two days, almost without ceasing, until every last body had been carried tenderly to its last resting place. I thought that with the soft wind carrying the scent of early gorse and the sea sparkling below, it was a peaceful place to leave our dead. Nothing could be done for Glenrannoch and his kin, and that grieved me; but perhaps the ruins of Ardverran Castle were a fitting mausoleum for a great warrior.

James Vyvyan, as a commissioned officer and the scion of an ancient Cornish line, deserved better. For such a young man, he had been surprisingly thoughtful on the subject of his own mortality; had talked often on the nature of the funeral he would prefer, or so Gale said. It was almost as though he had lived in the certainty of his imminent demise, this brave and noble young warrior, whom I had maligned so unjustly. Thus it was that on a splendid, sun-filled Scottish day, we committed his body to the deep of the sea-loch before Ardverran. We shrouded his corpse in the flag of Saint Piran, and as his body slipped into the waters, weighted by cannonballs at head and foot, John Treninnick sang an old song of Cornwall, a lament for another time and another place: *My agaran rosen wyn mar whek mar dek del dyfhy*. Coxswain Lanherne kept up a translation: "The first time I met you, my love, your face was as fair as the rose, but now your dear face has grown paler, as pale as the lily-white rose." The men of the *Jupiter*, lining the sides and manning the shrouds, took up the refrain in their own tongue:

"I love the White Rose in its splendour
I love the White Rose in its bloom
I love the White Rose, so fair as she grows.
'Tis the rose that reminds me of thee."

It was eery and beautiful music. I saw tears running down not a few faces, for young Vyvyan had been dear to many of these rough, weather-beaten tars. I mourned him hard then; mourned the friendship that might have grown between us. I do not know — perhaps I wept too. As the Cornishmen's song of farewell died away, the *Jupiter*'s muffled guns began their salute, joined in thunderous echo across the loch by those of the *Wapen van Veere*, then by the guns of the ship named by her temporary captain as *Le Martyr Royal*.

With due respect paid to the dead, we, the living, made our repairs. Cornelis and the mourning-clad stewards of Glenrannoch sent men to assist, but in a land with virtually no trees, it was inevitably slow and difficult work. For me, there was little to do beyond encouraging the carpenter's crew and the other work parties, for Penbaron was still too weak to do so. Almost every day brought a letter from Cornelia, full of anguish and advice concerning my recuperation; several posts brought parcels containing increasingly foul-smelling potions that she swore would expedite my recovery. I later learned that only a direct command from my brother had prevented her riding post-haste for Scotland, alone, to act as my nursemaid. As it was, my wounds healed, the musket graze to the thigh more rapidly than the deep gash in my arm, whose scar I bear to this day, and which occasionally sends forth an unexpected pain to remind me of that long-ago battle off Ardverran's shore.

In the early days, too, there were interrogations of the survivors of the *Royal Martyr*. From them I learned how Godsgift Judge had carefully chosen his crew from men he knew to be loyal to what they called the Good Old Cause, all fanatics committed to bringing down the monarchy and making Britain a Puritan republic once more. All, that is, except one, for Judge had not been able to get his candidate for lieutenant approved, and had been forced instead to take Nathan Warrender; a man as devout as any of that crew, but divided in his loyalties and his sense of honour between the cause that he had served for so long, and the royal authority that had newly commissioned him.

Warrender, it seemed, had been deeply troubled to learn of the plot. Himself a man of honour and conscience, he had strenuously objected to the stealth and disloyalty of their plan. He had remonstrated with his shipmates, with Judge, but to no avail. And so, although he doubtless knew he was placing his own life in jeopardy, he had arranged — presumably with the help of his cousin on the *Jupiter*, Pengelley — to meet Harker ashore and expose the conspiracy to him.

It would remain a mystery to me whether they did or did not meet. It must have been hard for Warrender to get away. I had a sudden memory of the two sullen men who had been his constant shadows. Not attendants, as I had thought, but guards. And then of course there was the anonymous note found upon Harker's person. *Go not ashore this day* . . . Was it penned by Pengelley? A fervent Royalist, he may have distrusted this kinsman who had fought against the king he loved. Or perhaps Warrender had belatedly discovered Harker's death to be part of the plan and was warning him to stay aboard? Either way, Harker had fatally ignored the warning and gone ashore. And there he was somehow poisoned by Judge's creature, Linus Brent, and shortly thereafter died, in full view of his men aboard the *Jupiter*. Pengelley, then, had fled for his life, but he had not got far. He, too, was dealt with.

As for Warrender, Godsgift Judge was no fool. Knowing full well that another death early in the mission would appear suspicious and bring down an inquisition from above, Judge kept Warrender under a close guard until he separated our two ships off Ardverran's shore, and no longer needed to maintain either his charade or Nathan Warrender's life. Why Warrender did not rebel against the masquerade that Judge forced him to play out is a mystery that I ponder to this day. Perhaps he thought that if he at least remained alive, he could find some way of destroying Judge's plot from within. Or perhaps he simply sought to cling to life for as long as he could, in the hope of escape. Who knows how each of us will react if we become but a dead man walking?

When I was a boy, I once witnessed one of old Jermy's curates at Ravensden sitting on the floor of the transept in our church. He was surrounded by thousands of pieces of stained glass that had been smashed by a fanatic mob bent on cleansing every last trace of so-called popery from our part of Bedfordshire. I remember the painstaking way in which he slowly reassembled the pieces into the precious pictures of saints that they had once formed, until at last the whole was there again, broken but plain to see. In those days at anchor before Ardverran, I felt much as our curate must have done, as more pieces of the great picture fell into place, and at last the whole foul plot became clear to my view.

I dined frequently with Cornelis in the fortnight before his ship sailed for home. Grateful as I was, I found that such frequent communion with my good-brother still stretched my patience to its bounds. Still, I had begun to suspect that perhaps this spoke more about my limitations than his; and meanwhile I was glad to learn from him how the Dutch side of the conspiracy unravelled. He told me that he had been secretly commissioned by Grand Pensionary de Witt. His mission was to obstruct the crypto-Catholic elements within the city of Amsterdam, who sought to

396

gain great trading concessions from the Pope and his family; all this had occurred long before Cornelis learned that I had been hastily commissioned to King Charles's complementary mission. As the king's spies had learned of the arms shipment, so had De Witt; but he, with his penetrating intelligence and suspicion of all men, had learned far more than our king. He knew the full scale of the plot and sent one of his best men to ensure that the Amsterdammers and the Catholics were prevented from accomplishing their goal.

We talked of Simic, the would-be assassin of Glenrannoch. They must have paid a high price to suborn him from his master. Glenrannoch would have had to die anyway to clear the way for the Macdonald army, but inadvertently we had presented our enemies with a far greater opportunity. Killing the general while Roger d'Andelys and I rode in his company would have allowed them to blame the death upon us, the king's men, with our dead bodies conveniently incapable of arguing any other case. Such a stratagem would undoubtedly have confused and divided Clan Campbell, turning them against the king and weakening them ahead of the Macdonald onslaught to come. Such a stratagem could have come from one of only two minds, those of Godsgift Judge or Countess Niamh. Out of misplaced chivalry, or perhaps some other emotion, I preferred to blame the former.

I spent much time with the newly abstemious Francis Gale. His terrible ghosts seemed to have been exorcized by the opportunity to cleave his avenging sword into so many Commonwealth's-men. He talked much of new ambitions for a quiet country parish, or perhaps a rural deanery, enthusing often over his schemes for young Andrewartha's schooling, whose intelligence and potential for a career in the Church would one day far outdo his own, or so he said. For my part, I found myself speaking openly to him of my own ghosts and demons. His conversations, both secular and spiritual, were a solace, for the deaths that had occurred under my command, both in the present and the past, weighed heavily upon me.

The comte d'Andelys, the sometime Roger le Blanc, eventually sailed with Cornelis for the Netherlands, there to sound fellow French exiles who had offended one or other of King Louis's ministers or mistresses about the feasibility of returning home. At our parting, he swore his undying affection and respect for me, kissed me after the French way, and exclaimed that we would meet again; as, indeed, we did, many times, and always to the peril of ourselves and the crowns we served.

Aboard the *Jupiter*, Phineas Musk revelled in his new status as acting purser, and delighted in the challenge of replenishing our battered storeroom at negligible cost to the king. Then he took a shore leave to which he was more than amply entitled, and disappeared for some "refreshment of the spirit". When he returned three days later, somewhat the worse for wear with his pocket torn off his coat and a black eye, he told a garbled story about a remarkably buxom woman in Oban and a complex misunderstanding with her many brothers. The effect was, surprisingly, to warm the crew to the old rogue, and despite his new airs and graces and his menacingly tight control of the ship's commodities, he seemed to find his own place, quite comfortably, in the hierarchy on board.

I spent long hours with the new and deeply self-conscious Lieutenant Farrell, who now held an acting commission from me. I did not doubt that such a promotion was illegal, but, as he said, by the time that news of the inevitable countermand got back to Ardverran's shore, several new forests would probably have grown on the hills of Mull.

By the end of that month, I had memorized the name of every mast, sail, and yard on the ship, if not quite of every rope or line. Far more important, though, I knew the name of every man in the crew, and passed easily from mess to mess every day, receiving nothing but respectful salutes and smiles. Several requested certificates of their good conduct, and I was happy to oblige; but many said that they would willingly follow me to another ship, if I obtained one, before they would seek berths with other captains. This gratified me in a way that I had never known, and I thought much on it. At other times, I pored over charts and waggoners, and could soon lay a course — on paper, at any rate — from Ardverran to Portsmouth, or Chatham, or Smryna. Kit, in turn, could spell correctly his full name, and mine, and could write any number of other words in an eccentric variety of ways, occasionally placing them into something approximating the correct order.

On what would prove to be my last day aboard the *Jupiter*, I was on the quarterdeck with Kit, who was pointing out the tides and currents of the sound, telling me how I could read them by sight alone, when I noticed a small boat coming out towards us. I assumed it was yet another fisherman or tradesman selling their wares and ignored it. A little later, however, I was called down to the newly repaired steerage by our acting boatswain, Monkley — the best of poor Ap's mates to whom I had given a temporary promotion. An immaculately dressed blond boy, younger even than poor dead Vyvyan, saluted me extravagantly.

"Captain Quinton, sir," he piped. "I am Bassett, king's messenger. I bring you the congratulations of His Majesty the king, His Royal Highness the Duke of York, and his highness Prince Rupert. His Majesty conveys his particular compliments, sir, and asks if you would be so good as to attend him at Hampton Court on the first of next month."

As I stepped off the deck of the *Jupiter* for the last time the crew gave me three hearty huzzahs. I returned their salutation by doffing my hat. As was his duty, Martin Lanherne commanded the crew that rowed me ashore, a crew that included George Polzeath, John Treninnick, Julian Carvell and young Macferran, all of whom grinned inanely at me for the entire passage to the shore. I left Kit Farrell in acting command of the ship, which, as he said, must have constituted one of the most rapid promotions in the whole course of naval history. My last sight of him on that voyage was seated behind the desk in my cabin, writing the proudest of superscriptions on the first letter that he had ever written in his life, addressed to his mother: *His Majesty's Ship the Jupiter, at ankur, Ardverin Casttle, Skottland; from Leftenant Christopher Farrell, Acting Captain.* His mother, whose own spelling was, of course, equally execrable, would no doubt be in raptures for a month. In fact, as Kit informed me later, she joyously served free ale to all her customers until the crowds flocking into Wapping forced the Middlesex justices to close her down temporarily after a man was trampled to death.

Meanwhile, king's messenger Bassett, Phineas Musk and I travelled light for the south. An escort of Campbells took us past Inveraray to the head of Loch Goil. From there a Campbell birlinn, still flying black ensigns to mark the passing of its chief, took us down brooding sea-lochs, past dark sea-girt Campbell towers that saluted us as we passed, across the broad Firth of Clyde and upriver to Glasgow. There, we took leave of our last party of Campbells. Of course, history tells us that the matter between the Campbells and the Macdonalds still had many hands to play out, most notably the massacre of Macdonald by Campbell that took place in the snowy wastes of Glencoe during the third year of the late King William's reign. Knowing nothing of such a future, only of that which awaited us in distant London, we took horse and rode down Clydesdale and Liddesdale, staying at wild Scots inns where we were looked on as kin to the men in the moon.

We crossed into England above Lanercost, where we heard of the arrival of the new queen in England and of her marriage to our king in the old garrison church of Portsmouth. The inns improved, but not our reception; not, at least, until we were well south of Coventry, and once more into a land of civilized speech and behaviour. I contemplated a route to London by way of Ravensden, where I could have spent the last night of the old month and still kept my rendezvous with the king on the morrow. But for all my desperate desire to see my Cornelia, there was the more troubling prospect of seeing my mother. Much as I longed to speak with her, I would have to tell her of my meetings with Glenrannoch and of his eventual fate. I had raked over the general's words more often than I could have wished in the cold, quiet nights of the Hebrides. What lay between them remained a mystery. It was important, perhaps. But something in me did not wish, quite yet, to think too hard upon their joint past. These were matters for another day, I decided, so we took the road through Stony Stratford, where I sent Musk off: first to the abbey to give my women a suitable account of events, and thence to Portsmouth to retrieve my horse, Zephyr, who no doubt had spent all this time contentedly siring mares in the stable yard of the Dolphin Inn. Bassett and I pressed on, and spent the last night of our journey at a pestilentially foul tavern in Barnet.

The next day, not long after noon, we came to the Palace of Hampton Court. This monstrous brick testament to the vanity of Cardinal Wolsey — and the rapacity of King Henry who stole it from him — was no longer a favoured royal residence; perhaps because, unaccountably, Noll Cromwell had liked it. Despite this taint, our noble King Charles had chosen it for his honeymoon. A peaceful interlude, thought I ruefully, before he introduced his queen to the tumult of scandal, politics and indecency that shook the windows of old Whitehall. Bassett disappeared to report our arrival while I stood alone in the great courtyard, uncomfortably unaware of the grime and dirt of my travelling clothes. It was not long before he returned with Tom Chiffinch, who acknowledged me curtly. Bassett made but a brief farewell, for he was a pompous, unsmiling lad; I never met him again, and I heard that although he bade fair to become the creature of a great man, the plague and a lime-filled grave-pit did for him barely three years afterward.

Chiffinch led me through the corridors of Hampton Court, so ancient yet ordered, and utterly unlike the chaotic warren that was Whitehall. The usual coterie of courtiers and petitioners lined the walls, made peevish at having to decamp so far from the comforts of London. There were not a few suspicious glances aimed at me; I must have seemed a young, saddle-dirty upstart. Young women, elaborately perfumed, elaborately gowned, and just as elaborately bosomed, looked curiously and sometimes keenly at me. Then we were beyond them, and out into the gardens behind the palace.

As was his habit wherever he lodged, the king was taking a brisk stroll amidst the trees and greenery, modestly attired in a light frock-coat, a great black wig and an equally great black hat. His dogs scampered around, keeping up with the lofty monarch while his morose entourage trailed him at a distance. On seeing me, he raised his hand, an unspoken command to the rest of his attendants to fall even further behind him, well out of earshot. I bowed, and he beckoned me to him.

"Well, Matt," he said grimly, "you almost lost my ship, after all."

I looked at him levelly, for I was one of the few men at his court tall enough to look the king in the eye. Charles Stuart's ineffably ugly face remained bleak and impassive for a second more, then broke into the broadest of smiles. His eyes twinkled and he grasped my shoulder.

"Well done, Captain. God's fish, well done indeed." His hand squeezed my shoulder a moment more then dropped away. "What a God-awful mess we bequeathed you. And of our own making."

He walked on, bidding me to fall in alongside him. The courtiers followed at a respectful distance, an interval enforced by the glowering presence of Tom Chiffinch, a few paces behind us.

"Bad business, Matt," he said, matter-of-factly. "Captain Judge a traitor. Murdered poor Harker, eh? Those who recommended him are abashed indeed. You know, he even turned down a plum command in the Mediterranean, confident that his friends would ensure we learned just enough about the plot in Scotland to despatch a squadron there? He knew he would be the only man qualified to command it. Ingenious, Matt. Devilish, but ingenious." The king sighed. "Then there's the Dutch, of course. I detest being crowed over by Meinheer de Witt, but for once I think he has a case against me. Thank God he had the wit to dispatch your good-brother and his ship when he learned of the conspiracy. Yes indeed, the wit of Witt, one might say. I like that, by damnation." He laughed loudly and slapped his knee. "Must tell the queen that one — though heaven knows she'll not grasp the jest. But then, maybe she'd grasp it better than Jamie, even though she can't speak English yet."

"Both my good-brother and my lady of Connaught told me something of the machinations of the Dutch, Your Majesty," I said quietly.

Charles Stuart's good temper suddenly evaporated. "There is no Countess of Connaught, Captain Quinton. She has no title recognized by my royal father of blessed memory, or by myself, beyond that of the Lady Macdonald of Ardverran." His black eyes glittered with frosty malevolence. "In any event, she is safe in her uncle's archdiocese, far beyond my reach." I learned only much later that the king had tried more than once to bring her within his reach in the most direct manner possible; but in their own land, Cardinal O'Daragh's Italian killers were more than a match for their English counterparts.

A long-eared dog snapped at the king's heel and gave a raffish bark. At once the amiable mask reappeared on the royal face. He threw a branch for the dog to chase, and said distractedly, "You know, Matt, that I must be in Portugal again tonight? My lady Castlemaine is furious, but she is so big with child that she has not the strength to throw her fists at me. Though God knows what price I shall have to pay after she is birthed." The king's mistress was ever noted for her temper. Charles Stuart looked moodily around him, at the great formal garden, at the courtiers, and finally at me. He seemed to recollect himself, and said, "Poor Campbell. I would have liked to have met him. He could have been a useful man for me, you know. I regret that I wrongly judged him for a traitor." He turned and looked at me directly, a sad, solemn expression on his swarthy features. His dog sat panting at his feet, waiting patiently for the game to recommence. "Even kings are fallible, Matt. Some, alas, are more fallible than others. But I shall learn. God's breeches, yes. I shall learn."

I knew that any audience with a monarch is short, and that whatever time remained to me was limited. Matters had been pressing on my mind, and I had to address them while my moment lasted.

"Majesty," I began, "if I may, my crew —"

"The survivors of your crew have already been granted substantial royal bounties," he said briskly. "All of them, of course, come with one condition, the same that I impose on you. Silence, Matt."

"Your Majesty?"

"Silence." He turned, walked slowly on and I followed. "Your brother can explain more of my reasoning when you see him next. Charlie knows far greater secrets than these, as Christ in Heaven knows. But these events," he waved a jewelled hand absently in the air, "they never happened, Captain. What comfort my enemies would take, if they knew of this threat to my Scottish kingdom. That Captain Judge had deluded me and my most trusted councillors, and that a full-scale sea battle had taken place in my own waters, between two ships supposedly my own! How weak would I seem, Matt? I am back barely two years on the throne of my ancestors, and if I am determined of one thing above all else, it is that I will not go on my travels again." He stopped and stepped closer to me, a few inches from my face.

"And what of my wish to reconcile the two sides that fought against each other so recently," he said in a harsh whisper, "if it becomes public knowledge that they have fought each other yet again? No, Matthew Quinton. Here is your new truth: the *Royal Martyr* and the *Jupiter* were ordered to Scottish waters on a surveying mission. There, they had the misfortune to venture into dangerous waters during a great storm. The *Jupiter* was damaged and many of her crew died, but she survived. Alas, the *Royal Martyr* was lost in the whirlpool of Corryvreckan with all hands, including her loyal and much lamented captain."

A new truth indeed. Now I am an old man, the oldest that I know, as my grandfather was in his time. I live in a world where there are new truths every few weeks — a new war, or a new minister, or a new king. A new religion, even, for religion seems but a very temporary truth these days. Truth is whatever men in power declare it to be, even if it is the highest treason of lies. Whoever is unfortunate enough to remember the old truths has to forget, for they are told to forget; and the *real* truth, the one abiding truth which we learn from the scriptures, is buried beneath all the rest. The last sixty years of my life, since that day at Whitehall, are proof of this: that it is possible to change, or cancel, or rearrange the history of nations to suit a purpose, especially if it is to suit the purposes of men of power. I learned that lesson for the first time, that afternoon in the garden at Hampton Court. I have learned it again many times since that day. I have even done it myself, more than once.

I saw the king looking for his dogs and turning toward his courtiers, and knew that his patience was almost gone. I asked him quickly what would befall those who had so inconveniently survived the destruction of the *Royal Martyr*. Their fate was already disposed of, it seemed: shortly, they would be shipped to the Indies, where they would be kept as slaves on the most distant plantations, along with the bog-Irish and men of Carvell's kind.

"There will be whispers and stories, of course," said King Charles. "But at bottom, Matt, who in London will give credence to such wild tales from the Scottish islands? All too far away, among people prone to exaggeration and myths, in a land about which few Englishmen care a jot. A battle in those parts, and a castle brought to ruin, in a land where blood feuds bring about such occurrences almost weekly?" His ugly face broke into a black-toothed smile. "No, none will care, or at least, none that matter. It will all become the rumour of a passing hour, as long as no testimony comes forward to support it from men of good credit. From a noble ship's captain, above all."

With that, the king extended his right hand. I paused but a moment, then bent to kiss the great gold signet ring he had been given at his coronation.

Today, I would react differently if a king asked me to lie, especially if the request came from one of those idiot Germans. Then, I was young, and believed as young men do in the purity of good and evil, not seeing that those two are but sides of the same coin, with much base metal between the faces. I bowed deeply to my sovereign who smiled with satisfaction and summoned Chiffinch with a clap of his hands.

Chiffinch stepped forward with alacrity, producing a paper from his frock coat which he handed to me. Wonderingly, I opened it: therein lay a commission, signed and sealed by the king, to a rank in his Horse Guards. I stared at my life's ambition. I could almost hear the pride in the voices of Cornelia and my mother when they learned of it. But I heard, or sensed, other voices, too. A decision had been made, either by me or for me. I took a breath and looked at my king.

"I am a seaman, Your Majesty," I said as evenly as I could, "like my grandfather before me."

Charles Stuart cocked an eyebrow, amused.

"I thank you, Sire. But I would ask . . ." I took a breath and went on, "I would ask only that you give me another ship."

Historical Note

Matthew Quinton is a fictional character, but he is based on a very real historical type, the "gentleman captain" of Charles II's navy. At the Restoration of the monarchy in 1660, the king faced the difficult task of creating a new officer corps out of two wholly disparate elements. During the 1650s, the low-born professional seamen — the "tarpaulins" who commanded the Commonwealth's ships — built up a formidable reputation for competence and victory in battle, particularly in the First Anglo-Dutch War (1652–54). That war, caused by competition for domination of the maritime carrying trades and by mutual suspicion of each other's political and religious principles, witnessed an increasingly comprehensive series of British victories consequent upon their adoption of the "line of battle", the system of broadside fire described by Matthew Quinton following the *Jupiter*'s disastrous gunnery practice off Islay.

After the Restoration, many of the Commonwealth's victorious captains were considered to have suspect political and religious loyalties, so to counter-balance them, and to reward his own staunch supporters, Charles II and his brother James, the Lord High Admiral (later King James II of England, VII of Scotland), gave commissions to young men of good

410

birth, even if they had little or no seagoing experience. Inevitably, in the early years there was much conflict between the two kinds of captain, and the royal brothers attempts to suppress past differences were not entirely successful.

The naval career of Matthew Quinton is essentially an amalgam of those a number of real gentleman captains of the 1660s. In this, the first of his adventures, the most influential real-life models for Matthew were Captains Francis Digby, second son of the Earl of Bristol; William Jennens (an uncle of Sarah, the future Duchess of Marlborough); and George Legge, later Lord Dartmouth, who (like Matthew) lost his first command within weeks. The character of Godsgift Judge is equally fictitious, but again, he is based on a very real type: the former Commonwealth captain, trying desperately to convince the new royal authorities of his loyalty, appears frequently in the pages of Pepys's diary. Judge is based most closely on Richard Haddock and John Lawson, both of whom had radical antecedents but conformed to the restored monarchy. Unlike Judge, neither betrayed their new loyalty; both died as knights of the realm. I explored the tensions within the Stuart officer corps in some detail in my two non-fiction books, *Pepys's Navy: Ships, Men and Warfare, 1649–89* (2008) and *Gentlemen and Tarpaulins: The Officers and Men of the Restoration Navy (1991)*.

There was no conspiracy to unseat King Charles II and restore the Lordship of the Isles, the history of which (and of its downfall) is as described by the Countess of Connaught. Nevertheless, in the tense and profoundly unstable years between 1660 and 1663, there were many real or rumoured conspiracies to overthrow the restored monarch and bring back the Republic. The most serious was the Fifth Monarchist rising in London in January 1661, which anticipated the imminent rule of Christ on Earth. The period is well described in Ronald Hutton's *The Restoration*, while contemporary London itself is splendidly evoked in Lisa Picard's *Restoration London*.

The tensions between the Clans Campbell and Macdonald following the execution of the Earl of Argyll, and the history of the lordship of the Isles, were essentially as they are described in this book (leaving aside my invention of an entirely fictitious Ardverran sept). Colin Campbell of Glenrannoch is also an invention, but he was intended to be a rather older and more martial incarnation of John Campbell, later the first Earl of Breadalbane. There are many accounts of the tragic conflict between Campbell and Macdonald: I used Oliver Thomson's *The Great Feud* and various older histories of the individual clans. Glenrannoch is also a representative of two very real historical types, the young Scots who flocked south to the court of King James I and VI, and the Scots who served with distinction in all the great European armies during the "Thirty Years War" of 1618 to 1648. The Countess of Connaught is based on no particular historical character (although the "flight of the earls" in 1607 remains one of the most important and poignant moments in Irish history). However her home, Ardverran Castle, was inspired by four very real fortresses on or near the Sound of Mull: Ardtornish, Duart, Tioram, and above all Mingary, where the remains of a Commonwealth warship only a little smaller than the *Jupiter*, wrecked during the little-known "Glencairn rebellion" of 1653–54, still lie among the rocks beneath its walls.

The birlinn is well described in *The West Highland Galley* by Denis Rixson; these direct descendants of Norse longships

412

were still being built in the eighteenth century. Unlikely though it may seem, the free library in the depths of the Highlands, where Francis Gale learned of the Countess's significant connection to the papal curia, actually existed (although it was not founded until 1680). It still does, although I have taken the liberty of transplanting it some hundred miles west from its actual location at Innerpeffray in Perthshire.

Prince Rupert's charge at Naseby, and the storming of Drogheda, both happened essentially as described, although the latter in particular causes controversy to this day: recent "revisionism" suggesting that Cromwell did not order the massacre of the women and children in the town, the line taken by Francis Gale, has caused considerable soul-searching in the Irish Republic and beyond. Tom Reilly's *Cromwell: An Honourable Enemy* is at the centre of this controversy.

The Byzantine structure and politics of the Dutch state during the seventeenth century were essentially as I have described them, although for the sake of clarity, I have simplified some of the even more complex realities of the situation. Good guides to the subject are Maarten Prak's and Diane Webb's *The Dutch Republic in the Seventeenth Century: The Golden Age* and Jonathan Israel's monumental *The Dutch Republic: Its Rise, Greatness and Fall.*

Matthew Quinton's grandfather and father, the eighth and ninth Earls of Ravensden, are both based to an extent on real people: the former equally upon George Clifford, fourth Earl of Cumberland, and John Sheffield, second Earl of Mulgrave, both of whom sailed against the Spanish Armada; the latter upon Lucius Carey of Great Tew in Oxfordshire, the second Viscount Falkland. Earl Matthew's extraordinary folding compendium is based on the so-called "Drake's Dial", an exhibit at the National Maritime Museum, Greenwich. Ravensden Abbey, the Quinton family's crumbling hotchpotch of a mansion built out of an erstwhile monastery, really exists: I have been there. Unfortunately it is not in the real Ravensden, a quiet and pleasant Bedfordshire village, but in approximately half a dozen other locations scattered across England and Wales, each of which provided one aspect of the whole.

Throughout, I have attempted not to twist the known historical record too far, but the story of Roger le Blanc's escape from France meant giving Marie-Madeleine, the famously loyal wife of Nicholas Fouquet (whose downfall took place as Matthew describes it), a distinctly more promiscuous character than she actually possessed. Conversely, Charles II and Catherine of Braganza did spend the first part of their honeymoon at Hampton Court; during the spring of 1662, most of the king's navy was indeed in the Mediterranean or in Portugal; and the whirlpool of Corryvreckan is still just as much a feature of West Highland waters as it was in Matthew Quinton's day.

Several of the lavish meals served to Matthew and his fellow officers were actually consumed, albeit not aboard any frigate named *Jupiter*; in several cases, I have taken the menus almost verbatim from the diary of Henry Teonge, who served as a naval chaplain in the 1670s and who always displayed a particular interest in the fare placed in front of him. Similarly, Malachi Landon's doom-laden readings of the astrological charts are taken from the journals of a contemporary seaman, Jeremiah Roach, who served as a lieutenant in the 1660s and eventually rose to command. For Roach, as for many others of

414

the time, astrology was seen as an essential and entirely legitimate adjunct of the science of navigation.

Although its author does not appear in person in this book (an omission that will be rectified in the next of the series), the influence of another contemporary diary, that of Samuel Pepys, pervades this story and heavily influenced some of the descriptions and assumptions within it. However, the demands of the plot forced me to take some liberties with the precise order of certain events in April and May 1662, notably the birth of the Princess (later Queen) Mary and the dating of Easter. I did so with a clear conscience, particularly in the case of the latter — bearing in mind quite how many liberties have already been taken with it by organized Christianity since at least the time of the Council of Nicaea!

Finally, I have not been able to find a definitive origin for "The White Rose", the wonderful Cornish lament that was sung at James Vyvyan's funeral and which I first heard many years ago on a memorable winter's evening in the ethereal surroundings of Truro Cathedral. The song seems to date from at least the eighteenth century, and its subject matter suggests that it was originally a paean to the House of York, in whose name Cornwall last rose in arms in 1497. Even if a performance of it after a sea battle in 1662 proves to be an anachronism, I am perfectly content to leave it where it is.

Acknowledgements

The origins of *Gentleman Captain* lie in the academic research into the history of the seventeenth century navy that I have been undertaking for well over twenty-five years. What began as a cathartic piece of light relief from supposedly more "serious" writing rapidly took on a very serious (and often all-consuming) life of its own, and as both Matthew Quinton and his creator took their first tentative steps, a number of influences soon began to shape both our journeys. I began my teaching career in Cornwall, spending several years learning to love that ancient land and its ferociously independent people, so it seemed fitting to cast the *Jupiter*'s crew as the heirs of An Gof and Flamank, and (perhaps) the fathers of Trelawny's "twenty thousand": *meur ras dhywgh hwi.*

Next, a special but belated "thank you" to the crews of the Clyde Fleet Tenders operating from HM Naval Base Faslane between 1988 and 1994. They introduced a very green Sub-Lieutenant RNR (CCF) to the scenic splendours and complex navigational challenges of the west coast of Scotland, and to much else besides — notably the merits of a bewildering array of malt whiskies, the elastic nature of licensing hours in isolated fishing harbours and the graphically anatomical reasons why one should steer well clear of a certain town in Argyll. The voyages of the CFTs instilled in me a love of those splendid, wild places that many subsequent visits have confirmed and deepened.

A number of old friends read drafts of the book and made many constructive comments. Ann Coats, Peter Le Fevre and my jacket artist, Richard Endsor, kept up their formidable reputation as probably the most knowledgeable, supportive and witty "discussion group" working in any era of naval history. Their unfailingly generous and selfless input into both this novel and my non-fiction books on the period has been above and beyond the call of duty, and truly in the spirit of the original musketeers: "all for one, and one for all"! But for illness, Frank Fox would have been counted with them. However, his contribution to my understanding of the layout and capabilities of Charles II's warships, and to the scholarship of the Restoration navy as a whole, was already incalculable.

Having taught me to sail long ago, David Jenkins again kept me afloat by ensuring that my passages about sailing did not stray from the realm of fiction into that of downright implausibility. Similarly, Sheena Boa and Christina Webb ensured that the exertions of Matthew Quinton's steeds did not exceed the capacity of any horse, then or now. My agent, Peter Buckman, displayed unwavering faith in the book, and Becky Senior, my editor at Old Street, provided many perceptive insights and rigorous but always constructive criticisms. Finally, though, my greatest debt is to Wendy, my sternest critic and strongest supporter, who read all of the drafts and acted as a surrogate stepmother to Matthew Quinton and the other characters. I dedicate this book to her, with gratitude and much love.

J D Davies
Bedfordshire
February 2009

Also available in ISIS Large Print:

To Do and Die

Patrick Mercer

It was Anthony Morgan's first time in battle, his first sight of a soldier from his company dead on the ground beyond him, his first awareness of the sounds of battle as the shells burst above them, the drums sounded and the wounded men screamed. Morgan, a subaltern in the 95th's Grenadiers, born and raised in Ireland, was determined to prove himself amid the more experienced officers, and his camaraderie with his men in particular his sergeant, brought him under suspicion.

But the over-confident British soon learnt that their enemy was a formidable foe, who used the rough terrain considerably better than they did. Several bloody engagements decimated the company. But gradually Morgan mastered his fears, learnt to fight fast and ruthlessly, and facing dire conflicts on — and off — the battlefield, he was going to be tested to his limits . . .

ISBN 978-0-7531-8548-3 (hb)
ISBN 978-0-7531-8549-0 (pb)

The Antigallican

Tom Bowling

Jersey fishing captain, Jean Cotterell is rescued by a French frigate — The Hortense — off the Grand Banks of Nova Scotia in May 1794. His fishing vessel has foundered and he is the sole survivor. The Hortense is part of Republican Admiral Jan Van Stabel's great fleet of over 100 ships bringing American corn to France. Lord Howe's Channel Fleet is off the French coast, hoping to intercept them.

Life on The Hortense is like France under the Terror; chaotic, ungovernable, obsessed with savage, radical political theories. Separated from the French fleet in the Western Approaches she is intercepted by two British frigates and battle is joined . . .

ISBN 978-0-7531-8352-6 (hb)
ISBN 978-0-7531-8353-3 (pb)

Pilgrim

James Jackson

What they seek is Truth. What they find is Hell.

1212 and the forces of Christendom are on the march again. Twenty-five years ago, the Christian army lay slaughtered on the desolate plain of Hattin, slaughtered by Mighty Saladin, ruler of the Moslem world. The Holy Land seemed lost.

But now the Pope has called for crusade. Many take the cross for pilgrimage and battle. Among them is Otto, a young noble in search of his vanished Hospitaller Knight Father. And then there are the children — tens of thousands of them, pledged to recapture Jerusalem. But nothing can prepare them for what they will face.

Treachery, horror, violence and dread beset the pilgrims' journey. There are allies at hand but they may not be enough. For the way ahead is perilous and some will not survive.

ISBN 978-0-7531-8284-0 (hb)
ISBN 978-0-7531-8285-7 (pb)

Absolute Honour

C. C. Humphreys

On his return voyage to England, Jack helps in the defeat of a privateer, gaining a friend in a charismatic Irishman, Red Hugh McClune, along with a large share of the prize money and a nasty dose of cholera.

Fever nearly kills him and his life is saved by his new comrade. The friendship takes him to convalesce in Bath and into a passionate liaison with the Irishman's beautiful relative, Laetitia. Yet neither cousin are all that they seem and tragedy strikes. Jack escapes with his life . . .but loses his honour.

Through betrayal and mutiny, grenades and cavalry charges and a climatic duel against an unbeatable foe, Jack seeks to restore that honour — with a consequence he could not have foreseen and a price to be paid in blood.

ISBN 978-0-7531-7796-9 (hb)
ISBN 978-0-7531-7797-6 (pb)

Captain Alatriste

Arturo Pérez-Reverte

Captain Alatriste is a swordsman for hire in Spain in the 1620s - a time when Court intrigue was high and the decadent young king had dragged the country into a series of disastrous wars. In this hotbed of hired assassins, court players, political moles, smugglers and pirates, the Captain hires out his skills as a dashing swordsman with a mind as sharp as his blade.

He is approached by two masked men to fake an attack on a pair of travellers who are stealing into Madrid in the dead of night. But things take a different turn when the Captain realises that this is no ordinary job, but part of a conspiracy that reaches to the highest levels . . .

ISBN 978-0-7531-7579-8 (hb)
ISBN 978-0-7531-7580-4 (pb)

ISIS publish a wide range of books in large print, from fiction to biography. Any suggestions for books you would like to see in large print or audio are always welcome. Please send to the Editorial Department at:

ISIS Publishing Limited
7 Centremead
Osney Mead
Oxford OX2 0ES

A full list of titles is available free of charge from:

Ulverscroft Large Print Books Limited

(UK)
The Green
Bradgate Road, Anstey
Leicester LE7 7FU
Tel: (0116) 236 4325

(Australia)
P.O. Box 314
St Leonards
NSW 1590
Tel: (02) 9436 2622

(USA)
P.O. Box 1230
West Seneca
N.Y. 14224-1230
Tel: (716) 674 4270

(Canada)
P.O. Box 80038
Burlington
Ontario L7L 6B1
Tel: (905) 637 8734

(New Zealand)
P.O. Box 456
Feilding
Tel: (06) 323 6828

Details of **ISIS** complete and unabridged audio books are also available from these offices. Alternatively, contact your local library for details of their collection of **ISIS** large print and unabridged audio books.